A tender, poignant portrayal of a mother/daughter relationship.
Sarah Vaughan

'A moving and thoughtful story about love and second chances.'
Sunday Mirror

Katie lives in south-west London with her family. Before being published she worked in healthcare, and her novels are inspired by the bravery of the people she met in hospitals and clinics across the country. Her first novel, *My Everything*, was picked by the *Evening Standard* as one of the hottest summer debuts of 2015, and her second, *A Life Without You*, was a Top 20 Kindle bestseller. *This Beautiful Life* is her third novel.

Katie loves strong coffee, the feel of a blank page and stealing her husband's toast. When not writing, she spends her time in local parks trying and failing to keep up with her daughter's scooter.

You can contact Katie on Twitter @marshisms, or on Facebook www.facebook.com/katiemarshauthor, or via her website www.katie-marsh.com

Also by Katie Marsh

My Everything
A Life Without You

KATIE MARSH

this
beautiful
life

HODDER

First published in Great Britain in 2017 by Hodder & Stoughton
An Hachette UK company

I

Copyright © Katie Marsh 2017

The right of Katie Marsh to be identified as the Author of the
Work has been asserted by her in accordance with the Copyright,
Designs and Patents Act 1988.

A CIP catalogue record for this title is available from the British Library

B format ISBN 978 1 473 63962 1
Ebook ISBN 978 1 473 63963 8

Typeset in Plantin Light by Palimpsest Book Production Limited,
Falkirk, Stirlingshire

Printed and bound by Clays Ltd, St Ives plc

Hodder & Stoughton policy is to use papers that are natural,
renewable and recyclable products and made from wood grown
in sustainable forests. The logging and manufacturing processes
are expected to conform to the environmental regulations of
the country of origin.

Hodder & Stoughton Ltd
Carmelite House
50 Victoria Embankment
London EC4Y 0DZ

www.hodder.co.uk

To Mel, Chris, Kate and the many
people who love them

My boys,

So. Now we know. That whirlwind ambulance to A&E. The pain that was cutting me in two. The shivering in a tiny hospital gown while people investigated parts of me that I normally keep private for a reason. And last week, under the clock that seems to be permanently set to 5 a.m, the surgeon gave me her verdict.

Cancer.

So, it seems I won't be celebrating my birthday tomorrow with a warm white wine or six at the pub near work. Instead I'll be flat on my back under bright hospital lights having some lymph nodes and a large section of my colon removed. Party on, people. I wonder what music my surgeon will listen to as she works. Pray to God it isn't Enya. I know I'll be under anaesthetic, but I swear I'll rise up and give them the fright of their lives.

Three weeks ago I was wondering whether I could still squeeze into my silver dress for my big 3-6 tomorrow. Now the world will be saved from that delight, because apparently I have cancer. Even when I see those words written down I can't bring myself to believe them. I was so convinced I was fine, telling myself I was glued to the loo because of my lifetime addiction to chilli sauce, or blaming my dad's dodgy home-brew for my apocalyptic stomach pain and for being so tired I was in bed by eight every night.

As I sit here in my favourite chair, I pray that miracles

can happen. That I haven't waited too long. That it hasn't spread. That I will get my second chance. I want more time with you. Seb and John. My boys. I'm not giving up – I will try and try and try to keep living. But I'm writing this and putting it away for you just in case – in case my story ends now.

Telling you two was the hardest part. I wanted to shield you and instead I had to drag you with me into whatever comes next. Even writing this is so hard. You would think that I of all people would have the words I need. You are always asking me to be quiet, and I never listen. I bubble with words. I love to share. I talk over TV programmes and when you're trying to hide behind the cereal packets at 7.30 in the morning. But now I have no idea what to say. I need to give you words you can treasure. Words to last a lifetime.

If I have to leave you now, there is so much I will miss. Not the crappy things, like the huge crack in the bathroom ceiling or pretending I know how to iron. But you two – the hearts and the laughs of you. John, I love the way you talk to the car when you think no one's listening, and the way you can make a party out of a packet of Doritos and some ancient sloe gin. I love the feel of your cheek against mine, your kindness, your incredibly complicated cooking and the way you always pretend to love my latest favourite band.

And Seb. Our beautiful son. I know my exclamations are random at best, but I love screaming your name every week as you sprint around the football pitch, a flask of coffee in my hand and the inevitable rain screwing up my mascara. Thank you for never disowning me, even when all the dads are staring at me like I belong in a padded cell. You are tall enough to lift me up and pat me on the head (SO annoying), but now when I look at you I see the boy who wouldn't let go of the front gate because he didn't want to go to school without me. I don't want to leave you. I don't want to let you down. You're sixteen and strong and I know you currently spend more time with your phone than with me, but I hate the thought of you growing up without me. Of not being there when you need an arm around you, or a smile, or to be told how bloody brilliant you are.

And then there are all the amazing things you'll do. I don't want to miss a minute. I want to see your face as your beautiful fiancée walks down the aisle. I want to meet your children – who will be funny and bright-eyed and insanely good with their left feet, just like you. I want to cheer as you get your exam results, or pretend I'm not crying as you cram your beloved football boots into your rucksack and head off on your adventures.

I know you're both angry that I have cancer. God knows, I am too. People keep telling me how brave I'm being, but the truth is I'm just furious. I keep asking why it's happening to me – wondering if it's payback for all those years of cheating on pub quizzes and pretending I had made the biscuits I took to school bake sales. It's all happening too soon and too fast. But as I sit here listening to Bob Dylan being tangled up in blue, I have faith in you both. I know how much you two will achieve without me if this turns out to be my time.

John – you could finally bike round the British Isles, like you've been planning ever since we met. Seb – you CAN date Chloë Grace Moretz (and good taste there, by the way) and become a surgeon, just as you planned aged ten after watching an episode of *ER*. And if a day comes when it's just this chair left and I am gone, please go to the shelf and take down the CD I've edged in silver. I know, Seb, nobody listens to them any more, but bear with me. You can write in the sleeves of CDs, and that's exactly what I've done. It's my survival playlist – full of the music that reminds me of the people I want to live for and the life that I don't want to leave.

So, John, turn off Radio 5 Live – I promise that your heart won't stop beating. And Seb, I know some of these songs are – whisper it – really old, but bear with me; they are keepers for a reason. They will be with me every day, the soundtrack to the weeks and months to come. The days when I'll head round the back of the hospital, past the bins and the staff ignoring the 'No Smoking' signs, into the world of clinics, chemotherapy and doctors staring at me with the sympathy I have already learnt to dread.

And as you listen to Queen and The Lemonheads, and to Black Beauty galloping home with his head held high, think of the best of me. Please. The moments when I managed to say the right thing, or to cook you a meal without using every single pan. The time when I had you both in hysterics when I put my neck out dancing to 'Walk Like an Egyptian'. My arms folding around you. And – let's not get too Hollywood about this – think of the rest of me too. Me shouting at you to pick up the turkey sharpish, that Christmas when I dropped it on the manky bit by the bin just before everyone arrived. Me delaying the start of yet another family outing as I endlessly searched for my keys. Me navigating us in a circle in Calais and ending up back at the ferry terminal just as Mum's sixtieth was due to start.

Whatever you think about, please know that I'll be thinking of you. I'll be loving you. And I'll be cheering you all the way to whatever your futures hold.

I lived over half my life before I met you both, and I hope with all my heart to live many years more. You two are the reason why. Always, always the reason why. That's not bravery – that's pure selfishness. I don't want to miss one minute.

I love you.

Abi/Mum xxx

September

'Don't Stop Me Now' by Queen

This one's for you, John, in memory of the heady romance of Noah and Jenny's wedding in that random barn in a field near Avebury. The smell of dung. The small fire started by a cigarette in a hay bale. Cider you could chew. I was uncharacteristically sober, which was just as well as, unbeknownst to me, Seb had already defied my unwilling ovaries and was growing inside me – our tiny polycystic miracle. This song (and five pints) got you up on the dance floor, and I realised that once you took off your jacket and tie you could actually MOVE. And then you fell to your knees, sliding halfway across the floor and coming to a halt at my feet with arms outstretched. What a smile. As I looked down at you, I knew that was it. My heart was yours. At least you didn't ruin those trousers for nothing.

Abi

'So, it's official. You've done it?'

Abi dragged her mind away from the expression she had seen on John's face last night and returned Lesley's smile. 'Yes.' She fiddled with the wedding ring on her finger. It was so loose now that she would have to go and get it resized. 'It's true. I am officially in remission.' The words didn't feel real. Not yet. She could still feel the race of her heartbeat as she and John had waited for the surgeon's verdict. The clutch of her breath as they had been called into the same consulting room where her world had screamed into nightmare twelve months before.

Lesley grinned. 'Bloody brilliant. I knew you could do it.'

'Did you?' Abi couldn't quite believe she had. She had to have blood tests every three months, but hopefully she wouldn't be seeing the bowel cancer team again until her annual check-up this time next year.

'Yes.' Her friend's face was full of a confidence Abi had forgotten how to feel. 'How about a celebratory dance later? You used to be unstoppable when they played "Ice Ice Baby" at that club next to our flat in Bayswater.'

Abi had used to be a lot of things. 'I'm not sure I'm up to that yet. It's been a while since I got my dancing shoes on.'

'OK.' Lesley thought for a second. 'How about some air

guitar instead, then?' She pulled her dark hair out of its sensible accountancy ponytail and fluffed it out around her face. She pinched more colour into her cheeks and her eyes snapped with mischief. 'I'll get some Oasis on later. That always gets you going.'

'Just as long as no one plays "I Will Survive".' Abi shook her head. 'I think I've heard enough of that one to last a lifetime.'

She looked up at the birch trees that framed the garden at the back of the pub, admiring the bright pink and blue flags tied to the branches. 'I love the bunting.'

'Yep.' Lesley pulled out a mirror and slicked on some lipstick. 'We thought you'd like that – you could barely move at your wedding without strangling yourself on the stuff. Your mum's had your dad up a ladder for most of the afternoon getting it all sorted.'

'Poor Dad.'

'Rubbish. He loved it. He even started trying to clean out the gutters, but luckily someone stopped him before he did himself any damage. The two of them bought up all the stock in the balloon shop too.' Lesley pointed to the colourful tangle of purple, yellow and silver by the back door of the pub. 'No expense spared, my friend. Not for your survival bash.'

Abi looked upwards, almost expecting a fork of lightning to flare across the sky. She had grown terrified of tempting fate. Every time she had thought that she was getting better, she had been given another unpleasant surprise. A post-operative wound infection that trapped her on the ward. A temperature that spiralled so high she needed a blue-light ambulance to A&E and on to ITU. A blood clot that caused her arm to swell to twice its normal size and ache remorselessly for days on end. For months now her body had refused to let her trust in a tomorrow. Now it was time for that to change.

If only she knew how.

Lesley dropped the lipstick back in her bag and folded her arms round Abi. 'Wow, there's really nothing to you any more, is there?'

Abi smiled into her friend's shoulder. 'The cancer diet. It's a real winner.'

'True. Think of all the money you've saved on gastric band surgery.'

Abi didn't laugh.

'Too early?'

Abi nodded. 'Yep. You can get going on the hilarious Big C jokes when I make it to forty, OK? I might feel safe by then.'

'OK.' Lesley hugged her even more tightly. She of all people knew how unfunny the last year had been. Despite being in the final throes of a vitriolic divorce, she had been right next to Abi through everything. From diagnosis to surgery to the shock of waking to a stoma bag she had hoped she might never need. Then onwards to chemo and yet more tests in windowless rooms where classical music failed to hide the relentless clack of the scanners. Colonoscopies. Enemas. Radiation tattoos. Scars that would last a lifetime.

Throughout it all, Lesley had never hidden. Never sent cheery texts and not followed through, like some of Abi's so-called friends. She had held Abi's hand as she was wheeled to theatre. Made soup. Made playlists blending her own shamelessly poppy taste in music with TV theme tunes from their childhood, distracting Abi from her chemo-therapy blues with 'The Wombling Song' or the merry flutes of the *Rainbow* theme tune.

She was so grateful for her thick-and-thin friend. They had been firm allies since their first year of primary school, when they had taken on the playground might of the Hammond sisters and their Scratch 'n' Sniff stickers together. Lesley could do the monkey bars and soon, despite Abi's initial reluctance, she had taught Abi to do them too. Lesley didn't believe in giving up and the last year had proved that beyond all doubt.

They pulled apart and Abi pressed her hand to the place where the stoma bag wasn't any more, feeling a pulse of freedom. No more emptying it. No more hiding it under baggy clothes. No more turning away from John when he walked into the room and she was in the middle of cleaning it, or staring at the floor when it got blocked and she was in such pain she had to ask him to help.

Over the past year it had become easier to view her body from the outside in; now she was struggling to feel like it was truly hers again.

'No more cancer jokes, I promise.' Lesley patted Abi's arm. 'I think it might be time for a glass of bubbly, though. Seeing as this is *your* party.' She pointed to the enormous banner hanging above the smoking barbecue. 'CONGRATULATIONS ABI' was spelt out in bright purple letters against a starry silver background.

'Sounds good.' Abi tried to ignore the nerves whispering inside her. It still seemed too soon to celebrate. Too much.

Lesley took two glasses of champagne from the rows lined up on a trestle table and gave one to Abi. 'Here's to you, my amazing friend. I'm so bloody glad you're OK. And I can't wait to see what you get up to now that it's all over.'

'Me neither.' Abi thought of the research she had done yesterday – the blossoming idea that was filling her with an excitement she hadn't felt in years. A new future. A fresh start.

She took a tiny sip of champagne, but it only made her feel sick. Bang went another one of her favourite things. Thanks, cancer. Lesley downed half her drink in one go while Abi put her glass down and thought again of the shadows on John's face last night. The grey strands starting to creep through his bright blond hair. The jiggle of his leg as he scanned the screen of his phone.

The window table in their favourite restaurant had never felt so wide.

'Keep up.' Lesley picked up her second glass as Abi jolted back into the present. 'Now . . .' she looked round eagerly, 'time to mingle.' Her phone bleeped. 'Shit.' She delved into her bag and checked the screen. 'It's work. Sorry. I've got to take this.'

'Well, if you will go and get promoted.' Abi patted her on the back. 'Go. Be busy and important. Do that deal. Sell that stock!'

'You do know I'm not starring in an episode of *Suits*, don't you?' Lesley rolled her eyes as she strode off. Abi stared at her back, thinking how much her friend had moved on in the year that Abi had been ill. Newly single. New job. New house. She was *carpe diem* personified. Now Abi had to catch up.

Lesley turned, putting her hand over her phone. 'Are you going to go and talk to that amazing husband of yours?'

'Of course.'

'Good.' Lesley's voice went up a gear. 'No, I wasn't talking to you, Simon.' She turned away again, her voice assuming the confident clip of the manager she had become.

The pub garden was filling up now. Sunglasses and white tops were out in force, as people showed off the last of their summer-holiday tans. They were all here. Abi's colleagues from the vascular admin team at the hospital, falling upon the breadsticks and booze like seagulls discovering a picnic basket. John's clients and colleagues talking top barbecue tips and which CEOs were still going to be in post at Christmas.

And most importantly of all, Seb was here, his normal football kit set aside for a smart black shirt and jeans, which were already on the short side after yet another bout of committed growing. His dark-blond hair was falling into his eyes as he and his girlfriend Jess hung around by the vat of Pimm's in the far corner, trying to sneak a glass whenever Rob, Abi's brother, wasn't looking. If he carried on gazing intently at the sky like that, their plan was very likely to succeed.

As Abi surveyed the familiar faces, she could almost see her former self laughing at the centre of the crowd, downing her favourite rosé and singing along to 'Viva la Vida' as it played from the speakers. How she had loved a party. The heat, the music and the sense of possibility as she stepped into a crowded room complete with maximum eyeliner and the brightest clothing she could find. But now that feeling was long gone. She felt like she belonged on the sidelines. Watching. Waiting for her old self to come back.

She felt a rush of affection as she saw the tall figure of her husband hard at work in front of the enormous barbecue, skilfully flipping sausages and burgers while holding a bottle of pale ale in his other hand. The pub had offered to cater, but John wasn't ever going to agree to that. He was born to barbecue. The flames, the meat, the oversized tongs – he even had a towering chef's hat keeping his hair at bay.

He jumped as a lick of flame shot alarmingly close to

his arm. She knew that frown only too well, and last night it had bitten so deep that she had barely recognised him. His phone had buzzed constantly as they were eating their celebratory dinner at the Japanese just down the road from his office. He had tried so hard for her – saying how happy he was about her test results, his blue eyes bright as he told her how much he loved her and talked about everything they had to look forward to. She knew he meant it, but she also saw that there was something else preoccupying him. For the past few weeks she had noticed him resetting his expression whenever she came into a room, or closing his laptop if she happened to glance at the screen. She had assumed her cancer had been the cause of this new secrecy, but last night she had realised she was wrong.

Against the quiet chatter of the clientele sharing sushi and edamame around them, she had tried to ask him about it, but got only reassurances and chinks against her glass as he raised yet another pint of Asahi to toast her recovery. She wanted to believe his denials, but she could see his long fingers worrying away at his napkin and the way he jumped every time his phone made the slightest sound. The last time she had seen him like this was when he was first setting up JCN Recruitment eighteen years ago. Two years living on credit and waiting to turn a profit. Chasing every client; interviewing reliable staff; finding the restaurants and hotels who needed back-of-house teams to clean kitchens or bedrooms overnight.

Back then, though, John had been excited. Hopeful. Last night he had just looked beaten.

Then this morning she had woken to see a different John by her side. He had smiled, joked and announced they were going to have a proper party to celebrate her news. All day he had been racing around texting and calling and doing supermarket runs, moving like a man possessed. All her offers of help had been kindly rebuffed. She must rest and get her strength back. She must look after herself and save her energy for tonight. Once she would have been in the thick of the action, but today, with every pacifying sentence, she felt further and further from the woman she had been before.

Still. He was only looking out for her. He had certainly had enough practice. During her treatment, if Lesley had been her right hand, John had been her left. He had been so kind and caring for so long – he deserved his moment of popping corks on a sunny September evening. Those tanned hands adjusting the burners had fed her ice chips. Changed sheets. Wiped puke off carpets and washed her thinning hair. They had stroked her hand during those endless nights on the ward, dispensed painkillers and dried tears. So many many tears.

He had turned away from the barbecue now, helping Abi's mum to lay out the cakes that various friends had made in celebration of this moment. Naturally her mum had beaten them all with a monster creation in the shape of a bottle of champagne. She was never one to be outdone. It was twice the size of the nearest contender, complete with frosted buttermilk icing with little bubbles arranged on a silver tray to simulate the popping of the cork.

Abi felt her stomach heave.

'Come on, Abi.' John held out a glass. 'Get this down you. It's time to get you dancing on tables at five a.m. again.'

Abi would rather put her feet up and watch *EastEnders*.

She gripped the glass. 'OK.' She took a deep breath and tried to force the doubts away. She would learn to trust her body again. And she was so lucky to be here – to be able to see these faces and hear these voices and be part of the big wide world again. She stepped closer to John and put her arms around him. Behind him, she saw her old boss undulating past, laughing with Simeon, one of John's biggest clients. It was the kind of laugh that belonged on a date that you both know isn't going to end when the bill comes. Abi knew that she and John had been on dates like that once. She wished she could imagine it happening again. A time when he could stop being her carer and start simply loving her again.

John pulled away. 'Are you feeling OK, Abi?' She hated the anxiety in his eyes. Once she had made him laugh. Had made him proud. Now she was another worry on his list. Well, she would change that. She would get things back on track. Tonight she would tell him what she was planning to do, and she knew how happy it would make him. He had been asking her to do it for years and now she was finally going to listen.

'I'm fine.' She tried to kiss him but he turned at the last moment and she lost her balance and nearly ended up joining the burgers on the barbecue.

'Good.' He turned back and kissed her forehead. He had never kissed her there in the old days. Always her lips or neck or the far more interesting places lower down. Now his kisses were dry. Careful. Cancer kisses. 'I'm sorry to nag.'

'It's not nagging.' She took his hand. 'But let's have a night off the *Casualty* routine. I'm fine now.' She ignored the tiredness that seemed to be weighing her down. 'OK?'

'Sounds good.' He let go of her fingers and turned back to the business in hand.

'Great.' She patted him on the bum, as she had a thousand times in the old days, wishing it didn't feel so forced.

They would get used to this. To the days and nights stretching out before them. To having a future.

She picked up her glass and tried to drink. Once again the bubbles tasted bitter on her tongue. She was so busy wondering how to swallow that it took her a while to notice that John was tapping on his glass.

Oh God. She choked the mouthful down.

'No, John.' She didn't want him to voice their luck out loud. She wanted to keep it close. To guard it like a hand over a flickering flame.

She felt everyone's eyes on her, and wanted to melt into the floor. Now she understood why Rob had always preferred to live in the shadows. It was calm there. Peaceful. She stared intently at her flip-flops, counting the tiny pink beads scattered across the straps.

John's voice trembled with emotion. 'You all know why we're here.' He took a deep breath. 'She made it. She gave us a few scares along the way, but our gorgeous girl bloody well made it.'

The crowd whooped and cheered. Abi tried to throw a 'save me' glance at Lesley, but her friend was too busy giggling with a man in red chinos to notice.

John waited until the noise had died down. He was always confident in front of a crowd – it came from a lifetime of pitching his business to people who generally didn't know they wanted it.

'I wanted to say a huge thank you to all of you. Thank you for helping. Thanks for all the casseroles and the soup and the *Game of Thrones* boxed sets.' His phone started to ring and a tremor crossed his face. He pulled it out and glanced at it as fearfully as if it was a hand grenade with its pin pulled out. Everything in Abi itched to see what was on the screen. He shoved it back into his pocket. 'Sorry, everyone. Yes, that's mine, and yes – you can all take the piss out of me later.'

He painted on a smile. 'Now please drink. Eat. Celebrate. Because our Abi's here to stay. And I couldn't be happier. And I couldn't be luckier. I am so very . . .' his eyes met hers and she felt tears start to sting, 'very happy that I get to spend more of my life with this beautiful, crazy whirlwind of a woman.'

Abi glanced at the sky again. It didn't seem to have fallen in. She realised her nails were digging into her palms and gently flexed her fingers.

John raised his glass. 'To Abi!'

'To Abi!' Everyone else followed suit.

Abi smiled, feeling a quiet glow of something she remembered as happiness.

Happy. Yes. She was. Deep down, she could feel that lightness that she remembered from her life before. Soon, she would learn to trust it.

Her husband held up his hand to quieten the crowd.

'So let's make merry, shall we? And nobody leaves until somebody's been sick and there's been at least one attempt to steal a picnic table.'

More whoops and applause. The crowd broke up into small groups. Abi breathed in the musk of the charcoal smoke as if it was the first time she had ever smelt it.

'You're not drinking fast enough.' Lesley was at her side again.

'I'm just warming up.' Abi took another sip and could already feel it giving her a headache. 'How was that?'

'Half-hearted.' Lesley narrowed her eyes. 'But it's a start. We'll get you back to normal soon.'

'I know you will.' It was only as Lesley turned away in hot pursuit of some cheese straws that Abi realised that she had no idea what normal meant any more. All these days she hadn't expected. A whole life to live. She could make plans now. She could make things happen. Dreams happen.

Then the music changed and 'Don't Stop Me Now' pulsed through the garden. John turned to her, hand outstretched.

'Come on. They're playing our song.'

She laughed. 'And there was me thinking you'd put this on because it's one of the few songs you've actually heard of.'

'Cheeky.' He held her tightly and then swung her away. Her head reeled but her heart was flying as he pulled her close again. 'You're taking the piss out of me, Abs. You must be feeling better.'

He twirled her around, faster and faster, and something in Abi caught alight. Joy surrounded them, in the smiles and glances from her friends and family. The people she had survived for. She forgot tomorrow. She forgot her fears. Instead, she nestled into John's arms and they swayed together and she was grateful. Grateful that her lungs were still working, that her heart was still beating, and that she was still here.

Seb

Dan was sending pictures of Gigi Hadid again.

Another buzz. Another beach. Another bikini.

Check this out.

Seb did.

Nice.

Seb raised an eyebrow, his thumbs poised to type.

Jess peered over his shoulder. 'Oh God. Boys are so predictable.'

Seb flushed and shoved his phone back into his pocket. He looked out of the pub window towards the garden, seeing his mum curled up on a bench in the corner, chatting to Gramps, wrapped up in that horrible grey cardigan. He bloody hated that thing. He had tried to charity-shop it, but of course she had just picked it off the pile so she could put it on and look like an invalid again. He sighed. His mum shouldn't wear grey. She should wear violet and polka dots and dresses designed by people who thought that orange went really well with lime green.

He angrily scuffed the ragged red carpet with his trainer and then glanced out at her again, muttering under his breath, 'She says she's better, but she's not.'

'What do you mean?' Jess twirled a strand of her cloudy dark hair around her finger. Her long black nails unnerved him. 'She looks fine. Stop stressing.'

He shook his head, irritated. 'You're not looking properly.

See?' He pointed towards his mum, who was nodding at something Gramps was saying. She looked cold and quiet. 'She's just sitting there. She's barely talked to anyone.'

'So? She looks pretty happy to me.' Jess squeezed his hand. 'She must still be a bit knackered. Her stoma reversal was only a few weeks ago.' Her fingers were warm against his. She always made him feel better. He had no idea how he would have survived the past year without her unerring ability to play the right song or say the right thing or simply to sit in silence holding his hand.

She rested her forehead against his for a second, before firing another charming smile at the barman. He shook his head firmly. 'No chance.' Their fake NUS cards had failed yet again. Seb would get that little shit from Year 12 tomorrow and ask for his tenner back.

'Oh well.' Jess shrugged. 'Back to the Pimm's, then. I've just seen your uncle Rob wandering off, so we've got the all-clear.' She chewed thoughtfully on the final McCoy's in the packet. 'Let's head outside. Seeing as this is my one night away from the books this week, I want to make the most of it.'

'Sure.' He was still thinking about his mum. Then he saw his dad turning around, waving those crazy tongs in the air, and he realised that outside was the last place he wanted to be. Last week had not been a good week in father–son relations, and after several days of successful evasion he didn't want to get caught out now.

Time for some camouflage tactics. As Jess stood on the threshold of the pub, he grabbed her hand, whirled her round and kissed her, pushing her back against the door frame, out of sight of his dad. Her mouth tasted of Diet Coke and cheese and onion and he tried to block his dad out as he kissed her.

'Ow.' She was wriggling out of his grasp.

'What?' He pulled back.

She reached out and took his hand. 'The door frame. It was digging into me.' She lowered her voice. 'But come here, babe.' She eyed the exit meaningfully. 'There's no one at home, if you want to go back there and . . .'

'I can't.' He saw his dad walking towards him and wished with all his heart that he could. 'It's my mum's big night. I have to stay.'

'But . . . when then?' That pout was increasingly visible nowadays. 'We've got so much to do before our BMATs, and you're doing that voluntary thing at the John Radcliffe at the weekend, aren't you? Like you need any more "I'm going to be an amazing doctor" points on your CV.' She shook her head. 'You're a dead cert to get into UCL, even if you never pick up a book again.'

He avoided her eyes. He was far from a dead cert for anything. She went to the girls' high school, so she didn't see him in class, fighting to keep his attention on the whiteboard. He'd fluked his A1s, but every time he'd tried to study over the summer his brain had refused to concentrate. There was too much else going on. Too many worries crowding in and keeping him awake till 3 a.m.

Jess placed her hand in his. 'I could do with some distraction, babe.'

'You know I'm happy to help.' He avoided her eyes. 'Dr White.'

She pushed him gently. 'I've told you not to say that out loud. Don't tempt fate.'

'What a load of crap.' He laughed. 'You'll ace your way into Oxford.'

'Seb.'

Shit. His dad. He kept Jess's hand in his, hoping he

could get away with a quick sweep out into the garden.

'Hi, Dad. Having fun?'

'Of course.' He had forgotten how piercingly blue his dad's eyes were, even when shadowed by eye bags so big that they belonged on an airport carousel. 'How was school today?'

Seb stood up straighter, emphasising the half-inch that he had over his dad in height.

'Fine.'

He flicked his eyes towards his dad's face and saw that he shouldn't have worried. His dad wasn't listening. He was busy scanning his phone, brow creasing into familiar furrows. His mobile seemed to be more a torture device than a way of keeping in touch with friends and family. His hands shook as he diverted the call and brushed his hair out of his eyes. Seb wished he would just cut it out and stop trying to pretend that he wasn't in his mid-forties. He clapped Seb on the shoulder. 'There's some bread out in the car – can you come and help me carry it?'

Seb had a feeling this wasn't just about carrying bread. His dad wanted the chat that Seb had been trying so hard to avoid. He looked around for an escape route, but The Antelope had always been lacking in trapdoors.

'OK.' He kissed Jess for just long enough to annoy his dad even more.

'I'll see you outside.' He turned back to her as he started to follow his dad, pulling one of the goofy faces that had mysteriously attracted her to him in the first place. Nando's. The ice cream station. That was where it had all begun.

They headed outside to the car park, where his dad started to perform his daily battle with the lock of the battered navy Volvo that had been in the family since the Dark Ages. His black Audi had mysteriously disappeared three months ago, along with his golf clubs and the over-priced mountain bike that Seb had been hoping to appropriate for himself. Seb had once felt he could ask his dad anything – well, anything except why Queen's Park Rangers never won the League. But he could still hear the slam of his dad's plate landing in the sink the night Seb had joked that he must have crashed the Audi after one too many whiskies after work.

His dad had looked like a different man that night, sucking on his beer like it was the only thing keeping him alive. 'I don't drink and drive, Seb. You know that.'

'OK.' Seb saw an anger that he had never known was there. His dad was the good-times dad. The one who took him and his mates to Wembley and bought them all burgers afterwards. The dad who let him try his first beer aged twelve. Yet he was more than that. He was also the dad who heard him screaming in the night when Mum first got ill and sat and read him the sports headlines until he went to sleep again. The dad who took him out every Sunday when Mum was sick – mountain-biking or running or watching the football in their local. The dad who was on his side.

But the night the Audi had gone, things changed. His dad's voice had been quiet. 'You should know me better than that, Seb.'

'I was only joking.'

'Well, it wasn't bloody funny.' His dad had opened his mouth to say more, but then shut it again as they heard footsteps overhead. The flush of the toilet. Silence. It was only eight o'clock and already Mum was on her way to bed. She should have been with them, forcing them to listen to bands with obscure names and cooking spaghetti bolognese that was at least fifty per cent red wine. Sadness had drained the air between them, and his dad had hunched forward over the table for a hopeless second before turning back to the fridge for more beer. He had wordlessly passed one to Seb and they had chinked bottles with all the joy of relatives on the way to a mortuary.

'Seb?' A plane droned overhead, and he blinked his way back into the car park. His dad had now won his battle with the car door and was leaning in to pull out what seemed like a thousand white bread rolls. 'Take these.' Seb held out his arms and was soon staggering under the weight of at least twenty packs of Hovis's finest.

'Things still going well with Jess, then?'

'Yeah.' Seb tried to hold onto the slippery packs with his chin. His dad had never had the best timing when it came to personal conversations, launching into the birds-and-the-bees chat on an open-topped bus in front of some toddler twins and their horrified parents.

'Good.' His dad leant back carefully against the door to close it, trying to ensure it didn't come off its hinges, as it normally did when anyone was in a hurry.

For once the door obliged him and clunked shut. 'And you're sure everything's OK?'

Seb bristled as much as a man could while carrying half a ton of white bread. 'What are you getting at, Dad?'

'Well, we still haven't talked about what happened last week.' His dad slid the keys back into the pocket of his jeans and reached out to take some of the rolls. 'You were lucky they didn't suspend you.'

Seb felt a prickle of guilt but pushed it away. 'Why are we talking about this now? It's meant to be a party, for fuck's sake.'

'We're talking now because you've been avoiding me. And don't swear.'

'Come on, Dad.' Seb shook his head. 'I'm not avoiding you – I'm studying. I've got exams, you know? And you're the one who taught me how to swear. All those football matches shouting four-letter words and chanting at the other team. Have you forgotten all that?'

A smile crept across his dad's face and for a second he looked like his old self. Despite himself, Seb began to smile back. For a second, it was like those times on the terraces, when they had grinned at each other over mugs of Bovril in celebration of QPR's latest goal.

His dad coughed. 'Look, I'm sorry if my timing's off, but I haven't seen you much, have I?'

'Well, it's not just me. You haven't exactly been around either.'

His dad nodded and ran a hand through his hair. 'Yeah. Well, there was your mum. And work's been a bit . . .'

'I know. A bit crap.' Seb felt like adding that his dad had spent more time going for very long runs recently than he had at home. It wasn't just work that was keeping him away. But he couldn't be bothered. He turned to walk back into the pub. 'Shall we get back in there now?'

'Seb?'

Seb sighed and turned around. 'Can't this wait? I know you need to tell me off and tell me not to do it again, but this is Mum's night and I want to be with her.'

'It's just . . .' His dad petered out, his eyes sliding away from Seb towards something – anything – else.

'What?' Seb felt a kick of irritation.

His dad chewed his lip in that new way of his as a yellow Skoda pulled into the car park behind him. 'I haven't told your mum about what happened at school – about what you did.' He shifted from foot to foot, seemingly incapable of keeping still. 'I didn't – I don't – want to upset her, which is why you've still got your phone and you're not grounded.'

Seb waited. He knew he had got off lightly and didn't want to jeopardise his freedom.

His dad puffed his cheeks out. 'Which means she'll go totally mad if she finds out. So you'd better not do it again, OK?'

'Got it.' Seb saw a pigeon taking a bath in a muddy puddle in the middle of the car park. It was definitely having a better evening than him.

His dad smiled. 'You kept her going, you know, Seb. You really did. You and your football and your A1 results and now applying for medical degrees.' His eyes softened. 'She has such high hopes for you.'

More pressure. Great. 'Dad, I—'

'So just keep on track, alright?' His dad held his eyes. 'She needs you to be OK, not getting into trouble at school. Thank God the office called me first and not her, that's all I can say.'

Seb clenched his fists as he thought of a thousand replies, none of which he could actually say out loud.

He kept it simple. 'Can I go now, Dad?'

'In a minute.' His dad swallowed. 'There's something else I need to tell you, before—'

'Sebastian!'

Saved. Seb turned to see Mrs Green, their neighbour with the bad breath and the lumpy cardigans. He had never been more pleased to see her.

Her eyes blinked behind orange glasses. 'How are you, dear?'

Too old to be called 'dear', that's for sure.

'OK, thanks.' The packets of rolls crackled and slid in his arms.

'How's the footie going?'

No one called it footie.

'It's great.' He started moving again towards the pub. She was his get-away ticket.

'Still playing for . . .?' Her forehead creased.

'My school.' He nodded. 'Yep.'

His dad stepped forward. 'He's captain of the first team this year.'

'Yeah.' Seb nodded. 'We're playing the Academy next week. We're going to—'

'Wonderful.' She clearly didn't know one end of a pitch from the other, and cared even less. 'And your mum?'

'She's great, Mrs Green.' He kept walking. Beer. And a secret smoke. That was what he needed.

She opened her mouth to ask more, but he was off. 'I'll see you inside, Dad.' He strode away, ducking his head to get it under the door frame, and carrying the bread through to the back. He put it down on the trestle table and walked over to his mum, sitting down next to her and flinging an arm around her bony shoulder. Once it had pillowed him through a thousand childish disappointments. Now it felt about as comforting as a carving board.

'Hello, Seb.' The exhaustion in her eyes pierced him, even as she tried to cover it with a smile. 'Are you having fun?'

He lied the latest of many lies. Lies to protect her. Lies to keep the smile on her face. 'Yeah, I'm great.' He leant forward, knitting his hands in front of him. 'I'd be even better with a beer, though.' He arched an eyebrow, hopefully.

She rolled her eyes. 'I wondered how long it would take you to try that one.'

'Well, I tried using my fake ID first.'

'Shit as ever?'

'Yep.' He nodded.

'You should take it as a compliment to your youthful good looks.' She tucked a strand of hair behind her ear. It was still so thin he could practically see her scalp, and she hadn't even put earrings on, despite being the Pat Butcher of Oxford before she got ill. He felt a familiar plunge of fear. She was better. She *was*. She had to be.

He thought back to that awful day when she had told him she had cancer, and all he had been able to think about was those Saturday football matches with a yawning gap on the touchline where she should be. He still relived that moment in nightmares. A series of snapshots. Her pale skin. The tracks of tears on her cheeks, but that big bright smile just for him. Her and Dad holding hands across the table, reaching out for his to complete the circle. He had grasped her fingers, reaching upwards to check the fast, febrile beat of her pulse. To check she was still there.

Later, when they were both in bed, he had got up, grabbed his phone and his last ten quid and run into Summertown. He had found a man to buy vodka for him in Budgens, then he had messaged his mates and they'd sat in the Parks till dawn, drinking and smoking and trying to climb the trees that were so tall they seemed to puncture the sky. Then he had gone home and got on with it. Washed up. Done the bins. Dealt with the clumps of hair in the sink and the locked bathroom door. Smiled and hugged the shuffling skeleton who had once been a mum who told dirty jokes and couldn't leave a party before midnight.

Now the doctors said she was cancer-free. But he couldn't rewind the time in between, back to the days when he could actually talk to her about everything that was on his mind. He wished he could. He wanted her help – to tell her what had happened at school last week and hear what she might say and how she might help. But she wasn't well enough for that yet – one look at her drawn face told him that.

He had to work it out by himself.

She was looking at him now, eyes shining with love. 'Are you OK?'

He opened his mouth. But then Jess was there. Short skirt, tight top, and a mouth made for kissing. She curled herself onto his lap and he held her there. He stroked her back automatically, feeling the warmth beneath the flimsy material and the jutting hooks of her bra.

'I'm good, Mum.'

He could see she didn't believe him, so he leant up and kissed Jess on the cheek. Her fingers entwined in his, holding so tightly it was as if she would never let him go.

But she would. If she had seen him last week at school. The shouting. The slam of his fist. The crunch of bone.

He couldn't forgive himself.

He might be here, at his mum's survival party, with his team captain shirt in his bag and this perfect girl on his knee. But he knew it couldn't last.

He knew it would all catch up with him.

Abi

'I'm just going to pull over for a second.'

'OK.' Abi gazed out of the windscreen at the trees towering towards the sky, drinking in the moon and the stars.

John swung the car over to the corner, coming to a halt just underneath Abi's favourite oak tree. The tall houses on either side looked on silently, windows dark and wooden gates shut across wide gravel drives. Even though central Oxford with its bells and chiming clocks and rumbling buses was only half a mile away, here it was still and peaceful.

'What is it, John?'

She turned towards him as the engine cut out, remembering how many of their conversations seemed to have taken place on these increasingly dilapidated seats. Next to her left leg was a tea stain from an ill-fated picnic, when the storm clouds had rolled in and they had been forced to eat their pasties inside the car. If she raised her hand she would find the indentation on the roof from toddler Seb's spirited exploration into the world of scissors, and if she looked to her right she would see that the wing mirror still bore a mark from the time it had coincided with the gate the night her stomach pain got so bad even she realised something must be wrong.

She loved this car. It had taken her to chemo. It had brought her back. It had kept her safe. It was one talisman among the many scattered around the house and garden. The statue of the little boy peeping round the roses that she had stared at from her chair in the sunny corner of the living room. The green candy-striped notebook that had been by her side throughout. Her yellow headphones. Her beloved Stone Roses album. The green record bag signed by Stevie Nicks, in which Abi had kept her chemo tablets and the huge purple glasses she had worn in a bid to distract people from the terrible sores on her skin.

The car was one more item in the collection that had kept her alive. Despite her tiredness, she smiled as she leant back against the less than comfortable seat. John had even proposed in here. Seventeen years ago, when she was twenty and wide-eyed and so busy partying that she hadn't even noticed that her period was late until she was eight weeks gone.

She turned to her husband, the street light highlighting the clench of his jaw, muscles bunching at the corner of his mouth as he prepared to speak. The drum of his fingers on the steering wheel told her it was something important, and she remembered his face last night. Something was wrong. As she watched him, she wondered what new fragment of their history the car was going to witness now.

He stared ahead. 'Did you enjoy the party, Abi?'

'Yes. Thank you.' She put her hand on his shoulder, squeezing it gently, feeling the tension in his muscles. She wished she knew how to take it away. 'I hope you did too.' Her heart twisted as she thought about how much pressure he had been under when she was ill. As well as managing his company, chasing new clients and contracts, he was the first contact for Seb's school – signing off on trips and reports, going to parents' evenings and topping up the

ParentPay account when it ran low. He also somehow found the time to organise her life too – coordinating her diary, dense with the medical appointments that had replaced fun outings to the pub or to gigs or the cinema as her world got smaller and smaller, until it was just the house, the car, and whichever treatment she was undergoing that day.

'I had a great night.' He nodded slowly. 'I'm so bloody proud of you.'

He leant closer and kissed her. For a moment she responded, running her fingers through his hair and pulling him towards her. Then the panic rose as it always did and she jerked away, feeling a kick of guilt as he sat back wordlessly in his seat.

She knew she should explain to him, but she didn't know how to begin. How to say that she still wasn't ready, even now. That she couldn't kiss him without reliving everything he had done for her. Carrying her to the bath. Dashing to the supermarket late at night to try to find some prunes to end her agonising chemo constipation. For years she hadn't thought twice about being naked in front of him – now she couldn't even take a sock off without wanting him to leave the room.

'I'm sorry, Abi.'

It took her a second to register what he had said.

'Sorry for what?' She took his hand in hers, trying to still his restless fingers. 'What on earth could you have to be sorry for?'

His mouth was working. 'I . . .' He stopped and then banged his fist against the wheel. 'Shit.'

'What is it?'

He leant his head against the steering wheel. 'There's something I have to tell you.'

She nodded. Waited. Whatever it was, she had been through worse.

'I'm afraid I've . . .' He faltered.

'John? You can tell me. It can't be that bad.' Whatever crime he had made up for himself, it couldn't be real. There was no way he would ever let her down.

His shoulders were hunched forward. He looked like a man defeated.

She rubbed his back, feeling its strength through his shirt. He was the one person she knew who actually used the weights stored under the bed. 'What is it?'

He shook his head. 'I just can't believe you made it through.'

She squeezed his hand. '*We* made it.'

'No. You.' He looked towards her and she saw panic in his eyes. 'I thought it would be like Noah all over again.'

'I know.' Abi squeezed his hand as she thought of his best friend who had died from pancreatic cancer two years ago. Big hair. Big smile. Six months from diagnosis until his ashes were scattered on the River Cherwell.

John closed his eyes. 'When you got ill, I didn't think you'd make it either, and the thought of losing you was such a bloody nightmare and I didn't know what I would do without you, and so I—'

She cut in. 'Don't think about that now, John.'

'But I never thought that . . .' He was crying now. 'I never thought we'd get this day. This night.'

She reached for him and kissed the tears away. Salt on her tongue. Warmth. For once it wasn't her who was in tears. She was the strong one.

'John. Stop.'

Tears were still running down his face. 'No. I've really screwed up.'

'John.' She kissed him. 'I owe you everything. OK?'

He took a tissue from the pack on the dashboard. 'Not quite everything. I think Lesley would want to take some credit too.'

Abi nodded. 'Of course.' She smiled. 'Please don't ever tell her I left her out. It would be a shame to be viciously murdered just after surviving cancer.'

He grinned, and ran his hand down her cheek. 'True. And death by Lesley – I dread to think what that would be like.'

She shook her head. 'It would probably involve a stiletto.'

'Ouch.' He was pulling her towards him again, pressing his mouth against hers. 'Through the neck?'

He felt so warm. So alive. 'Through the heart, more likely.' She would do this. She could do this. She kissed him back, harder and harder as his hands moved to her hair. His breath was soft against her as he lowered his head, dropping kisses onto her neck. She had been so tired just a second before, but now every nerve was wide awake. It had been so long. Too long. She arched her back as his mouth moved lower. Collarbone. Lower. This was living. This was why she had survived.

He stopped as he reached her bra. 'Are you OK?'

'Yes.' She fumbled behind her to pull off her top and undo her bra strap, but as usual it didn't have romance as its primary priority. Her fingers slipped and she cursed as she tried again. This time it relented and soon John's mouth moved downwards until she had almost forgotten what it would find.

The scars.

She tried to block them out.

His mouth was so warm. So hungry.

She could do this.

She wanted to do this.

She thought of the slashes across her white skin. One where they had cut the tumour out. One where the stoma bag had been.

No.

She wasn't ready. Not yet.

She pushed him away.

'Abi, please? I just want to hold you again.'

She heard his frustration. His need. But there was nothing she could do. The thought of him seeing her now – really seeing her, all bone and tissue – filled her with horror. She couldn't even look at herself in a mirror. She pulled her top down and folded her arms tightly across her chest, fighting back tears like a teenager left alone on the dance floor at a school disco.

'Damn.' John wound down his window and Abi could feel the night air cooling her burning cheeks. She tried to get up the courage to reach out and take his hand, wondering how things had got this far when once upon a time they had been addicted to each other. They had lived in total chaos at first, their lives punctuated by tangles of credit cards and unpaid bills and a tendency to get home on Sunday night with very little memory of what they had done since they had left work on Friday. But then Seb had happened. And as a girl with the kind of ovaries that didn't exactly make it easy to conceive, there was only ever one choice after that.

John had stepped up. He had started JCN, and stuck it out through lost contracts and economic downturns and colleagues leaving and taking big clients with them. He had bought a small flat and they had moved in. Two years later Abi's stereo was in pride of place in the living room, while Seb's clothes were hanging off the radiators as he proceeded to jump into every muddy puddle in the entire city. The bookshelves had been taken over by her collection – albums by David Bowie, The James Taylor Quartet and The Rolling Stones – while the lone shelf John was in charge of carried a selection of football books and thrillers.

John was speaking again. 'Are you angry with me or something? Is that why you won't . . .?' He tailed off but his eyes gave her no doubt what he was referring to.

'No. How could I be angry with you?' He couldn't be further from the truth, but she was too tired to tell him why. 'I'm just wiped out.' She took his hand. 'Let's get home, OK?'

'I didn't mean to pressure you.'

'I know.'

He made a visible effort to smile. 'OK.' He wound the window back up and started the engine. 'I just feel . . .' He sighed. 'Like I don't know how to touch you any more. Like I keep getting it wrong.' Distress was stamped across his face.

She was so used to seeing it now. A couple of times tonight the cloud had lifted, as he had placed a perfectly done burger in a bun for his mate Andy, or rolled his eyes and laughed when her mum had told him that he should have used her recipe for marinade. Then she had seen the old John. At ease. Happy.

But now here was the new John – the man the past year had created.

She wanted to help. 'John, just stop worrying, OK?'

'I'll try.' He nodded. 'I just want to make you happy.'

'You do. You make me so happy.'

He was shaking his head and she had no idea why. She was the one in the wrong here – the one who turned away from him when the lights went out. Meanwhile he had been so damn saintly throughout her illness that he might as well have had a pair of wings and a fast-track pass to the pearly gates when his time came.

He swallowed. 'I just worry that I'm going to let you down.'

'You could never let me down.' She squeezed his arm with her hand. 'Never. It'll turn out all right. Isn't that what you always say?'

'Let's hope you still think that tomorrow.'

'I will.' She nodded with absolute conviction. 'Of course I will. Oh, and I've got something to tell you.'

'Oh yes?' He drove round the corner towards their house. 'Have you finally persuaded Oasis to get back together?'

'If only.' Abi grinned. 'I'll tell you when we get inside.' Their white gate was open and the dog next door had performed his traditional 'welcome home' stunt of leaving an enormous branch just in the spot where they parked the car. John braked and Abi undid her seat belt and opened her door, dragging the branch across the gravel onto the lawn.

She walked towards the house, digging for her keys in her handbag. The window boxes she had bought on a whim last week were wilting in the unexpected heatwave and she made a mental note to water them tomorrow. And then, as she raised her key to the lock, she felt his hand in hers. She turned, and he pulled her across to sit on the wide stone step that led down to the drive. He stared down at his feet for a moment, and then he began to talk, finishing the story he had tried to tell in the car, his voice juddering and hesitating as he laid out what was before them. What he had done.

When he finished, she stared ahead, feeling the future dissolving before her. She wouldn't be telling him her plans later. Those plans were over, just pointless files on her laptop that she might never open again.

Because now she knew what was about to happen. Now she understood.

And she had absolutely no idea what to do.

October

Black Beauty theme tune ('Galloping Home')
by Denis King

I know you claim to prefer jazz, but this one's for you, Rob. Or Bobby, or Bob-Bob, or Dingbat, depending on how annoying I'm being. Happy memories of us galloping down the stairs, neighing and pissing Mum off by accidentally knocking her glass ornaments off the hall table. We always had Superglue on hand after that. And I know you always pretended you didn't like *Black Beauty*, but I used to see you peering out from your Lego corner when Vicky, Kevin and the rest of their unbelievably wholesome friends were trying to work out how to take down yet another incompetent criminal. You didn't fool me, little bro. Not for one second.

Abi

'Is it warm enough for you in here?'

Abi put down the box she was holding. It was definitely warm enough in here. She rapidly undid the zip on the thick parka that had been protecting her against the sting of the harsh October wind and ripped off her turquoise beanie and gloves.

'It's great, Mum.' She didn't want to start the day on a negative. Not when her parents were being so kind. She dropped her garments onto the dark wooden chest in the hall, only to pick them up again when she saw the suppressed grimace on her mum's face. The clench of her lips took Abi right back to the day she and Rob had been caught finger-painting the posh red wallpaper in the living room only minutes before one of their parents' wine and cheese nights. Abi had genuinely thought her mum was going to throw them both out of the window until Dad had come in and saved them by claiming that the artists whose work he sold at his shop would love it. He had been right, and they had all added their own paintings to the 'collection'. Abi hadn't dared look at her mum's face when an immaculate yellow cock and balls were discovered behind the sofa the next morning.

'I can turn the heating up a bit more if you like?' Her mum was wearing the purple 'Supermum' apron that Abi and Rob had bought with Kellogg's Corn Flakes vouchers and a precious fifty-pence piece during the late eighties. 'We don't want you catching cold.'

This seemed unlikely, seeing as Abi's bra was already damp with sweat. 'No, Mum, honestly. Thank you, though.' Over the past year it seemed that her mum's main anti-cancer strategy had been to keep her daughter hotter than the earth's core. Whenever her mum had visited, Abi had woken to find a large duvet on top of her, or a fan heater stripping all the moisture from her already dry skin.

She persuaded her coat to squeeze onto the tip of one of the hooks by the front door, turning away quickly before it inevitably fell onto the floor. She picked up her box again, praying the albums inside didn't melt in these tropical temperatures. She noticed some leaflets sticking out of the drawer of the oak dresser, covered in pictures of happy people staring out at a postcard-blue sea.

'Are you two planning a holiday, Mum?'

A flicker of uncertainty passed across her mum's face before she followed Abi's gaze and shook her head. She smoothed a lock of her precise grey bob back into place, her long nails painted the pale pink they had been since time began. Abi saw the lumps twisting her fingers out of shape and wondered if her arthritis was getting worse. She felt a twinge of guilt. They shouldn't be here, invading like this. She had created enough anxiety for her parents recently, without turning up on their doorstep with the possessions they couldn't manage to sell and nowhere else to go.

Her mum pushed the leaflets deeper into the drawer and slammed it shut. 'No. They're Ellen's from next door. She came over to tell me all about her trip and must have left them behind. We're not planning anything.'

'Lucky her.' Abi heard the note of regret in her mum's voice and resolved to bring this up again later. One thing at a time.

Her mum held her hands out for the box. 'Let me take that – you shouldn't be carrying it. You should have got movers in.'

'They cost too much, Mum.' Abi was too tired to sugar-coat things. 'Better to do it all ourselves. And I can carry it, no problem.'

Her mum's chest swelled in a way Abi recognised only too well. Words were on their way. Many, many words. Her fingers twisted the golden locket at her throat as if it was to blame for Abi's woes. Then she shook her head. 'Well, at least let me help.'

'No, Mum. We've got it covered.' Abi had nearly made it to the stairs when she tripped on a huge pile of news-papers that were waiting patiently for her dad to remember to take them out to the recycling bin. She was dangerously close to her mum's treasured line of ornaments on the dresser, and in grinding slow motion she watched the box fly forward and knock a glass dragon towards a fatal colli-sion with the hall floor.

It shattered across the widest possible area.

'Shit. Sorry, Mum.'

Abi saw her mum press her hands to her eyes in a brief moment of struggle. Then the true Brit in her was trium-phant. 'It's fine.'

Her tight lips told Abi that the opposite was true. She knew her mum had been collecting these for decades. 'It wasn't the one from . . .'

'. . . from the Mitford Collection?' Her mum's voice was unusually high. 'Yes. It was.'

'Oh God. I'm so sorry.'

'Never mind.' Her mum's face was so taut Abi was scared it might crack.

'Can we replace it?'

It was only a glass dragon. It couldn't have cost *that* much.

'No.' Her mum shook her head.

'Really?' Abi frowned. 'But . . .'

Her mum held up a hand. 'It's worth five hundred pounds, Abigail. It was a present from your grandmother.'

Uh-oh. Day one, hour one and already she was being called Abigail.

Still. Her mum had a point. They really couldn't afford to replace it. Not now. Abi felt a renewed rush of shame. Her parents were in their early seventies. They shouldn't have to deal with this kind of chaos. She placed a hand on her mum's shoulder, surprised when it was seized for a kiss.

'It really doesn't matter.' Her mum's mouth was trembling.

In her eyes Abi saw pain and fear. Pain she had been resolutely shielded from since her hospital visits had begun.

'Oh Mum. I'm so sorry.'

'Don't worry.' Her mum took one last look at the smashed glass on the floor. Abi actually thought she could see her upper lip stiffening. 'I'll just get the dustpan and brush.'

As her mum walked straight-backed into the kitchen, where she would probably indulge in a silent scream and a Werther's Original or five, Abi stood listening to the tick of the grandfather clock and staring at the shards lying on the old blue rug that had been here for as long as she could remember. When she had thought about what she would do with her second chance, moving back in with her parents hadn't exactly been top of her list. She had wanted to finally go back and finish the psychology degree she had abandoned when Seb came along. Or enter a Race for Life and not collapse before the end. Or have a week . . . a day . . . an hour when she didn't think about cancer at all. When she felt safe.

But not this. Not moving back into the house she had left with her clothes falling out of bin bags and her car stereo blasting Jamiroquai nineteen years before. Not back to the house that was so far away from Seb's school that it would take him well over an hour to get there. This wasn't a fresh start. This was a door slamming shut.

Her mum was back, dustpan in hand.

'Let me do that, Mum.' Fortunately they were saved from the inevitable argument by the doorbell. Abi opened the front door to see John teetering beneath a large white mattress.

'Why have you brought that?' Her mum frowned. 'You could have sold it, along with everything else.' Abi felt her spirits deflate a little more. She would miss their house. She couldn't bear to think of other faces in their garden, or other shoes in the hall or other writing on the big blackboard at the far end of the sunny kitchen.

Her mum sniffed. 'We do have beds here, you know.' Abi could see a lifetime of make-do and mend in her disapproving expression. She looked behind her to where John was struggling to bring the mattress inside, and wondered again where on earth Seb was, and why he wasn't here to help. Since John's news he had been using his headphones as a shield and retreating into monosyllables – the only sign that he was living with them at all being his dirty football boots by the back door and the fact that there was never any bread.

'It's an orthopaedic mattress, Mum.' Abi bent down to

47

pick her box up again. 'I still need extra support at night.' She thought of the dusky lump of a mattress that she knew was up there in the attic – the same one her mum had put on her bed in order to deter any illicit liaisons during Abi's teenage years. There was no way she was sleeping on that.

Her mum gave a tight shrug. 'Well I don't know where you're going to put the one that's up there already.'

'We'll think of something.' Abi moved towards the stairs.

'How many flights is it?' John pulled the mattress inside and shut the door. His face was bright red and she could see the sweat through his pale-blue shirt. As a man who regularly wore shorts in snowstorms, the temperature in this house was going to prove a problem.

'Just another two flights to go. I can put this down and give you a hand if you like.'

'No.' In her husband's voice she heard a savage kick of guilt. She reached up and stroked his cheek, only for him to turn away.

Abi felt a rush of sympathy. Yes, he had concealed things from her. Yes, she wished that she had known that he had been overspending, getting through first their overdraft, and then his company's too. She wished he had shared the fact that he had just lost several key contracts to Rachel, who he had trained straight out of university, and who had rewarded him by starting up a rival business and stealing as many of his clients as she could.

But she had been otherwise occupied and he had only been trying to protect her. And much as her mum might huff and puff about John and his flashy lifestyle – she had never really forgiven him for owning an Audi – Abi understood. She really did. He had only spent so much money because he had been trying to help her survive. The money had paid for all the things he had bought for her. The

Ayurvedic massages recommended by Alison, the sixty-year-old who sat in the chair next to hers in the chemotherapy suite. The highest quality organic food. The trips to the spa with Lesley to cheer her up and the post-chemo holidays to places with guaranteed sun and so much space that no one would stare at the woman with haunted eyes wrapped up in ten sarongs under the palm trees.

After the party he had wept as he had told her everything. He had apologised again and again as she held his hand, saying that he hadn't thought the future mattered without her in it – that he had taken risk upon risk to try to help her get better and to keep her positive. That after losing his best friend, he was determined to do everything he could to help her to stay alive.

She had kissed him and stroked his hair and listened. Despite his distress, she felt calm. His business was in trouble. They were in serious debt. He would have to work every hour he could to turn things around and things would be tough. But what really mattered was that she was still here. And she would do her damnedest to help. She had put the house on the market, sold as much as she could on eBay, and even tried to offload the Volvo before realising that she would have to pay to persuade anyone to take it away. After everything John had done for her, it was the least she could do.

Living with her parents wouldn't exactly make things easier, but she was ready. John had told her that he could turn things around pretty quickly if they really cut back on their spending, and moving back to her childhood home was the obvious choice. Seb wasn't helping – he had chosen this precise moment to broaden out and was urgently in need of clothes they couldn't afford. He was currently playing football in boots that were one kick away from falling apart, and Abi had been mortified last week when a particularly dangerous tackle saw his shorts rip up to the bum. While some of the teenage girls watching had enjoyed the view, Abi was left trying to blend into a tree as other parents glared accusingly at her, the mum who was letting the school captain take to the field in rags. She was seriously considering stealing the relevant kit from the enormous Sports Direct in Cowley, while the teenage staff were busy Snapchatting on their phones, but getting a criminal record was another thing that wasn't exactly top of her post-cancer list.

'Come on.' She started walking up the stairs, seeing the same pictures still on the walls and the same chip in the banisters from Rob's unsuccessful attempt to skateboard down the stairs aged six and a half. The carpet still suffered from an overdose of 1970s burnt sienna and the squeak of the top step would surely expose Seb's night-time exploits in the same way Abi's adventures with her first love Steve had been revealed in years gone by. It was all so familiar it was almost comforting, like stepping into a pair of soft pyjamas at the end of a long day. And yet so much time had passed. She was meant to have achieved things. Made her mark.

As she forced her tired legs up the second flight of stairs, she encountered the picture that had been taken on her first ever day of school. She stopped and stared at this younger version of herself. That resplendent bowl of white-blonde hair. Those chubby cheeks. Those bright bright eyes.

She shook her head and moved away.

It was time to look ahead now.

She bent her head to enter the attic bedroom she knew so well. This room had held dreams of becoming a psychologist, and finally getting to snog Gideon from her drama class at school. Nails had been painted and hairstyles tried and discarded. She could remember sitting at the dressing table, wreaking misguided havoc with her first ever Boots eyeshadow palette. The scarlet lips. The neon-blue eyelids. The world had seemed infinite then – full of boys, songs, careers and adventures. Today she could feel claustrophobia prickling across her skin. The cast-iron bedstead was still tucked under the sloping eaves, and sun spilled in through the casement window. The old mahogany wardrobe stood dustily in the corner. If she opened it, she half expected to see the platform trainers and sequinned boob tubes of her teenage years. Time had stopped in here.

Or at least it had until John flopped down onto the bed with the orthopaedic mattress. There was a brief struggle for supremacy, before the mattress won and landed squarely on his face.

'Shit.' He groaned. 'Can you help, Abs?'

She looked at the way he was writhing around underneath it, and for the first time since the rental van had juddered to a halt on the cracked tarmac of her parents' drive, she felt herself smiling.

She walked towards him. 'Well I think we know who's winning this particular encounter.' She lifted the corner, surprised by quite how heavy it was. Between them they managed to shove it onto the floor, revealing the yellowing expanse of the one her mum had chosen so many years before.

'Me?' He smiled sheepishly as he sat up. 'You mean that I won, don't you?'

'Sure.' She looked at the dust settling on his blond hair. 'It's all a bit Bernard Cribbins singing "Right Said Fred" today, isn't it?'

He nodded. 'Who knew that would be our song?'

She inhaled and the dust caught in her throat. It tickled and she started to cough. And cough. And cough some more.

His smile vanished. 'Oh God. Are you OK?'

'I'm fine.' She pushed his hand away, covering her mouth with her own. 'I had bowel cancer, not consumption.' She took a heaving breath and wiped away a tear. 'You have to stop worrying about me. It's just the dust – Mum hasn't moved this mattress since "Beetlebum" was number one.' She walked to the window, grappling with the catch just the way she had when she had stuck her head out for fag breaks when she was revising for her A levels. Eventually the window opened and she gulped down the crisp air. She didn't know how to turn round and face him. She knew the concern she would see.

Over the neatly clipped hedge she could peer into the next garden, complete with a big trampoline and a lopsided swing. She guessed it wasn't Mr and Mrs Hedges living there now. Their children had already been downing vodka and setting off firecrackers by the time Abi's parents had bought this place back when she was five. Her eyes moved across to the wide circle of her parents' garden. At the back was the swing she and Rob had sucked ice lollies on when she had mumps at the age of six. Then in the centre of the grass by her dad's beloved shed was the wooden bench on which she had pondered a thousand teenage moments. First dates, first kisses, first listens to new bands on her Walkman. The bench had seen them all. She would lie on it for hours, staring up into the branches of the willow tree as she mapped out her future. Seeing it now calmed her. Grounded her.

Now she was living her future. And every second was precious. She turned to face her husband. He was still her

John. The same blue eyes. The same tan. The same blond hair, constantly pushed back from his face with his hand in a manner her mum called 'fussy'. This was the face that had got her through her illness. These were the hands that had brought her whatever she asked for. His love had kept her strong – she couldn't start resenting it now. She tucked her hair behind her ears and pointed at the old mattress.

'Shall we get this off the bed?'

'OK.' They both started to pull. It was clearly very much enjoying its current position, and refused to budge. Then suddenly it moved, leaving them both flattened against the wall. John took a step forward and cracked his head on the sloping ceiling.

'Shit.' He rubbed his forehead. 'This place is going to be seriously bad for my brain cells.' He laughed a laugh that was undercut with sadness. 'Not that anyone will notice the difference.'

'Don't say that.' She focused on the task in hand. 'You'll turn things around. I know you will.'

Worry darkened his face. 'I hope so.'

'You told me you could. And I believe you.'

Silence.

'So there's no problem, is there?'

He still said nothing.

'John? You promised you'd tell me everything. You have, haven't you?'

'Of course.' He looked her straight in the eye. 'No more surprises. Full disclosure. I promise.'

'Good.' She kissed him lightly on the lips before patting the old mattress. 'Now. Where shall we put this beauty?'

He pointed under the bed. 'How about squeezing it down here?'

'OK.' She watched as he pushed it beneath the bedstead, lifting up the corners to make it fit. Then he stood up and dragged the other one into place. 'OK.' His smile was strained. 'So. Now we have somewhere to sleep. What's next? Is your mum going to start telling me I should get a proper job while we all have a cup of tea?'

She shrugged. 'I don't know. But she might well mutter darkly about the Audi.'

His shoulders sloped downwards and she took his hand. 'I told my folks about the business the other day. They were so kind I felt worse.'

'That must have been tough.'

'At least they're so far away up there in the Lakes that they don't have to see us crammed in here.'

'True.' If this was tough for her, she could only imagine how it made him feel. 'Maybe now we're living here for a bit we could regress completely and start watching *Neighbours*, eating Pop Tarts and wearing DMs.'

He shook his head. 'I never liked Pop Tarts.'

'What? How have I only found this out now?' She stared at him in mock-horror.

'I dunno.' John scratched his stubble. 'But it's so hot in this house, you could probably cook one on the radiator.'

'True. But don't worry, I know where the thermostat is.'

For a second they smiled at each other and she remembered the old them. He squeezed her hand and she enjoyed the strength of his fingers around hers. He kissed her gently. 'Look, you were going to tell me something. The night of the party. Something about what you wanted to do.'

No. She couldn't make him feel any worse by talking about going back to do her psychology degree. It would cost too much. Take too much time away from her earning the money they needed. She shook her head. 'It was nothing important.' She made herself look him in the eye. She had to convince him. Had to block thoughts of the excitement fizzing through her as she found the course she wanted to do and how she could apply.

'I was thinking that it's time I went back to work.' She ignored her plunge of despair.

'At the hospital? But you hate it there.'

'No I don't. It'll be fine. Besides, it's only temporary. It won't be long until we're back on our feet.'

'If you're sure.' He nodded. 'God, it's good to hear you talking about the future.'

'It is.' She felt a band of pressure lifting. 'It really is.' She took his hand. 'Now let's head downstairs and tape down all her ornaments before getting the rest of our stuff in. We don't want to be kicked out within an hour of arrival.'

They walked down together to see Seb hunched over the kitchen table. Ever his gran's favourite, he was already the recipient of a mug of tea and an enormous slice of chocolate cake.

Abi kissed the top of his head before he could deflect her. 'Seb. Where have you been? Or was it your hospital volunteering day today?'

'Nah. That was last month, Mum.' He shrugged. 'I've been at football.'

'Well, can you get outside and help with the boxes?' John's voice had an edge of irritation.

'When he's finished his cake.' Abi's mum put a protective hand on Seb's shoulder. 'He's such a big boy. I must look after him while he's here.'

Abi saw a vein standing out in John's forehead. 'That's lovely of you, Carol, but it would be great to get all the stuff in now, so we can get sorted.'

Seb chewed his cake without replying, tipping his chair

back from the table in a way that Abi definitely wouldn't have got away with when she was young. She turned round and walked into the hall. She could almost see her younger self, dashing in from school and down the hall to see the latest episode of *Black Beauty*.

She heard the low rumble of Seb asking for another slice of cake and her mum reminding John that it was no phones at the kitchen table in her house.

She shook her head, anticipating the clashes that were to come once her mum revved up and started talking about cleaning rotas and how the spice rack had to be arranged just so. She took a step forward and found herself staring at the burn mark on the pale pine of the dresser. She pressed it with her fingers, remembering the way she had frantically rearranged plates and Yellow Pages to try to cover it up all those years ago. Before cancer, before John, before Seb, and before she had possessed even the faintest inkling that life might not work out exactly as she had planned. She remembered the click of the pink Bic lighter in her hand as she lit a cigarette on a night when her parents were away. The flare of excitement in her heart.

She took her hand away and remembered where she was.

'What are you doing, Mum?' Seb was beside her and she saw that his legs were splattered in mud.

'Daydreaming.' She reached out and hugged him. Surprise was her weapon nowadays – the times when he would run into her arms at the end of his day at nursery were long gone.

'Sure.' He nodded. 'So which is my room, then?'

'It's the small one at the top of the stairs.'

'Uncle Rob's old room? The tiny one?'

'Yep.' Abi nodded. 'I'm so sorry about this, Seb. We'll get things sorted.'

He shook his head dismissively. 'It's not your fault.' He headed towards the front door, his trainers slapping against the carpet. 'And I've got way more to worry about than that, anyway.'

'Like what? Your BMAT results?' He had taken the exams a couple of weeks before. 'I'm sure you aced it.'

His face looked like he thought this was almost funny. 'Nah.' He shook his head and a bit of twig fell out of his shaggy hair. 'That's done now. Nothing I can do. No, it's . . .' He stopped, and she sensed an opportunity had been lost. 'It's just that we've got a big game coming up. That's all.'

There was no way that was the truth. 'Seb? Is there something you need to—'

'I'll go and get the boxes in.' He opened the door and headed out.

She was left staring at his retreating back, feeling a prickle of unease. She sensed secrets swirling around her. She was out of touch. Even though he had been at her side only a moment ago, her son had never felt further away.

Seb

'What are you looking at?'

'What?' Seb pulled his white T-shirt over his head and stared at his mate Dan. The rest of the team had already left, and as usual he was waiting for Dan to stop dicking about and get ready to go.

'I know. Great gains.' Dan flexed the biceps he claimed to have been nurturing since Christmas in a bid to impress the girls at the high school. 'Rock hard. Can't take your eyes off them, can you?'

'Something like that.' Seb turned round and shoved his boots into his rucksack. 'Though I think you might have got a bit further if you'd actually taken those weights you got for Christmas out of their plastic wrapping.'

Dan squirted deodorant on and reached for his shirt. 'Yeah, yeah, you're just jealous.'

Seb checked his hair in the mirror. Out of control, as usual. Ah well, it would just have to do. He was only going to work. None of his friends would see him there. No one at all saw him actually, seeing as he was glued to the sink most of the night, rinsing dried curry stains off endless white china plates. Jess kept threatening to come in at the weekend, but then her revision timetable got the better of her and she ended up messaging him at 11 p.m. asking him to come round when he was done as her parents were away again.

He loved cycling through the dark streets to her gate and letting himself in with the key her parents didn't know he had. Not that they knew much about their daughter and who she spent time with, given that they were away on business fifty per cent of the year.

'Are you pouting, Seb?'

Seb realised he was still in front of the mirror.

'No. Don't be a twat.' He rolled his eyes and picked up his rucksack. One strap gave way and it slid to the floor. Shit. More stuff to buy with money he didn't have.

Dan had his shirt on now – the red The Weeknd one that he claimed had been signed by the man himself. Seb had his doubts. His friend zipped his Adidas hoodie up over the top and turned, his blue eyes red-veined from his latest *Game of Thrones* marathon.

'Are you heading back to mine? I'm on to Season Five now. Same as you?'

'Nah.' Seb shook his head. 'Can't.'

'Turning me down again for that bird of yours?' Dan still hadn't quite forgiven Seb for getting a girlfriend. Before Jess it had always been Dan disappearing off for Netflix and chill sessions with various babes, while Seb simply headed out to kick some more balls around and wondered when his time would come. Then, a year and a half ago, there she was. Dan had been seeing a redhead from the off-licence at the time, but had still managed to be jealous, claiming that Jess was the girl of his dreams, largely on the grounds that she had long dark hair and wide brown eyes and a touch of Selena Gomez about her. But nothing had made Seb hesitate. Not for one second.

He had kissed girls before. He had taken off bras and giggled under duvets. But he had never opened up like this. When his mum got sick, Jess didn't lie, or talk shit about fighting and battles – she just held his hand and hugged him and watched Sky Sports with him and was just . . . there. A pair of arms around him in the darkness.

He had never doubted her for a second. It was only recently that he had started to doubt himself.

'Hello! Earth to Seb?'

Dan's face was inches from his and Seb could smell the wax in his short dark hair. 'So. Are you headed to the gorgeous Jess's?'

'No.' Seb slammed his locker door shut. 'Some of us have jobs to get to.'

'Again?' Dan frowned and followed Seb to the door of the changing rooms. 'Bloody hell. You must have earned enough for some new boots by now.'

'Minimum wage, Dan.' The heavy door swung shut behind them. The long corridor in front of them was dark and their shoes squeaked against the wooden floor. 'I should have got enough by next week, if they let me do enough hours.'

'You're not getting the Messis, are you?'

'Yep.' Seb nodded. 'They're my lucky charms.'

'Don't be gay.'

Seb bristled. 'What did you say?'

'Don't be gay.' Dan shook his head. 'Just get some cheap boots and stop spending all your evenings surgically attached to a washing-up brush. It's almost like you're trying to avoid her.'

'Who?' Seb pushed the door open with undue violence, conscious that something in Dan's words was making his heart beat faster.

'Jess.' Dan arched an eyebrow. 'If she was my girlfriend, you wouldn't ever keep me away.'

'Even if Selena herself turned up?' Seb knew he had to joke his way out of this. Something was cutting too close to the bone and he didn't want to think about what it might be.

'Well, maybe not then. I mean, she'd be all over me.' Dan grinned.

Seb clipped him gently round the ear. 'In your dreams, Danny boy.'

Dan shrugged. 'You just watch me.'

'And in the meantime? Who's next on your famous hit list?'

Seb's chemistry teacher appeared at the far end of the corridor and Seb decided that now was definitely not the right time to talk to him.

'This way.' He pulled Dan through a fire exit and out into the playground. He was spending increasing amounts of time ducking into doorways or lurking in the school's many fire escapes, trying to avoid awkward conversations with anyone who was expecting homework from him any time soon. Every night he tried to sit down and study, but he was too tired and his brain refused to concentrate, whirling through thoughts and feelings that he could no longer ignore. His BMATs had been a nightmare, and glowing though his UCAS personal statement was, he knew that soon he would have to face his parents and admit that he had failed.

Dad would go ballistic, but his mum was the one he worried about. There would be that moment when her eyes would widen, just before she summoned up her most supportive smile. That moment when he would know how much he had disappointed her. He felt a trickle of dread in his stomach, but stuck his chin out and forced it down. He could always catch up on schoolwork later. He had football boots to buy. A team to lead.

Dishes to wash.

Not so exciting.

Dan was still pondering Seb's question. 'I think Hope might be into me.'

Seb couldn't help it. A guffaw exploded from his mouth. 'Hope?' The daughter of his mum's best friend Lesley was generally to be found welded to her boyfriend, Zane, who had the joint benefits of being nineteen and owning a car. Dan didn't stand a chance.

'What?' Dan spread his arms wide. 'I tell you, she was hot for me at that party. She was practically drooling. If I'd got her on her own, I could totally have had her.'

'She was hot for the joint you had in your hand, mate.' Seb rolled his eyes, sick of the macho banter that only made him feel how much he was starting to stand out. He headed back a football that had been kicked in error by a scrawny junior with tufty black hair. The boy waved in thanks and Seb remembered the days when he had looked at the school football captain with eyes like saucers, hoping against hope that one day he might become his friend. If you set the endless bloody homework and looming A2s aside, being in Year 13 definitely had its advantages.

'Nah.' Dan strode out through the rusting metal gate. 'She was twirling her hair round and round her finger. She was into me, I'm telling you. It was a sign.'

'Yeah. That you're deluded.' Seb went up to the tangle of bikes on the racks outside school. His stood out purely because it was ninety per cent rust. As he unlocked it and pulled it out, he heard a squeal of protest from the brakes. Clearly they were warming up for his journey to the restaurant – past Queen's and all the other colleges full of people who hadn't screwed their lives up – before they inevitably failed as he reached the roundabout at the bottom of the High Street.

He felt another stab of anger at his dad. His mum kept asking him if he was angry about the money, but it was more than that. He could earn his own cash. It was that he and his dad had got on OK when his mum was ill. And now she was better, his dad seemed to be doing his best to turn into that dickhead dad from *Modern Family*. He kept giving Seb advice about applying to university without knowing a damn thing about the endless crazy of UCAS or BMAT or anything, and it was all Seb could do not to laugh in his face.

He didn't want to have to listen to him any more. And the best way of doing that was to avoid his dad for as long as possible. 'I could come round later, yeah? We could get pizza and play FIFA?'

'Sure.' Dan frowned. 'If my dad's not being too embarrassing. I borrowed his phone the other day and saw that he's on Grindr now. Like him coming out hasn't messed things up enough, now he has to shag someone wherever he goes.' His eyes were heavy with disgust. 'Makes me want to puke. So when you come over, I'll let you in at the side door so you won't have to talk to him.'

Seb nodded. Dan's dad had come out last year by turning up to Dan's family birthday dinner with his new boyfriend. Dan's mum had moved back to her family up north, leaving Dan with no choice but to live with the dad he now hated while he finished school.

Dan grinned. 'Bring me some curry if there's any left.'

'I'm not a delivery boy, you dick.' Seb shook his head as he climbed onto his bike. 'Get your own curry.'

'Whatever. Worth a try.' Dan turned to head off to the bus stop.

Seb shook his head, settling the rucksack on his shoulders before kicking off without looking. He was only prevented from crossing the path of a white van by a hand grabbing his shoulder.

The white van man lived up to expectations by sticking his head out of the window and yelling 'Bellend!' at the top of his voice.

Seb felt a jolt of adrenaline and turned to thank whoever had saved him.

'Shit. It's you.' He turned away again.

'A thank you would have been fine.' Marc's green eyes gazed at him impassively. His short bleached hair was shaved close and his leather jacket was tight around his shoulders. 'But then you're not a big fan of those, are you?'

'Just piss off.' Seb made to set off again, but was prevented by the approach of a learner driver who appeared to be terrified of going over ten miles an hour. He was trapped. Right next to the one person in the world he was trying to avoid.

'Look.' Marc came closer and Seb automatically moved his bike backwards. He didn't want it happening again. The thing he couldn't tell his dad about. The secret that lay behind the punch he had thrown.

'What?' In a minute he would go and drive the learner driver's damn car himself. Anything to get out of here.

'Look, I get that you have an issue with me. But I wasn't trying to piss you off, Seb. I just misread things. You know?'

'Yeah, you did. We were in the playground, for God's sake. What the hell were you thinking?' Seb folded his arms across his chest. 'You might have asked me, before . . .' He realised he didn't want to complete that sentence.

'I'm really sorry.' Marc's voice was soft, but Seb refused to go any closer. There was danger in that, and God knows he had enough shit going on already. 'If it's any help, I felt like a total loser. I thought you wanted me to kiss you. You

64

were leaning so close and I'm new here so I didn't know if you—'

Seb looked around to check no one was listening. 'I was leaning close because those kids were screaming their heads off playing basketball behind us.'

'Well I didn't know that!' Marc shrugged and Seb saw a glimmer of vulnerability beneath his smile. 'But don't worry. Your knuckle sandwich made things perfectly clear. You're not into me.'

Despite himself, Seb could feel a smile starting to form. 'Knuckle sandwich? Are you twelve?'

Marc's lean face broke into a smile. 'I certainly sound it.' He shoved his hands in the pockets of his skinny jeans. 'Shows you how many fights I've been in.'

'None?'

'You got it.' Marc arched an eyebrow. 'Damn. And I've been trying to cultivate such a butch image since I got here.'

'Really?' Seb glanced at his watch. 'Can't say I'd noticed. You've been at this school for nearly two months; how long is it going to take?'

Marc's eyes were lasering into his. He had to get away. He looked over his shoulder. Learner driver had finally made it past him.

'It's OK, I'm not going to do it again. I'll resist you.' Marc glanced at his phone. 'I'm off to meet someone now, as it happens.'

'Oh yeah?' Seb attempted a casual air that he suspected he couldn't pull off. 'Who's that?'

'No one you know.' Marc smiled a smile that belonged in a dark corner of a sweaty nightclub. 'Just a guy from the gym.'

'Right.' Seb swallowed. 'Well, great.'

'So I won't be trying it on with you again.' Marc shook his head. 'It's strange. My gaydar is normally so reliable.'

'Well not this time.' Seb tried to slow his breathing.

'If you say so.' Marc stayed for one more disconcerting look. 'Have a good evening. I know I will.'

'See you.' Seb felt the urge for more explanation. For a lie. 'I'm with Jess tonight. My girlfriend.'

'Good for you.' Marc raised his hand. 'Enjoy.'

'I will. She's gorgeous.' Seb pushed his bike towards the road. 'See you. And . . .'

Marc turned and raised his eyebrows. 'Yes?'

'Sorry. For punching you.'

Marc shook his head. 'Don't worry about it. Made me look way more rugged than usual. Never a bad thing.' He grinned. 'Just as well we cleared that up, seeing as we'll be seeing more of each other now.'

The words were a slap. 'Why?'

'Because you've moved in next door to me.' Marc grinned. 'There's no escaping me now.'

As he crossed the road, Seb felt a rush of frustration. Great. He was living next to Marc. Bloody hell. Marc's mum would tell his mum what he had done and he would have to explain and she would have even more to worry about and it would all be his fault. For the past year all he had wanted was for her to survive, and now that she was still here, he was on the verge of totally fucking things up.

He sighed and set off on his bike. He thought about Marc heading off to meet his new man. He thought of the moment those lips had touched his.

No. Definitely not his scene.

Jess. She was the one for him.

For sure.

Abi

Abi dropped the needle onto the record, loving the crackle before the first chord kicked in. Her dad had brought this beautiful wooden record player home from a *Blue Peter* bring-and-buy sale when Abi was ten. Mum had wanted him to buy a mower. Abi was very happy he had been distracted.

'How's this for an eye-opener, Dad?' She grinned as the opening chords of The Jackson 5's 'ABC' bounced through the speakers that her dad had lovingly installed at every corner of his shop. Gryff's Gallery was dedicated to his two loves – music, and the art prints and limited editions that he sourced and sold to supplement the picture-framing that lay at the heart of his business.

'Pardon?' He was leaning against the wide counter in the middle of the shop, thick grey hair standing on end as he peered intently at a letter that he had found on the doormat amidst a tangle of flyers and junk mail. Abi walked towards him. The counter was piled high with paints, pens and rulers and the card machine was buried beneath a pale-blue football shirt and a tiny pair of ballet shoes with pink ribbons wound round the soles.

Her dad was still engrossed, his fingers playing absently with the corner of the letter.

'There's nothing like a bit of The Jackson 5.' Abi smiled and tried out a twirl, only to trip against a pile of pictures wrapped in brown paper that were lying on top of the navy carpet. She started to move them, only to discover they had obviously been strategically positioned to cover a very large stain. She hastily put them back. 'Is there, Dad?'

'No, darling.' He clearly wasn't listening. His thick black glasses were low on his nose, and his brow was creased in concentration.

'What's the letter about?' She walked towards him and peered over his shoulder.

'Nothing.' He crumpled it up and shoved it in the pocket of his ancient Levi's. Then he turned and headed towards the kettle that he kept in the tiny kitchen at the back. 'Nothing at all. Tea?'

'Yes please.' Abi walked back to the door and switched on the lights, discovering that they made very little difference to proceedings, except for their uncanny ability to highlight the areas where the shop was at its most chaotic. One feeble spotlight was trained on a disorderly pile of posters emblazoned with the names of various European cities, while another picked out a pile of paint samples and a tower of cassette tapes that really should have been in the tip.

The doorbell jangled and her brother appeared, huddled into the leather jacket that was a remnant of his last shopping trip with his ex-girlfriend. It was two years old. He had a habit of holding on to the past. It was probably why he was still working here, soldiering on in the framing room downstairs, despite once nurturing ambitions to become an artist himself.

'Abi!' His face broke into a smile. 'Good to see you. To what do we owe this honour?'

'Hey, Dingbat.' His childhood nickname never got old. 'I just fancied a visit. I haven't insulted you in over a week, so I thought it was time I got some practice in.'

'I see.' His brown eyes crinkled up at the corners. 'Well, let's see who gets the most insults in today, Batfink.' They hugged. He smelt of paint and toast and she loved the familiar scratch of his beard against her cheek.

'You'd better be quick if you want to get any more in.' She checked her watch. 'I'm off to the clinic in a bit. I'm meeting my boss to talk about returning to work. Dad was heading in here, so I thought I'd hitch a lift.'

Rob gave a low whistle as he shrugged off his jacket. 'You're going back to work already? Wow, you don't mess about.'

Abi ignored the thickening dread in her stomach at the thought of spending her days typing up letters and answering queries in the same hospital where she had been treated. Even going in through the front doors made her chest feel tight and despite the fact that she worked in a different specialty, she couldn't shake the feeling that everyone around her had seen the inside of her colon. She had returned to work there in between bouts of chemo, and had vowed that once she was in remission she would find something new. A fresh start.

But now that their circumstances had changed, getting some money coming in was their priority. Since they had moved in with her parents two weeks ago, John was putting in longer hours than ever, trying to dig his company out of its financial hole. He was chasing new clients and doing his best to woo old ones back to the fold. He was focused and determined – up at five for a run before leaving the house an hour later to head to the office, a slice of toast clamped between his teeth and his hair still damp from his speedy shower.

He was so busy she really only saw him at weekends, but even when they had Sunday breakfast together or shared an afternoon walk across the University Parks, she could feel that he wasn't really with her. There was a darkness beneath his smile; a loneliness in his eyes. Abi kept trying and failing to bridge it.

When she had been diagnosed they had sustained themselves with the things they would do after she got better. Visiting the Bodleian. Strolling across Christ Church Meadow or around the Botanical Gardens. Driving across Canada. Taking Seb to watch the World Cup. Spending a week at the Edinburgh Festival. Now all they talked about was paying bills and how to save more on food.

Abi sighed. It was only temporary. Everything would be all right.

Yes.

'Are you OK?'

She smiled at her brother. 'Sure.'

'Good.' He rubbed his hands together. 'Man, it's freezing in here. Is the heating still broken, Dad?'

'Yes, but I'm going to fix it today.' Her dad risked pneumonia by taking off his battered tan jacket to reveal his ancient leather tool belt. 'I've come prepared.'

'Oh Dad.' Abi cringed. He didn't have the strongest DIY track record in the world. 'Are you sure? I mean, you could get someone in to help.'

'No.' She could see the smears of dirt on his glasses as he vehemently shook his head. 'That's not how I do things, Abi. You know that.'

Abi raised her eyebrows at Rob. She knew they were both thinking of the same thing. The great gas explosion of 1990, when their dad had lost most of his hair and all of his DIY credibility when he had decided to mend the gas oven just as their mum was about to put in the Sunday roast. It had been sandwiches for lunch that day.

'Well, can you give us a warning?' Rob's eyes glinted. 'So we can run?'

'I will do no such thing.' Their dad stretched his hands above his head, as if warming up for a running race. His sweatshirt had once been emblazoned with the Gryff's Gallery logo, but all that remained of it now were a few crumbling dots that indicated where the letters had been.

'Quick! He's going in. Duck for cover!' Rob jumped behind the counter and crouched down as if under fire.

'Here.' Abi picked up two big square mount boards and held one out to him. 'Protection.'

The two of them giggled as their dad huffed his way to the radiator on the wall behind them. 'That's it.' He sighed. 'No inheritance for you two.'

'Like that's a threat.' Rob shook his head.

Their dad was detaching an alarmingly big wrench from his belt. This was a scenario that never ended well.

'Seriously, though, this place is in a bit of a state, isn't it?' Abi looked around. 'I mean, there are cobwebs up there that are so thick they could be in a Disney film, just before the chirruping birds come in to clean.' She peered at the carpet beneath her feet. 'And are those mouse droppings?'

'Maybe.' Rob shrugged. 'Though God knows they could find warmer places to stay.'

'And what's that massive hole in the wall?'

His voice was low. 'We'll sort it. We've been busy.'

'Really?' Abi looked around. 'God knows how, given the state of this place. I would think customers would be running screaming to that new place in town. The Arthouse, or whatever it's called.'

'Fine. Sorry we haven't done a better job.' His lower lip was protruding now.

'Oh God, sorry, Rob.' Her and her massive gob. 'That wasn't what I meant. It's just that—'

Her brother was already standing up. 'No. You're right.'

'What?' She looked at him, bewildered. 'Why are you so cross? I was only saying.'

Her brother's shoulders sloped downwards. 'It's just been difficult. With . . . things.'

'What things?' Abi blinked and stood up herself.

Rob shook his head. Abi seemed to be getting that a lot nowadays. 'Nothing. It doesn't matter.' His words held all the petulance of their childhood arguments over dens, or the stripy spade that both of them claimed as their own. Once again Abi felt like someone watching the light disappear as she was shut out of a room. She felt a kick of irritation. She didn't need the kid-gloves treatment any more.

'What is it, Rob?' She put a hand on his arm.

'Nothing.' He had never been one for discussing his feelings. When she had been ill, he hadn't once talked about his fears or how watching her go through treatment had made him feel. Nor had he ever used the word 'cancer'. On his visits bearing DVDs or books he hadn't even mentioned her illness – he had just sat and talked about the latest exhibition at the National Portrait Gallery or what he had watched on TV the night before. Yet she had known how worried he was. It was there in his tight hugs. The heavy silences as he stared out of the window, avoiding looking at her face.

She searched for a change of topic. 'How's your painting going?' Once upon a time Rob had been the toast of his art college. His canvases had been big. Bold. Joyful. They had sold well back then, but afterwards he had tried to change direction and orders had slowed. And then stopped. Every now and then there was a flash of excitement – a big commission or a new idea – and Mum would be straight on the phone to all her friends. But then things quietened down again and the family went back to hoping that one day his big break would come.

Rob sighed. 'It's not.'

'Why? You were really into it when we last talked about it.'

'Yeah. But that was over a year ago.'

'Was it?' She felt a wave of embarrassment. She had let things slide.

'Yeah.' He fiddled with the strap of his bag and she saw that his fingernails were bitten to the quick. 'There was that scholarship. In Italy?'

'Oh yes.' She frowned. 'What happened with that?'

'It didn't pan out.'

'I'm so sorry. Why not?'

'Doesn't matter.'

'Rob?'

He looked at her and in his eyes she saw the truth, just as she had always been able to see it. The time he had told their mum that she was in the garden having a joint, because he was furious with her for stealing the gold lighter Grandad had given him. The time he had lost her Barbie doll at nursery and she had instantly seen through his lie.

She stared at him. 'Oh God. Was it because I was ill?'

'Yeah.' He shrugged. 'I turned it down. But I wouldn't have been anywhere else but here. No bloody way.'

Tears pricked her eyes. 'Thanks, Dingbat.'

He looked her in the eye and nodded. 'No worries, smelly pants.'

'Hey.' She checked her watch. 'It's not even nine thirty yet – it's too early for pants-related insults!'

He smiled sweetly, combing a hand through his messy

brown hair. 'Well, you did say you were heading off soon. I couldn't resist.'

She went to whack him, but he ducked away and soon she heard the heavy tread of his feet on the stairs as he headed down to the framing room.

His timing was good, as their dad chose this moment to clank the wrench against the radiator valve. He beamed as it started to turn. As he leant forward to exert more pressure, the letter fell out of his pocket, and Abi bent down to pick it up.

She read the header without even meaning to. *Offer for Cowley Road property.*

She read on, her pulse starting to accelerate. 'Someone's offering to buy the shop? Why, Dad?'

'Oh, I don't know.' He tried to turn the wrench again. 'Don't worry about it.'

She ignored him. 'It says here they've been having discussions with you. That there have been negotiations.' She stared at him. 'Dad. What's going on? You can't sell this place. You love it. You built it up from scratch.' She averted her eyes from the patch of mould she had just noticed on the ceiling. 'You can't sell it to a . . .' She read on. 'To a bloody estate agent. Like the world needs any more of them.'

Her dad was focusing squarely on the wrench. 'Well, it's only an idea.'

'But why, Dad? Why?'

He sighed. Turned. She could see that he was revving up to say something difficult. First sign – repeated wiping of hands on jumper. Second – pushing glasses carefully up his nose. And the third and conclusive sign – rapid blinking. She waited. Her dad was a man of few words, but when he did get a sentence out it was normally worth listening to.

'Look . . .' Down went the hands again, and she saw

how the veins stood out above the fading tan of his skin. They looked like an old man's hands, and the sight made her feel afresh the fragility of everything around her. No matter how hard she tried to shore life up, to feel safe, she knew now that the shadows would always seep through and try to choke her.

'What is it, Dad? Are you OK?'

'Erm . . .'

No. NO. Her voice was a whisper. 'You're not ill, are you?' She couldn't bear it.

'No.' His eyes widened and he squeezed her arm tight. 'Not me. Nor your mum.'

Sadness clouded his face. When she'd got cancer, she knew he had wished it had been him.

'We're right as rain.'

She took a deep, shuddering breath. 'Thank God.'

'It's just that your mum was wondering . . .'

This was never a good start. Abi did the maths. If her dad was actually saying this out loud, that meant her mum must have been on the warpath for at least two weeks. He could normally head her off for that long by strategic trips to the potting shed or by putting in longer hours at the shop.

'She was wondering whether I should sell up.'

'Why?'

'Her arthritis is getting worse and we were thinking of trying to take things a bit easier. Maybe moving somewhere sunny. Once you're all back on your feet, of course.'

Abi remembered the leaflets in the dresser drawer. The sunny skies. She should have known.

But no. Not the shop. Not Dad's shop.

'It's not really making that much money, anyway.' Her dad's face told her that this was probably one of his infamous understatements. 'So . . .'

'No.' After so many months of living on pause, it was such a relief to know what she wanted for once. 'Don't. Please don't sell it. I'll work here. I'll manage it. You won't have to do a thing.'

'I can't ask you to do that. Not when you're just getting your health back.' He shook his head. 'It's too much for you.'

'It's not.' She was full of an energy she had forgotten she possessed. 'And I'm not ill any more, Dad.' She ignored the dreams that still came – dreams of murky tunnels sucking her downwards into a place she never wanted to see again. The way she saw every twinge and ache as a potential symptom. The daily checks and endless googling to try to prevent the next disaster. She still couldn't trust her body. It had betrayed her too many times.

The dangers were everywhere, but maybe the only way to escape them was to try even harder to live.

Her dad squeezed her arm. 'I can't ask it of you. You're not yourself yet, Abi.'

She stopped, surprised. She had been trying so hard to convince everybody otherwise. She had been telling bad jokes and eating her greens and drinking her smoothies.

'But I've worked here before.'

He scratched his head. 'A long time ago. And I don't know . . .'

She had to convince him. For once, her way forward was clear. 'Please, Dad. Let me try.' She held his eyes.

He exhaled. 'Are you sure?'

'Yes.' She nodded. 'I am.'

'I'm fairly sure your mother will want to kill me if I say yes.'

Abi kissed him on the cheek. 'Well that's nothing new, is it?'

He reached his arms round her and pulled her close. 'I'll make sure you're paid properly, mind.'

She drew back. 'You'd better. You don't want us living in your attic for ever, do you?'

He smiled, and he saw the tiredness etched across his face. He had grown old in the past year. She had never had the clarity to see it until now.

'It's so good to see you smile, love.'

Tears were glazing his eyes and she felt another kick of guilt at what she had put them all through. That had been the worst thing about having to tell them about her diagnosis – seeing the fear in their faces and realising quite how much she would be missed. She kissed his cheek before walking over to the huge shop window, currently housing a tired *Alice in Wonderland* print and a Spurs poster in a bright yellow frame.

'I think I'll start here. With the window.' She grabbed her jacket. 'I'll go and talk to my boss, but I'm sure it'll be fine. They were holding my job open but they'll have a temp in to cover until they get someone permanent.' She giggled, full of a rush of freedom at the thought of never sitting at that desk again, surrounded by piles of medical notes and dictation tapes. Now she understood how words in bold on a white sheet of paper could change lives. She needed to get away from all that.

Her dad picked up his wrench again. 'Shouldn't you talk to John first?'

'John?' She stopped with her fingers on the door handle. 'Of course.' She nodded. 'I'll call him now.' The bell jangled as she opened the door. 'See you later, Dad.'

She dialled John's number and left a voicemail before turning left and walking down the Cowley Road, past the deli with the huge raisin pastries in the window, and then on past the second-hand shops where she had spent so much of her school holidays hunting records or books or long flowery skirts with bells on.

She was so busy thinking about window displays and how to source local artists that she wasn't concentrating on where she was going. She slammed into someone at speed, her head colliding with his shoulder as he walked the opposite way.

'Shit.' She put a hand to her head, rubbing it to try to take the piercing pain away. 'I'm so sorry.'

The man pulled his headphones out. 'Are you OK?'

'Yes.' Abi pressed her head one more time. No blood. Good. 'Lost a few brain cells, but they're probably the ones containing all the lyrics to "Saturday Night". No biggie. And you?'

'I'm OK.' He grinned. 'Tough guy, me.'

She stared at him. That smile. The tiny mole above his lip.

It couldn't be.

'Steve?'

His eyes were widening with recognition too.

'Abi?'

There he was.

His black curls were shorn and he wasn't wearing the denim jacket that he had barely taken off during all their time together. But his brown eyes were dancing. His smile was wide. And he still wore the same aftershave. The tang that took her back to sweaty gigs in random pubs and the knowledge that the man up on that stage was hers, all hers.

'How are you?' They spoke in unison.

And then they hugged, right there in the middle of the street, and Abi felt seventeen again.

She pulled away and grabbed his phone.

'Hey.' He blinked. 'What are you doing?'

She tapped on Spotify. 'Just checking.'

'Checking what?'

She scrolled through his playlists. *Rock. Sunday mornings. Saturday nights. Camping. Hangovers.* She saw bands she loved. Albums she had queued outside Our Price for hours to obtain. She saw her youth. Her first love.

She handed the phone back. 'Excellent taste. Just checking you haven't changed.'

He threw his hands wide. 'Of course I haven't.'

She grinned. 'Good.'

'And I'm guessing you haven't either?'

Abi debated for all of a nanosecond. She could tell him about cancer and debt and how she hated looking at herself in the mirror. But it would be so much more fun to keep it to herself. She shrugged, feeling the weight of the past year lift from her shoulders.

'Not one bit. Not one single bit.'

At last, someone was looking at her without concern in their eyes.

It felt fantastic.

November

'Get Happy' by Harold Arlen and Ted Koehler (performed by Ella Fitzgerald and Billy May and His Orchestra)

Gran and Gramps, this one's for you. It has your beloved Ella. It has a full orchestra and it doesn't have one of those unsubtle finale key changes that you hate so much. I can see Gran dancing round the kitchen to this, preparing endless vats of jam or chutney, while Gramps wound the unreliable grandfather clock in the hall. I remember Gramps saying Ella was the only woman he'd ever have left Gran for, but only if she promised to sing to him every day and to learn to make a decent cup of tea. This makes me think of the two of you, and of blackberrying and playing pick-up sticks and fighting with Rob over who got the last hot cross bun. You two, scones, climbing trees and Ella. My summer holidays in a nutshell.

Abi

'Lesley. Hi!' Rob spilled his coffee down his front.

'Smooth, Rob. Smooth,' Abi muttered under her breath as she walked round from behind the counter to hug her friend. 'How are you doing?'

'You know. Glamorous as ever.' Lesley's dark fringe was stuck to her forehead and rain dripped down her neck. 'I'm on my fifth emergency brolly from Boots and it's only the beginning of November. Maybe this is the year I'll break my all-time record and make it to fifteen. Or I could save time by setting fire to two fifty-pound notes and shoving my head in a bucket of water.'

Abi grinned. 'Where did you leave the last one?'

'On a bus. Classic.' Lesley lowered herself into a soggy bow. 'But I accidentally put one in a rubbish bin on the high street the other day, which was a new low.'

'What did you mean to throw away?'

'My chewing gum. Which then glued my fingers together just to really make my day complete.'

'Nice.' Abi nodded. 'But still probably more fun than the time you forgot to wash that bleach out for a whole day and ended up having to shave your head.'

'Definitely.' Lesley nodded. 'It took Dean Mackelthwaite two years to stop calling me Willis.' She looked at Rob. 'As in Bruce.'

He nodded. 'I was just about keeping up with that one.'

He glanced up at the ceiling, as if in thanks for getting a coherent sentence out.

'I hear bells.' Lesley held up a finger as her phone chimed. 'Pushy teenage daughter has signed me up to some ridiculous dating site, with a stunning' – she made quotation marks in the air – 'picture of me in the mid-nineties attached.' Another chime. 'God, they're going to be so disappointed when the real me turns up, no matter how many of those new-fangled BB creams I use.'

Rob opened his mouth and then closed it again. Abi shook her head. His unrequited love was destined to last for some time yet, it seemed.

'Their tongues will be hanging out, Lesley.' Abi hugged her. 'There'll be jaws hitting floors all over town now you're back on the scene again.'

'*This* is why you're my best friend.' Lesley's eyes swivelled to her bag as her phone chimed again. 'No, I am not obsessed. I am NOT.' Her eyes glinted. 'Though, of course, it might be work . . .'

Abi nodded. 'It might be. Now you're a manager and all.' She saw her brother staring intently at the floor and felt a pulse of pain for him. His crush on Lesley had begun at the age of six when she had dug him out of the sandpit after her older sisters had buried him up to his neck. It was still going strong now and his descent into monosyllables whenever he saw her wasn't exactly helping his cause now she was divorced and actually available.

Lesley fished her phone out of her bag. 'I think I'm still too damp to use this.' She looked around. 'Got a tissue or something?'

'I'll get a towel.' Rob started walking left. Then right. Then left again.

Abi sighed. 'They're in the kitchen.'

'Oh. Yes.' He headed out the back, returning with a Bodleian Library tea towel with a huge coffee stain across the top.

Abi took it from him, leaving him alone with Lesley for a minute while she replaced it with a clean one. Maybe this could be his moment. He could finally come into his own. But when she returned, she was unsurprised to find that conversation was not exactly flowing.

It turned out he had beaten any previous small-talk lows. Lesley was repositioning her bright yellow umbrella against the wall, and this appeared to have inspired Rob to tell her all about the time he and Abi had experienced a vomiting bug so extreme that their dad had been forced to get professional carpet cleaners in.

She looked at him despairingly as he talked on and on, his voice sounding increasingly strangled, stepping in to rescue him just as he reached the 'carrot chunks' phase of his monologue.

She handed Lesley the tea towel. 'So how do you think the place looks now?'

Rob dropped his head in defeat and Abi felt a beat of sympathy. He dug his hands deep in the pockets of his insanely skinny grey jeans, scuffing his dark blue Converse against the carpet.

'It looks amazing.' Lesley mopped her face and hair with the towel, then shrugged off her raincoat, hanging it on a bust of Charles Dickens that had lived at the back of the shop ever since Abi could remember. She had moved it nearer the door, positioning it high up on the wall, where the giant of Victorian fiction made a rather resplendent coat stand.

'You must have worked really hard.' Lesley dabbed her shoes with the towel. 'Are the spiders homeless now?'

'They are.' Abi smiled. 'And they're not happy about it. I think they've all gone to the bookies next door.'

'Sensible. Plenty of dark corners in there.' Lesley nodded and turned to Rob. 'Has she tornadoed through your framing room downstairs, too?'

'No.'

'His space is sacred.' Abi was pleased to see him smile. 'And I'm scared of what I might find.'

'Abi.' He flushed.

Three more chimes from Lesley's phone. With each one Rob's shoulders slumped lower. 'I'll head back down there now. Lots to do.' He raised his hand and dropped it again. 'I'll see you later, Lesley.'

'Sure.' Lesley was hunched over her phone. 'That's three messages now from Mr Academia. And two from Mr "I'm a pilot, honest". Oh, and one from a doctor.'

'Really?'

'Hope said on my profile that I'm up for "anything, any time". I'll be killing her later, after she's got her UCAS form sorted, of course.' Her words were belied by the warmth of her smile. Her daughter was the kind of girl who ended up on the front of school prospectuses. She played the flute. She got endless A*s. She had never had a ridiculous tattoo or turned up puking on the doorstep with a bottle of cheap vodka in her hand. 'Look at *this* guy.'

Abi peered at the screen as her own phone started to ring.

'Bloody hell. He's gorgeous.' Lesley was swiping away. 'In real life he's probably seventy-five with a drink problem.' She sighed. 'But a girl can dream.'

Abi answered the phone, still looking at the photo. 'Hello?'

'Hello, you.'

She blinked, instinctively turning away from Lesley.

The voice continued. 'Dilemma time. I've got an Everything Everything ticket in one hand, and a Benjamin Clementine ticket in the other. Which do you want?'

She leant back against the counter, remembering the twist of the phone cord in her hand as she crouched in the hall as a teenager long after she should have been in bed. The same voice. The same subject. 'Benjamin Clementine, of course.'

'Why?'

'Because nothing could be more exciting than Benjamin Clementine with a Steinway.'

His laugh was low and made her think of pints in pub gardens or the crackle of a match as it lit a cigarette.

'Damn right. And how are you, Abigail?'

'I'm well, thanks.' She still couldn't say that phrase without feeling a bite of disbelief. She knew how magical it was for her body to be healthy.

'Fancy coming out next week?'

'What?' She panicked. She had to shut this down. She didn't want to think about what 'this' meant. 'I'm sorry, I can't. I'm pretty busy at the moment.'

'I know, I know. Family and stuff.'

'Yeah.'

His voice was warm, and she could imagine his smile. 'It's just that I've got these spare tickets to see The National. And I thought it might be your kind of thing.'

It was. It really was. For a moment she allowed herself to toy with the idea.

She could feel Lesley's eyes burning into her back. No.

'Sorry. I wish I could.'

'Shame. Maybe next time?'

'Yeah. Maybe.' She felt her cheeks burning. 'I've got to go now. Take care.'

'OK.' He sounded surprised. 'Laters.'

It was the same sign-off as the old days. The Britpop days. The days half a lifetime ago when she wore her Oasis T-shirt and her DMs and spent every weekend with him up in London blagging her way into the Camden Palace or the Brixton Academy. She was sixteen. She was in love. She was going to university to study psychology. The way ahead was clear.

How long ago it all felt. She sighed and tapped her phone against the counter, which, despite her best efforts, was still littered with cloths, receipts and the Post-it notes that made up her dad's filing system.

She put her phone down and turned round.

'And who,' Lesley's arms were folded, 'was that?'

'Just a friend.'

'No no no.' Lesley held up her finger, her blue eyes gleaming. 'I know that expression.' She took a step towards Abi.

Abi decided that now would be a very good time to give her friend a tour of the shop.

'Do you like the new window display?'

She pointed at the series of Penguin cover prints arranged diagonally behind the glass, next to a watercolour of a couple holding hands on a bench and looking out to sea. Getting things in shape here had made her happy. At night, her dreams were clearer and the apocalyptic shapes that had haunted her were visiting her less frequently. When she woke to hear the bedstead springs straining as John got up, she didn't roll over and fall asleep again – she got up and got on with her day.

Lesley came and stood next to her. 'It looks amazing, but I'm not letting you off that easily.' She peered at her sternly.

'It was just Steve.'

Lesley's eyebrow shot upwards.

'Steve your ex?'

Abi knew she needed to tough it out. 'Yes. We bumped into each other a couple of weeks ago. We had coffee – that's all.'

'And you gave him your number?'

'Sure.' Abi adjusted a print of a butterfly against a vivid orange sunset, which was hanging off-centre. 'Why wouldn't I?'

'Ooh, let's see.' Lesley looked at the ceiling and pretended to stroke her chin. 'Well, there's the heartbreak, of course.'

'That was years ago.'

'True.' Lesley nodded. 'And then there's John.'

'What's John got to do with it? It was only coffee.' Abi walked over to the record player, realising it had stopped playing. 'What do you fancy? Some Van Morrison? The Clash?' She ran her finger along the album covers. 'Madonna?'

'Don't try to mollify me with the Queen of Pop.' Lesley glared at her.

Abi took it out of the sleeve anyway and dropped the needle onto the record, and Lesley started shimmying her shoulders before remembering that she was meant to be in interrogation mode and stopping.

'Now.' She leant her elbows on the counter. 'Steve aside, let's get serious. How are things with John?'

'Fine.'

'Really?'

'Yes.' Abi nodded.

'Had any sex yet?'

'What? Lesley!' Abi looked round the shop. 'I can't talk about that here. Not with Rob downstairs.'

Lesley walked to the top of the stairs and listened.

'If he can hear anything down there over those screaming saxophones I would be very, very surprised.' She pushed the connecting door shut for good measure. 'Now. Spill.'

Abi shook her head. 'A customer might come in.'

'Fine.' Lesley walked over to the shop door and turned the sign to *Closed*.

'But it's not six yet.'

'It's five forty-nine. No picture is *that* urgent. Now, stop avoiding the question.'

'I don't know what to say.' Abi felt her cheeks flush with embarrassment.

Lesley squeezed her arm. 'Look, I know it's difficult, getting used to things again. Especially as you haven't had sex for such a long time.'

Lesley had no idea how long it had really been.

'Just get back on the horse.' She giggled. 'So to speak.'

'I can't.' Abi sighed. 'I don't feel ready. I don't feel . . . sexy.' She kept her eyes lowered, not wanting to see pity in her friend's eyes.

Ha. Fat chance.

'You've got to get over it.'

'What?' Abi's head jerked upwards.

'It's true.' Lesley arched her eyebrows. 'You know it is. Just leap on him and see what happens. He must be gagging for it. Give it a go.'

Abi grimaced. 'Well that makes it sound appealing.'

'But you know I'm right. At the rate you two are going, you'll be turning seventy before you kiss with tongues again.'

Abi folded her arms across her chest. 'No we won't. It's just . . . temporary. And living with my parents doesn't help. My mum's night-time gargling regime is hardly an aphrodisiac.'

'You're just making excuses.'

'If you heard how loud she is you wouldn't be saying that.'

Lesley shook her head impatiently. 'Abi, for God's sake, you love that man. You know you do. You two have been through the kind of terrible time people make movies about, and then the actors win Oscars and everyone cries and applauds and thanks God it didn't happen to them. And here you are now, barely even seeing each other. It's not right. So go home and give him a snog, for God's sake. Please?'

'Why are you so upset about this?'

Lesley was pacing now. 'Because this is meant to be your happy ending. This is the ordinary day you dreamt about having. You used to talk about it when we were sitting in that horrible chemo suite with all those other people who were scared they were going to die. You with your drip, and me sitting there trying desperately to chat my way through the fact that I might lose you.' Lesley took a shuddering breath. 'We used to talk about you and John all the time. Don't you remember? About how kind he was. How strong. About how once he took his clothes off, you couldn't get enough of him, even though he was ten years older than you. Even though he actively hated Del Amitri and The Stone Roses and going to gigs. We talked so much about him and how much you wanted to stay alive to be with him.' She stopped for breath. 'Do you remember?'

'Yes.' Abi felt a rush of shame. 'I do.'

'So please enjoy it. Enjoy him. I know he's fucked up his company, but that just makes him human.' Lesley grinned. 'Thank God. When you were ill, I was starting to suspect he might be so superhuman he rescued people from burning buildings in his spare time.' Her eyes widened. 'Maybe that's how you get things started again. Role play?'

'Stop!' Abi was having a return to the hot flushes that had plagued her during chemo. 'Seriously. Enough.' She giggled.

'OK.' Lesley picked up her phone. 'By the way, what's up with Seb and Jess?'

'What do you mean?'

'Hope told me that he's spending way less time with her nowadays. Jess is up to her eyeballs in Oxford entrance prep, but she's pretty pissed off by all accounts.'

'Really?' Abi frowned. Seb had told her only that morning that things were great with Jess, just before driving her mum scatty by making a four-tier bacon sandwich and leaving the unwashed frying pan on the hob. 'That's weird.' She counted up the number of nights he had been out late last week. Three. She wondered where he had been, and felt that tingle of uncertainty that nagged at her every time they were in the same room. The feeling that what he was saying and what he was thinking were nowhere near the same thing.

Of course, he was a teenage boy and no one really knew what the hell was going on in their heads. But right now things felt different. As if he was putting on a shield when he pulled his school jumper on.

'I'll talk to him.'

'Good luck with that.' Lesley arched an eyebrow.

Abi nodded. 'Well obviously I'll warn him.'

'And no going into his room when he's not expecting you.'

'No.' Abi shook her head. 'Absolutely not.'

'Good.' Lesley smiled. 'Now, before you go home and get all Victoria's Secret, please help me decide who to go on a date with.'

Abi laughed and flung her arms around her friend. 'OK.'

She squeezed her tight. 'And thank you.' She paused. 'You do know that Steve having my number doesn't mean anything, don't you?'

Lesley narrowed her eyes. 'I did. Until you asked that question.' She shook her head. 'Just be careful. OK?'

'Careful about what? I knew him a hundred years ago.' Abi flicked her wrist dismissively. 'Besides, you're the one who should be careful, with that rampant pilot about.' She whistled. 'That's quite a message he's sent you.'

'Has he?' Lesley looked at the screen. 'Shit. How am I meant to reply to that?'

'Well, start by turning Caps Lock off. OK?'

'OK.' Lesley pressed her lips together. 'This isn't really my area of expertise. I haven't been on a date since Bros were in the charts.'

'I'll help you.' Abi pulled one of the high stools across and clambered up. 'It's not just window displays I'm good at, you know.'

But as she talked and giggled with her friend, her mind was turning over their earlier discussion. About John. About her. And about whether she could ever reach for him again without worrying that he didn't want her any more.

Seb

If there was a fate worse than being stuck outside a Topshop changing room on a Saturday afternoon, Seb didn't know what it could be. The bright lights and the smell of plastic were giving him a headache, but despite this he pushed his headphones tighter into his ears. Unfortunately even Stormzy's 'Shut Up' on full volume couldn't drown out the shrieks from the cluster of girls behind him. They were gaggling around some doll-sized tops, exclaiming so excitedly they were like prospectors finding a glinting speck of gold.

He sat back on the 'bored boyfriend' sofa, watching a shop assistant in grey skinnies who was carrying some silver dresses in his arms. He had dark hair and brown eyes and was so thin that Seb could practically see his ribs sticking out beneath his tight black 'Topshop Crew' T-shirt.

Seb jumped as one of his headphones was removed and Jess spoke straight into his ear. 'You can stop staring at that guy now.'

'What?' He whipped his head round to look at her. 'I wasn't. What are you talking about?'

She put her hand on his arm. 'It's OK, I get it.'

'Get what?' He felt a churning panic, and didn't want to understand why.

She smiled and pointed at the sales assistant. 'I get it.

You want a black T-shirt for Christmas. You can stop staring at it now.'

It hadn't been the T-shirt he'd been looking at. The thought flashed through his mind before he could stop it.

He stood up, skin prickling with heat.

'What's eating you?' Jess flicked out her long dark hair. 'And how do you like the dress?'

Shit. He hadn't even noticed the dress, which was insane, as it was absolutely bloody gorgeous. Purple folds clung to her curves and the material stretched tight across her body. Her legs were endless and the colour brought out the pale glow of her cheeks.

'You look stunning.' He kissed her lightly on the lips.

'Thank you!' She held her arms up and did a twirl. 'Do you think it's birthdayish enough, though?'

He had no bloody clue. He just wanted to get the hell out of this shop. 'Sure. Absolutely.'

The sales assistant walked towards them, a stud glinting in his nose. He glanced at Seb and a slow grin crept across his face. Seb felt a jolt of alarm and grabbed Jess around the waist and kissed her.

When he pulled away, the sales assistant had gone. Seb gazed at his girlfriend, taking in her wide eyes and her beautiful mouth. He was so lucky to have her. He knew that. He pulled her close and gently kissed her hair.

'Down, boy.' She pulled away from him and smiled. 'God, this really *is* the right dress. Sorted.' She turned away. 'I'll just go and change.'

'OK.' Seb sat back on the sofa again, his rapid heartbeat starting to calm. As the November winds had got colder, he had been increasingly bothered by a feeling that something was missing. No matter how much he practised his football or worked in the restaurant or tried and failed to concentrate on his coursework, he couldn't get into any of it. He kept finding himself staring at things he had never noticed before. Googling topics he had never cared about and then deleting his search history, just in case one of his friends or family should see.

He sighed and stretched his legs out in front of him as a girl paraded out of the changing rooms in a silky blue dress that left him in absolutely no doubt about the size of her tits. He looked away, relieved when his phone bleeped with a new message. It was Mum, asking if he would be back for dinner. She was trying so hard to make things normal, but it wasn't working. And there was no way he wanted to go back for dinner. Dinner meant chat. Dinner meant his mum asking about how things were going at school (not well) and his dad coming in late – if at all – and frowning as his phone lit up with even more messages telling him how broke they were.

He messaged back. No. Sorry. With Jess.

Shame. Have fun. See you soon?

He felt a twinge of guilt. He really wanted to talk to Mum, but he couldn't cope with the family mealtimes, with added Gran and Gramps talking about what university he would get into and how he'd be finding the cure for cancer by the age of thirty. He didn't want to think ahead. It was all he could do to get through today.

Sometimes he would creep back into the house after everybody was asleep and open his window wide. He would lie back on his pillow on the narrow bed in his cupboard of a room and stare at the sky, smoking his way towards dawn. He would think back to how things had been once upon a time – memories of family football matches and days when his mum and dad had held hands and finished first each other's sentences and then each other's ice creams.

Then, the world had been a safe place. A place for dreaming. He was going to play football for England. Simple. Whereas now, as the maths and chemistry and biology coursework bore down on him, he could see less and less point in even trying. He knew that life wasn't in his control. He knew it because he'd been trying so hard to ignore something – to push it away beneath layers of training and Jess and bad vodka from the corner shop. But now he realised he couldn't, and he wanted to clench his fists and punch the world in the face.

He was so tired. As tired as the middle-aged man next to him, with his baggy eyes, his terrible stonewashed jeans and his endless carrier bags. Seb rubbed his hands through his hair and told himself to get over it. He had Jess. The team had won their last match. He should be happy.

Yes. He nodded. Happy.

Jess reappeared in a different dress, the affection in her eyes overwhelming him.

'Sorry. Had to try just one more.' A dimple danced in her cheek. She looked amazing. Turquoise material against pale skin. Teeth gently biting lip. Dark hair cascading over her shoulders. She was every boy's dream.

He stood up and took her hand.

'You're gorgeous.'

'Yeah?' She folded her arms. 'You know you've said that about every single dress so far?'

'Yeah.' He held her close, feeling the beat of her heart against his chest. 'That's because it's true. You're beautiful.' He picked her up and held her high, loving the warmth of her smile, which was only for him.

She giggled. 'Beautiful enough for you to take me into the changing room and have your wicked way with me?'

Despite himself, he tensed.

'Definitely.' He took a breath to gain time. 'If only there weren't so many people around. Including kids.' He gestured at a little girl in a Peppa Pig T-shirt. 'If they weren't around, I'd be in with you in a second.'

'Boring.' She turned on her heel and started to walk back to the changing room. The girl in blue whispered something to her boyfriend as Jess walked past. He laughed, and his hand settled comfortably on her bum and gave it a squeeze.

Seb watched them out of the corner of his eye. They looked so easy together. As he sat down again, he realised that he never felt relaxed any more, except on the football pitch when the ball was at his feet and he was sprinting down the wing. Then, he could forget everything. Forget the mess and the fog and the fact that he felt like everything was about to fall apart. The fact that Jess was going to get a full set of A*s and go to Oxford and he was going to fail everything and end up working behind a checkout. His mum hadn't survived cancer for him to let her down like that.

There was that bloody sales assistant again with another armful of clothes. Seb scowled as he watched him kissing another boy on both cheeks. His white teeth flashed as he pulled away, his voice carrying to Seb, laughing that it was only an hour to go now until the end of his shift and that he couldn't wait to get to the gig later.

Lucky him, going to gigs. Seb was going to do some more washing-up.

The other boy turned and Seb blinked.

It couldn't be.

'What's eating you?'

It could.

Seb would have leapt out of his seat, but the sofa had him firmly in its clutches. 'Hi, Marc. How's things?'

'Just visiting my new man.' Marc grinned and waved at

the sales assistant, receiving an air kiss in return. 'What are you doing out here by the girls' changing rooms?'

'Jess is in there.' Seb leapt away as Marc sat down next to him.

'God, you're jumpy.' Marc's green eyes glinted with amusement. 'This is a public place, you know. And my boyfriend's standing over there. Nate.'

He waved again and Nate waved back.

Seb felt slow. Clumsy. 'Sorry.' He tried to smile. 'I've been here a while. All the sequins must be getting to me.'

'Well . . .' Marc reached out and took Seb's dangling headphone. He put it to his ear. 'Thank God you've got some Stormzy to get you through.'

'Do you like him then?'

'Yeah.' Marc nodded. 'No need to sound so surprised. I love it when he takes everyone to Nando's. Amazing. Have you seen that?'

'Of course I have.' Seb flicked through his phone. 'How about this one outside his house?'

'Yeah.' Marc leant towards him and Seb could smell the musk of his aftershave. He was still holding the other earphone to his ear. 'Yeah, that one's amazing.' He turned and looked up into Seb's face, and Seb could see the tiny mole under his left eye and the length of his dark eyelashes as he blinked. They both paused, and Seb's pulse started to rise.

'I'm finished now.'

Jess smiled as Seb jerked away from Marc and leapt to his feet.

'Great.' He grabbed her hand as if it was a life raft. 'Let's go and pay.'

She wrinkled her nose in confusion. 'Aren't you going to introduce me?'

'Yes.' His voice sounded ridiculously high-pitched. 'Yes.' Now it was insanely low. Excellent. Talk about playing it cool. 'This is Marc. He just started at my school this term.'

'Hi.' Jess smiled at Marc.

'Hi.' Marc grinned. 'I'm also Seb's new next-door neighbour.'

'Really? No wonder I haven't met you.' Jess arched an eyebrow. 'I haven't been allowed over to his new place yet.'

'You've been too busy studying.' Seb was well aware that this was only an excuse. The truth was, he couldn't bear her to see the cramped chaos of life at his new home so far out of town. He barely wanted to see it himself. He turned to Marc. 'Jess is about to interview for Oxford.'

'Wow.' Marc raised his eyebrows. 'I'm still struggling to sound exciting on my UCAS form.'

'Yeah, it's a tough one.' Seb nodded.

'What are you talking about?' Jess frowned. 'Yours is so glowing it probably has a halo.'

Seb shifted uncomfortably. He knew his results wouldn't match up. 'I feel Marc's pain. That's all.'

'Sure.' Jess nodded and he felt a jolt of envy. Her world was so ordered. Goals clear. Mind tidy. Her study schedule stuck up on the wall of her bedroom, alongside chemistry equations and long lines of photos of her with her friends and of the two of them at parties or in photo booths. Eyes bright, smiles wide.

He was a disaster in comparison. His grades were dropping. He couldn't focus. He didn't even know if he wanted to be a doctor any more – he had spent too much time in that world of needles and antiseptic and pain, and now he just wanted to be doing something that helped him to forget how ill his mum had been. Every time he tried to study, he wondered why the hell he was sitting there wasting his time.

He was trying so hard to reconnect with his former ambitions, but not for himself. For his mum. When she had been ill she had talked so much about her hopes for him. He sighed, wishing he could just talk to her about it, but he didn't want to make her worried. Frequently he found himself staring at her number or lurking outside the kitchen and then disappearing without saying a thing.

'Let's head to the tills.' Jess smiled at Marc. 'Great to meet you.'

'You too.' He glanced at his phone. 'I'm off to check the jeans out.'

'See you.' Seb raised his hand and then dropped it again.

'He seems nice.' Jess looked up at him. 'How come I've never met him before?'

'I don't hang out with him that much.' Seb took the dress from her, desperate to change the subject. 'Let me buy this for you.'

'What?' She shook her head. 'No way. I know you're skint.'

'I'm fine.' He wanted to give her this. 'And you deserve it.'

She stared at him with her head on one side and then gave a little nod. 'Thank you.'

'No problem.' Seb put his arms round her as they arrived at the queue, resting his chin on the top of her head.

She leant into him. 'Are we OK, Seb?'

'Why?'

'Because I feel like you've been avoiding me.'

'No.' He shook his head, while feeling a thud of recognition. 'Not at all.' He sighed. 'Things are just mental, living with Gran and Gramps, and school and the team and stuff.'

'Really?' She sighed. 'Because I'd rather you were honest with me.'

'I will be.' He stroked her hair away from her face. 'I am.'

'OK.' The happiness in her voice made his guilt smoulder. 'Good.' She turned to kiss him. 'I love you.'

He shifted uneasily. 'God, this music is terrible. Why does everybody have to play bloody One Direction all the time?'

She was watching him. Waiting.

Now it was his turn. His turn to say it back.

'Jess, you know I love you.'

'Do I?' Her breath was sweet, just as it had always been. Her eyes were clear.

'Yes.' He pushed away his doubts. 'You know I do. I love you.'

And he kissed her. The music was too loud. His body was too hot.

But he had made her happy. And that must count for something.

He bloody hoped it did.

Abi

It was very difficult to have a romantic date when your parents were talking about walking holidays in the next room.

'But we can see the bluebells if we go to the Lake District.' Her mum had raised her voice over the sound of the *Crimewatch* theme tune.

'I'm not sure they're at their best in February,' her dad replied mildly. She heard a clink as he put his beer can down.

'Coaster!'

Abi sighed, singing the words to 'Time Warp' under her breath. This hadn't been the plan. Fired up by her conversation with Lesley, she had suggested that she and John should go out to their favourite pub for a drink to celebrate his first new contract in months. He had been out working so much recently, and then last week he had gone up to Birmingham to pitch to a chain of restaurants who needed new overnight cleaning staff fast. He messaged and called whenever he could, but he was still feeling increasingly unreal. She wanted to see him. To talk to him. To look him in the face and see his smile.

She had turned up to the pub to find that he was already there. Something in her ached at the sight of him, hunched over his phone, a frown cutting deep into his forehead. He had been through too much. Noah would have cheered him up, taking him for an air-hockey marathon or a trip to a climbing wall or simply for a few pints in the pub. Now it was her turn to help.

As soon as he saw her, the frown disappeared.

'Hi, gorgeous.' He looked almost too tired to smile. 'How are you? Did you have a good day?'

'Yes, thanks.' She kissed him lightly on the lips. She felt stilted, like an actor trying out some last-minute script changes. 'It's lovely to see you.'

'You look beautiful.' His eyes had the old glow and her heart leapt. She had felt the familiar flutter as she got ready in the tiny toilet at the back of the shop, shivering as the wind penetrated one of several large cracks in the ceiling. It had been so long since they had been out together that she thought she would make an effort. Dress to impress.

'What can I get you?' There were dark shadows beneath his eyes.

'Just a lemonade, please.'

The corner of his mouth lifted. 'You're such a cheap date nowadays.'

'Just as well really.'

His face fell and she felt a pulse of regret. 'Sorry. I didn't mean it like that.'

He shook his head. 'No. It's fine. And you're right, aren't you?'

She tried to reach up and hug him but he had already moved away towards the bar.

She sat down, playing nervously with the silver charm bracelet on her right wrist. He had given it to her the night before her first operation – the night when neither of them had slept so they had migrated to the sofa, where they held hands and critiqued the hairstyles in her favourite 1980s films, *Weird Science*, *St Elmo's Fire* and, of course, *Dirty*

Dancing. At about 1 a.m. Seb had come down and quietly joined them, his long legs encased in his favourite black tracksuit and a big bowl of popcorn on his knee, crunching his way through the hours until dawn and departure.

Abi watched her husband as he leant against the bar, chatting to the girl in charge of pulling a pint of his favourite pale ale. This situation was so familiar and yet felt so new. Once they had spent hours talking and laughing and debating whether Doritos were better than Quavers. Now she found herself wondering what to say.

As he paid, she saw him reach into his pocket to grab his phone, and the way his face instantly set into those familiar lines. She felt a pang of fear, wondering again whether there was something he wasn't telling her. When he came back to the table it was as if the phone was now part of their date. And it certainly wasn't bringing any fun with it.

'Cheers.' He chinked glasses with her, but the phone was now in between them and his eyes flicked down towards the screen before rising to meet hers again.

'Cheers.' She debated taking the phone and putting it in her pocket. Nope. Too extreme. She would try to distract him instead. 'Seb scored a goal today against Woodbury.'

'Did he?' John's face lit up and once again he looked like the man in the wedding pictures she had been looking at last night, trying to remember the couple they had once been. 'Bloody brilliant. He's had a great season, hasn't he?'

'Yeah.' She nodded, wondering if she should mention their son's ominous silence on all things academic. No grades being shared. No talk of interviews.

No. Celebration. Reconnection. That was what they were here for.

His phone lit up and he stabbed the screen with his finger.

'Shit.'

So much for celebration.

'What is it?' She sipped her lemonade and watched him.

'My client pitch hasn't gone through. I bloody knew that connection was dodgy.'

'Which client?'

'The Scottish restaurants. The steak-and-ale ones. You know.' He tapped the table impatiently. 'They want it tonight and my battery's nearly flat.' He shook his head. 'I'll just try it now.' He swiped. Tapped. Swore.

'Shit. It's dead.'

'So use that charger you always carry around.' She put her hand over his, trying to calm him. She knew he was under pressure, but deep down she felt the first smoulderings of resentment.

'That's out of juice too.'

'OK.' She took another sip. 'Well, can it wait?'

He paused for a second, before giving a brusque nod. 'Yes. Of course. Sure.' He visibly tried to cheer himself up. 'How was your day?'

'Good.' She twirled her straw between her fingers. 'I got some deliveries in and met a new artist I'd like to stock, and there was more Mrs Amos action too.'

John scratched his nose. 'Mrs who?'

Abi took a deep breath. She had talked to him about Mrs Amos only last weekend.

'She's one of our regulars.' She smiled. 'And she likes to bring in things that are totally impossible to frame. Today she brought in a sculpture made by her four-year-old nephew – a giant multicoloured hedgehog roughly the size of a Jack Russell, made out of milk cartons and shoeboxes. Rob wasn't impressed.'

'No. I bet he wasn't.' John's eyes slid to his phone again.

It had no battery and it was still more interesting than her. They were ten minutes into their date and already she felt like she was losing him. She tried to think back to before she had got ill, and wondered if things had actually been as different as she remembered. If he had ever really held her eye and laughed in the right places and remembered what she had told him.

He nibbled on his lower lip, then picked up his pint and downed half of it in one go. Abi watched him. He looked really worried. Maybe she should give him an out.

'Let's go back, John.'

'No.' He didn't meet her eyes. 'It's our night out.'

'We can still talk at my parents' place.' She refused to call it home.

His body was taut. Poised. 'No. We said we'd—'

'We've got the rest of our lives, John.' She wanted to remind him. Remind him of how lucky they were to have a future. 'This is temporary. You just need a few months to turn things around. Don't you?' She wished he would look at her.

'Yeah.' His tone was unconvincing to say the least.

'Let's go.'

'Thank you.' It was his first real smile of the evening. He put his hand over hers. Once it had made her feel secure. Safe. Not any more. 'Sorry.'

'That's OK.' It wasn't. She didn't want to go back to the cramped politeness of her parents' house, with its constant repetitions of 'Oh no, I'll make the tea' or 'Are you going to take that washing out of the machine soon, Abigail?' She wanted to stay here, with the buzz of the city outside – the spires reaching into the dark sky, Magdalen Bridge just past the roundabout, and the sense that everyone she could see was on their way towards something exciting.

Concerts. Dates. A night that would begin with a pint and end in a bacon sandwich at dawn.

She swallowed her disappointment and scraped her chair back. One day their life together would start again. Just a bit longer. She didn't ask for much – just the odd drink in a pub garden and a walk along the riverbank with no particular destination in mind. Looking up on beautiful days and appreciating the way the clouds floated across the sky. Sharing headphones. Laughing in the car. The feeling of a hand in hers.

She missed that most of all.

As she put her coat on, the couple behind them caught her eye. They were wearing T-shirts that told her they were off to see Jools Holland in concert at the New Theatre and they both looked so bright-eyed. So joyful.

She wondered briefly how she and John must look to them, but rapidly decided this wasn't a positive line of inquiry.

'Let's go.'

'I'm sorry, Abi.'

'No problem.'

They didn't talk all the way home.

And so here they were, in Mum and Dad's kitchen, with John's phone charging on the side while the two of them scooped up the remains of a butternut stew that her mum had made earlier. She had 'just happened' to have food left over so much recently that Abi was starting to suspect she was making double quantities. She appreciated the kindness, just as she appreciated the fact that they had heating and running water and a roof over their heads. But as the weeks went by, the need to hang the tea towels on the correct hook or always put tap water in a jug before drinking it was starting to grate.

'That was delicious.' John scraped up the last of the rice on his plate. 'Thank you.'

'I didn't make it. Thank Mum.' Abi was surprised he had noticed the taste as he had inhaled the food so fast. She was barely halfway through her helping.

'Another glass of red?' He had already lifted the bottle to fill his own glass for a second time.

She indicated her water glass. 'I'm not drinking, remember?'

'Oh.' He nodded. 'Of course.'

She gritted her teeth. He was preoccupied. That was all.

But still the thoughts persisted. She just wanted him to remember *one* thing she had told him. Just one. He only seemed to tune in if she said she had a headache or that she was really tired – looking so anxious that she had rapidly learnt to keep her constant health worries to herself. It turned out cancer didn't end with a clear scan – it took up residence in your mind and loomed with every twinge or sting, colouring the world black and sending Abi running to make yet another GP appointment. But she couldn't talk to John about it. Not at the moment.

That was what was new. That was what scared her.

He sloshed the rest of the bottle into his glass and a splash of red fell onto the flowery tablecloth her mum had been using since the 1970s. It had a bare patch near the middle and was fraying at one end, but her mum's make-do-and-mend philosophy knew no bounds. Abi had found a teapot without a spout in the cupboard the other day, next to a pile of yellowing doilies and a Soda Stream that had last been used when she and Rob thought a Blue Peter badge was the pinnacle of life's achievements.

'Shit.' She leapt up and grabbed the salt, emptying a small heap over the stain.

'Sorry.' John gazed longingly at his phone on the counter.

Abi rolled her eyes. 'You could help me, John. We need to keep things nice for them, you know. They're doing us such a favour.'

His voice rose. 'Do you think I don't know that?'

She had poured on enough salt to totally disguise the stain. Job done. She sat back in her chair.

He tried to smile. 'You shouldn't worry so much.'

He didn't know her mum like she did. She absolutely should worry that much.

She took a deep breath. *Date night. Yay.*

'Have you managed to send the pitch yet?'

'Yes.' He downed about half his wine in one go. 'I think it's a winner.' His face relaxed and he reminded her once again of the man she had married. The man who had practised swaddling for weeks in advance of Seb's arrival, only for their son never to stay still long enough for it to work. The man who whisked her away for weekends in wood-smoked pubs with velvet sofas and twenty kinds of cheese. The man who used to pop home in his lunch break to bring her a brownie and give Seb one more cuddle. The man who would have done anything for them.

That was what he was doing now. She needed to remember that.

'Great. My fingers are crossed.'

'Thanks.' He sighed. 'I'm sorry it's so manic. Lots of big contracts are coming up, so I just need to keep pushing. I'm taking some potentials to the Varsity match next week – did I tell you?'

'No.' She stroked her glass with her finger and thumb. It wasn't the first time she hadn't been informed.

'Sorry.' He reached for his wine again, but she stretched

out her hand and held his. She had to push through what-ever this barrier was between them.

His fingers rested in hers. 'And you, Abi? How are you?'

Now. Now she could finally talk to him. 'The shop's great. More customers. More orders. And I've sourced some fantastic new artists. I'm really enjoying it.' She inhaled, trying to steady herself. 'And I was thinking—'

His phone pinged, and within a second his hand was gone from hers. She felt the chill, despite the tropical heat in the kitchen. She sat back in her chair, staring at the plump wire basket dutifully holding the eggs of a brood of free-range chickens down the road.

The glow of the screen highlighted the lines on his face.

'John. Stop. You said you sent it.'

'I did.' He didn't even look at her.

Abi got up to close the kitchen door, aware again of her parents in the next room. 'Why don't we ever talk any more?'

'We do.'

'John.' She walked across and took his phone out of his hand. 'We don't.'

'I need that.' The desperation in his eyes scared her. 'Just a couple of minutes. We've got an issue at the Randolph – some of the staff paperwork hasn't gone through.'

'You always have an issue.' She hated the harshness in her voice. 'Why don't you have someone to help you?'

'Because my number two buggered off with three of my biggest clients and I haven't had a chance to replace her yet.' A muscle flickered in his cheek. 'You know that.'

Bloody Rachel. What a cow.

'But I'm here too, John.' She shouldn't have to beg like this. 'And I . . . we . . . it's just that . . .'

Suddenly he was back in the room with her. 'Oh my

God. I'm so sorry. Are you feeling OK? Do we need to get you to a GP again?'

'I'm fine.' The panic on his face broke her heart. 'That's not it at all.'

'Oh, thank God.' He exhaled. 'So what is it you want to talk about?'

'I just want to see you, John. I want us to be a couple, OK? I saw you more when I was in and out of hospital than I do now.'

'You needed me then.'

'What?' She looked at him in total incomprehension. 'How does that even make sense? Yes, I needed you then, John, and thank God you were there. Sleeping in that awful chair in the hospital. Telling me terrible jokes.'

'They were some of my best!' At least he was smiling.

She forced the words out. 'But I still need you now.' She felt a pulse of embarrassment.

He put his head in his hands, which somehow hurt more than him getting angry. 'But I'm trying to put things right. You know that. I'm trying to get us a home. I'm not out having a laugh. I'm at the office every day, and then I'm trying to wine and dine people back into using my company rather than one of my many rivals.' He sighed. 'I'm trying to get more money coming in than is going out. I took my eye off the ball when you were ill.'

'I know.'

'So now I have to work twice as hard. OK?' He took her hand. 'I thought that was what we agreed.'

'Of course it is.' Abi heard the creak as her dad got up from his chair in the next room. 'What do you think I'm working so hard for too? It's not just you who's trying to sort things out.'

'I know.' He squeezed her hand. 'Thank you.' The tenderness in his eyes touched her. 'And I promise we'll be through this soon. We will.' He raised her hand and kissed it. 'And then we can go out all the time. We can talk so much you'll never want to hear my voice again. And we can go and see the Raging Fannies, or whatever your latest favourite band that I *have* to love is.'

Despite herself, she laughed. 'Even I don't like *them*, John.'

'Well, we can go and see Barbed Wire. Or that Benjamin guy who always seems to have a piano with him. Whatever. But we will do those things again, Abi. We just need to wait a bit longer.' He moved closer, stroking her hair with the strong hands she loved so much. 'Please?'

'OK.' He kissed her and she kissed him back. Naturally this was the moment that her mum chose to bustle in, her cheeks flushed from the glass of red wine she always pretended she wasn't going to have. The two of them leapt apart.

'Don't mind me.' Abi's mum opened the fridge and pulled out the Thorntons selection box that she kept in pride of place on the top shelf. She put it down on the table and scraped the top tray out of the box.

Behind her, Abi suppressed a giggle as she reached for John's hand, squeezing it in hers. She mouthed, 'I love you,' feeling a warm glow as he mouthed it back. He had been her rock for so long. Now it was her turn to support him.

Her mum selected a caramel cream with all the ponderous intensity of a surgeon choosing a scalpel. She popped it in her mouth, eyes closing in appreciation, before putting the box back in the fridge. She turned, brushing imaginary fluff off her deep-red polo neck, then swooped in and took Abi's plate. 'Have you finished? I'll just clear this up.'

'I . . .'

The plate was already in the sink. More fool her for saving the best bit till last.

Her mum was running the tap and the boiler was clanking into action. Being here was now about as restful as standing next to a power drill.

Abi sighed. *Hot date. Not date.*

She moved towards the door. 'Well, I think I'll leave you to it.' John was back spending time with his phone. 'See you later.'

She stepped out into the hallway. The door to the living room was open and her dad was standing on the big red hearthrug, bent over his record player.

He turned his head and beckoned. 'How's this for a gem, Abi?'

She stopped and walked towards him, grinning as she heard the ritzy opening of 'Get Happy', her grandparents' favourite song.

She sat down beside him on the sofa. He had on his yellow cords with the rip above the knee, and the blue jumper that her mum had patched up at least fifty times.

'Gramps will be singing along.' She nudged him. 'Won't he?'

He laughed, the deep, comforting rumble that was one of the main highlights of living here. 'I have every faith that wherever he is – up there or down there – he will have cornered Ella and persuaded her to sing it for him.'

Abi smiled. 'He's probably trained her to make apple crumble too.'

'And custard.' Her dad smiled. 'Lots of custard.'

'Oh yes!' Abi remembered swimming pools of yellow sweetness. 'He was a fanatic.'

'He was.' He waved his arms as the song built to its climax. 'Are you ready?'

'Hell, yeah!' She grinned and they put their heads back and sang in unison, ending with arms raised and smiles splitting their faces as the brass screamed and the crowd roared.

'That was one of our best.'

'It was.' She beamed back at him. 'I doubt Mum thinks so, though.'

'She'll just be happy to hear you singing again.' His eyes dimmed for a moment, before he looked away, frowning at the crossword that was resting on the arm of the sofa.

Ella moved on and started singing 'I Get a Kick Out of You'. The fire flickered and Abi looked around the room at all the familiar objects on the shelves. The misshapen sheep Rob had made in DIY class. The crown she had adorned herself with in a school production of *A Midsummer Night's Dream*. The picture of her and John on her wedding day. Seb, aged five, already rebelling against his school uniform.

Tears appeared in her eyes. This room held too much that was precious. Too much that mattered.

'Is everything all right, darling?'

'Yeah.' She thought of the worry on John's face. The tension in his jaw. She wondered if he was keeping more secrets. If he was still protecting her, even now, when they really needed to work together.

No. He wouldn't do that. He'd promised.

But later, as she lay next to him, fingers running over her scars in the dark, she wondered if she was right. There were too many doubts. Too many shadows.

She wondered if she could cut through them all and set them both free.

December

'In the Bleak Midwinter' by Harold Darke
and Christina Rossetti (sung by the choir of
King's College, Cambridge)

Well, Mum, this is the one you sing every year with your
choir and I can't listen to it without thinking of you and
of the year that your friend Helen fainted just before
the final verse. I love this carol. I've murdered it in the
shower. I've murdered it in countless churches, and best
of all, I've made you all listen to me singing it every
bloody Christmas since I was old enough to know the
words. It makes me think of the snow that never comes,
of Mum adding too many cloves to the mulled wine,
and of the sheer bloody love and beauty of Christmas.
I know we fight every year. I know that Dad always
wants the wishbone and never gets it. I know we all
hate Trivial Pursuit and play it anyway, until Mum falls
asleep and wakes up protesting she could have beaten
us all if only she hadn't nodded off. I know we always
mean to go for a walk and then opt instead to drink
sloe gin on the sofa. I know it all. And I love it all. Just
as much as I love all of you. Happy Christmas x

Abi

'You used to love surprises!'

'Steve.' She flushed as she looked at the bright bunch of gerberas in his hand. 'Thank you. I wasn't expecting to see you.' She put a hand to her hair, hoping it didn't look as wild as it had when she had returned from her lunchbreak earlier.

'They're a bit squashed.' He shrugged as he looked at one flower that had very few petals left. 'My car isn't the best place for fragile items.'

'Still full of guitars and amps?' She reached out to take the flowers.

'And old bits of sandwich. And chocolate wrappers.' He grimaced. 'God, I'm not painting myself in the best light, am I?'

'Bit late for that.' She smiled. 'I know all your deep dark secrets already.' She hovered for a second, wondering if she should kiss him on the cheek or not.

'True.' He solved the problem by leaning in and taking the lead. She brushed against his leather jacket and remembered when she was seventeen and he had thrown it around her shoulders in a Glastonbury field, the summer before he went to university.

She blinked herself back into the present.

'Well, it's lovely to see you.'

'Yeah.' He sat on a stool and picked up a pencil, tapping

it against the counter. 'I thought I'd come in and see what you've done with the place. Great window display. Very Christmassy.' He nodded approvingly.

'Thank you.' She found a vase and started to take the wrapping off the flowers.

'I remember when you used to work here when we were at school.'

'Yeah.' She put the stems into the vase. 'I earn a bit more now.'

'Glad to hear it.' He beamed. 'Have you been here the whole time, then?'

'No.' Her voice was sharp, and she took a deep breath as she went out the back and filled the vase up in the kitchen. 'I worked at the hospital. In their vascular admin team, and cardiology before that.' She came back in. 'John was setting up his business, so I was the breadwinner for a while. When he was starting out.'

Steve nodded. 'He sounds like quite a go-getter, your husband. I'd love to meet him.'

'Great.' She smiled, while knowing that she would never let that happen. 'We can fix something up some time.' She put the flowers on the counter. 'They're gorgeous. Thank you.'

He shrugged. 'No problem. I haven't got anyone else to buy them for.'

'No?' She didn't know why her pulse had quickened.

'I split up with my girlfriend a while back. She wanted to travel. I'd had enough of it. Wanted to stay here and put down some roots. You know?'

'Sure.' She started to tie some picture cord onto the back of a framed print of the Lake District.

'And bumping into you again – that was amazing. Fate. It must have been.'

'Yeah.' It had been pretty crazy.

'You still look the same, you know.' He leant forward on one elbow. 'Makes me feel sixteen again.' Their eyes tangled and she couldn't look away, then the bell jangled and a tall figure loped in, wrapped up inside a thick grey hoodie.

'Seb!'

Her son eyed Steve. Steve eyed Seb.

Oh God.

'Seb, this is my old friend Steve. He just popped in to . . .' No. She couldn't mention the flowers. 'To look at the new prints by Scott Naismith.'

'Oh.' Seb rubbed his nose. 'Sure.'

'I'll head off, I think.' Steve got off the stool. 'Thanks for showing me the prints. See you soon, I hope?'

'I hope so.' She smiled and raised a hand. Behind Seb, Steve gave her a lingering smile before disappearing into the street. She felt a beat of disappointment. Of loss.

Seb slung his rucksack onto the floor and took his turn on the stool. He peered across at the library book she had been reading when Steve came in.

'What's this, Mum?'

'Nothing important.' She pushed it to one side and went round the counter towards him. 'Go on. Let your mum give you a hug.'

He shook his head, thick eyebrows lowered in a frown. 'I'm way too cool for that now, Mum.'

For a moment she stopped moving, disappointed. Then she saw his mouth twitch.

'Come to Mama.' She grabbed him and pulled him close, savouring the warmth and the height of him. 'New after-shave?' She drew back and ruffled his hair.

'Stop it, Mum.' He pushed her hand aside.

She shrugged. 'It's not like it'll actually move, Seb. Not with that amount of crap in it.'

'Wax, Mum.' He rolled his eyes. 'It's wax.'

'If you say so. Feels like concrete to me.'

There was a splash of mud across his broad nose and his trainers were caked in grass.

'Good practice today?'

'Yeah.' He sighed.

She watched him. Normally even the tiniest mention of football was guaranteed to ignite his smile.

He reached out for the book again. *The Art of Choosing*. His eyes sped over the blurb. 'What are you reading this for? I thought you were more of an *NME* type.'

Abi smiled. 'Well, of course, that's in my bag for the bus home.'

'Thought so. But what made you choose this?'

'Oh. You know.'

'No.'

She picked the book up and put it on the shelf behind her. 'When I was younger I wanted to be a psychologist, so sometimes I read books about it.'

'Oh yeah. That degree you never finished.'

'Exactly.' She pushed away thoughts of the aspirations she had nurtured only a few months before.

'Because you had me?'

'Not really.' She shrugged. 'I could have kept going – taken a year out and made it work. But somehow I never got around to it.' She straightened the jars of mount rings in front of her. 'And it's never going to happen now. I'd have to do a four-year degree and then a masters and it's all too much.'

'Why?'

She didn't want to share her disappointment with him.

'It's a bit late now.' She shrugged. 'Besides, I'm happy with what I've got.'

'What, living with your parents and never seeing Dad?'

His sharpness surprised her. When he was at home, he spent so much time in his room that she had convinced herself that he hadn't noticed John's frequent absences.

'Is everything OK, Seb?'

'Sure.' He tore at a thumbnail with his teeth. 'Is the psychology thing why you were reading that Oliver Sacks book that time?'

'Yes.' She nodded.

His face clouded. 'Just before you . . .'

Her heart surged. 'Just before I got that infection and had to be ambulanced in on your birthday.' She winced at the memory and put a hand over his. 'Worst birthday ever. I'm sorry.'

He shook his head. 'Not your fault.' He got up and started roaming around the shop. 'Wow. You've certainly gone all out on the decorations in here.' He banged his head on the Christmas wreath hanging from the ceiling. 'Are there any paper chains left on the planet?'

'Nope. It's amazing what you can get in Poundland.' She grinned. 'Did you like the window?'

His blank expression told her he hadn't even noticed it. It had taken her hours – full of giant snowflakes, bold superhero prints, three dachshund cartoons against festive red backgrounds and all the tinsel she could find.

'Well I hope you're enjoying my Christmas carols then.' She hummed along to 'In the Bleak Midwinter'. In her head she could sing it as beautifully as any member of the King's College choir. In reality, Seb's face told her otherwise.

'Make it stop, Mum. Make it stop!' He put his hands over his ears.

'Oi, Scrooge.' She gently clipped him round the ear.

'Got any . . .?' He looked around hopefully.

She might have no idea what else was going on in his head, but this time she knew what to say. 'Trying to find these?' She opened a drawer and pulled out the shop's current pack of chocolate digestives.

'Yes. How did you know?'

'Seventeen years of mumming will do that to you.' She pushed it across to him. 'When you were younger, you used to be able to sniff them out.'

'Really?'

'Really.' She nodded. 'It was your party trick. Didn't matter where I hid them – you would always hunt them down.'

'God.' He took one out and crunched. 'So good.'

'So what made you pop in today? Apart from the biscuits.'

His face shuttered and she kicked herself. 'What do you mean? Do I need a reason?'

'No.' She must tread more carefully. She was too shut off from his world – she didn't know where the landmines were. 'I just wondered if there was anything . . .'

'No.' He slid another biscuit out of the pack. 'Is there any tea?'

'Of course.' She swallowed her frustration. She knew he was preoccupied. He might be annoyingly tall now, but he was still the boy who had once eaten all the flapjacks in the cake tin before confessing that he had cut a hole in her favourite scarf while trying to make a tent.

Maybe he would talk once he had tea in his hands.

'I can make it.' He started to stand up, but she remembered the bag she had tucked under the counter and realised that there was no way she wanted her teenage son to see that. Chemo had been bad enough, but this would scar him for life. She thought of what she had planned for later and felt a kick of nerves. She could do this. She wanted to do this.

Maybe.

She flicked on the kettle and walked back towards her son.

'Where's Uncle Rob?'

'He's off today. Why?'

'Just fancied talking to him about something.' The packet was nearly empty now.

'Can I help?'

'It's just . . .' He crunched another biscuit. 'It's . . .'

'Yes?'

Silence, then he shook his head, as if dismissing whatever he had been about to say.

'You. And the psychology thing.'

'Yes?' Another diversion.

'It's not easy doing what you want, is it? Being who you want to be.' He mashed the packet with his fingers, keeping his head lowered.

She leant on the counter. 'Seb? What do you mean? What's happening?'

'Nothing.' He sighed the sigh of an old man on a hospital ward. 'Nothing's happening.'

Despite his size, his strength, the fact that he could kick a ball from one end of the football pitch to the other, he was still vulnerable. A child in need of help.

She walked around the shop straightening pictures as she worked out what to say. Maybe reassurance would help. 'You're doing so well, Seb. Your BMAT results were great, weren't they? You seemed really happy with them. And you've got your UCL interview next month. Don't put more pressure on yourself. You just need to charm them, get your grades and then the world's your oyster.'

'Yeah. Like it's that easy.' He scrunched the packet between his fingers, his face telling her their conversation was over.

She had lost him.

'Is everything OK with Jess?'

'Of course.'

'Are you sure?'

'Yes, Mum. Stop worrying.' He jutted his chin out. 'It's all good.'

'OK, then.' She knew there was a large elephant in this room. She had to keep tiptoeing forwards until she found it. 'And is there anything else? You can always talk to me, you know.'

'Can I?'

'Of course.'

He took a deep breath and rasped his hand over the stubble on his chin. 'Mum. I'm really worried that I don't—'

The doorbell jangled. Damn. Of course it was Mr Withers, a customer with whom there was no such thing as a quick chat. He talked at the speed of a dying cassette tape and liked to share stories of his friends at the church lunch club and their battles with various maladies. Abi never talked cancer as much as when Mr Withers turned up. It wasn't a welcome topic at the best of times, and she always found afterwards that she was doing extra lumps-and-bumps checks when she got home. Just in case.

'Seb. Wait.'

He shook his head. 'I'll see you later, Mum. OK?'

'OK.' Abi stared after him as the door swung shut. She turned to her customer. 'Now, Mr Withers, how are you today?'

'Well, I've got a very sore hip . . .' He rubbed it with an arthritic hand. 'I'm going to the doctor tomorrow, because you never know, do you?'

'No. You don't.' Abi smiled kindly and settled down for a very long session indeed. She kicked the carrier bag further underneath the counter, wondering about what Seb had been about to tell her.

She wondered if it was something he wasn't even ready to tell himself.

'John?'

'Up here.'

Perfect. She pulled her purple dressing gown more tightly around her as she padded up the stairs. Despite years of dedicated practice, she appeared to have forgotten how to put on eyeliner, and had abandoned the attempt after ten minutes of grappling in which she had ended up looking like she had been punched in the eye. Her hair was now thick enough not to look as if it had been stuck on, but was too short for styling, and all her brushing had simply succeeded in making it so static that she looked like she had a halo. Still, her toenails were varnished. Her armpits were shaved. And the fruits of her lunchtime Primark shopping trip were on. Uncomfortable, but on.

She heard a sound behind her and turned, panicking that her mum and dad had come back early from the concert at their local church. Nothing. Seb was out. The coast was clear.

Tonight was long overdue, and yet still she clung to the worn banister, unwilling to take that final step. What-ifs clouded her mind. John might not want her any more. He might not like her surprise. Then she thought about the fierce text Lesley had sent her. Get on with it. You love him.

He loves you. Chuck the abstinence ring in the bin and just jump him. You won't regret it.

She hoped not. Her heart was thumping so hard she could barely breathe. She looked around and realised she was staring straight into a portrait of her late grandad. Not the greatest aphrodisiac.

Get on with it, Abi.

She stepped forward and laid her hand on the door handle. Over a year of trauma lay between her and the man inside. Her husband. The man she loved.

Enough. She opened the door and raised her hand, aiming to pose seductively in the doorway. Naturally she forgot about the step down into the room and ended up tripping forward, catching herself on the end of the bed.

He didn't even look up.

Disappointment started to seep through her, but she clenched her fists and carried on. She had to fight for this. For them.

'Hi.'

'Hi.' His fingers never stopped moving, and his worried face was highlighted by the glow of the screen.

OK, so being ignored hadn't featured in all the scenarios she had imagined. She had no idea what to do. She stood there feeling marooned and foolish, thinking of the flimsy triangles and elastic beneath her robe. They belonged on someone else. In another life.

But she couldn't give up now. She walked towards him and sat down on the bed. She steeled herself and put her hand on his laptop, before snapping it shut.

'Ow!' His finger flew to his mouth.

'Oh, sorry. Did I hurt you?'

'Yes.' He looked at her askance. 'What did you do that for?'

Keep going. She had a seriously *Titanic* feeling about this now, but there was no choice. It reminded her of the time she had insisted on performing the Bucks Fizz Eurovision entry for some of her dad's friends, only to realise that one of them was laughing at her before she had even got halfway through. She remembered the sheer loneliness of standing there at the end, arms raised, heart in her boots.

She took John's hand and gently put the laptop on the floor. She ignored his look of panic as it was taken away – so similar to the expression on Seb's face as a baby if she dared to remove a yoghurt from his tray before he had eaten every last bit. Tiny fists pumping on plastic.

Nope. That wasn't quite the vibe she was going for.

She turned his hand palm upwards and kissed it.

'I went shopping today.'

'Oh yeah?' He nodded. 'Did you get any loo roll? It's our turn, I think.'

Oh God.

'And food waste bags.'

OK. Enough talking. She leant over and kissed him.

Well, that had shut him up, at least. She took his hand and slid it underneath her dressing gown.

He stopped to take a breath. 'Oh. *That* kind of shopping.'

'Yes.' She hadn't seen that glint in his eyes for a long time. Her heart quickened and she put her hand under his shirt and grabbed his belt. She pulled him towards her and they kissed, his lips on hers becoming more and more urgent until the dressing gown was off, the shirt was off and they were in a tangle of limbs and breath in the middle of the bed. This was what she had been waiting for. This was what she needed. Him. And her. Together. At last.

'God, you're beautiful.' He stared at her and the lights were on and she saw nothing but admiration in his eyes.

All these months of hiding. Of pulling up the sheets and buttoning up her pyjamas. When all the time there was . . . this. She curved up into him, nibbling his neck, caressing his hair with her fingers. She forgot the scar. Forgot the blood and the pain. Forgot the months of trying and failing to get up the courage to reach for him in the night.

This was who they were meant to be.

She dropped her hand lower and lower, until it touched the soft skin of his thigh. His breath was coming in gasps. Raw. Primal.

This felt so good. She could see he thought so too.

Then she heard a buzz.

'Shit.'

Not exactly the word she had dreamt of hearing.

She ignored him, running her hands up his legs.

'Oh God. Stop.' He sounded like he was in pain.

Anger and frustration made her breathless. 'What the hell is it, John?'

'I've got . . .' He pointed at his phone. 'I've got to get that.'

'Are you fucking serious?' She flicked her hair out of her eyes and plunged downwards again. She wouldn't stop. She would make this happen.

'Abi!' He pushed her away.

She stared at him, this man who had once been unable to resist her, and suddenly she was only cheap underwear and scars and she knew it wasn't his phone that was stopping him. She knew he had been looking for an excuse. Any excuse to get away from her.

To think she had felt sexy. To think she had felt excited.

What a fool. John had put Bonjela on her mouth ulcers. He had spoon-fed her, and he had found her burning up and delirious in the middle of the kitchen floor.

They could never get past that.

The thought was quiet. Heavy.

Tears started to slide down her face.

'Oh God, sorry.' He pushed up and turned away from her. 'I can't get anything right.'

She wiped the tears away, reaching for the dressing gown to cover up her ugliness. 'It's OK. I get it.' Her voice was tiny.

'No, you don't.'

'I do.' She forced herself to look at him. Forced herself to see what had become of all that love.

His eyes were full of pity. She had known it must be there, but still it stung.

'Abi. Come on. It's been months since we had sex and then you just spring it on me, and I told you I have to work tonight trying to pull in staff to cover that hotel, and . . .' He stopped. Threw his head back in a grinding howl. 'Why the fuck won't anything work out any more?'

Four months ago, all he had wanted was for her to live. Now here she was and everything was falling apart.

She didn't have an answer for him. She was too tired. Too crushed.

'I'm sorry.' He shook his head.

'Me too.'

He stood up and pulled on his pants. 'We just need more time, Abi.'

'What – one and a half years isn't enough of a break between shags?'

'Don't be stupid.'

'I'm not.' She shook her head. 'Just honest.' The bloody dressing gown had wound itself around the bedpost. She tugged it. She was cold now. She looked down at her matching bra and pants. They looked ridiculous. A stupid whim. She should have known they wouldn't solve anything. She gave up on the dressing gown and wriggled back, pulling the covers over her body. Throughout her illness she had wanted just one more Christmas. Now here it was and the man she loved didn't want her any more.

John looked utterly defeated. 'I'm sorry, Abi.'

'Sure.' She shook her head. 'I know.' The covers were thick but she couldn't even begin to get warm.

He picked up his laptop again. 'I'll go and work downstairs.' He didn't meet her eyes. 'I'll leave you to get dressed.'

'Sure.' Abi stared out through the skylight at the stars in the sky above. Stars she had wished on. Stars she had prayed to.

She looked at him as he stopped in the half-light by the doorway.

'It's Tuesday, isn't it?'

He stared at the floor. 'Yep. It's never been our night, has it?'

'No.' Abi shook her head, remembering their Chemo Tuesdays. They were the same every time. She was scared. He was worried. They both said things they wished they could take back and John always ended up going on a very long run or bike ride until both of them had calmed down enough to be civil again.

And now the tradition was continuing.

He tried to smile. 'Everything will be OK. You'll see.'

Absolutely nothing in her believed him.

Seb

'Well, I guess we nearly christened it, babe.' Jess reached across to his bedside table and took a sip of water.

'Yeah.' Seb raked a hand through his hair and pushed himself up to a sitting position. His head collided with the wonky shelf that had inexplicably been placed above his narrow single bed. He looked around, his mind still racing over what had just happened. Or what hadn't happened.

Part of him wasn't even surprised. The part he had been trying to ignore for the last few months.

His mouth was dry with embarrassment, and he rubbed his hair and wondered how soon he could ask her to leave. All he wanted right now was a football and a very big field to kick it around in.

Jess sat up to cradle him, breasts pressing into his back. Her purple nails ran gently over his chest in a way he knew was meant to turn him on. Right now they felt about as appealing as barbed wire.

'I can't wait for next time.' She lowered her voice suggestively, her long dark hair tickling his neck and back.

Oh God. She was being so bloody nice. If she would shout or stamp then they could at least have a fight and he could unleash some of his frustration. But all this understanding – there was no way he could feel anything but shame.

He had to get out of there. 'I need to head out soon. Got a shift at the restaurant.'

'Oh, right.' She lingered, her hands on his skin. 'How are you going to keep that going? With mocks coming up?'

'I don't know, but it's not like I have an allowance any more. Not like you.' He sounded churlish but he didn't care. He stood up and she collapsed back onto the pillows, and the shelf had its moment with her too.

She rubbed her head. 'Shit. That hurt.'

He knew he should go to her and see if she was OK, but he wanted his clothes on – the safety of a barrier between them. A step away from the raw humiliation of their afternoon playing hooky. No school. No revision. Just the two of them here at a time when everyone else was out. They had held hands and giggled as they ran up the steps, kissing as they opened the front door and then again as they made their way up to his room.

That ease had gone now. Now, it was him and her and some rumpled sheets. It seemed sad. Sordid, even.

He sighed. Ever since he had tipped Coke all over Jess, the hottest girl at Oxford High, and she had mysteriously found this attractive, he had known he was the luckiest guy in school. That day she had sat with him and laughed about the amount of food he was eating (Wing Roulette, garlic bread, two corn on the cobs and a large mash – not even his biggest meal) and then they were an item and then his mum was diagnosed and Jess was with him every step of the way.

But recently he had started to wonder how much of a future the two of them could have. However hard he tried, he couldn't get away from the thing he still couldn't artic-ulate even to himself. Where his eyes were drawn. The faces that lit up his dreams. He couldn't even imagine how to tell her – how to say that they were over.

He would work it out. Later. When the shame had died down.

She watched him from the bed. 'We could try again, couldn't we?'

No. Not again. Not yet.

'Sorry. Like I said, I've got to go.' He swiped his phone into life. A second later, Bugzy Malone blasted over the speakers, handily destroying any remnants of romantic atmosphere.

He turned back towards her, feeling self-conscious in only his boxers. This was when he should be happiest. Beautiful girl. Empty house. He had spent years dreaming about this kind of thing.

'Seb?'

He couldn't look into those liquid eyes. Not now. He turned around and pulled his jeans on, then glanced at her over his shoulder. 'Gran and Gramps will be back soon, anyway.'

Jess smiled and patted the pillow next to her. 'Well, why don't you get back in here until we hear them come in?'

'No.' It came out too loudly. 'I haven't got time. I . . .' As usual, he ran out of words. He turned away again to try to find his T-shirt. 'I don't think . . .'

She grabbed his hand, kneeling up on the bed with the covers slipping downwards. If only he wanted to touch her. If only he wanted to kiss her sadness away.

He wished he did. He wished it with his whole heart.

'Look, Seb, it's OK. It happens to everyone sometimes.'

No, he wanted to say. It's not that. This is not just once. It's going to happen again. And again. Until I do something about it.

She was pleading now, and every word only made him feel like more of a shit. 'You've got a lot on, babe. Your mum's only just got better, your dad's in trouble. You know.'

She gestured round the room with its tragic 1980s decor. 'It's a lot to deal with.'

He clutched at the straw she was offering him. 'Yeah.' He felt like a bastard, but it was better than thinking about the last sixty minutes. Her dark hair soft against the pillows. The excitement in her eyes as she pulled off his jeans. Her fingers tracing soft curves over his bum.

Oh God. Fresh air. Now.

'Thanks, Jess.' He pressed his hand over his eyes as if he was crying, before realising that tears were in fact starting to fall. Even more embarrassing. She reached out and pulled his hand, drawing him into a hug. The bed was starting to feel like a giant magnet full of everything he didn't want to face or think about.

He extricated himself from the noose of her understanding and pulled his T-shirt over his head. As she started getting dressed, he opened the thin curtains, still scattered with the *Star Wars* figures his Uncle Rob had chosen for his childhood bedroom. His eyes roamed across the garden. Neat rows of broad beans and carrots criss-crossed the vegetable patch at the back of the lawn, and the willow tree arched over the bench in the centre of the grass. Two names were on it: Gryff and Carol. His mum used to joke that she and Dad would get a bench sometime, but that didn't seem likely now. They needed other things, like food and toothpaste and some very cheap Christmas presents for each other and for him.

He sighed. He had expected things to get easier once Mum was better, and of course they were. The aching anxiety was gone. The feeling that every call might be the end. But he missed seeing her holding Dad's hand. Missed their two heads next to each other on the sofa as they watched the Bear Grylls survival shows that they both adored. He missed feeling part of a family.

'You're still OK for my birthday party, yeah?' Jess had most of her clothes on now and was fluffing her hair out around her face while checking Instagram. He hoped this afternoon wouldn't feature on her feed. It was definitely one to forget.

'Of course.' He took a deep breath. 'I wouldn't miss it.'

'Great.' She stood up and slid her feet into her boots, leaning over to zip them up.

'Well.' She looked up at him, eyes full of doubt. 'I'll see you.'

'Yeah.' His voice cracked and for a moment he thought he was about to cry again. 'And good luck. Knock 'em dead at your interview.'

She grinned, but he knew how hard she had been working to get into Oxford. How many late nights. How many 5 a.m. starts as she steadily ticked off the sections on her revision schedule. Meanwhile he had done . . . nothing. He had even lied about his BMAT results to his parents. Miraculously, he had done OK on the aptitude and scientific knowledge sections, but his written results were way below expectations. His head of year had asked him why, and all Seb could do was to say he'd found the questions too hard. It was easier than admitting that his brain just couldn't focus long enough to get any of the answers down. That he had sat there staring at his paper, wondering how on earth the other candidates had enough words in their heads to fill up all that space.

The school had contacted his dad too. Seb was so grateful that his mum wasn't back on their contact list yet that he had agreed to everything his dad suggested. Yes, he would start revising properly. Yes, he would cut back on his hours at the restaurant. Anything to stop his dad telling his mum what had happened. And his dad had gazed at Seb with those exhausted eyes, and asked him if he could really turn things around before his mocks in January. And Seb had said yes.

Given his current form, though, he would soon be found out. Time was running out.

He hugged Jess close. 'You deserve this. Oxford would be lucky to have you.'

'Yeah, right.' She pulled on her coat. 'Just got to beat ninety per cent of the competition. No problem. Clever you, choosing UCL.'

'It's pretty competitive too.' He swallowed. 'But you can do it, Jess.' He held her by the shoulders, his grip strong and firm. He might be a disaster in the sack, but this bit he could do. 'I know you can.'

'Are you sure?' Her voice was so quiet.

'One hundred per cent.'

The gleam was back in her eyes. 'Well it must be true then.'

He smiled back at her, enjoying the unusual feeling of having actually helped someone.

When she had gone, hair whipping round her face as she walked to her car, he opened the door at the back of the kitchen and stepped out into the garden. The wind cut through his hoodie, but he needed the cold to clear his head. He was tired of the swirling anxiety now; he wanted something – anything – to become clear.

'Hey.'

A head appeared over the fence.

'Hey.'

'Fancy some of this?' Marc waved a joint in the air.

'Definitely.' That would improve his mood. He ran towards the hedge and tried to vault over it. The yew tree had other ideas and he fell backwards, blood stinging across his forehead. 'Shit.' He scrabbled around in the mud and encountered one of the local fox's early morning craps. 'Oh for fuck's sake.' He really *really* wanted to cry.

Next thing he knew, a pair of Converse had landed lightly beside him. It must be easier to get over the fence from the other side. Marc's hand was underneath Seb's chin, tipping it upwards.

'That hurts.' Seb writhed away.

'Don't panic.' Marc's voice was calm. Must be all that weed.

'I'm not.' Seb sat up and grabbed the joint from his hand. It was still lit. Thank God.

Marc narrowed his eyes. 'You've got a fairly major cut there. Luckily . . .' he dug a hand in the pocket of his jeans, 'I have a toddler sister, so I come prepared.' He pulled out a Peppa Pig plaster.

Seb inhaled deeply as Marc pressed the plaster on with light fingers. He coughed. 'Shit. That stuff is strong.'

'Just the way I like it.' Marc sat back on his heels and Seb could see the hair on his leg through a rip in his jeans. He moved his eyes away, staring up at a robin twittering happily on a branch above him. Lucky sod. Food, sex and territory. What a simple life.

'And don't worry. I won't tell anyone that you had a pink plaster stuck to that manly forehead of yours.'

'Shut it.' Seb pushed himself up until he was standing. The world tipped for a second. Hard to tell if it was the weed or the fall.

'You do like talking in monosyllables, don't you?' Marc tilted his head sideways. 'Very primitive. Very football boy.'

'Fu—' Seb realised he was conforming to type. He winced as Marc's fingers found their way towards his. 'What are you . . .?'

'Doing? God, you're jumpy.' In the dusk he could see Marc's white teeth as he smiled. 'I'm just getting my joint back.' He put it between his lips and Seb saw the tip glow as he inhaled.

Despite himself, Seb wanted to prolong the conversation. 'Doesn't your mum mind you doing this?'

'Don't your grandparents mind?'

Seb could feel his mind softening. The wind whistled. The world was shit and his mum was probably about to discover quite how much he had screwed things up, but . . . but. The joint was in his hand again and all he had to do was inhale. Exhale. Inhale.

At last he had found something he could do right.

Abi

Naturally the oven decided to break an hour before Christmas dinner was due to be ready.

'Bollocks.' Abi took a sip of the brandy she was planning to douse the Christmas pudding in later, wincing as she was reminded yet again that she no longer enjoyed booze.

She had just tried to deploy the microwave to see if she could get her pre-made gravy to defrost, but it had taken one look at the dark brown bowl and taken the sensible option and exploded. Her dad was currently 'mending it', aka snoozing in front of *Happy Feet* with a screwdriver in his hand and filaments and wires littered across the carpet.

'Are you OK in here?' Her mum popped her head into the kitchen, her suspicious expression only slightly negated by the jangling red antlers holding her hair back from her face.

No oven. No microwave. Yes. Everything was peachy.

'It's going really well, Mum.' Abi was starting to regret putting on her nylon Mrs Santa outfit so early in proceedings. She had the back door wide open, but it was still thrush-inducingly hot inside the bright red dress. Having made a huge fuss about cooking the full works this year, after last year's nightmare of sitting limply on the sofa trying to swallow, she was determined that it would go perfectly. Not the case so far. Maybe she would have to resort to Lesley's tactic and just try to get everybody drunk.

She picked up the nearest bottle. 'Would you like more Prosecco, Mum?'

'No thank you.' Her mum's cheeks already had a familiar pink tinge. 'I'll wait till the food's ready.'

'Might be a while yet.' Abi lit the gas under the potatoes.

Her mum homed in on the oven. 'Why isn't this on?'

Abi sighed. 'I don't know.' She dabbed her forehead with a tea towel and wondered if she could just hop into the freezer for a second to cool herself down. 'It switched off a minute ago.'

'Well, you probably had it too hot. It cuts out when you do that.' Abi heard the click of her mum's knees as she bent down to open the door. She peered over her shoulder. Inside, the turkey still looked determinedly raw.

Her mum tutted under her breath and switched the oven back on again. 'Look, Abi, do you need some help?'

'No.' Abi shook her head. 'I want you to relax. To enjoy yourself.'

'Well I'd enjoy myself a lot more if you'd just let me help.' Her mum adjusted a rogue antler, which was leaning forward towards her nose. 'I can do the sprouts. And I can help you to get the roasties sorted out.'

'Mum, I . . .' Abi saw her mum walking over to the packet of bacon on the side, intended for the turkey later if it ever deigned to cook. Saw her take the scissors and try to cut. Saw the pain flickering across her face as her arthritic hands refused to comply. She put the packet down again.

Abi needed to do this herself. 'Mum. I'll do it all. I promise. You go and relax.'

'No.' Her mum was at her most resolute. 'I'll start with the sprouts.' She picked up the bag. 'And I'm shutting the back door. It's freezing in here.'

If only. Abi sighed and got the carrots out of the fridge. She had entertained visions of honeyed roasted vegetables and making her own stuffing, but inevitably that had dwindled when faced with the reality of cooking her first major meal in well over eighteen months. She could manage a casserole or a stew or a quick plate of pasta, but her multi-tasking abilities seemed to have abandoned her.

Seb was meant to be helping, but instead he had eaten all the pigs in blankets for breakfast and then disappeared. She felt a rush of concern, and turned up 'Fairytale of New York' to try to drown out the whispering in her mind. She wished she was as drunk as Shane MacGowan sounded. That might reduce her stress levels.

John wasn't helping either. Christmas was always a bad time for him, as ever since they had met at school, he and Noah had always made sure they spent Christmas Eve in whatever pub was their current favourite. John would re-appear in the small hours, with beer on his breath and a Santa hat on his head, and snuggle into her and tell her how much he loved her. This year he had stayed in with a cheap bottle of whisky while she had sat in a chair in the corner, wrapping their paltry Christmas presents and wondering if he needed to talk.

He showed no sign of it. Eventually she had given up and gone downstairs to join her mum and dad and Rob in their annual game of Racing Santas, while Seb pretended he wasn't interested enough to watch. John stayed upstairs, and when she went back up, the whisky bottle was nearly empty.

If only he would talk to her. It would be the best Christmas present in the world.

Rob wandered in, grabbing yet another nut from the bowl. He was the only member of the family who ever ate the walnuts that her mum always bought in bulk for Christmas. He picked up the nutcrackers and slotted his next victim into place.

'Do you want me to lay the table?'

'No.' Their mum shook her head. 'We're not quite ready yet.'

'Not long now.' If Abi said that every ten minutes for the next two hours, she thought they'd probably get there. 'Drink?'

'Yes please.' Rob cracked the nut with evident glee and popped the kernel in his mouth. 'And I'll have some more of these. Just to tide me over.'

Abi poured him some Prosecco and handed it over.

'Thanks.' He took a swig before returning to the nuts.

'You seem very cheerful.'

'Yeah?' Rob crunched another shell. 'Must be all this tinsel. Gets me all excited.'

'You've certainly gone to town on your outfit.' Abi looked at his stripy green elf jumper with amusement. 'It's not a subtle message, is it?'

'You can talk.' Rob went for a third nut.

Abi wiped her hands on her short red skirt. 'True. But why are you in such a good mood? Did you have something particularly nice in your stocking?'

'No.' Rob shook his head. 'But things are good. Better than they've been in a long time.' His eyes glanced towards her and away again.

'Oh yes?' Abi started to peel the carrots. 'Tell all.'

'I . . .' Rob's nut flew out of the crackers and landed under the sideboard. He dived after it. His voice was muffled as he hunted around. 'Wait a sec.'

She watched for an agonisingly long time, as the nut ran rings round her brother. Coordination had never been his thing. She could still remember his attempt at the high jump at school. Somehow he had totally missed the double crash mat and ended up in A&E with a broken wrist.

Eventually he reappeared, nut triumphantly clasped in his hand.

'Well?' She looked at him, seeing a new light in his eyes. 'What is it?'

'I've started—'

'Nuts!' Seb stumbled in, all bare feet and baggy tracksuit. Rob stopped talking and turned to him. 'Yeah. Want one?'

Seb blinked slowly and looked around. 'Mmmmmm.' He grabbed a handful, trying to eat one without taking the shell off.

'Hello, Seb.' Her mum continued calmly putting crosses in the sprouts. 'Just woken up again?'

'Gran.' His beam went from ear to ear. Rob quietly took the nut out of his hand and handed him one with its shell removed.

He crunched it up and turned to Abi. 'Mum.' He swayed gently. 'Love the costume!' His smile was slow. Warm. And came with a cloud of Diamond White, if she wasn't much mistaken. She took a step towards him and smelt the unmistakable musk of weed.

Her son was stoned. And drunk. She was all for holiday relaxation, but it was only 12.15 on Christmas Day.

He should know better than this.

'Can I have some?'

He was reaching for the Prosecco. As if he needed any.

'No, you can't.' Abi kept her voice even, conscious of her mum's flapping ears only centimetres away.

Seb put his hands together as if in prayer. 'Pleeeeeaaaaase?'

'No.'

145

'Oh go on.' The antlers always unleashed the devil in her mum. 'Give him some. It is Christmas, after all.'

'Yesh!' Seb staggered and grabbed on to Rob for support. Abi put the knife down. Better to avoid sharp objects, given the circumstances.

Rob sidestepped under the weight of his nephew and no doubt got a choking waft of cheap lager for his pains. He glanced at Abi – a look of conspiracy born of year upon year of their mum trying to get them to come out and 'enjoy' pruning the roses or tying back the broad beans. 'Shall we go outside and play football, Seb?'

Thank God. Abi shot him a glance of pure gratitude.

'Good idea!' She practically shoved her son towards the back door.

Seb shook his head. 'But you're crap, Uncle Rob.'

Abi winced. 'Seb, don't be rude.'

Seb shrugged. 'OK.' He held up his hands. 'But don't be surprised if I thrash him.'

Rob took one more nut. 'For strength.'

Abi topped up his glass. 'For patience.' She mouthed a thank you to him behind her son's back, and then quietly lined Seb's trainers up correctly before he stumbled out into the garden.

Her mum looked on fondly through the window. 'He's exactly like you, you know.'

'A bit taller, surely.'

'Yes.' Her mum smiled. 'But I bet he smokes out of the window too. And climbs out to go and meet his girlfriend.'

'You knew I did that?'

'Abi, you were hardly subtle about it. I could smell Marlboro as soon as I got in the front door.' Her mum sighed. 'Let alone the time I found condoms in your school bag.'

Abi winced. 'Well, at least I was being safe.'

'Yes. You and that Steve.' Her mum coughed. 'I suppose you could say that.'

Steve. Abi felt a twinge of regret. She still hadn't called him and he had now stopped calling her. He had got the hint, though now she was struggling to remember why she had driven him away. Why shouldn't she have a laugh? Spend some time with someone who actually smiled when he saw her?

'TUNE!'

Oh good. Here was the other member of her family.

John wandered in, putting his head back and launching into the opening lyrics to 'Last Christmas'. Abi turned the sound up. It didn't help.

She held in a scream. He only ever sang when he was drunk. Great. Anger flared inside her.

'John. I thought you were meant to be giving me a hand.'

'Sorry.' His eyes struggled to focus. 'I got distracted.'

'By what? Another whisky bottle?' She felt her mum watching her, but couldn't keep the impatience out of her voice. 'I could have done with some help, you know.'

He held up his hands and she saw the hole in the elbow of his blue jumper. 'Sorry.' He didn't sound sorry. He sounded relaxed and mellow and all the things she wasn't.

He looked out of the kitchen window. 'Great. Football.' He looked as if he was going to go and join them. No. That wasn't happening.

She held out the bag of carrots. 'Here. You can peel these and slice them.'

'Me?' He blinked with all the innocence of a baby lamb. 'But I thought Rob might need saving. He's taking a hammering out there.'

'How noble of you.' She rattled pans around, making

more noise than all of Wham!'s synthesisers combined. Mariah Carey launched into 'All I Want For Christmas Is You' and Abi got a strong urge to swear at the speakers.

Instead she had another sip of brandy. Still disgusting.

'Please help me, John.' She glared at him, and her look clearly penetrated his alcoholic fog. She couldn't hold it in any more. The hurt of that night was with her – had become part of her. The rejection. Being pushed away so he could answer his bloody phone. She leant close to his ear. 'For once, just do something useful.'

She hated herself as soon as she had said it. He nodded, mouth tight, and took the bag from her hand.

'Thank you.' She knew she sounded like a petulant child, but she had no idea how to climb out of this hole, where she had become a shrew and he had hurt ingrained in his face.

He put the carrots down again. 'I'm just going to the loo. Is that allowed?'

'Of course it is.' She slammed the parsnips on the hob. 'Just be quick, OK?'

She could feel her mum's eyes on her back. Years of those admonishing stares. She braced herself for whatever came next, but her mum surprised her by simply saying mildly, 'He's trying, Abi.'

'Since when were you on his side? You've always thought he was too flashy. All style and no substance.'

'Yes.' Her mum carefully sipped her drink. 'But he proved me wrong, didn't he?' Abi stared at her. 'And he's working so hard to try to get you out of this mess.'

Abi stayed silent. That was all anyone saw from the outside. But in her heart she knew that their finances weren't the real problem. It was the distance between them.

'He loves you.'

Abi longed to turn to her mum and explain. But she couldn't. Because saying it out loud would make it real. He didn't want her any more. She was skin and scars. That was it. Nothing more. No more flirtatious glances. No more leaning in towards each other, fingers magnetically attracted to fingers. That was gone.

Sweat trickled down between her boobs. This dress was yet another thing that made her feel ridiculous.

Her mum coughed. 'Abi, if you ever want to talk . . .'

'No.' Abi shook her head. 'Honestly, Mum. It's just a blip. We've always fought . . .'

Not true.

'It's just we're all in close quarters here, you know?'

'Of course. Just be careful.'

Abi felt white-hot rage. 'Mum. I am. OK? I'm four months out of treatment, so forgive me if I'm still getting used to things.'

Her mum stood up, muscles bunching at her jaw. No doubt she was angry. No doubt she thought Abi was getting it wrong. Great. Maybe it would be best if Abi just went up to her bedroom and slammed the door, like she used to do in the good old days.

Then a hand appeared on her shoulder. A light squeeze, and it was gone. Abi stood. Breathed. In her mum's terms, this was the equivalent of being picked up and whirled around the room.

'You'll work it out, Abigail.'

She looked at her mum, tears filling her eyes.

'Will I?'

'Yes.' Her mum sat down again. 'You've got through worse than this.'

Abi opened her mouth to ask what she should do, but then the potatoes boiled over, and the next five minutes were lost to turning down the gas and mopping up the spillage before it seeped into her mum's precious oak worktops.

When the mess was cleared and the cloth was wrung, she sighed. 'I thought we'd done the hard bit. I thought we might get a moment now – some time to be happy. And part of me is so angry that it's been taken away.'

'I know.' Her mum put her knife down and looked out into the garden. 'But I remember when your gran died. Dad – your grandad – spent every day regretting all the things he hadn't said. All the ways he could have made her happier.' Her mum flexed her fingers, mouth pressed in a thin line.

'Are you OK, Mum?'

'It's just more painful in the cold.' Her mum smiled. 'Your grandad always wished he'd made the most of being with her. Done more. Laughed more.' As usual, she was delivering her message with all the subtlety of a boxer in the ring.

'I'll try, Mum. I promise. We'll try.' Abi wondered if John would agree.

She leant against the worktop, absently riffling through the pile of papers that was lying there as Band Aid launched into 'Do They Know It's Christmas?' This CD really did have all the classics.

'Maybe you should go out there.' Her mum pointed to the garden. 'Take John with you. You could all do with some fun.'

'But . . .' Abi gestured at the destruction that lay all around her. Pans bubbling. Salt scattered across the work-tops. The vinegar lid swimming in its own personal pool of oil. The Christmas pudding glaring at her malevolently from the top of the bread bin. 'I can't leave you with all this.'

'Yes you can.' Her mum stood up. 'Listen to your old mum.'

'No.' Abi grabbed a tea towel and started to mop. 'I want to do this.'

Hopefully Seb wouldn't have passed out by the time the turkey was cooked. Hopefully they could have the family meal she had dreamed of.

'Then I'll just carry on helping, OK?'

'OK.' Abi smiled.

'Good.' Her mum went back to the sprouts. 'And there was me thinking I'd lost my air of authority.'

Abi shook her head. 'God, no. I was always terrified of you.'

'Even when you were stealing my lipstick and sneaking out of your window to meet Steve?'

Steve again.

'Even then, Mum.' Abi picked up the pile of papers, which was about to get caught up in her cooking extravaganza. As she carried it to the table, one sheet fell to the floor.

It had Seb's name at the top.

She reached down and picked it up. She scanned the page, her frown deepening, and panic started to churn inside her.

Then she looked out towards the garden as the happy scene outside turned to grey.

She had been right about Seb. Her beautiful boy. The one who was going to take over the world. There was something wrong. She had the evidence now – right here in her hand. The doubts she had tried to ignore hardened inside her.

She put the paper down. At least she knew now what she had to do.

She needed to find a way to help Seb. To get through to him.

And she needed to do it fast.

January

'She's Electric' by Oasis

This one's for my youth. Oh what fun you were. The platform trainers. The screw-top Lambrusco. The white trousers that were so tight I devoted entire nights to standing up to avoid splitting them. And – of course – Noel and Liam, and the merry havoc they played with my sensitive teenage heart. How much I loved you and how embarrassingly often I kissed the enormous poster of you that I had on my wall. How much I screamed when I finally got into one of your gigs, and how often I listened to this song, convinced that somehow you were singing it just for me. What a song. What a band. What a decade.

Abi

'Just let me finish this.' John took another huge bite of his muffin.

'We don't have time.' Abi checked her watch again. 'We're late, thanks to you.' She pushed open the gate as they were buzzed in and started to walk along the wide concrete path towards the towering white expanse of the main school building. Willow trees drooped around a circular bench just in front of the main entrance, and behind them the playing fields stretched away towards the main road. 'And given the situation, I don't want to make things any worse. OK?'

'OK, OK.' John shoved the rest of the muffin in his mouth. 'I said I'm sorry.' The words were ninety per cent crumbs.

He was right. He had. But she was still finding it hard to forgive him.

Reading the letter had been like a jab of adrenaline – a call to action. It told her that Seb had lied to her. That his written results on the BMAT weren't as high as had been predicted. And it turned out that John had known about it all along. That was what really hurt.

All his talk of honesty, and he had kept this to himself. However hard she tried, however much he told her that he hadn't wanted to worry her – that he'd wanted her to enjoy being cancer-free – she couldn't shake the sting of betrayal. If she had known, she could have done something earlier.

Instead, here they were, meeting Seb's head of year to discuss his future. He had done so well to be admitted to this high-performing Academy; now she was worried he might be asked to leave.

She looked up at the clock carved into the wall above them. It was dangerously close to the hour.

She turned to John, forcing herself to make conversation. They needed to be a team today. 'I wonder why I always feel guilty when I come in here.'

'Your misspent youth?' He wiped the muffin crumbs off his coat. 'Memories of detentions and doing a hundred lines a day?'

She pulled a face. 'I didn't go to school in the eighteen hundreds, you know.' She smiled. 'Not like you.'

'That's right. Mock my immense age.' He smiled down at her and held out his hand. She took it, and for a minute she could forget the anger that had been bubbling inside her since Christmas Day.

They walked up to the huge blue door, which opened automatically. Inside, the spacious atrium was light and covered with pictures done by the students here. Trees against dark skies, babies with bright red cheeks, mosaic faces in blues and greens. A small girl in the school's purple V-neck and grey trousers was pacing up and down, muttering some kind of speech to herself, while a group of students sat in a circle on green chairs, talking intently about what sounded like the Second World War.

As they walked towards the curved reception desk, emblazoned with the school motto – *Be the best that you can be* – she saw the football teams coming in from practice. Seb was walking with a cluster of his team-mates, a bag of balls slung over his shoulder, his head thrown back as he laughed. He looked like he didn't have a care in the world. Since she had seen his results she had tried to talk to him again and again. She had asked him what was wrong. Asked him about his revision schedule. Told him to stop his part-time job and focus. With every attempt he looked at her with more and more contempt and she felt further and further away from the mum she wanted to be.

Every approach was met with a slam of a door or an 'I'm going to my room.' Every reminder of the medical career he had once dreamt of was received with one of those shrugs of the shoulders that were starting to make her really miss booze. Again and again she was left standing there feeling as if she had somehow failed, while her mum made tea or hung up the washing and told her that Seb reminded her of Abi at the same age.

Abi felt a pulse of nerves as the receptionist checked them in. The last time they had been here was when Seb's team won the ESFA U17 national trophy last year. Then it had been all cake and congratulations. Now she had a feeling it would be bad coffee and stale Rich Tea biscuits.

'Come in, come in.' Mrs Chambers appeared, all smiles and pinstripes. 'How are you?'

Abi's mouth was dry. 'Very well, thanks. And you?'

'As well as I ever am in January. It's not my time of the year.' She showed them into her office, which was a glorified cupboard painted a pale cream with a view out over the basketball hoop in the playground. A scratched desk dominated the room, and Mrs Chambers settled into a red chair behind it. Abi and John took their places on two low chairs facing her.

Abi looked at the desk. Just a jug of water and three glasses.

Not even coffee. This must be bad.

She crossed her legs and reached for John's hand.

Mrs Chambers coughed, smoothing down her thick blonde bob. Her hair was shiny. Thick. Abi would bet she was the kind of woman who actually used her NutriBullet every day.

Mrs Chambers started to speak. 'It's been great to see Seb on the football field recently, showing the leadership and determination that we all know he is capable of.'

Abi could actually feel her hands sweating.

'But now we have to get his grades up to the standard he is capable of too.' Mrs Chambers looked straight at them. 'Before it's too late.'

Abi blinked. The head of year had a reputation for not taking any prisoners. She could see why.

'Seb did his mock exams this week.'

'Well, that's good.' Abi had been worried that he might not turn up.

'But as far as the invigilators can see, he has written very little down.'

Abi struggled to process this information. 'But . . . that's crazy.'

'No.' Mrs Chambers' gold studs glinted as she shook her head. 'Not crazy at all. We think he's struggling to concentrate.'

Abi felt resentment start to burn. 'As you know, I was only made aware of his academic situation at Christmas.' She refused to look at John. 'And I hope that now I am better I am back on your contact list. But since I found out what's been going on, I have made every effort to help him.'

'Of course you have.' Mrs Chambers steepled her fingers together. 'And as Seb is nearly eighteen now, we have also tried to work with him directly to resolve these issues.'

Abi removed her hand from John's and began pleating her cardigan between her fingers.

'Now.' Mrs Chambers sipped her water. 'There may be issues at home that are affecting Seb's behaviour. We have asked him, but he's not willing to talk about it. Is there anything we should know about?'

Abi thought of the fight she and John had got into last night. A fight about how much money he appeared to be spending on wining and dining potential clients. She had found a receipt in the wash and her searing frustration had exploded into a row. She remembered hearing a door closing upstairs, and wondering if it was Seb. Guilt started to churn inside her.

'What are you implying?' John's left leg was jiggling up and down. 'That it's our fault?' He lowered his head, strands of grey dulling his blond hair. 'I just thought he was having a few off days. You know, like all kids do. He's been through a lot, you know.'

'We are aware of that.' The wedding ring on Mrs Chambers' finger gleamed. 'And so we have given him a lot of leeway. But the time has come when we need to decide how best to help him. We can't let things drift.'

Abi shook her head. 'But he's studied so hard.'

'Not recently.'

Abi needed to defend him. 'Well he did while I was ill. He was amazing. Look at his A1 results. And I'm not having him missing out on his future because I got ill at the wrong moment.' Once again she felt the fierce pain of having let him down. Of putting him through too much, too soon. His future had been so bright – she had to help him save it. 'Look, I understand that this is difficult, and I promise we'll do everything we can to help him. But . . .' She took a gulp of air. Her head felt too slow for this. Too sluggish. 'But it's still a few months until his exams. We can turn this around. I'll help him.'

John shifted on the chair next to her. '*We'll* help him.' He took her hand and she decided to let him.

Mrs Chambers put her head on one side. 'We'll monitor the situation for the next couple of months, then. And if we don't see any improvement . . .' She let the words hang.

'You will.' Abi wanted to get up and pace, but there wasn't enough room. 'I promise.'

'Well, classes are about to finish for the day, so I suggest you take Seb home and work out a way forward.'

Beside her John was taut as an arrow. 'I've got a meeting, Abs, but I could—'

'You're coming with us, John.'

He held her eye for a second and then nodded. 'Sure.'

'Excellent.' Mrs Chambers stood up. 'Now, I'm sorry, but I have another appointment.'

Abi got to her feet. She opened the door to the office to see the next set of parents waiting to be told off. Poor sods. She looked at them. They looked so bright-eyed and happy. That wouldn't last long.

Half an hour later, the three of them were sitting on stripy seats in the Story Museum café on Pembroke Street, nursing drinks in painted mugs that looked far more cheerful than they did.

Abi put her mint tea down. 'We need to make a plan, Seb.'

'Do we? Why?'

'Because at this rate you're not going to get any A2s, let alone ones that are going to help you become a doctor.'

Seb wiped a blob of cream from his lip. 'Maybe I don't want any. Maybe I'm like you and your psychology degree. Destined to let things slide.'

His words hurt. 'Don't talk bollocks.' She felt the need to justify herself. 'And I didn't let things slide. I had you.'

'And now I'm going to let you all down.'

His coldness shocked her.

John put his cup down. 'Seb, it's not about letting us down.'

'Isn't it, Dad?' His lips twisted into a smile. 'I thought that's exactly what it was about.'

John shook his head. 'No. It's about making the most of what you've got. Like you always have.'

'Have I?'

John looked to Abi for help, but her brain helpfully went blank. The meeting with Mrs Chambers had shaken her up, exposing how out of touch she had become, and shining a light on all the cracks in her marriage. She felt bruised and defensive. She tried again. 'You've always wanted to be a doctor, Seb. Off doing volunteer placements, always watching random documentaries about anything medical – and always working so hard. So why stop now? I don't get it.'

'I've been trying to study, Mum. That's what you don't seem to understand. But I can't concentrate.'

'Then try harder.' John's voice was a slap.

Frustration blazed across Seb's face. 'I am. I have. You just assume I'm being lazy and I'm not.' He looked out of the window as if desperate to escape. 'You just don't get it.'

'You're right. I don't.' John finished the last of his coffee.

Seb folded his arms. 'Maybe I've just changed my mind.'

Abi shook her head. 'I don't believe you.'

'Fine.' He spread his hands wide. 'Well I haven't got any interviews anyway. My BMAT scores are way too low for UCL. So I don't really see the point now.'

There was something more, she was sure of it. If only she could see it. She looked at the huge Roald Dahl display in the centre of the café. *Matilda*. Charlie. *The Witches*. She had loved reading the books to Seb, hearing his gasps at the galumptious words and the bravery and daring of the characters. If only she could sit him down now and cuddle him like she used to. But no. Those times were long gone. Now she found herself wishing that she could crack his head open and take a look at what was inside. It would be so much easier than this constant guessing.

'Seb, come on.' She leant towards him, seeking a connection that seemed to have been burnt out. 'I know you. And I know you can do this.'

'Well maybe I don't believe you, Mum. It goes both ways, doesn't it? Trust.'

'What?' No matter what other mistakes she had made, she had always been honest with him. His words stung like the shards of glass in her knee when she had run into a French window aged six.

He slammed his mug down and the little girl playing by the door turned her head curiously. 'You and Dad? How's that going?'

She knew he was trying to rile her, but could only stare at him. *Words, Abi. Find some words.*

'We're fine. We're happy.' She reached out and took John's hand. It was cold and gave her no comfort whatsoever.

'See?' Seb rolled his eyes. 'You're lying. You're looking me straight in the eye and lying to me.'

Abi squeezed her husband's fingers. 'I'm not. That's not fair.'

She knew it was.

John played with the packets of sugar in the bowl at the centre of the table. 'Your mum and I are fine, Seb.' She had heard more convincing lines on *Take Me Out*. He shrugged. 'But this isn't really about us, is it?'

'What?' Seb gazed at him in annoyance.

'You're just avoiding the question. *You* need to decide what you want to do. Not us. You're eighteen in April – you're nearly an adult now. If you want to screw everything up, then that's your choice.'

Abi pulled her hand from his. This wasn't the support she needed. He was undermining her, right in front of their son.

She would have to convince Seb alone.

'Look, I can help you. We can do revision together. I can quiz you. Like we used to do with your spelling tests.'

'I'm not six any more, Mum.'

'I know, but I'm here and I'm ready to help.'

'When?' Seb's voice was quiet. 'Dad's never home. You're at the shop. When, exactly, are you meant to give me all this help?'

'In the evenings. At weekends. We'd make it work.'

'Just like you're making things work financially?' She could hear the anger in his voice and again sensed that there was something else going on here. Something funda-mental. Something that was tearing her son apart.

If only he would share it.

She reached out for his hand and briefly he let her hold it. 'Seb, what is it?'

He shook his head, finishing the last of his hot chocolate and reaching for his bag. 'It doesn't matter, Mum. We used to talk sometimes and it was easier, but now . . .' He bit his lip. 'Now there's too much in the way. And you two can't even agree on the advice you're giving me. That just about sums it up, doesn't it?'

He scraped his chair back and stood up. So tall. So strong. So lonely.

'Seb!' Abi got to her feet to try to stop him. The little

163

girl wasn't the only one looking at them now. They were the afternoon's entertainment. 'Seb!'

He didn't stop.

She turned to John and sat down. He had already got his phone out.

'Put that bloody thing away or I swear I will smash it into a million pieces.' Her voice was raised now. 'Seb is throwing everything away. How can you just sit there and fanny around on that thing?'

He had the temerity to laugh. He held out the phone. 'You're right. Feel free. Smash it. Go ahead.'

She stared at him. 'Why?'

'Because if you do, then I won't be able to read the really shit news that keeps coming in.'

She rubbed her eyes, exhausted. 'What's happened now?'

'I've lost another three clients. A supermarket. A hotel. And a chain of ten restaurants.'

'Shit.' She put her head in her hands. 'Why?'

'Because I can't keep on top of things any more.' He puffed out his cheeks and she saw nothing but shame in his eyes. 'I can't get the staff I need. I can't manage things. I just can't do it any more.'

'John . . .'

'Please don't be sympathetic.' His eyes were so sad. 'I don't deserve it.' He slumped forward, looking like he was about to slide his head down onto his arms and rest it there for ever. 'And a major client has defaulted on payments dating back over a year, so . . .'

'Yes?'

'The bank are threatening to call in the administrators.'

'What?'

John sighed. 'You heard me.'

'Shit.'

He had tears in his eyes. 'I've fucked everything up.'

'But you said you were turning things around. You've worked flat out, pitching and chatting up new clients and fire-fighting. We've barely seen you. And now . . . this? I don't get it.'

'I'm so sorry, Abs.'

She waited for him to say he had a plan. That everything would be OK. Instead he bowed his head. His sadness moved her, despite her shock. She awkwardly tried to reach out but he moved and her hand landed on the smooth surface of the table.

'What are we going to do?'

He raised his head. 'Is there still a we?'

She summoned the strength she knew she had. Deep down. Somewhere. Beneath the doubts and the distance from this man who had stood beside her through so much.

She took a breath. She had survived. Now she had to survive this too.

'Of course.' She drew herself up. 'We can fix this. And Seb. And . . . everything.'

'Can we?' His voice was tiny. 'Really?'

And she stared at him for a second too long, because the truth was she didn't know.

All she knew was that they had to try.

Seb

'Not you again!' Marc pushed through the gaggle of smokers until he was at Seb's side. 'Can't keep away, can you?'

Seb ground his cigarette beneath his heel and took another swig of his drink. 'Well, seeing as I was here first, technically you're the one following me around.'

Marc nodded. 'Yeah, but I told you I'd be here.'

'And I told you I'd be here too. Jess's eighteenth birthday. Remember?'

'Oh yeah.' Marc leant against the wall next to Seb. 'Got a spare?'

'Sure.' Seb handed over the pack. 'Here you go.'

'Thanks.'

Seb could see the raindrops glinting on Marc's bleached hair as he tapped the bottom of the pack, then reached into the pocket of his skinny jeans and pulled out his lighter. He had a sudden urge to reach out and stroke those long fingers. Instead he shook his head and took a gulp of nicotine-flavoured air. Jess's birthday. He must get in there and be the boyfriend she wanted him to be.

He straightened up and moved to go back inside the club.

'Wait up.' Marc exhaled and sent a plume of smoke snaking into the sky. 'I won't be long. Besides, we need to chat about why the music in here is so damn bad tonight.'

His eyes glinted in the darkness. 'I mean, "Mr Brightside"? Really?'

'Not a fan, then?'

'Not drunk enough for it. Nowhere near.' Marc took another drag. 'My mum loves it, though. Plays it all the time in the car.'

The music from the club boomed through the walls, vibrating beneath Seb's feet. He thought of his mum and wondered whether she liked it too. Once they had shared music. Now he used his headphones as a shield. Still. Silence suited him just fine. Silence and booze. They helped him to avoid the feeling that everything was falling apart.

'Hey. Smile. It's Saturday night.' Marc had finished his cigarette and was in front of him now, their faces only inches apart. 'It's party time.'

Seb could smell the Marlboro on his breath. He was looking straight into his eyes. He felt heady. Reckless.

'What?' Marc's voice was low. 'What is it?'

'I just wondered.' Seb looked down at the ground. 'I just wondered how you knew?'

'Knew what?'

'That you were . . .' Seb hated himself for petering out. 'That you were gay.'

'Oh.' Marc nodded. 'That.'

'Yeah.' Seb forced himself to look Marc in the eyes. 'That.'

'Honestly?' Marc shrugged, folding his arms against the January chill. 'I always knew. From when I was ten and I saw Freddie Mercury on TV and thought I liked the look of him.'

'Right.' Seb nodded. 'Makes sense.'

'How about you?' Marc's voice was a whisper. 'When did you know?'

Seb looked at him. Swallowed. 'I . . .'

'Yes?'

Seb leant forward. 'Maybe . . .' He stopped himself. 'Is Nate here?'

'What?'

'Your boyfriend?'

Marc rolled his eyes. 'Well, no, funnily enough. He's not really my boyfriend anyway. It's a casual thing. Now . . .' He was centimetres away now. 'Where were we?'

'When did I know?' Seb grinned and put his hand gently around the back of Marc's neck. He could feel the softness where the hair had been clipped away.

He heard a wolf-whistle and saw a guy with red hair pointing them out to his mates. Seb found he didn't care. This was the moment he had been waiting for. Something true. Something real.

He leant forward. Closer. Closer. He forgot about the club. He forgot about Jess. Nothing mattered but this.

'What the fuck are you doing?'

Seb pushed Marc away and whipped his head round.

'Dan, I . . .' He couldn't look his best mate in the eye. 'It's not what you think. It's . . .'

Dan whistled between his teeth. 'So let me get this straight. In there,' he jabbed his finger towards the club, 'it's your girlfriend's eighteenth birthday party. She's on the dance floor, enjoying herself on her special night, waiting for you – her *boyfriend* – to come back from having a fag and actually pay her some bloody attention. And you're out here? With this loser?' He jerked his head towards Marc.

Seb risked a glance and saw that Dan's eyes were pure steel. He felt frustration and shame pulsing through him. Every morning as he got dressed or brushed his teeth he ran a constant monologue. All questions. No answers. How he definitely wasn't gay. How he definitely was. How he would tell people. What his mates would think. What the team would think. What he was going to do about Jess. Whether he needed to do anything about her. On and on in a world where there was never anyone to help him to find his way through.

He didn't know who to start with. Definitely not his dad. And his mum seemed so preoccupied. Even thinking about saying the words out loud made him feel exposed, but increasingly it was the only thing he could think about. He had convinced himself that things would sort themselves out. But here with Marc so close and yet so far, he saw how stupid he had been.

But he couldn't tell Dan. Not right now. He took a step towards him. 'Look, mate, I—'

'Don't bloody mate me.' Dan's dark eyes were slits, but even through the slur in his voice, Seb could hear the hurt loud and clear. 'You're as bad as my bloody dad. Sneaking around behind my back, keeping secrets. And what about Jess? God . . .' He ran a hand through his hair. 'It makes me so fucking mad.'

'Calm down.' Marc took a step forward and put a hand on Dan's arm.

Seb winced. Waited. One second. Two.

Then it came. 'Get the fuck off me!' Dan's face was a snarl.

Marc was tall, over a foot taller than Dan. But Seb knew that Dan was scrappy. He had always been scrappy. Ever since they had hit puberty and Dan had realised he was only ever going to be tall enough to reach most people's chins.

Dan clenched his fists. 'Don't make me hit you.'

Marc folded his arms. 'What is making you so mad?'

Dan jabbed his finger towards Seb. 'The fact that he's a bloody liar.'

Marc took another step. 'Just because you like her yourself.'

Dan's eyebrows were up to his hairline. He turned to Seb, holding his arms wide. 'You told him I liked Jess? Fuck. Unbelievable.' He looked Seb full in the face. 'Now. Either I tell her about you and him. Or you do. Got it?'

Seb felt like crying, but he held firm. Now that he had seen the reaction he was going to get, he knew he wasn't ready yet. Wasn't ready to say those words.

He stuck his chin out. 'I was only messing about, wasn't I, Marc? It was just a joke.'

Marc looked at him, shaking his head slowly. Seb felt a jag of sadness but carried on. 'I was just messing.'

Dan shook his head. 'Don't be a dick. I saw you. You were about to—'

'Nah.' Seb shrugged. 'You know I'm not like that.' He hated himself already, and with every word he hated himself more. But a hen party in bodycon dresses and tiaras were flocking around them now, lighting Silk Cut and downing Jägerbombs. Now really wasn't the time to get into this.

Dan's eyes were narrowed. 'You'd better not be lying.'

Seb tried to assume an ease he didn't feel. 'I'm not. You know that, mate.'

'I'm starting to think I don't know you at all.' Dan was still taut. Ready to fight.

They were attracting glances from the bouncer at the back door of the club.

'You do know me, mate.' Seb faked a smile. 'Shall we get back in there? Get some shots going on?'

'OK.' Dan still eyed him suspiciously.

Marc shook his head and blocked Seb's path. 'You know,

I always thought you were a bit of a loser, but now there's no need to wonder any more. I thought you might have grown up a bit, but no. Still a dick.' His voice was bitter. 'Still a liar. I'm out of here.'

'But . . .' Seb didn't want him to leave. Not now. Not ever.

Dan's voice was harsh. 'Let him go, Seb. What a fucking loser. Who gives a shit what he thinks?'

Marc stood for a second, his eyes fixed on Seb, as if waiting for him to intervene. To stand up for him. But Seb just dropped his eyes, and a minute later, Marc was gone.

In that moment he wanted to talk to his mum so badly it hurt. To talk to her back in the good old days, before the bloody cancer had started. Like that night when they had been out to a gig by one of those singers she loved – a Greek guy – and they had ended up Cossack dancing, or trying to, and having beers (or a Coke Zero in Seb's case) with the band afterwards. They had gone on to a late-night Greek restaurant and feasted on feta and crunchy greens and dolmades and moussaka.

They had laughed and he had let her ruffle his hair on more than one occasion. They had walked home sharing her late-night playlist, one earphone in her left ear and one in his right. Stevie Wonder. Beyoncé. And then the ultimate night-time song – 'Get Lucky' by Daft Punk. He missed their closeness so much a lump was forming in his throat. Now he just felt as if he was disappointing her every day and in every way. She kept looking at him as if he was the end of the world. Just when she was here again for good.

He couldn't call her, so instead he headed back into the club – past crowds screaming out the lyrics to 'Uptown Funk' and a girl being sick on somebody else's Nikes – following his oldest friend: the boy who had frozen under a misshapen tent with him on a Duke of Edinburgh expedition in Snowdonia. The boy who had played football with him every evening after school. The two of them had played together since primary school. They had talked first crushes. First phones. First dates. If anyone knew who he was, it was Dan.

But not any more.

Oh God. He was here in a room packed with people and he had never felt more alone.

Seb's hands were shaking and the cold outside had penetrated his booze blanket and was biting into his bones. More drinks were needed. He knew he had to finish it with Jess but he had no idea how to tell her what he had only just realised himself.

He grabbed Dan's arm and gestured towards the bar. Anything to get more time. Anything to put off finding the birthday girl. The girl who loved him. The girl who had held his hand while his mum was ill. Who had always been there for him.

They waded through the crowds to get to the bar. Seb ordered as many tequilas as he could afford and the two of them downed them all. Oblivion. That was the answer.

Then he went over and danced with the girl whose heart he was about to break.

Abi

'Oh go on. Be a devil. It's not as if you don't deserve a drink or ten.'

'No thanks.' Abi pulled off her woolly hat and scratched her sweaty head. 'Sorry, Lesley. But the thought of drinking that still makes me want to spend the night in the toilet.'

'Wow.' Lesley stared at the mojito jug in front of her. 'Well.' She sat up straighter. 'It's a tough job, but somebody's got to do it. I will heroically try to down every last drop. Promise.'

'Noble.' Abi stared unexcitedly at her bottle of still water. Despite multiple attempts at Christmas, she still couldn't seem to get on with alcohol. It made her hot and it made her feel scared. It wasn't worth it. She sighed and poured the water into her glass.

'How was your Christmas?' She leant back in her chair and looked at her friend. Lesley's long dark hair was piled up on top of her head and she was wearing a low-cut green top that Abi hadn't seen before.

'Stop!' Lesley raised her hand. 'No questions yet. Not before I've had a chance to anaesthetise myself.' She took a long drink. 'OK. Ready now.' She took a breath. 'We eventually made it up there after three delayed trains and several random Accessorize purchases to kill some time. Mum lost the remote before we even arrived, so we were forced to play hour upon hour of Trivial Pursuit, which always leads to Dad stomping off to his den muttering about how the questions are all slanted towards women. Meanwhile Hope was so busy messaging Zane that she barely uttered a word, leaving me to down all the crème de menthe and wonder how soon we could go home. Chuck in my brother's toddler brood and you have a recipe for a terrible Hollywood comedy, starring Robert de Niro in his later years.' She lifted her glass and drained it. 'Happy New Year, that's all I can say.' She slammed the glass down on the table. 'And you? Love and peace and joy to all mankind?'

'Not exactly.' Abi drummed her fingers against her glass, watching the group at the next table out of the corner of her eye. They looked like office workers celebrating making it to the end of the week. One of them pushed her chair back and stood up, staggering slightly as her body tried to adjust to the amount of alcohol in her system. She had a red bra on over her blue dress. Abi wasn't entirely sure if it was a fashion statement or if she had lost some kind of office bet. The woman held up her finger and teetered dangerously on her tapering heels, her voice carrying above the music. 'What are we having again?'

'Tequila,' the group chorused.

Abi grinned at Lesley. 'Those were the days.'

'Weren't they just?'

Abi sipped her water. 'Mind you, I'm out past ten p.m. In recovery terms, this is huge.'

Lesley poured more mojito into her glass, her neon-pink nails vivid against the frosted glass. 'And Christmas? What happened?' She leant forward. Abi could see a tiny slick of salt on her upper lip. 'You're feeling OK, aren't you?'

Abi nodded. 'Yes.' Bar the odd twenty checks per day on various parts of her body, she was absolutely fine. The shadow of cancer would never leave her. She understood that now. She took another sip. 'In fact, maybe that's the good thing about all this. I have new shit to worry about.'

'Er . . . great?' Her friend smiled. 'You'd never have imagined that a year ago, would you?'

Abi grinned as 'Parklife' blasted through the speakers. The woman with the external bra unwisely decided to try to climb on a chair with her tray of shots and one of the men ended up wearing most of them. He thought it was hilarious and simply stuck his tongue out and licked his face as the liquid streamed down. 'Where's the lemon?' he roared.

Lesley tapped Abi's hand. 'Christmas?'

Abi turned back to her. 'I found Seb's BMAT results.'

'OK.' Lesley nodded. 'So far so not exactly exciting.'

'His scores weren't great. Too low for UCL and the other universities he wanted.'

'What? Seb who was glued to his toy stethoscope from the age of six?' Lesley twisted her straw between her fingers. 'He's always been so set on being a doctor. What happened?'

'I have no idea.'

'Really?'

'Yep.' Abi nodded.

Lesley rested her chin on her hand. 'But it just doesn't sound like Seb. Have you managed to sniff out any clues?'

'No.' Abi sighed. 'We've tried everything. I keep trying to talk to him and I swear that with every single conversation I get less of an answer. It's like he's tuning me out.'

'Welcome to parenthood.' Lesley folded her arms. 'The only time Hope talks to me is when she's used up her data allowance, or to ask to borrow the one top of mine that she doesn't hate.'

'I don't believe you. You two have a great relationship.' Abi knew her friend was just trying to make her feel better. 'But the worst thing . . .'

'There's more?'

'Yep.' Abi bit her lip. 'The worst thing is that when he does bother to do any work, his marks are dropping off a cliff. And all the things he's hoped for – and worked for – seem to be slipping away.'

'God, he's packing five years of teenagerdom into twelve months.'

'I suppose he is.' Abi smiled for the first time in about a week.

'He never got a proper go at rebellion while you were ill, did he?'

'I suppose not.' Abi shook her head.

'Well, I'd stop asking him about it directly for starters.' Lesley took another sip. 'You just have to lurk at the kitchen table until he tells you what's going on.'

'But Seb and I have always talked.'

'That makes you the exception that proves the rule.'

'I suppose so.' Abi digested this as the gang on the neighbouring table moved on to their next shots. She envied them their oblivion. 'And then last night John told me that Seb punched someone from school too. Back in September. And they both kept that quiet too. All this time and no one told me.'

Lesley shrugged. 'They probably didn't want to upset you.'

Abi felt a stab of frustration. 'But that's not OK, is it? I mean, I understand Seb trying to hide it, but not John. He knows I want to be involved. It's not right to leave me out.'

'He didn't leave you out. He was trying to protect you.'

'Yes, but if you had—'

'If I had a partner?' Lesley arched her eyebrows.

'Well, yes.' Abi swallowed. 'When you were with Paul

176

– in the good times – you wanted him to be open with you, didn't you?'

'Mainly, yes.' Lesley nodded. 'Until he started having affairs, that is.'

'Of course.' Abi nodded. 'So I have a right to be angry, don't I?'

Lesley wrinkled her nose in thought. 'John's got a lot going on, Abi. His business must have been going to shit for months. He's probably not thinking straight.'

'That doesn't make it OK.'

Lesley poured more cocktail into her glass. 'So the sex didn't work out then?'

'What?' Abi felt a flush of shame.

'You seem so angry with him. I just wondered . . .'

Abi didn't want to talk about it. 'Things are fine, Lesley.' It was easier to lie. 'That's not the problem. It's just that we're meant to share things. And if we're not a team, then . . .'

'Don't be so hard on him.'

'Why not?'

'Because no one's perfect, Abi. So, he hasn't told you a thing or two. So what? You've got to cut him some slack.'

The punch. The bad results. The house. The rejection. She had cut him plenty of slack.

'So you admit he should have told me?'

'Yes.' Lesley pushed her chair back. 'But I think he was just trying to help. I need a wee. Back in a sec.'

'OK.' Abi stared after her, wondering if Lesley was right. Before her illness, Abi had been the parent who was called or emailed or accosted by teachers. But since she was diagnosed, things had changed. She had been forced to tune out the world to get better, and John needed time to get used to the fact that she was back now. Able to make decisions. Able to help.

'Penny for them?' A bottle of Heineken landed on the table.

She knew that aftershave.

She turned and blinked up at the new arrival.

'Oh my God. Steve!' She found herself wishing that she had changed before coming out. She had been clearing the only remaining dusty corner of the shop this afternoon, making space for the arrival of springtime prints by Sam Toft and Dave Thompson, and she wondered if there might be the odd dustball still in her hair.

'No need to get up.' He pulled up a chair and sat down in his old way, turning it round and leaning forward against the back. She could see a sliver of leg through a rip in his dark-blue jeans. She prayed she didn't have spinach in her teeth. Or chocolate.

She took a breath. She was being ridiculous. But seeing him was like a passport to the past, back to the days when she was obsessed with Pulp and learning how to smoke without coughing and her main goal in life was growing her hair down to her bum.

Steve was a year older than her. He was sixteen when they met. One afternoon he had beckoned her over to the bus stop and cupped his hands round hers as she lit a cigarette and from that moment they were inseparable. Her world had never felt complete unless his arm was around her shoulders. They had argued about lyrics, clambered into festivals and danced like crazy people in sweaty tents until dawn. For two years they had drunk wine out of teacups, written love notes on napkins and called or seen each other every single day until he had gone to university in St Andrews and never come back.

There had been tear-soaked letters. Cheap gin. Moody fags out of the window. And then finally John had appeared and Steve's memory had finally started to fade.

'I should have known this would be your kind of bar.' He took off his leather jacket.

'Why's that?'

'Indie music – tick.' He smiled. 'Great cocktail menu – tick. And, if I'm not mistaken, they have nachos.'

'Yeah.' Abi remembered nights when the two of them had spent hours fighting over the ones at the bottom of the pile that were soggy with olives and tomato and soured cream.

Looking at him now, in the dim light, she could feel the past coming back to comfort her. 'Do you remember that pub with the guitars on the wall?' She leant towards him. 'The one where the barman used to let you play them if you helped out washing glasses after they closed?'

'Oh my God, YES.' He clapped his hands together and she saw that he still wore that thick silver ring on his first finger. 'We spent so many nights there.'

'We did.' She smiled. 'Though I'm not sure all that whisky had a great effect on the way you played.'

'True.' She loved the hint of mischief in his smile. She saw a girl at a nearby table gazing admiringly at him. Some things never changed.

He swigged some beer from the bottle. 'So what the hell have you been up to since we last saw each other and you started screening my calls?'

'Not a lot.' She felt a rush of heat to her face. Helpful. 'I'm out with Lesley.' She ground to a halt.

'Lesley from school?'

'Yep. We're still mates.' *Oh God.* Her small talk really did need a bit of work.

'Great.'

'Yes.' Her world sounded very small.

'And still a party animal?'

'Sure.' She would not be cancer girl. Not with him. No way.

He peered at her drink. 'So that's vodka, is it?'

'G and T, actually,' she lied.

'Nothing changes.' The shark-tooth pendant round his neck shifted as he picked up his beer again.

'Well, what a surprise.' Lesley was back, standing over the table looking like an owl discovering a hunter with a hand in her nest. 'Steve? What are you doing here?'

'Hi.' He grinned and stood up to kiss her on both cheeks. 'Lucky chance.'

'I see.' Lesley arched an eyebrow.

'He just bumped into me.' Abi felt unaccountably guilty.

'Of course.' Lesley sat down, crossing her legs decisively. 'So tell me. What have you been up to since breaking my Abi's heart all those years ago?'

Steve put his head on one side. 'Oh. You know. This and that.'

'Yeah?' Lesley poured herself another generous measure of mojito. 'Tell us more. Broken any more hearts?'

Abi felt a flush of embarrassment rushing to her cheeks. It had been a long time. Lesley should let him off the hook.

Steve, though, seemed impervious to Lesley's tone of rebuke. 'Oh. You know. A few. I've had mine broken too, just for balance.' He smiled. 'Anyone for another drink?'

Abi shook her head. She didn't want him asking why she wasn't drinking. 'No thanks.' She didn't want that light to go out in his eyes when he heard the 'C' word.

'OK.' His eyes lingered on her for a second longer than

was strictly necessary. Then he turned on his heel and strode towards the bar.

'God. Arrogant as ever.' Lesley was practically inhaling her mojito. 'What a dickhead.'

'Mmmm.' Abi watched him as he pushed his way through to the bar. Wide shoulders. Long legs. Hair just long enough to curl against the collar of his black shirt.

'All he needs is a guitar on his back and his tragic tosser status would be complete.'

'Yeah.' Abi was still staring at him.

'Hello?'

'What?'

She became conscious of a hand flapping in front of her face.

'Calling Abi.' Lesley sighed and rolled her eyes. 'God, anyone would think you still fancied him or something.'

'No way.' Abi forced herself to focus on her friend. 'It's just nice to see an old face, that's all. Takes me back a bit.'

'Yeah, well you were wearing tight white trousers and DayGlo trainers back then, so don't get too nostalgic.' Lesley dug into her bag for her phone. 'Shit. It's Hope. She's got some mates over and is threatening to cook. Must just check she hasn't burnt the house down.' She tapped the screen. 'Hello?' She stood up. 'Back in a sec.' She stalked over to the door.

Abi felt relieved, and didn't want to think about why.

'Where's Happy Face gone?' Steve sat down with a beer for him and another jug for Lesley.

'She's on the phone.' Abi looked at him. 'Weird to think that when we last spent an evening together, the only mobile phones were the massive ones in Hollywood films. The ones as big as phone boxes. Do you remember?'

'God, don't talk about that. You're making me feel old.'

Abi shrugged. 'Forty is approaching. That's all I'm saying.'

'You're killing my mood.'

'That's what they all say.' She played with her straw, feeling as nervous as she had on their first date. Apple Day Fair, 1994. She remembered looking up at him, silhouetted against the night. His hand reaching for her as she leapt onto the waltzer. The thrum of music and the smell of toffee apples and cider in the air.

'So . . .' He took a swig of his beer. 'What are you listening to nowadays?'

Of course. That was what they always talked about. Music. 'I like Chvrches. Have you heard them?'

'Have I heard Chvrches?' His eyes widened. 'Have *I* heard Chvrches?'

She rolled her eyes. 'Not a difficult question, buddy.'

He shook his head melodramatically. 'I just can't believe you'd even ask such a thing.'

'Just answer the question. Unless . . .' She looked around. 'Unless you need to go? Are you waiting for someone?'

He grinned. 'No. I'm not waiting for anyone. Nobody at all. I just popped in for a quick beer before heading home.'

'Great.'

'So? What do you think of "Every Open Eye"?' He started to peel the label off the beer bottle.

'It's amazing.'

'Why?'

And here it was. The conversation they had enjoyed on buses. In lunch queues. On dates in dark pubs. Different bands. Different venues. But always the same passion.

It took her back. Back to the girl she had once been. The girl with dreams and CDs and pictures of bands and singers plastered all over her wall. It felt good to meet her again. And as 'She's Electric' started to play, Abi dived in. She didn't let herself think ahead. She didn't think about home. She just thought about bands and music and lyrics and the joy of finally talking to someone who loved them too.

It was only later, as Lesley sat back down, that Abi realised that – for the first time in months – she had felt like herself again. Her old self. The one she could see reflected in Steve's smile.

February

'The Promise' by Tracy Chapman

For John. It's only right you get more than one, after all. In case you don't remember (highly likely), this was the song that was playing as I walked down the aisle. The one that people welled up to, the song that people weren't expecting and the song that I love above all others. It means love to me. It means you to me. It means everything that I'm surviving for. It means the world.

(And yes, I love it so much, I gave up irony for the duration of this note. A compliment indeed.)

Abi

'So why don't you just ask her out, Uncle Rob?' Seb carefully submerged a chip in ketchup and put it in his mouth. At the rate he was eating you would think he hadn't been fed for a month, when in reality he had polished off half a lemon drizzle cake only an hour before they had left.

Rob seemed to shrink into his beard. 'I don't know what you're talking about.' He picked up his burger in a bid to terminate the conversation.

Fat chance. During this meal so far approximately ten conversational topics had been introduced, all of which had ended in people slurping their drinks in silence. Her parents' vision of a family celebration of Abi and John's wedding anniversary wasn't going according to plan. In fact it was going so badly that Abi had decided to have a red wine or two to speed things along. She was tired of living life with her shoulders up around her ears.

She added more ketchup to her veggie burger and took a bite. She should have known not to trust her mum. She had never been one to leave a situation well alone. Two weeks ago. 7 a.m. Her mum ready for her day of volunteering at the local Oxfam shop, dressed in her red polo neck and the chunky pendant Abi's dad had bought her on her seventieth birthday.

Abi had been in her dressing gown, gasping for some tea.

'Well, of course it is *your* anniversary. But you must celebrate it.' Her mum put her cup down in its saucer. She pushed the muesli box to one side, and Abi's last defence was gone. Her only remaining weapon was silence. She stared downwards and dipped her spoon back into her bowl.

Yes. It was their anniversary. The one they had thought they might never get to celebrate. All those weeks of chemo, with Lesley or John sitting next to her with magazines and an iPad loaded with US shows and gigs by her favourite bands. Days spent staring at her bedroom wall, listening to Bob Dylan or The Stone Roses and wondering if the nausea would ever go away.

Back then the thought of her boys had kept her alive. But now the distance between the three of them was so great that even sitting around a table with them didn't feel honest any more. John was steadily chewing with all the joy of someone waiting to have an ingrowing toenail removed, while Seb was making the most of looking eighteen and was already on his seond beer.

She wished she could reach them. She wished she could help.

Rob shifted in his seat. 'Look, Lesley's just a friend. OK?'

'You're a terrible liar, Uncle Rob.' Seb sat back in his chair, kicking the table leg.

'Yeah, well you're a terrible stirrer.' Rob sipped his beer. 'Just because you're such a hit with the ladies.'

A shadow crossed Seb's face and Abi itched to know what had caused it.

'Everything OK here?' The young American waiter was undoubtedly the most cheerful person in the vicinity.

'Another beer, please.' Seb glared at Abi as if expecting

her to veto his order. She was definitely the bad cop in his world. When he was little they had sat together making spaceships out of cardboard boxes and tinfoil, zooming to far-distant planets where they snacked on raisins and cheese.

Now, part of her was terrified about what he was hiding while part of her was furious that he was throwing his life away. But at the same time her heart was full of desperate guilt that what he was going through was her fault. Her fault for getting cancer. Her fault for letting him down.

She sighed as the restaurant decided to really put a dampener on things by playing 'Our House'. Across the High Street, a group of students chatted on the wide stone steps leading into Queen's College. They looked so young. Like they held the world in the palm of their hands. Abi wanted Seb to feel like that, but right now he looked about as carefree as a prisoner in the dock.

She wished she knew what to do.

She wished she could trust John to help her.

She gulped her water, aware that the wine was going to her head. Soon they would all finish eating and go home, and she could sit on the bench in the garden and think – really think – about how to make things better. There would be fresh air. Daffodils. She would listen to Tracy Chapman and Amy Winehouse and try to remember how to find her way back to the man who had given her so much, but who now seemed only capable of taking things away. Affection. Certainty. Trust.

Her mum finished her salad.

'Do you remember the day you two met?'

Oh great. Nostalgia. Just what they needed.

'Mum.' Abi attempted to introduce a warning note to her voice, but as ever her mum didn't pick up on subtext.

'Abi was temping in that horrible office.' Her mum

looked at her dad for confirmation and he nodded in return. 'The one where they had found that body a few years before. They talked about it on that Channel 4 documentary. Do you remember?'

Abi caught Rob's eye. Their mum had a strong track record of sitting down to watch worthy documentaries and then falling asleep five minutes in, leaving the rest of them to endure tales of bodies or abuse or drug trafficking until the credits rolled.

'Anyway, it was the Christmas holidays, I think. Your first term at university.' Her mum's smile was soft. 'And you were temping, and you'd dyed your hair pink and you were paid to put accountancy brochures together. Then one day you came home and you had this smile on your face. I knew that smile.'

Abi stared at her plate.

'And then you kept him from us for a while.' Her mum laughed. 'Which meant you definitely liked him. And then there you were one day, John, and you were holding hands in the living room and telling us you were going to have a baby.'

Seb smiled at the waiter as his next beer arrived. 'Sex out of wedlock. What a disgrace.'

'It was a bit of a surprise.' Abi's dad put his knife and fork together and dabbed his mouth with a paper napkin.

Abi arched an eyebrow. 'Mum barely spoke for a week.'

The corner of her dad's mouth rose. 'It was quieter around the place than usual.'

'You didn't like him, did you, Mum?'

'Well, I've already said I was wrong, haven't I?' Her mum smiled at John, who looked infinitely grateful for her kindness. Abi felt a twinge of guilt. She should be more understanding. More supportive. If only she could get past his secrets. Past the way his back was turned towards her every single night as she slipped between the sheets.

She realised she was stabbing a chip to pieces with her fork and rapidly put it down.

John sat up straighter, a hint of a smile on his lips. 'And our wedding – what an amazing day.'

'Really?' Seb's voice dripped cynicism. 'Didn't me being in your tummy ruin the dress?'

'Not at all.' Abi shook her head. 'It was bright green. From a charity shop. We just let it out, didn't we, Mum?'

'Sounds like you didn't have much choice.' Seb gulped more beer.

'Well, we didn't mind.' Abi tried to connect with him, but his eyes slid away. 'We were so happy to have you.'

'If you say so.' Seb sighed and shifted in his chair.

A slow smile crossed Rob's face. 'They were, you know.' Abi felt a pang of envy as Seb looked at her brother with genuine interest. 'I've never seen them happier. Most people would have freaked out – dating for only a few weeks before you were on the way – but not these two. They were straight off to Mothercare, buying annoying mobiles that played nursery rhymes on pan pipes.' He winced. 'God, I hated that thing.'

Abi laughed. 'Did you? I used it *all* the time.'

'I know.' Rob nodded. 'I remember. It's burnt into my brain for ever. But don't worry about it, guys. No hard feelings.'

Abi started to hum 'Rock-a-Bye Baby'.

'Make it stop!' Rob put his hands over his ears.

Seb was actually smiling. 'Maybe I should take up the pan pipes.' Another cloud crossed his face. 'Or maybe not.' He signalled for yet another beer. Abi knew she should stop him, but couldn't find the stomach for another fight.

'Shall we raise a glass?' Her mum blinked round the table.

'Yes.' Her dad held his up. 'To Abi and John. To many more years of happiness.'

'To Abi and John.' Rob dutifully followed suit, while Seb just muttered into his beer.

Something in Abi snapped. 'What is it, Seb? This is meant to be a celebration. Why are you sitting there looking so damn miserable?'

'Do you really have to ask?'

'Yes I do. Because you're being bloody rude.' She glanced at her mum. 'Language. I know. Sorry.' She looked back at her son, feeling a pulse of rage at his sullen face. The face that could light up the world if only he let it.

'Well, you made me come with you.'

'Because it's a family occasion. And you're part of this family, whether you like it or not.'

'Some family.'

'What did you say?'

'You heard me.' His voice was a growl.

'I beg your pardon.' She leant towards him, shaking. She wasn't afraid any more. They were going to have this out now.

'I don't get it, Mum.' The pain in Seb's eyes was real. 'You survived. This is meant to be the happy-ever-after bit. And you two are fucking it up.'

'We're not. Things have been difficult, that's all.'

'But you were the one, Mum.' Seb jabbed a finger at her. 'When you were ill and you were talking to me about the future, you were the one who said to me, don't worry about getting things right or wrong, just be happy. Life's too precious to waste.' He threw his arms wide. 'And here you are doing exactly that. Throwing it away. You're still wearing that horrible grey cardigan, just like you did every bloody day you were ill.'

Abi pulled the grey wool closer around her. 'It's not horrible. It's warm.'

'It's horrible.' His face was twisted in rage. 'It's everything that's wrong with you. You never wore that colour before. Before . . .' He was swallowing back tears.

'It's just a cardigan.'

'No. It's you giving up, Mum.'

She knew he was right. She remembered the day they had talked about making the most of every day. She could feel the warmth of the sun through the window, see the robin hopping onto the holly bush outside, touch the warm mug of tea in her hands. Things had been so clear then. She wished she could feel that certainty now.

'So that's why I didn't want to come.' Seb grabbed the next beer from the waiter's hand and started to drink. 'Because this is all just – wrong.' He put the bottle down. 'Still. At least it gives me a chance to make my announcement.'

'What announcement?' Abi pressed her forehead into her hands. Her temples were starting to ache. The wine. The tension. The sight of her son's furious face turned to hers.

'That I'm not going to uni next year.' Seb shrugged. 'No clearing. No nothing. I'm taking a year out.'

'Seb, no.' She wasn't going to let him chuck all the hard work away now. 'Medical training is so long – you've got to get started. It's what you always wanted. Please . . .'

His chin jutted forward. 'You know you said to me once – wrote to me, in fact – that you had faith in me to make the most of my life.' He practically spat the words across the table. 'Well, that was clearly a lie. You think I'm going to screw everything up. You want to make my decisions for me. Well it's not going to happen. OK? Not any more. I'm tired of trying to be who you want me to be. So I'm getting another part-time job, playing football, and once the summer term is over, I'm off to London. And if you don't like it, tough. It's happening.'

He pushed back his chair and stood up. 'I'm sorry, Gran and Gramps. And Uncle Rob. I really am. You're bloody lovely and the food was great. But I'm just done playing along. I'm not toasting an anniversary when they'll be divorced in a year because neither of them will make a bloody effort. OK?'

He turned and was gone, practically running out of the door and dodging an Oxford Tube bus and a taxi to get away across the road as quickly as possible.

The five of them stared at the checked tablecloth for a moment or six. Even her mum was silenced. There was nothing to be said.

Abi's dad broke the silence. 'Shall I pay?'

Normally they wouldn't let him. Normally she or John would leap in with a credit card and a smile.

Not this time.

It was the final sliver of humiliation.

Abi clasped her glass, hoping against hope that John would reach out and try to take her hand. That he wanted to make this work. That he wanted her.

He didn't move.

Seb

'Come on, Seb. At least give up the job. Give yourself a chance.'

Seb stared at his dad. His hair was too long and was falling into his eyes, which were red-veined and pouchy with tiredness.

'Dad. I don't know why you're bothering. We've talked about all this. You being here is pointless.' He had wanted to come here by himself and have a pint and spend some time with the BBC sports headlines before seeing Jess later. He had wanted to work out what he was going to say.

You could hide yourself in this pub – it was one of the reasons he liked it. The bar staff never checked ID, and rock music drowned out pretty much anything else, even the huge man bellowing into his mobile phone over by the bar. Seb had nearly made it out of the house unnoticed, but then his dad had seen him and insisted on coming too and trying to follow through on the dismal conversation of the week before.

Seb knew it was a waste of time. There was nothing new to say.

'Look, your mum just wants to help.'

'She has a funny way of showing it.'

'Sure. But give her a break.'

Seb was tired of this. 'Why are you standing up for her? You two are always arguing. Stop pretending you're on her side.'

'I am on her side. And I'm on yours too. I know things have been tough for you.'

Seb shook his head, tired of saying that it wasn't about the cancer. This was about him. About something that he was only just starting to admit to himself. Something that would take him out of his easy football captain existence and into a life on the outside. He was terrified. He had seen his dad ladding about with his work colleagues or with Noah – always at the centre of the crowd with his pints and his gorgeous wife. There was no way he would understand what Seb was going through. No way he could help.

'Dad, if you're on my side, can you just leave me alone? Because that's what I really need.' He imagined broaching what was bothering him and was filled with a wild laughter. 'I've told you what I want. I want to move to London for a year. I want to try something new.'

'But your education . . .'

'Fuck my education.' Seb shook his head. 'I can study later. Once I've figured things out. Besides, education hasn't got *you* very far, has it, Dad?' The words came out unchecked. 'You've lost your house and your company's screwed, and now you're scraping to find the change for a pint.'

His dad sat back in his seat, staring into his glass. A muscle flickered in his cheek. Seb felt a jolt of panic. He had gone too far.

'OK.' His dad's voice was disturbingly quiet. 'OK. You're right. Who the hell am I to give you advice?' He stood up. 'But you've got a lot going for you, Seb. So much. And I want you to know how proud I am of you. No matter what shit you give me. No matter how angry you are. OK?'

As he turned to leave, Seb almost stopped him. Almost.

But something held him back. His loneliness was easier to bear than the disappointment in his dad's eyes.

He sat and stared into his pint, losing himself in his seething thoughts. Minutes passed and his glass was empty, so he got himself another pint and sat down again.

'Hi, Seb.'

He had forgotten she was coming. 'Jess. Hi.' He stood up and bumped his knee against the table, which jerked forward. He leant across to kiss her on the cheek, and as he did so, he knocked his beer over. Smooth.

Golden liquid poured down her white jeans. Shit.

'Oh my God, I'm so sorry.' He ran over to the bar and grabbed a handful of napkins. Jess stood still as he tried to mop up the foaming mess, her eyes never leaving him as he sweated and swore his way around the table and dabbed at her jeans. He noticed that the enormous man had stopped talking and started staring at Jess's bum. Then upwards at her chest. He felt a stab of protectiveness and blocked the view with his own body. The man went back to his phone.

'Would you like a drink?' For a very cold February day he was ridiculously sweaty. He could practically feel himself shining.

'Sure.' She sat down and put her bag on the table as he went over to the bar.

'Gin and tonic, please.' The tattooed barman nodded and took a glass from the stack behind him. 'And another Beck's.'

He pulled a tenner from his pocket, thanking God again for the part-time job he had started last week, after filling out an application form, having an interview and downloading an App. He didn't enjoy the massive bag or the ridiculously shit gears on his bike, but he did like the cash. A lot.

He took the drinks and headed back to the table. Jess

was sitting straight-backed, the sunlight bringing out the auburn highlights in her hair.

'Thanks.' She reached her hand across the table and he took her fingers in his. So warm. So familiar. A lump came to his throat and he didn't fully understand why.

'Do you know that's the only time we've touched recently?'

'What?' He picked up his drink. Half the pint disappeared in one.

She took a sip and then put her drink down on the table. The move was deliberate and determined, and the woven silver ring he had given her back in the good old days when he had known who he was and what she meant to him glistened on her middle finger. He touched the leather bracelet she had given him for his seventeenth.

'What do you mean?' He was horribly aware that he sounded like his dad only a few minutes before. He forced himself to look her in the eye.

'Look.' Her voice was gentle yet he heard the bravery beneath. 'I don't think things are working out with us, do you?'

He looked at her, surprised. He felt jolted. And guilty as hell.

'Erm . . .'

She arched an eyebrow. 'I think that says it all.'

Her lips glistened as she sipped again. He struggled to find words, but the things he had to say were too big and too jagged and he didn't know how to get any of them out of his mouth.

Impatience flickered across her face. 'I thought as much.'

'What?' His brain appeared to have buggered off just at the time he needed it most. He knew he should tell her. About Marc. The near-kiss. The realisation that when he looked at a guy it wasn't just to see if he would be good at football.

She carried on, looking worryingly calm. 'You barely touch me. You never want to stay over, and you say your bed is too small for the two of us so I can never stay with you. You kiss me on the cheek. So there's only one conclusion I can come to.' Her forehead was pinched and he hated knowing that he was the cause.

He forced himself to speak. 'What conclusion is that?'

Her eyes were steady and determined. 'I think you're into someone else.'

Seb flinched.

She twisted his ring round her finger. 'I mean, fuck knows who.'

He felt relief seep through him. He hadn't been found out yet.

'Maybe it's that blonde cow who runs the pub, or that girl with the crazy nails in Budgens – I don't know. But I'm not waiting around to find out. I may feel like shit about myself right now, but even I can see that I'm not getting a lot out of this.'

God, he hated himself for being such a dick. He had to tell her. 'Jess, I—'

She held up a hand. 'No. Let me finish. I've been thinking about it for ages now. What could be wrong with me. Why you can't just love me like I love you.' She was staring into her glass but then raised her eyes to meet his. 'Because you did, didn't you? Once?'

The courage in her eyes made him honest. 'I do love you.'

'But as a friend, right?'

Shit.

'Yes.' He leant forward and reached for her, but she pulled her hand away. 'I'm so sorry.'

'Me too.' Her smile was tight and unconvincing. 'Maybe you just needed me to get through your mum's illness. Is that it?'

'No.' He shook his head, horrified. 'I thought . . . that it would grow.'

'So you lied to me? When you said you loved me?'

'Jess . . .'

'No.' She downed the rest of her drink and tears glistened in her eyes.

'Please. Listen.' His voice appeared to have gone up an octave.

'Why should I, Seb?' Now her anger was breaking through. 'Why the hell should I, when all you give me is evasion and lies and bollocks?' She threw her arms wide. 'I deserve more than this.'

'I know.'

'And I don't understand what the hell is going on with you, or why you can't talk to me about it.'

'I . . .'

'What?' Impatience was stamped across her face. 'WHAT IS IT?'

Her shout penetrated the AC/DC playing on the speakers, and now the whole pub was watching them. The huge man was fully tuned in, mouth hanging open, eyes bright with curiosity. Seb would bet a tenner that he was the kind of guy who would pick up his phone and film if things got any more interesting.

He kept his voice low, hoping she would follow suit. 'Jess. I know I haven't been talking much recently.'

'Or turning up much.'

'Or that.' He swallowed. 'But I've been going through a lot of stuff, and—'

'Oh. *You've* been going through a lot, have you?' She

shook her head, but at least she had stopped shouting. 'Because there was me thinking that it was *me* going through a lot. Exams. Interviews. My parents never *ever* being here.' She took a shuddering breath. 'And I kept thinking that maybe it was to do with your mum, and her being ill, or the fact that your parents aren't getting on, but then I realised that I could only give you so many chances.'

She was crying openly now. God, he had never meant to be so cruel.

'I was so stupid, putting up with all your shit. I didn't care who you spent time with as long as you also spent time with me. Which now you don't. So it's time. I've got to focus, even if you can't be bothered any more. I have to get out.'

He stared at her. Part of him wanted to say something to save this. Part of him knew it was impossible. That it was time to face whatever music he had coming to him. 'I'm so sorry.'

'Me too.' He saw how her hands shook as she reached for her bag. 'Because I really love you, Seb.' Her eyes were burning into his face. He knew how much she wanted him to confound her expectations – to leap up and say he loved her too.

But he couldn't. All these months of being at each other's side, and now he knew that it was over.

'Jess?'

'Yes?' The hope on her face cut him to the heart.

'You're amazing. I hope you know that.'

She shook her head.

'You do talk a load of shit, don't you?' She picked her bag up and got to her feet. 'Some things never change.'

She took a deep breath, raised her head and walked steadily away from him towards the door. And then she was gone.

He picked up his phone. Scrolled past his dad's number to his mum's. He paused, remembering their chat the night his great-gran had died and he had realised that the world wasn't necessarily always safe. That people could leave. That the ground wasn't solid beneath his feet. It would be so great to talk to her.

Then he put the phone down again.

She was too angry with him. He had disappointed her too much. The only thing he could do now was to stay out of her way.

He waited a second, then went to the bar. Nothing else to do. Nowhere else to go.

He was going to stay here and drink until this feeling went away. This feeling that everything was over.

Abi

'I can see you. Feeling it in your fingers. Feeling it in your toes.'

'Oh my God.' Abi dipped her pitta bread into the olive oil. 'I forgot about that bloody song.'

'Yep.' Steve put down his beer. 'Ninety-four. The year of Wet Wet Wet and Hugh Grant's incredibly floppy hair. And you discovering pitta bread, of course.'

Abi put her head on one side. 'Or the year of Whigfield. Depending on your point of view.' She sat back in her chair and threw her hands out in the moves her brain appeared to have remembered perfectly, despite choosing to erase useful information like her PIN and where she kept the VAT book. 'Saturday night, I feel the—'

'Stop!' Steve held up his hand.

Abi laughed. He had never had any tolerance for pop, particularly when it was served up daily on every radio station in the world that summer. Abi could remember him now, baggy jeans, Fred Perry polo shirt and long curls, shoving his hands over his ears when they had walked into Woolies to get a copy of 'Definitely, Maybe' only to be assailed by Whigfield and her endless song.

Steve sat up straight and spread his hands wide, clearly very proud of whatever idea had struck him. 'It wasn't the year of Whigfield. Or Wet Wet Wet.'

'Oh no?' Abi sipped her juice. 'Who was it then?'

Steve's face was a picture of mock-solemnity. 'Blur, stupid. *"Parklife".'*

'Yes. It came out in April. I remember because I listened to it while eating the last of my Easter eggs.'

'You really haven't changed.'

'Thanks.' Abi tucked a strand of hair behind her ear. 'Do you remember the fights we used to have about Oasis and Blur?'

'Only that I won them all.' Steve folded his arms.

'Still deluded, then.' Abi arched her eyebrows. 'Do you remember, though? All of us queuing by that one crappy payphone at school, waiting to book our *(What's the Story) Morning Glory?* tickets?'

'Yes!' Steve grinned. 'And I remember telling that dick Larry that we'd got the last two – the look on his face.' He shook his head. 'Serves him right for punching me at primary school.'

Abi munched her bread. 'So you're still good at forgiving and forgetting then?'

'Yep.' Steve nodded. He looked around at the chattering bustle of the bar. 'This is great, isn't it? Out on the town – just like the good old days.'

Abi laughed. 'The very old days.'

'Well, at least we've got a bit more cash now.' Steve stared at the menu. 'Which is just as well, looking at these prices.'

Abi kept silent. It was a bit depressing that her spending money had decreased since her teenage years. Then, thanks to a weekend job stacking shelves and the odd shift in her dad's shop, she had been able to afford to go to gigs and buy Adidas trainers and a bottle of cider or two on a Saturday night. Now, her salary from the shop went out of her account as soon as it went in, disappearing into the vast black void of their overdraft.

She sighed.

'I'm so glad you could make it tonight.' Steve leant towards her and she was conscious of her wedding ring burning a hole in her finger. 'I never thought you'd be able to come out at the last minute like this.'

'Me neither.' Abi twirled her straw around her glass. She had done a runner. She should be at home looking at spreadsheets with John. She should be trying to save whatever was left between them. But ever since their anniversary she had been increasingly aware that life was passing her by. That she needed some fun. A lift.

And when Steve had texted, she hadn't hesitated. She needed this. She needed to kick-start herself again. In the past few days she had revisited her cancer diary – full of anticipation of everything she would do if she could only get better. *When I am well I will make the most of every day.*

Well tonight she was going to do just that.

'So what happened?' She leant forward. 'Who stood you up?'

His face fell and she kicked herself. Her big mouth had clearly pulled off another peach.

'Someone with no taste.' His lips twisted into a smile. 'I met her online.'

'I see.'

'Sometimes the real-life version doesn't quite measure up.'

'Sure.' She struggled to think of something to say. 'Have you done much online dating, then?'

He shrugged. 'A bit.' He drummed his hands on the table in that way she remembered from a hundred teenage nights. 'Anyway, plenty more fish in the sea.' He looked around at the packed bar. 'Even if they are all half my age.'

'Watch out, world.'

'Yep. Got it in one.' He waggled his eyebrows and she laughed.

He played with the coaster under his beer. 'You know, I was thinking on the way here about the first time I saw you.'

She flushed. 'It was the school uniform that did it, wasn't it?'

'Well, obviously I was rocking that school V-neck myself.' He pretended to preen. 'And my pants were hanging out of my trousers, just for added sex appeal.' He leant forwards. 'It's amazing you resisted me.'

'I don't think I did.' She looked down at the table.

'It's so good to see you again.' He undid the cuffs of his black shirt and rolled the sleeves up.

'You too.' She finished the last of her lemonade. 'Last time we saw each other I had a CD Walkman the size of a small dog. Scary.'

'I remember getting jealous of that thing. Sometimes I thought you loved it more than you loved me.'

'Never.' She stopped, aware that a line had been crossed.

But he seemed unperturbed. 'The thing I loved about you was the way you started dancing whenever you heard music. The world was your dance floor.'

She laughed. 'Like the time we danced in the bus queue?'

'Yep.'

'Or outside the showing of *Trainspotting* at the Phoenix?'

'Yeah. Didn't the police show up to that one?' Steve threw his head back and guffawed. 'Because you were trying to climb a lamp post or something?'

'Shit, yes!' Abi's hand flew to her mouth. 'I'd forgotten that.'

'You were limping for weeks.'

'But I still went to Glastonbury.' She smiled. 'In Ewan Ingram's Lada.'

'Yes.' Steve nodded. 'You were bitching the whole way about his shit taste in music.'

Abi grimaced. 'All that bloody trance. I hated it.'

'I remember.'

'No bloody tune.' She rolled her eyes. 'Just give me a TUNE.'

'Well, there's a tune.' Steve gestured to the room next door. 'They sound like they're getting going now.'

'Who are they again?' Abi looked towards the door.

'A new band. Local.' Steve consulted his phone. 'Apparently they're up for the BBC Sound of 2017 award.'

'I can't wait to hear them.'

He smiled. 'What was the last gig you went to?'

In reality it was Professor Green in 2012. Ages ago. But she wasn't going to say that out loud. Tonight she was the old Abi. Giggler. Dancer. Adventurer.

'Oh, I can't really remember. I got traumatised by breaking our cardinal rule.'

'The rule where you have to love a band before you book tickets?'

'Exactly.' She nodded.

He sucked air between his teeth. 'Oh dear.'

'And it was outdoors, but not at a festival.'

'You broke two rules in one night?' She loved the way he remembered them just as vividly as she did.

'Yep. Fatal.' She felt her phone beep and pulled it out of her shoulder bag. It was John. They communicated far more by text than in person nowadays. This was a classic. Are you back tonight? She had just told him. She had bloody told him an hour ago.

She was depressingly unsurprised that he hadn't listened.

Irritated, she turned her phone off. She wanted tonight.

One night to herself with music and smiles and a companion who had no idea that she had ever had cancer.

She dropped the phone into her bag.

'Another drink?'

'Sure.' She nodded. 'And make it interesting this time. Vodka cranberry?' Little by little she was getting her drinking mojo back.

'What happened to the Strongbow days?' Steve stood up. 'You were a cheap date back then.'

She ignored the pulse of excitement she felt at the word 'date'. This wasn't a date. It was a gig. With an old friend. Lesley would scoff at the idea, but it was true. Sure, she and Steve had once been in love, sneaking their way into the Reading festival and disappearing on adventures with fags in their hands and vodka on their breath, but not any more. Now they were just two people who loved a night out.

As he went to the bar, she remembered one night when she had been locked in her room with only her homework for company. The scrabble of stones against the window. A deep laugh when she had opened it to see precisely bugger-all in the garden. Peering out with rain lashing her face to see a plastic package appear in front of her attached to the end of a very long broom handle.

It was a mixtape. Of course. A mixtape that told her he loved her in the language of Leonard Cohen and The Beatles. A mixtape she still had, hidden away in the corner of her wardrobe underneath the shoe polish that she never used.

She remembered tucking herself down on the floor that night, crossing her legs and sliding the tape into her cassette player before listening to it over and over again. Later, when her mum had stopped prowling around and was safely in bed, she had crept down and picked up the phone in the hall. She remembered the buzz of the dial tone as she wrapped the cord in eager fingers and dialled Steve's home number. If he really loved her he would pick up. If it was really true.

And it was. He was there. And she had told him she loved him too, and then they had stayed together through her GCSEs and his A levels and gigs and albums until the day he had called her from a university pay phone and said he was never coming back. She stared into her glass as she remembered the pain of it. The tears. The melodramatic train journey to see if she could change his mind.

Steve slid back into his seat. 'So what's the best gig you've ever been to?'

'Primal Scream.' Abi grinned. 'Brilliant.'

'And worst?'

'Barenaked Ladies. They were amazing, but I was too far away and nobody danced in my section. Hammersmith Apollo. Hate that venue.' She shook her head. 'But Seb enjoyed it. He was ten at the time.'

'Getting him started early then?' Steve smiled.

'Yes. And how about you? Best gig?'

'Blur. The reunion.'

'Oh my God, you got tickets to that?'

'Of course.' He sipped his pint. 'I was on the website in seconds. There was no way I was going to miss that.'

'And how was it?'

'Spectacular.' He smiled as he used the word they had swapped so frequently in the past. About lyrics. About food. About sex.

She flushed and dived into her drink.

'What?' He frowned. 'Are you OK?'

'Yes.' Her voice sounded strangled, so she drank some more. 'Totally fine.'

'Good.' He smiled. 'Don't want you conking out halfway through.'

'You don't have to worry about that.' She shook her head, thinking how shocked he would be if he knew how close she had been to genuinely conking out for ever. 'I'm game for anything tonight.'

'Really? Well that's good to know.' His eyes were intense, focused on her face. 'God, it's as if no time has passed at all, isn't it?'

'Is it?'

'Yes.' He nodded, his long fingers curving round his glass. She watched them, transfixed. 'I missed this, you know. When we split up.'

'Yeah, well, it was your choice.' She shook her head. 'Anyway, it was a long time ago.'

He tapped the table with his fingers. 'And you look great, Abi. Really great. You could still be in your twenties.'

She thought of the scars beneath her dress, and for the first time, she didn't feel sad. Pride flickered back to life. 'That's very kind, but—'

'Not kind. Honest.'

She was unnerved by the admiration on his face and sat back on her bar stool. He leant forward, his face so close to hers. She felt that familiar flutter inside her and realised how much she had missed it. Then John's face flashed into her mind and she knew she had to move. To break this moment.

'Shall we go in?' She downed the rest of the glass, feeling the pump of alcohol through her veins. 'Right now?'

'OK.' He stood up. Slow. Easy. 'If you insist.'

'Well, it would be a shame not to see who's opening, wouldn't it?' The charm bracelet John had given her glinted in the lights.

'Sure.' He fell into step beside her. 'Great to see you've got your DMs on, by the way.'

'Of course.' She grinned. 'What else would I wear?'

'True.'

They walked through the door and the darkness swallowed them up. Up on the stage was a band dressed in bright T-shirts, their jeans tight above white trainers. A boy was singing into the microphone, his voice raw and poignant. A girl wandered the stage, her bass slung round her neck as she accompanied him. At the back of the stage the drummer clutched both sticks in her hands, nodding in rhythm as she waited to join in.

And then a long chord kicked in and they all started playing together. The lights swooped around the venue and the band started jumping up and down in time with each other. The beat was fast. Rocky. Addictive. Abi could feel it in her feet. In her body. In her heart.

This was one of those gigs. The ones where you walked in a human being and ended up feeling like you were immortal. She couldn't stop smiling. Couldn't stop moving. This was music. This was adrenaline.

This was life.

And for these precious moments the distance between her and John didn't matter. And it didn't matter that Seb loathed her.

None of it mattered in here. Because the music was playing. The lights were bright. And the audience was high – high on the chords and the heat and the words and the energy and the knowledge that everyone around them was flying too.

She felt alive. At last.

Steve turned to her and lifted her up and whirled her round. Just as he had done so many times all those years ago. Just as she had wanted him to ever since she had decided to come here and meet him.

And it was right then that she saw him. Just at the moment when a smile was splitting her face and the world was hers again.

Seb. Staring at her from only feet away, with all the hatred in the world in his eyes.

March

'Faith' by George Michael

For Lesley. Ye of the terrible taste in music and strange addiction to Steps. Here is the one song we can agree on. I know I always pretended to like Kylie, but I was lying. Don't spin around, just give me some decent guitars and I'll be happy. But I'm not here to moan about your music taste (again!). I'm here to say thank you. For everything. I don't know what I'd do without you. I mean, I'm sure I'd drink fewer cocktails and spend more time reading worthy books, but where the hell is the fun in that? I love you, my whirling dervish of a friend.

You're the Diana Barry to my Anne Shirley. Only with much MUCH better hair.

Abi

'Can you turn that yowling down?'

'It's not yowling, it's Primal Scream's finest album.' Abi shook her head. 'You're beyond hope, you are.' She turned the volume down.

'Give me Katy Perry any day.' Lesley's mouth was set. 'And please say that again. What you were saying before.' She leant forward against the counter, placing her chin on her hand. 'I got lost around the Steve-texting-you bit. And of course I'm still blushing from the embarrassment of bumping into John when – apparently – I was meant to be with you.' She picked up a ball of string and started to tug absent-mindedly at the end. 'Just as well I'm such a good liar. I told him you were back at mine keeping the sofa warm while I popped out for more wine. I felt like such a shit.'

'I've said I'm sorry.' Abi finished bubble-wrapping a print of the Thames at night, and placed it back on the counter with unnecessary force. 'It was just a spur-of-the-moment thing, OK? I wasn't doing anything else, and—'

'And you thought it would be a great idea to go out with your ex? Rather than – ooh, I don't know – your husband? I know you two are broke, but surely you could have shared a pint and a packet of peanuts at the pub.' Lesley reached into the packet in front of her and crunched another Frazzle into oblivion.

Abi placed the print on the floor with the other

completed orders. The Christmas rush had kept on going and Rob could barely keep up with the flow of things to frame. Babies' shoes. Rugby shirts. A selection of pictures of cricket and football teams and one of girls wobbling on tiptoes in some sort of Christmas ballet show. A beaming mini-Joseph with a tea towel on his head standing hand-in-hand with a Mary who appeared to be doing her best to decapitate the toy baby Jesus under her arm.

'Look, I thought I'd go out and have some fun for a change.' She swallowed as she thought of Seb's face when she had tried to talk to him after the gig. The set of his back as he had run out of the door. His shuttered expression. Him sweeping past her to the bathroom, refusing to acknowledge she existed.

She forced the thoughts away. 'I just wanted a night out, Lesley. I'm still allowed those, aren't I?'

'Of course you are.' Lesley finished the packet and licked her fingers. 'What did John make of it? When you told him where you really were?'

'John?' Abi swallowed.

'Oh my God, you still haven't told him.'

Abi ignored her pulse of shame. 'He's too stressed to want to talk about stuff like that.'

'Well isn't that convenient?' Lesley was drumming her fingers on the counter.

Abi prickled. 'Look, you don't know what it's like at the moment. I was just trying to be spontaneous, that's all. Do you remember being like that? Once upon a time?'

'Vaguely.' Lesley slurped from her water bottle. 'But I think that mainly led to waking up next to men who couldn't remember my name.'

'I just needed to feel free. Just for a night. I went through all that shit when I was ill . . .'

Lesley blew a strand of hair out of her face. 'You all went through it, Abi. Your whole family. Including John.'

'I know that.' Abi didn't want her friend taking away the joy of her night out with Steve. Despite Seb. Despite his anger, the memory of Steve's arms around her made her glow as she and John ate their quiet breakfasts and headed out for the day. It sustained her through the dense silence in the car, with Seb oozing disdain behind her, before John dropped her off at the shop and went into the office to continue his final attempt to turn his company around.

She had tried to talk to John. She really had. But he just muttered about how he just needed a bit longer, and she ended each exchange feeling even further away from him than she had at the start.

She knew how much he had done for her. She knew how much he had loved her. But she couldn't see a way back to him, not now when all they talked about was who was going to use the bathroom first or which one of them was taking the car. She looked at her friend. 'Lesley, I think . . .' She stopped, unwilling to say the words out loud. She was boiling and she started wrestling with the window next to her, needing some cool air on her face. The window wasn't in a helpful mood. She tugged and tugged until the sweat was sticky against her skin.

'Damn it.' She gave up, exhausted, only for Lesley to stand up and open it with irritating ease.

'I know what you went through.' Lesley kept her voice low. 'I get it, I really do. I was there, remember?'

'I know.' Abi bit her lip.

Lesley sighed. 'But you have to keep trying with John. Don't just give up and bugger off on the town with your first love. That's not leading anywhere good, is it?'

But I felt alive. Abi clamped her mouth shut to keep the words inside and took a breath. 'I know last Saturday sounds mad, Lesley, I really do. But I just didn't think.' She knew this wasn't true, but she carried on anyway. 'You know how much I love going to gigs.'

'Sure.' Lesley's voice was dry. 'Unless it's Take That.'

Abi winced. 'Yeah. Unless it's them.'

'Excuse me!' Lesley whacked her on the arm. 'I saw you dancing to "Shine", despite your ridiculous Indie kid snobbery. I saw you getting your groove on.'

'Getting my groove on? We're not living in the 1970s!' Abi laughed. 'Are you kidding me? Hasn't Hope taught you anything at all?'

'Nope.' Lesley shook her head. 'Shame that gig was before the era of the mobile. All I've got is a grainy photo with a thumbprint bang in the middle to prove that you like pop music too.'

Abi picked up another painting, ready to wrap it.

'Ooh, can I do that?' Lesley held her hand out for the bubble-wrap gun.

'Yes, but please don't bubble-wrap your hand to the picture like you did last time.'

'I won't.' A smile played around the corners of Lesley's mouth.

'Oh God.' Abi held the gun back. 'I mean it, Lesley!'

'OK, OK.' Lesley slumped down again. 'Spoilsport.'

She was silent for a minute, bending over her task, as Abi ran through the catalogues of new prints, searching for something new for spring. Something exciting to focus her window around. But no matter how hard she looked, she hadn't found it yet.

'And Steve? How was it spending time with him?' Lesley was focusing on her bubble wrap, but Abi knew all her senses were trained on the interrogation. She might as well have a bright light and a polygraph machine.

'It was great.' Abi spoke carefully. 'We talked about old times and did a lot of jumping around to loud guitars.' She skipped over Seb. She was too ashamed. She sipped the last of her tea. Stone cold. 'Just like the old days, really.'

'Well, let's hope it wasn't too much like the old days.' Lesley glowered. 'Because let's not forget that you two used to have sex by the football pitch and that half the team had seen Steve's bum by the end of the summer term.'

Abi giggled. 'I'd forgotten about that.'

'Well those poor footballers haven't.'

Abi thought of the bed she shared with John. It didn't make a happy comparison. Once they had cuddled but now they lay back to back, unable to reach across the divide. With every passing day it got harder to try. He didn't want her. She knew that. Sometimes she caught him staring at her, eyes wide with regret, but by the time she could say anything he was bent over his phone or had reached across to change the channel. At weekends she would take her tea out to the bench in the garden, and gaze up into the branches of the willow tree, wondering how they had let things slip away.

She opened the till to cash up. 'There were definitely no bum sightings on Saturday. I promise.'

'And his chest?' Lesley glanced up and Abi had to look away from the laser beam of her stare. 'He used to like getting that out too.'

'Yeah. I remember.' From what Abi had seen beneath the black shirt, it was still as hairy as ever. So different from John's smooth skin. She shook her head. She shouldn't be comparing.

She must change the subject. 'How about you?'

'What?'

'Your dates?'

'Oh. Total disaster.' Abi could hear the frustration beneath Lesley's light tone. 'I deleted the App.'

'Really?'

'Yes.' Lesley shrugged. 'I started missing Paul. That's when I knew it had to stop.'

'God. That's really bad.' Abi thought about her friend's ex-husband and the fights they used to have.

'Think I'm going to take a break.' Lesley finished her wrapping and reluctantly put the bubble-wrap gun down.

'Sounds like a good idea.'

'Yeah.' Lesley stretched her arms above her head. 'You should tell John, you know. About Saturday. He's not jealous like that, is he?'

'No.' Somewhere way down deep, Abi wondered if she wished he was.

'So tell him. Why wouldn't you?'

'Because . . .' Abi knew she was blustering. 'Because I don't see the point.' Deep down she knew that wasn't the reason.

'The point is what he might think if he finds out you've been keeping secrets.'

'Well so has he!' Abi's words rang out far louder than she had intended. 'So many bloody secrets I don't even know where to start!' She bit her lip. 'I know you're a big fan of his, Lesley, but frankly it just feels like we're stuck.'

Her friend watched her, silent.

'It's hard, feeling this lonely.' She waited for the kind arms around her. They didn't come.

Lesley took another Frazzle. 'Don't you think he's tired too?'

'What do you mean?'

'There's something you're not telling me here, Abi.'

Nobody trusted her any more. 'No there isn't.'

'Bullshit.' Lesley put her head on one side. 'Did you kiss him? Steve?'

'What?' Abi shook her head. She hadn't. She wouldn't. 'No. How could you even ask that?'

Lesley's face was so sad. 'But you wanted to, didn't you?'

'No.' Abi shook her head again, stung. 'Why are you being like this?'

Lesley stood up. Walked towards the window. Turned. 'All the shit John went through – half of which he has never let you see, by the way—'

'What?'

'He's got used to protecting you, Abi. Things happened while you were ill. And he dealt with them without bothering you.'

'I know. Like Seb's school stuff.'

'Way more than that.' Lesley wound a strand of hair around her finger. 'Like the time your boss was about to fire you for being off sick for so long, and John spent a fortune on legal fees to stop him, only for you to bloody resign before even going back.'

'What?' Abi stared at her in total incomprehension.

Lesley counted the items off on her fingers. 'Then there was the time that Seb totalled the hire car and John had to replace it without you knowing.'

'No way.' Abi shook her head. 'I would have known about that.'

'Oh, and that other time.' Lesley's voice was a knife. 'The time when you were so sick with the UTI, and you wouldn't call the clinic like you were meant to, and you collapsed and he found you on the floor muttering about some band you wanted to see at the Royal Albert Hall. He had to drag you to the hospital, and then he spent weeks making sure no one with even the tiniest hint of an infection went anywhere near you, while pretending that people were away on holiday. He told you Seb was on a school trip, for God's sake.'

'He was.' Abi blinked.

'For two weeks?!' Lesley shook her head. 'The state sector isn't *that* committed, is it? No. Seb was staying at Dan's place, because he had flu and you were so weak that John thought you might die if you had contact with him. Just like Noah had died. Can you imagine what that does to a man? You should have seen him, Abi.'

'I did see him.'

'No. *Really* seen him.' Lesley shook her head. 'He put on a front for you, you stupid arse, but I saw him just after he left you one day. Standing there by the hand-gel dispenser, just staring at the floor like that crappy blue vinyl might have the answers he needed. He believed his world was ending, because it wasn't a life for him without you in it. And he'd lived it before with Noah.' She exhaled loudly. 'Of course he tried to buy everything on the planet to save you. Of course he took his eye off his company and tried to deal with Seb himself. Of *course* he did.'

Her voice caught and Abi could see a tear gleam in her eye. 'I would kill for love like that, Abi. Everyone fucks up sometimes. So don't just chuck him away for someone you already know isn't for you. Please.'

Abi stared at her friend as a car beeped in the road outside. She reached out and held onto the counter, seeking a certainty that had long been lost. To be this misunderstood. By Lesley. It was too much. There was so much her friend didn't know. John wasn't perfect. He was the one who was shutting her out.

'I just went to see a band. That's all. OK?'

'Stop saying that.' Lesley frowned. 'Stop deluding yourself. I see the smile on your face when you talk about Steve. I know what you're feeling, even if you can't admit it to yourself.'

'I don't know why you're attacking me like this.' Abi was shaking now.

But part of her thought back to when Steve had picked her up and held her high. It had felt like coming home. A home where Cancer Abi was dust. Where she was just Abi again, a girl who liked Wrigley's and playing Portishead at top volume.

'Come on, Abi. Be honest.'

'I am being honest.' She turned round and cranked up the volume on the radio. 'Faith', her friend's favourite song.

Lesley wasn't deflected. Not for a second.

'No you're not.' Her eyes held all the chill of winter.

'You should believe me.' Abi looked her in the eye. 'You should.'

Lesley got her bag and coat. 'OK, OK. If you say so. Look, I've got to get to a work thing. Do some of that schmoozing I'm paid for.'

'Sure.' Abi felt a pang of sadness.

Lesley turned at the door and then walked back to kiss Abi on the cheek. 'I'll see you soon. Drinks? Next week?'

'OK.'

Lesley held up a finger. 'But never, ever get me to lie for you again, OK?'

Abi stood staring at her departing back, trying to ignore the squirming feeling that perhaps some of what her friend had said might be right.

An hour later, Abi pressed Rob's buzzer. Nothing. She tried again. She thought he had planned to cook her supper tonight. He had certainly implied that when he had left the shop to head home earlier.

She waited a minute before trying to push the door. It was open. Typical Rob, worrying endlessly about the words that came out of his mouth, yet leaving his door unlocked so that any old person could get into his flat.

She walked along the entrance hall towards the battered door at the end. The hall hadn't changed much over the years Rob had lived here. The paint was still peeling. The stain on the carpet was still the colour of wee. The smell of fried food was already implanting itself on her hair and clothing.

At the end she tapped on the door and eventually her brother stuck his head out. His eyes were red-veined. His skin was pale. She glanced down and saw that he was wearing some kind of overall. There were red stains all over it and she had to look twice to check that it wasn't blood.

'Oh. Abi. Hi.'

'You look surprised to see me.'

'Oh. No, I just lost track of time, and . . .'

'Aren't you expecting me?' She pushed her way in, aiming for the living room. He blocked her way, folding his arms.

'You can't come through here.'

'Why not?' She noticed the paintbrush in his hand and something clicked into place. 'Oh my God. Are you . . .'

'No.'

He was.

She tried to get past him. He sidestepped.

'Rob, you have to let me see!'

'No. It's not ready. I . . .'

She dodged round him and headed for the living room.

'This is so exciting!' She was nearly at the easel now. 'I love your paintings.'

'You do?'

'Yes. I had that one of the girl at the piano on my wall for years.'

'I thought that was just because you felt you should. Not because you liked it.'

'Why on earth did you think that?'

He scratched the top of his head. 'I don't know. It just seemed . . .'

She was in front of the easel now, and her breath stopped. The dark silhouette of a woman was standing in front of an enormous tear, edged with sunlight and shadow. Blues and silvers spiralled their way up to the top of the canvas and a rainbow arced above the woman's head, which was tipped up towards the light.

'It's beautiful.' She reached out a fingertip, only for him to nudge it away.

'Don't touch it. It's not dry.'

'Sorry.' She sat down and gazed at it. 'You've got so much detail in here.' She peered more closely at the tear and saw that it was full of tiny needles. A miniature pillow. An oxygen mask so small you might think it was a cloud. 'It's amazing.' She put her head on one side. 'You can tell she's brave, even though you can't see her face.'

He coughed. 'Well I had some pretty good inspiration.'

'Yeah? Who was it?'

'You.'

'What?' She looked at the woman again. The shape of her chin in profile. The determined tilt of her head. 'No way. She looks far too ballsy.'

'Just like you.' He paused. 'I wanted to tell you at Christmas. To ask your permission, really. To paint you. I was looking at the pictures we took on your birthday – when you came round from that first operation and you insisted we took a photo of all of us. And then I got this idea.' He pointed at the canvas.

Tears sprang to her eyes.

'I can honestly say I have never felt as brave as her.' Abi swallowed. 'If only.'

'You always seemed that brave to me.'

'Really?'

'Yeah.' He shuffled from foot to foot.

'Then why do I feel so scared, Rob? Why is everything falling apart?'

He met her gaze. 'Because life knows you can handle it.'

'Can I?'

He took her hand and gave it a brief squeeze. 'I reckon you can, Batfink.' He pulled away. 'Now, can I stop being nice to you?' He gave a wry smile. 'It's a bit too much for me on a Tuesday night.'

'Sure thing, Dingbat.' She couldn't take her eyes from the picture. 'I love it.'

'I was just messing about, really.'

'No, Rob.' She looked at him. 'This isn't messing about. This is brilliant.'

'Well, you can have it, you know. I—'

'No.' She took his hands gently. 'Don't just give it away. You can do a series. For the shop. Not about me.' She flushed. 'But a series of these silhouettes. It would be amazing in the window. People would snap them up.'

'Oh no.' He shook his head. 'I couldn't. I really couldn't.' He was starting to shake. 'I don't want people to see them. No one would buy them and I'd be . . .'

'Be what?' Her voice was soft.

'Be devastated.' It barely came out as a whisper. 'It's easier when my pictures are here. With me.'

She put her arms round him and hugged him until she

felt his shoulders relax. 'Then I'll just have to make sure that I make them look really good.'

'No.' He shook his head again. 'I can't.'

'You can.' She nodded, remembering a time before she had her final chemo when they had spoken these words in reverse. His strength in the face of her doubts. 'Trust me.'

In his eyes were a thousand questions. 'OK, Batfink,' he said eventually. 'Let's do it.' Then he pulled her close again.

'Don't think this gets you out of making dinner.' She heard her phone ringing and walked over to look at it.

'I know.' Rob walked towards his tiny kitchen. 'I'm on the case.'

'Good.' She checked the screen. It was Steve.

She felt a jolt of excitement, but Lesley's words stayed with her. She shouldn't talk to him. Deep down she knew that.

So she rejected the call and put her phone back in her bag, wishing that her heart wasn't telling her to do the opposite.

Seb

'Here. Over here!' Seb sprinted down the wing, his lungs rasping.

Dan passed to Ant instead and Seb swore under his breath as the ball was predictably intercepted by one of the opposing team. They must have been thirty minutes into a key league match and he had touched the ball twice. As team captain he wasn't exactly having an influence on the game.

'What's wrong, faggot?' The guy marking him ran past, boots heavy on the muddy grass.

'What?' Seb stared after him, hoping he had misheard. The ball flew past him to a chorus of groans from his team.

'You heard me.' The guy shook the rain out of his bright red hair and suddenly Seb knew where he had seen him before. Jess's birthday. The club. Marc.

His stomach started to churn right at the moment Ant intercepted the ball and tapped it back to him. He went to send it along the touchline but it glanced off his foot and into touch.

Shit.

Their coach, Mr Vanger, was on the touchline, wearing his familiar tracksuit in a vibrant shade of korma with cracked white stripes running up the side. His wild pacing showed that he was not a happy man. He cupped his hands to his mouth. 'Come on, Seb! Get it together.'

Seb swallowed, still thinking about what the guy had

said. He tried to force himself to concentrate. He stretched to intercept the ball, only to see it bounce off his foot and into the path of the opposition striker.

More groans. Then the redhead was back. 'You're having a shocker, aren't you? Must be all that time you're spending on Grindr.'

Ant was sprinting past and turned his head. 'Shut the fuck up, loser.'

Seb felt panic rising. When he had imagined telling the world he was gay, it hadn't involved being outed in the middle of a football match.

The redhead waggled his bum in its very tight red shorts. 'Or maybe I'm just too distracting? Fancy a bit of this, do you?'

'Shut it.' Seb tried to blink the rain out of his eyes.

But being quiet was definitely not on the redhead's agenda.

'Or is it my biceps that are turning you on?' He flexed his arm at a right angle.

'That's not very likely, seeing as you don't seem to have any, mate.' The ball was in their penalty area and Seb prayed that Dan would be able to keep it out. He watched as his friend dived to the left just as the striker thumped the ball past him into the right-hand corner of the net.

Shit. Now they were two goals down. The referee blew the whistle for half-time and Seb jogged over to the touch-line, where Mr Vanger looked like he was doing his best to have a cardiac arrest.

'What the hell is going on?' Seb dropped his eyes to his boots as he realised that the coach was mainly talking to him. 'This isn't the formation we talked about.' A fleck of spit shot out of his mouth and landed on Ant's purple team shirt. 'This isn't the energy or the tempo that we talked about either. We talked about what Thame are like. How we need to keep on the front foot and never give them an inch. And what are you lot doing?' His face was reddening now. 'You're pussyfooting around, passing it back and forth and never actually getting it anywhere, and you're making so many mistakes that you might as well just hand it to them on a bloody platter.' His fists were clenched. He had always wanted to win the league. This was his final year on the staff, so no wonder he was pissed off.

As the others went off to have a drink and an energy bar, Mr Vanger turned to Seb. 'And what the hell are *you* doing?'

Seb felt a pulse of resentment. 'I'm trying, sir.'

The redhead sauntered past and stuck up his middle finger. Seb dug his nails into his palms and brushed his wet hair out of his eyes.

'You're normally so up for it, Seb. You can't get enough of the ball usually, but today you look like you're actively trying to screw things up.'

'I'm not.' Seb kicked the ground with his boot, sending a clump of mud flying. 'I'm just having a slow start.'

Mr Vanger raised his eyebrows. 'Well any slower and you might as well be playing netball. Sort it out. Get your team in order. OK?'

'OK, OK.' Seb looked at them, clustering round the sidelines, legs and hair streaked with mud. Before, he would have known what to say. How to get them fired up. But now he didn't know how to start.

He forced himself to walk towards them, noticing as he went that his mum was pacing along the far end behind the goal, phone in hand. It pissed him off – her pretending that she was supporting him when all she wanted to do was chain him to a desk and force him to live out her perfect-son fantasy happy ending. And all the while she was having a bloody affair with that dodgy bloke with the shit hair and the even shitter jacket.

Anger flamed inside him. The only thing keeping him going was the thought of going to London and finally feeling free.

He called the team over to him, and they all hunched forward in a huddle.

'Do you want me to punch him in the face, Seb?' Ant pointed at the redhead.

'No.' Seb shook his head. 'Just leave it.'

'But he's saying you're a faggot.' Ant shook his head. 'He's trying to psych you out.'

Seb's heart rate spiralled. 'Yeah, well that's not going to happen. Let's just ignore him.'

'That's not like you, Seb.' Dan's blue eyes were bright with suspicion.

Seb thought about the club. Thought about what Dan had seen. Things hadn't felt the same between them since then – all surface and no foundation. Too much macho chat in the changing rooms with Dan staring at Seb until he felt forced to join in. Tits. Legs. Girls reduced to body parts and marks out of ten. With every sentence Seb uttered he hated himself a little more.

Dan was watching him. 'You normally get right up in people's faces.'

'We need to focus on winning the game.'

Dan wiped the rain off his face with his sleeve. 'Well we're all trying, but you're in a world of your own today. You're so busy taking shit from the opposition that you can't even see the ball when it's right at your feet.'

Seb couldn't contain his impatience any more. 'Will you just shut up?' He jabbed a finger at the other team. 'We have a couple of minutes till the next half. Just listen to me and let's get on that pitch and show them who we are.'

He hadn't realised that the redhead was right behind him. He leant round Seb's shoulder, squeezing him delicately on the arm. 'I doubt you and your fairy dust are capable of that.'

Seb felt his face blazing. He saw Dan shaking his head and turning away. It made him want to punch someone. To scream.

But he had a team to lead.

Ant's face was screwed up in a grimace. 'Why's he keep saying that?' He turned and towered over the redhead. 'What the fuck is your problem?'

'Oh, you know.' The redhead smiled slyly. 'I was at a club back in January and saw your captain kissing some guy with bleached hair.'

'Oh fuck off.' Ant laughed in his face. 'Seb's just finished with the hottest girl at the high school. He's no faggot.'

Seb winced. No wonder no professional footballers ever came out with this kind of crap going on. He saw his mum laughing into her mobile and suddenly he knew where to target his rage.

'Back in a minute.' He ran towards her.

She finished the call just as he got to her. She was smiling, her cheeks flushed against the March breeze. Probably on the phone to that loser he'd seen her with. He clenched his fists.

'Great game.' Her smile wavered. 'You're playing so well.'

She clearly hadn't watched any of it.

'Look, I know you're angry with me, but I really wanted to be here. I'm sorry if . . .'

Months of anger ripped out of him at last. 'Well, I don't want you here. OK? God knows I've given you enough hints. Everything's shit, Mum, and you're only making it worse.'

She took a step towards him. Fair play to her. She always stood her ground. 'It's not what you think.'

'Oh please!' It came out as a roar. 'Just stop lying, for God's sake. I saw you. In his arms like some saddo losers on a first date.' Heads were turning and he didn't give a shit. It was such a relief to shout.

'Seb, please . . .' She reached out but he slapped her hand away. He didn't care if he hurt her. He just wanted her to disappear.

She stared at him, shocked and he looked away, staring at this pitch where once he had felt so free. He was gay. And nothing in him wanted it to be true. He wanted to fit in here. He wanted to talk about girls when he went out with his team. He didn't want them covering themselves in the showers. He didn't want the awkward silences or the suspicious sideways glances as they remembered that he wasn't going to join in with their analysis of who was the hottest Kardashian.

He didn't want to be gay. He hadn't asked for it. And now here it was. An epic pile of shit just dumped in his life, taking up his energy and his brainpower right when he deserved a bloody break.

It all came together in his head and made him want to scream.

His mum tried again. 'Is it Jess, as well? The break-up? Because I'm sure you two can get back together. She loves you, I know she does.'

Great. That was her solution.

'This has got nothing to do with Jess. Nothing at all. This is all about you and that bloke and Dad and everything going to shit.'

'Seb, I'm not . . .' She looked to her left and right and lowered her voice. 'I'm not shagging him.'

'Oh piss off, Mum!' He gave an anguished howl. 'I saw you. It was . . .' He gulped air. 'It was fucking embarrassing. So stop pretending you don't know what I'm talking about. You're getting divorced, aren't you?'

'No.' She shook her head. 'We're not. Never.'

'Stop pretending.' He shook his head. 'I know you haven't told Dad about that night. I know you're lying to him, just like you're lying to me. Just piss off. I don't want you here.'

'But Seb—'

'No!' He roared at her, feeling a vicious pleasure as tears started to slide down her face. 'I'm not listening. Not one fucking word more.'

He turned his back on her and ran back onto the pitch. His blood was pounding in his ears but it couldn't hide the fact that everyone was staring at him. Or that there was an eerie silence hanging over the pitch. A silence he had created.

The whistle went and the game restarted.

He didn't glance behind him to see her leave. He didn't care.

He didn't.

But after the match he couldn't help himself. He turned and looked for that familiar blonde hair.

She was gone.

Abi

Steve had just texted her when John arrived. Her hand shook as she remembered the contempt on Seb's face, and she deleted the message without reading it.

'Hi.' She took a breath to steady herself, and stood up to kiss her husband on the cheek. For the first time in ages he was clean-shaven, and she was shocked by how surprised she was to see him smile.

'Hello.' His blue eyes were bright and he looked years younger – once again a man who could swim a mile in a freezing lake, or have a relaxed evening talking about the world's top ten cheeses.

He looked like the man she had married.

He took her hand and squeezed it. 'Good to see you.' Conversation stopped. They were like two strangers meeting on a first date. Abi couldn't believe that the other occupants of the restaurant were still smiling, chewing and chatting, oblivious to the thick fog gathering over the corner table.

She stared at the white lights strung along Little Clarendon Street outside as she struggled to think of something to say.

'Can I take your coat, sir?' Fortunately their waiter appeared and filled in the conversational gap.

'Thank you.' John shrugged off his black jacket and brushed a thread off his denim shirt.

'Would you like a drink?' The waiter's dark hair was tied

back neatly in a ponytail. Behind his glasses his eyes gleamed, and Abi found herself wondering if he was a student who solved complex equations in his spare time. A student like Seb would have been. Seb who hated her. Seb who she loved so much.

She had lost him. They had lost him.

And they had lost each other.

'What would you like to drink, madam?'

Abi's stomach was fluttering with untold fears. 'I'll have a red wine.' She didn't think she could get through this without some alcohol in her system. There were things to say. Decisions to be made.

John ordered a beer. Behind him Abi could see a woman with long grey hair and sparkling eyes dipping her spoon into a bowl of soup. As she brought it to her mouth her companion made her laugh, and she tipped her head back, the ruby pendant at her throat glinting in the lights.

John leant towards her and Abi suddenly wished they had a TV or a radio or anything to crowd out the silence between them. He took her hand and she nearly flinched in surprise. She looked down, tracing the grain of the tabletop with her finger. It was easier than looking at his face.

'It's good to be back, isn't it?' His thumb stroked the back of her hand.

'Back?'

'At our place.'

'Oh.' She nodded. 'Yeah.' She felt her phone vibrate in the bag at her feet and wondered if it was Steve again.

She must concentrate. She raised her head and met his gaze.

'Can we afford this? I mean . . .' This had been their place in balmier days, when John's company had just landed its first contracts with big London hotels and restaurants. But they hadn't been here in years. Not since well before her diagnosis. Everything was the same – the menus, the blue awning and the steaming kitchens visible at the far end – but Abi felt so different. Like she had fought to cross a finishing line, only to see that everything she had expected to find there was gone.

'Yes.' John nodded with a certainty she hadn't seen for a while. 'We can. It's on me.'

She decided not to ask any more questions and smiled at the waiter as he put her red wine and John's beer on the table. The stem of her glass was long and elegant and shone in the flickering candlelight. Abi took a sip, looking at the red rose in the vase between them. The wine was rich and she could feel warmth seeping through her. As she swallowed some more, she remembered all the evenings they had enjoyed here testing the prix fixe menu. Bouillabaisse. Moules frites. Pâté de volaille. She had forgotten that they used to have nights out. Fun. Laughter. The kind of nights that didn't end in lights-out before the end of the ten o'clock news.

'I thought you might like a surprise.' He smiled. 'I hope that's OK?'

'Of course.' She nodded. 'Always.'

'Great.' He pressed his lips together. 'I feel like I need to make it up to you. Things between us have been so bad recently and it's all my fault.'

Steve's face flashed through her mind and she picked up the menu to cover her blushes.

She took a breath. 'It's not your fault.'

He reached out and brushed a stray strand of hair behind her ear. 'I know I've been stuck in my own head too much. Shutting you out.'

Lines cut deep into his face.

'Things have been hard for you. I know that.'

'Yeah, but I should have talked to you more.' He shook out his napkin. 'There was no need for me to be such a tool about it.'

The waiter reappeared and Abi dived into the menu, ordering the moules and the risotto. John went for the snails and the steak-frites. He always did.

'Nothing changes.'

'Yeah.' *Everything changes*, Abi thought.

She sat upright in her chair. Time to make an effort. 'There's no need to apologise, John. You must have got used to keeping things to yourself when I was ill. About Seb. The business. Everything.'

He shrugged. 'Yeah. It seemed easier that way. But I don't know why I carried on when you got better.'

Abi played with her heavy silver cutlery.

'And then all the company stuff . . .' John sipped his beer. 'I'd tried and tried to keep it going and it felt so hard and I was so embarrassed that I'd screwed up. All those years of being so proud of myself for starting my own business, and I ruined it, just like that. And every night I was out with clients or on the phone scrabbling for staff, I just felt worse and worse. Like I was missing out on what was truly important.'

She met his eyes.

'Missing out on you.'

She swallowed. Here was the love she had been looking for. Here was the emotion that had been missing for so long.

Maybe they could still turn this around. Maybe.

'And I've got news.' A smile flickered at the corners of his mouth.

'What kind of news?' She felt a strange urge to joke. 'Has Mum finally decided to get a new doorbell?'

'No.' John shook his head. 'Though obviously we all live in hope.'

'Honestly, I wish she'd get on with it. We've had six weeks of her complaining about how she never gets anything she orders on Amazon.'

'Your dad has threatened to mend it.' John grinned. 'That's bound to solve the problem.'

'Oh God.' Abi shuddered. 'Anything but that.' She braced herself. 'So what's this big news?'

John arched his eyebrows and leant close. She could smell the gentle fragrance of his aftershave. She breathed him in, transported for a second to the pubs and cafés and parks of their first few weeks of going out. Her hand reaching for his and always knowing it would be there.

Maybe this was it. The moment at which they would find that their problems were over. She had to remind herself to breathe.

'Well, the good news is that I chased down the late payments and some of them came through – so JCN Recruitment is finally breaking even.'

'Oh my God, that's amazing!' Abi lifted her glass high in the air. 'Let's drink to that.'

'But . . .'

Damn. She put her glass down.

'But?'

'But there's more.'

'Which is?'

He grinned. 'Now things are going better, I've decided to sell the business. I got an offer from a big recruitment firm in the city who want to get more of a foothold in the restaurant trade.'

'Pardon?'

He didn't seem to see the confusion that must be written on her face. 'And I'm taking a job with a new firm.'

'A job?' Abi struggled to keep up. 'With a salary?'

'Yes.' He laughed. 'I'm certainly not doing it for free.'

More wine. Now. She took a big gulp. 'But you always said you didn't want to be an employee again.'

He shrugged. 'Sure. But things are different now. And when I signed the contract, I—'

She held up a hand. 'What? You've signed a contract already?'

'Yes.' He didn't even look remotely abashed.

Anger started to swirl. 'But didn't you just tell me that you were sorry for shutting me out?'

'Yes. And I am.'

'But now you've made this huge life-changing decision and you're telling me about it afterwards? After you've signed the contract?'

'Yes.' He looked puzzled, which only served to make her more angry.

'And you think that's OK?'

'I knew you wanted me to sort things out.'

'Really?' Her voice was too loud and heads turned. She tried to calm down. 'And how did you know that? Telepathy?'

'Don't be like this, Abs. This is meant to be a celebration.'

'Of you making yet another decision without me?' She raised her eyes to the vaulted ceiling. It didn't have any answers. How did they get from designing the JCN logo in their lunchbreaks to this?

John's fingers were drumming against his glass. 'It's a way out, Abi. The company sale won't get me much, but my debts will be paid. And I'll get a regular salary and a big signing bonus to get up and running again.'

Abi noticed the way that he was only using the words 'I' and 'my'. Never 'we' or 'our'. Once it had been the three of them. Now they were one plus one plus one.

'That's great, John.' She filled her water glass. 'Well done.'

'You don't sound like you mean that.'

Abi sighed. 'Of course I mean it. But you've made all these decisions on your own. I asked you to talk to me. I asked you to stop protecting me. But now you've done it again. You've done all this by yourself, and completely left me out.'

His wounded expression was back. 'I wanted to surprise you.'

'I know. And that's really sweet.' She felt a surge of frustration. 'But I want to be involved. I want us to feel like a team. To talk things through, you know?' She wanted to feel useful, like an equal with something to say. No more protection. She wanted to get out there and shout her thoughts and feelings to the sky. She wanted to drive life again, not sit back and react.

'And . . .' John stretched his legs out, 'it means that we can move out. Of your parents' place. Accommodation comes with the job, you see.'

Abi knew she was meant to feel excited, but instead she found herself wondering what on earth they would say to each other when it was just the two of them again.

The expectation on John's face gave her a pang of sadness. He was expecting her to be delighted – thrilled that he had ridden in on his white charger and made everything all right. But that wasn't how she felt. Loneliness pierced her, right here in 'their' restaurant, opposite the man she had married.

John took her hand. 'There is one other thing.'

Great.

'What's that?'

'It's in Cambridge.'

'What is?'

'My job. Which is great, as it's beautiful over there. And . . .'

Abi stared at him. His mouth was moving but he didn't seem to be making any sense. Cambridge? Since when had she wanted to live there?

'. . . I'll be heading up recruitment for one of the big touring companies.'

'I . . .' Her mind was still screeching through what he had just said.

'Yeah. It's perfect, isn't it?'

'For you, maybe.' She swallowed. 'But what about Seb?'

John scratched his head. 'He's moving to London anyway. It'll be just as easy for him to come to Cambridge as it would be for him to come to Oxford.'

'Right.'

He missed the sarcasm in her voice.

'Yeah. A new start, Abs.

'No.' Abi shook her head. 'I don't . . .'

'You don't what?'

Abi shook her head impatiently, wondering why John couldn't understand that she might be annoyed that he was suggesting they should move to the other side of the country. For a second there she had felt hopeful. Optimistic.

More fool her.

It was time to face facts. 'I can't go with you.'

It was his turn to look puzzled. 'Why?'

Because wherever Seb went, she wanted to keep things stable for him, just in case. Because she wanted to be here. Near her parents. Near her friends. Because she didn't want to start again. She wasn't ready. Not yet.

And there was another reason.

'The hospital, John. My team. My check-ups. My surgeon and all those amazing nurses and oncologists. They're all here. And I need to be near them.' She felt a prickle of nerves at the thought of her annual check-up in August.

'Ah.' He sat up straighter. 'I've thought of that.'

'You have?'

'Yes.' The more he smiled, the more she wanted to turn and run. Every word he said was building obstacles between them. 'Addenbrooke's. One of the best hospitals in the country. We can send all your notes over in advance. They'll look after you, I'll make sure of it.'

She sat there, speechless, wondering if they would ever connect again. He clearly had no idea how much she trusted the team that had made her well again – the group of men and women in scrubs and gloves who had calmly and kindly helped her body through. She couldn't leave this city. Couldn't walk away from them.

Her voice was a husk. 'John, I don't know what to say.'

'Just say yes.'

He didn't understand anything. He thought he was offering her everything she had ever wanted, when in reality the opposite was true.

'I can't go with you.'

'But you don't really want to work at the shop for ever. Do you?'

'I don't know, but—'

'So let's just go. Your parents get their space back. We get to start again. It's the ideal solution.'

'No.' She shook her head. 'Not for me.'

'But why?'

'I'm not ready for a move like that. How many times can I say it?'

'We can just give it a go. Live a little. Like we always said we would.' He sat back with a satisfied air that made her want to scream.

'John, no.'

He threw his hands wide. 'Why, Abi. Why?'

Because he hadn't asked her. Because she was still bloody terrified of the cancer coming back. Of turning her back for one second and finding herself on a trolley staring up into the grim lights of NHS doom.

And – far worse – she knew that she couldn't go anywhere with him. Not with things as they were. She didn't feel like she knew him any more. And it was blindingly obvious that he didn't know her either.

'You don't want to be with me.' His head bowed. 'That's it, isn't it?'

'No.' She stopped. 'It's just . . .'

His eyes were dark with disappointment. 'Oh come on, Abi. Be honest, please.'

Her voice shook. 'We're too far apart at the moment – I don't know what's left.'

'You do. I'm John. Your John.' His voice was urgent. He reached for her, but the waiter reappeared, bearing two plates full of delicious food Abi suddenly didn't want to eat.

She waited till he had gone away again before speaking. 'I just don't know if we can make this work. You in Cambridge. Me here.' She had to bite her lip to stop the tears falling.

'We can.' John shook his head. 'We've been through too much. There's no way I'm letting go of this.'

'Letting go of what? We don't talk. We don't have sex.' The heads at the next table turned, but she didn't care. 'We certainly don't discuss things.' She threw her arms wide, feeling all those years of understanding and trust and partnership disappearing like the steam from the food on her plate. 'We can't stay together because I once had cancer. We have to stay together because we're a team.'

'But we are.'

She shook her head. 'No, John. You just decided to move us halfway across the country and didn't even mention it to me until you'd signed on the dotted line.'

'But . . .' He exhaled, puffing his cheeks out as he struggled for words. In some ways he was so familiar. Still the old John. But maybe the problem was that she wasn't the Abi she had been. Maybe it was time to admit that. Time to start again.

She looked down at her plate but couldn't bring herself to eat anything.

'John. You've done so much for me and I can never thank you enough. But cancer – it's changed me. It's a part of me now and it always will be. There's so much I haven't told you, and . . .'

'So tell me now.'

'It's not that easy.' She looked towards the window, only to see that it was darker outside and the two of them were reflected in the glass. Two people having dinner, with no hint of the momentous discussion taking place. She forced herself to look at him.

'I think I need to do things differently. I don't know how. And I don't know where it will lead. But I do know that I have to try. Because we can't go on like this, John. Neither of us is happy. Do you see what I mean?' She twisted her fingers in her lap as she waited for his reply.

His face was heavy with sadness. 'You don't love me any more.'

'John. No.' She reached for his hand but he moved his away before she could reach it. 'It's not about loving you or not loving you.' Words whirled through her mind as she tried to make him see. 'It's about what we've been through, and where it's left us. Do you see?'

'No.' He finished the last of his beer. 'I don't. Not at all.'

Frustration rushed through her. 'You really don't see why I want to stay in Oxford? The place I got better in? Near my friends? My family?'

'The place you got sick in. The place Noah got sick in. Do *you* really not see why I want a fresh start?' He gestured angrily outside. 'Everyone thinks it's the city of the dreaming bloody spires, but to me it's just a place where I remember who I've lost.'

'But you haven't lost me.'

'Haven't I? Are you sure about that?' His mouth was pressed into a grim line. 'Because right now I'm wondering if you've found someone else.'

'No.' She thought of Steve, hating herself for lying.

'Are you sure?'

She was so tired of hiding. 'Well, I went out to a gig a couple of months ago. A guy called Steve. It was nothing, but—'

'But you haven't mentioned him till now?' His eyes narrowed. 'I see.'

'No, you don't see. Nothing's happened. Nothing. I promise.'

'But it might?'

Her silence lasted too long.

He shook his head and stood up. 'Right. Well, *now* I understand.' He threw his napkin down on the table. 'I'll stay at a hotel tonight. I can come and pick up my things at the weekend.'

'No. John.' This was too fast. Too much. 'Please stay. We can talk. We can work out what to—'

He shook his head. 'I think we're finished here, don't you?'

She stood up too, the table biting into her legs as she leant forward. 'No. We're not finished. You're not listening. We—'

'You don't think we can make it work, Abi. That's what you said, isn't it?' He blinked, waiting.

'Yes. No. I don't know.' She didn't feel sure of anything.

'So let's have a break.'

'I just want you to listen to me, John.'

'Oh, I'm listening.' He shrugged. 'And I'm hearing you loud and clear.'

'John!' She tried to grab his hand but he didn't hesitate. Didn't even turn his head. She sat down again, dazed, watching him walk away, as two plates of food cooled on the table in front of her.

So. This was it. This was starting again.

She bowed her head and began to cry.

April

'Summer' from *The Four Seasons* by Antonio Vivaldi

Dad. Oh Dad. It could have been the slow movement of the Ravel piano concerto. It could have been Tom Petty's 'Free Fallin''. It could even have been the theme tune from *The Muppets*, which you love slightly more than you love your children, I suspect. Here is your song, my man of very few words. I can't listen to this without thinking of you and the way you've gently steered me away from the edge again and again and again. What would I have done without you? I don't even want to begin to imagine.

Abi

'Seb?'

Nothing.

'Seb?' Abi and John walked towards their son as nervously if he was an unexploded bomb.

No reaction.

Abi stepped forward and pulled one of the headphones out of his ears. 'Seb. We need to talk to you.'

Seb raised his hand to shield his eyes from the lukewarm April sun. Around them the garden was coming back to life. The grass was turning from sludge to green. Daffodils circled the base of the willow tree and Mum's beloved snowdrop anemones were starting to appear in the flower beds by the back door.

Seb sat back on the bench, planting his hands on his knees as he looked at them. He was in the bright red T-shirt she had got him in Kalamaki, that spring holiday after her chemo last year. He had soaked his last clean one diving to spot the turtles and she had wandered to a stall and bought a replacement. She remembered the tang of salt on her lips. The ice cream melting down her fingers. Breathing in and out, watching as John and Seb tried to replicate the Eiffel Tower out of the endless golden sand.

A lifetime away. As John sat down at one end of the bench, she wondered how on earth things had got this far.

Seb spoke slowly. 'Well, this can't be good.'

251

'What do you mean?' She perched on the other end, her hand draped along the back, close, but not quite touching him.

He grunted. 'You two – together. There's only one thing you're going to be telling me, isn't there?'

If only he wasn't right.

She glanced at John, seeing the dark shadows beneath his eyes. She wondered if he'd go first but he was just staring into the middle distance, a frown on his face.

It was down to her then. 'Seb, I'm afraid your dad's moving out for a while.'

Seb brushed his shaggy blond hair out of his eyes. It was so long now that he could almost make a ponytail. He rubbed his broad nose – so like John's – and shrugged.

'Right.' He pulled out his phone as casually as if they had told him they were going out for Sunday lunch. 'Sure. No problem.'

'No problem?' She dared to place her hand on his shoulder. 'Is that all you've got to say?'

His face was as blank as his iPhone screen, which had a jagged crack across the centre. He kept jabbing the home key with his thumb. When he spoke, his voice was a sarcastic drawl. 'Well, I was right, wasn't I? I told you this was coming.'

Once Seb had spent hours Sellotaping their legs together so she would have to come to primary school with him. Now, their bodies were inches apart, yet he was so far away.

'Yeah. You did.'

'I knew you didn't love each other any more.'

'That's not true.' She was surprised at the violence of the words. She looked to John for reassurance, but he was just watching their son with infinite sadness in his eyes.

'Look. I know you're going through a lot, Seb.'

He shook his head. 'You don't know the half of it.'

'So tell me.' She touched his shoulder, only for him to flinch away.

'Yeah, right.' He went back to staring at his screen.

Abi dug her nails into her palms. It didn't help. She glanced towards the house, to see her mum staring out at them, tea towel in hand. As soon as she met Abi's eyes, she turned away.

Abi sighed.

John finally decided to speak. 'I'm moving to Cambridge, Seb. I've got a new job.'

'Yay.' Seb's voice was flat. Cynical.

'And I've sold the company.'

'Double yay.'

Abi was sorely tempted to rip the phone out of his fingers. Then a thought flashed through her mind.

'You don't think this is your fault, do you, Seb? Because of all the stuff at school?'

She saw his shoulders tense. He didn't answer.

'Because it's not. That has nothing to do with—'

Seb's face was iron. 'No. I wasn't thinking that, but thanks for bringing it up. Just what I bloody needed.'

He stood up, and now Abi was the one shielding her eyes as this boy-giant turned towards them. He looked every inch the adult he would become on his birthday next week.

'I don't know why you needed the big announcement by the way. It's not like anyone is surprised.' He turned to John. 'Did she tell you? About her big night out with Steve?'

'Yes.' John gazed at the ground. 'She told me.'

If Abi was expecting points for honesty, she didn't get them.

'Well.' Seb shrugged. 'At least that's one thing you've done right.'

253

She couldn't hold his eyes. She fingered the red material of her dress as the rest of the world got on with its Saturday afternoon around them. Gardening. Doing their nails. Reading the newspapers.

Lucky them.

Seb reached into his pocket and pulled out a tin and some Rizlas.

'Seb, you know you shouldn't . . .'

He shook his head and turned away. 'Whatever.' He strode off towards the house.

Shame coursed through her.

'Well, that went well.' John ran a hand across the bark of the tree.

'What are we doing, John?'

His hand was so close. 'I haven't got a bloody clue.'

She could have turned to him. She could have leant in and sought comfort. But it was too late. She had known it at the restaurant. There was too much misunderstanding. Too much hurt. So instead she took his hand and kissed it, half a lifetime of hugs and cups of tea and late-night confidences in her heart.

Then she got up and walked away.

Her mum was lurking in the kitchen, pretending to rearrange the perfectly alphabetised cookbooks on the shelf above the cooker. Abi walked towards the sink, leaning against it and taking a deep breath. She picked up her mum's Diamond Jubilee tea towel, wetted it and pressed it against her face. Then she took a long shuddering breath and dropped it in the sink.

'Don't leave that there! Washing machine, please!'

'Sorry.' Abi picked the towel up and walked over to the machine. After nearly six months here she still hadn't inter-nalised the fact that nothing was allowed to remain in the wrong place for more than a nanosecond. She did manage to hang the bath mat on the heated towel rail ninety-nine per cent of the time, and she was pretty damn good at never using the washing machine on a Monday night (aka the towel session), but any more than that was beyond her.

'What happened out there?' Her mum folded her arms and leant back against the kitchen counter.

Abi crouched down and threw the tea towel into the washing machine. 'I don't want to talk about it.'

Her mum pointed at the garden, where John was still sitting, staring ahead of him. 'Whatever it was, it obviously didn't go well.'

Abi shook her head. 'Not now, Mum.'

Her mum dusted an invisible speck from the row of mugs hanging from the dresser. 'Seb's just stormed through here. That's a very upset boy you've got there.'

'I know that!' Abi stood up, sadness and frustration exploding from her. 'For God's sake, I'm not blind.'

'Well . . .' Her mum's duster moved with even more vigour.

'I am trying, Mum, you know. I really am. So stop making me feel like I'm a failure. Stop judging me.'

Her chin was up. 'I'm not judging you.'

'Yes you are! Peering out of the window. Pointing out the bloody obvious – that Seb's not happy. I'm well aware of that. I'm not stupid!' She knew none of this was her mum's fault, but she couldn't stop. 'Just leave me alone, OK?'

She stared out at John. The man who was energetic and enthusiastic and always knew where the car keys were. The man who brought home strawberries, or songs with her name in them, and who wanted to hear about all the things she had done that day. The man she could tell anything to.

The man she could tell that she had cancer.

She took a breath, remembering that moment. The bottle of wine in his hand. The puzzled smile on his face as he headed out to find her in the freezing garden, where she was curled up going over and over her surgeon's words. Searching for a loophole. A way out. Finding nothing but fear and a net drawing tight around her.

It had been so hard to tell him. Noah had loomed large as she forced the words out. She remembered the way John's face had sagged only for a second – almost as if someone had taken all the air from him in one greedy breath – and then he had rallied. He had started talking about second opinions and cancer diets and Swiss treatments and vitamins and she remembered sitting in her chair, watching the frost gripping the garden and observing the way her breath curled up into the air. She had counted each precious white plume, wondering how many she had left.

Now she turned away from the kitchen window. She would miss him.

'Anyway, I'd better go and . . .'

'And what?'

Abi was nearly out of the door. 'And iron things.'

Her mum frowned. 'But you never iron anything.'

'I do.'

'Well why's your dress so creased then?'

'Later, Mum. OK?' Abi slid out of the room, seeking refuge. She stood in the hall, where the clock was still determinedly telling the wrong time, before going into the living room, where Dad was sitting in his high-backed armchair, a beatific smile on his face.

She listened to the violin soaring.

'Vivaldi?'

He turned round to smile at her. 'Indeed.'

'"Summer". I love this movement.' She closed the door behind her and sat down in the leather chair that had seen many of her more dramatic childhood moments. The crack in the leather on the arm represented her first ever cup of coffee – there had been spilling, and she could still remember her mum flinching as it flowed out of the cup onto the then pristine leather. And that stitching there represented the time she had split up with Tommy Martin when she was fourteen and had, in her rage, stabbed the chair that had seen her weep her way through most of the previous week. She ran her fingers over the puckered material, snapshots of those times still as clear as if they had been immortalised on an Instagram feed.

She sat back, trying to remember how to breathe.

'Do you know what makes this even better?'

'Nope.' She shook her head. 'What?'

'One of these.' He grinned and threw a cardboard packet across to her.

'Bramley apple pies.' She gave a shuddering laugh. 'Perfect.'

He bit into his and chewed with evident satisfaction. 'Don't tell your mum I've got these in here.'

'Dad.' Abi slid one out of the packet. 'You do realise that Mum knows absolutely everything you do, don't you?

'Allow a man his fantasies.'

'OK.' She leant back and closed her eyes. As she listened, Abi thought back to the night she had first heard this music. The cloisters of Magdalen College. A summer evening. Her dad beside her, their tummies full of Big Macs and McFlurry. Him sipping a glass of wine. Her chewing on a sweet red bootlace and thinking of the boy she had kissed that afternoon.

Thinking of Steve.

Things had been simple back then. She was going to be a great psychologist. She was going to have Findus Crispy Pancakes for tea tomorrow. She was going to hold Steve's hand on Saturday night. All this she had known as she sat in her chair with her dad next to her and the ancient stone of the college towering towards the sky around them. X would follow Y as surely as she would reach into the bag to get another sweet when this one was finished.

'Abi?' She came back to the present to realise that she had tears pouring down her face.

'What's wrong?' Her dad was waiting patiently for her reply. Crumbs of pie were scattered down his old blue jumper.

She shook her head, unable to stop the tears falling. The violins were building, on and on, towards their frenetic climax. They seemed to be cutting her in two, ripping down all her defences and her denials and her ability to put one foot in front of the other. All she could see was what she had lost.

She heard the creak as he rose. He padded over in his slippers, resting on the arm of her chair and putting his arm round her. She leant into his comforting bulk. He smelt of earth and pencils, just as he always did.

She looked up at him through tear-soaked eyes. 'John's leaving and I don't know what to do.'

'He's leaving?' His face sagged. 'I'm so sorry.'

'Me too.' She looked out into the garden again but her husband was gone.

She bent over, tears falling fast now.

'I've messed it all up.'

'No.' He shook his head. 'Not you. Not my girl.' His arms around her were so steady and sure. 'You'll work it out.'

'Will I?'

'Yes.' His smile held such faith in her. 'You will. You'll work out your next step.'

She stared into the empty garden.

She only hoped he was right.

Seb

The team were discussing Jess's new boyfriend. It wasn't making the best end to Seb's day.

'He's butt ugly. She must have gone for him because he's older.' Ant slammed his gym locker shut. 'Fucking slick bastards with cars.' He rubbed his torso dry with his towel. Seb felt Dan watching him from across the room, his expression not exactly at the friendly end of the scale.

'I'm not bothered.' He made sure he stood as tall as he could. He was just about on a level with Ant on his tallest day. 'I don't care anyway. It's not like it was going anywhere.'

'Got your eye on someone else, have you?' Ant raised his eyebrows. 'You sly dog. I knew those guys at the match had it wrong, calling you a faggot. You've always had your fair share of action, haven't you?'

'For sure.' Seb pulled on his shirt. 'And no, I haven't got my eye on anyone.' He put his muddy football boots in his bag, shoving his shorts on top.

'Really?' He flinched at Dan's cutting tone. 'That's not what I heard.'

'Oh yeah?' Ant was so eager to know who it was that he put both feet into the same leg of his fake Calvins. 'Who? Who?'

'For fuck's sake.' Seb rolled his eyes. 'Dan's talking shite.'

'Am I?'

This was the problem with Dan. He could never leave anything alone.

Ant stood in front of Seb, all challenge and Lynx. 'Come on then. Spill it.'

Seb averted his eyes. There was too much flesh on show here and he didn't even want to think about how he was reacting to it.

Last night he had wandered online, trying to find someone else like him. Captain of the football team yet secretly attracted to men, too scared to admit who he was out loud. Next thing he'd be launching into some Judy Garland number and his *Glee*-episode life would be complete. At 2 a.m. he had got out a bottle of vodka and sat there downing it in his bedroom, eyes blurring as he thought back to when life had felt simple. He had wanted to call Jess. Or go to the attic and talk to his mum. But of course he couldn't. Not after everything that had been said.

God. He would be snivelling in a minute. He had to get it together.

He looked Ant dead in the eye. 'That girl in the Summertown Costa. The blonde? With the tits?'

'Samantha.' Ant was practically licking his lips. 'Yeah. You're not getting it on with her, are you? You lucky bastard.'

'Yep.' Seb shrugged, hating himself as he felt the lie grow inside him. He picked up his bag. 'Well, you've either got it or you haven't.'

What a load of crap. He was fairly tempted to punch himself in the face.

He caught Dan's eye as he left. What he saw there didn't make him feel any better. As he walked away, he tried to tell himself he didn't care. He didn't need anyone.

He moved at speed, rounding the corner and slamming

into someone coming the other way. Their bodies collided, and his head snapped forward and bumped against bone.

'Shit.' He put his hand to his eyes, which were protesting very painfully indeed. 'God, that hurt.'

'Yeah. Well it wasn't exactly fun for me either, you know.'

The voice was muffled but he knew who it was, even from behind his hands.

'Marc.'

The other boy nodded. 'Yep. It's me. Or rather it was me before you cannoned into me like some kind of crazy person and attacked my nose. Again.'

'It takes two, you know.' Seb's whole face was stinging. 'Christ, are you made of *steel*?' He risked pulling his hand away from his head. His face didn't fall off. Result.

'Nah.' Marc was still holding onto his nose. 'Fuck, this hurts.' He sighed. 'Bang goes my audition for *First Dates*.'

Seb stared at him. 'You wouldn't?'

Marc kept a straight face and then collapsed into giggles. 'Of course I bloody wouldn't!' He shook his head. 'I'm more of a *Love Island* type.'

'Really?'

'Yep.' Marc nodded, looking pretty jaunty for someone whose nose was twice its normal size. 'I'd love it on that island. Roaming around looking hot in my board shorts.' He did a practice strut. 'I'd be on a bad US TV channel in days. From there straight to a soap opera, and then Hollywood would be knocking on my door. Global superstar by twenty.' He bowed. 'Thank you very much.'

'Whatever you say, mad man. Now, if you're definitely OK, I've got to go and work.'

'What kind of work?'

'Delivering takeaways that rich people can't be bothered to go and get themselves.'

'Oh. Still doing that, are you? Enjoying it then?'

'Having the time of my life.'

'Oh God, that's my sister's favourite song at the moment. I thought she was too young for *Dirty Dancing*, but apparently not.' Marc rolled his eyes. 'So. Have you come out yet?'

'Piss off.'

'Just wondering.' Marc's eyes gleamed with amusement. 'So what else is going on?'

Seb opened his mouth to reply and then closed it. Mum flat-hunting by herself – check. Dad miles away – check. Grades tanking – check. No. Nothing he wanted to talk about there.

Inspiration struck. 'Heard the new Chvrches album?'

'Does the Pope wear a cross?'

'What do you make of it?' They fell into step beside each other.

Marc put his head on one side. 'Clever lyrics but not sure about the final few songs. A bit too orchestral for me.'

'I know!' Seb nodded. Once he would have chatted to his mum about it as she got the pizza ready for their Saturday-night *Match of the Day* session. The three of them all crammed onto the biggest sofa, grabbing pieces of cheesy pepperoni and piling it on their plates.

He realised he was humming the theme tune under his breath.

Damn it.

Marc looked at him and he stopped, feeling flushed and foolish.

'*MOTD* fan?'

'Used to be.' Seb hitched his bag higher up his shoulder. 'You watch it too?'

'Nah.' Marc shook his head. 'Not since Dad decided to

get Sky. No point now. Though I do weirdly miss that gathering-round-the-TV thing. My folks are out and about all the time. Mum does shifts. Dad works weekends a lot. You know.' He scuffed the floor with his toe.

'Yes. I do.' Seb peered more closely at Marc's face. Something red was oozing from his nose. 'Wait.' He tipped Marc's chin up with his hand. 'You're bleeding.'

He was just digging in his pocket for a tissue that was never going to be there when he heard Dan's voice again. 'Ah. A corridor liaison. How romantic.'

He turned. 'Yeah. Teachers round every corner and twats kicking footballs around.' He nodded at a group of juniors near the doors at the far end. 'Always turns me on.' He was sick of his friend's insinuations. 'Piss off, Dan.'

Dan pantomimed concern. 'Am I ruining the atmosphere?'

'No, but you're definitely not enhancing it.' Marc's voice was calm and cool. Everything Seb wasn't. 'If you really were an obstacle in a romantic comedy, then you'd at least have to be funny. Right now you're just annoying.'

'Annoying, am I?' Dan's jaw clenched and he pushed his dark fringe out of his eyes.

'Yeah.' Marc shrugged, even as blood trickled down to his chin. He pulled his sleeve down over his hand and pressed it to his nose, tipping his head forward as he did so. 'I mean, I thought you two were mates. Fuck knows why you're picking fights all the time.'

Seb saw a muscle flicker in Dan's cheek. 'Turns out I didn't know him at all.'

Marc laughed and glanced up for a moment. 'Do you mean the kiss? The one that never actually happened?'

'Yeah.' Dan clenched his fists.

'Haven't you ever kissed a guy?'

'No way.' Dan shook his head.

Marc sighed. 'Well, Seb was just trying things out. Experimenting. Right, mate?'

His eyes were wide as they looked at Seb. He was giving him an out.

Seb stood there as the world pressed in on him.

He could sidestep. Escape. Carry on hiding.

Or he could speak out. Become the person he was destined to be.

And here, in a corridor smelling of blocked toilets, he decided it was time.

'No. I wasn't just experimenting. I'm . . .'

Say it. SAY IT.

Dan folded his arms, but Marc's face was full of encouragement. Seb stared at it as if he was drowning. Stared at those eyes and those lips as he finally said the words out loud.

'I'm gay.'

Dan rolled his eyes. 'Well I'd worked that one out.'

'And I only just realised.'

'Yeah, right.'

Seb shrugged. 'It's true.' He slung his football bag higher on his shoulder. 'And no, I don't fancy you, Dan.' He saw Marc suppressing a grin. 'So you've got nothing to worry about, OK?'

He folded his arms and stared Dan down. He felt as if a hundredweight of stress had just rolled off his shoulders. He felt as if this might be the beginning of the beginning. As if it all might just be OK.

'Any questions?'

Dan appeared to have run out of words. Unusual.

'Great.' Seb nodded. 'Good to chat.' He smiled at Marc. 'Let's head outside, shall we?'

Marc nodded. 'Sure.'

As they walked off, Dan shouted from behind him. 'So, is he your boyfriend now, then? I guess he's all right if you ignore the dodgy hair and the terrible taste in clothes.'

'Piss off.'

'Just asking.' Dan was still going. 'Because Samantha will be gutted, won't she? Wait till I tell the guys about who you're dating now.'

Seb swallowed but kept walking. He couldn't stop Dan any more than he could stop himself wanting to follow Marc out of here.

Dan's voice was strident. 'Poof!'

Seb stopped. Turned. He walked back to Dan, hating every single part of his small, shrewish face. 'What is it about me, Dan? Why can't you get the fuck out of my face? Who gives a shit if I'm gay? I still like Stormzy. I'm still the best winger in the school. I still love cheese and pickle sandwiches and eating you under the table at the all-you-can-eat Chinese. I still read manga and love McDonald's at four a.m. and hate the bloody Brontës, and I still really hope that you get the grades you need to go to Loughborough and wear a tracksuit for the rest of your life. And you know what?'

Dan's head was lowered.

'I'm not like your dad. He lied to your mum for years, having that boyfriend on the side, and believe me I'm angry with him too for what he did to all of you. I'm not leaving you – at the moment you're the one leaving me. But this has happened to me – this *is* me – and it's huge. It's not something I asked for. It's not something I wanted. But I have to get through it, because apparently that's how life works. My mum got through her shit. And now I'm facing mine. So I don't need your comments. I don't need your shit. So you can choose what you do. You can try to turn

266

everyone against me, or you can just shut up and accept the fact that I fancy boys. Your call. All right?'

He stalked as far as the door, where he realised that he had forgotten his bag.

Damn.

He retrieved it, avoiding Dan's stare, and then walked out into the fresh air of a whole new evening.

Marc held out an ear bud. 'Fancy a listen?'

'Only if it's loud.' Seb put the bud in and Marc turned the volume up to full. He hoped it could drown out his thoughts. His fears. His reality.

Because now the deed was done, he was absolutely terrified. About what people would say and about what would happen next. He had spent his whole life fitting in without even having to think about it. Now he was going to have to learn about standing out.

Abi

'It's so good to see you.' Steve stood up and kissed her on the cheek. 'Have a seat.'

'Thanks.' Abi sat down, blinking at the sun that was pouring through the window next to them. 'Sorry I'm late.'

'How's the flat-hunting going?'

'Crap.' So far she had learnt that anywhere within her budget was either so bijou that it had a toilet in the bedroom or so far out of Oxford that it would take her a year to get to the shop.

'I'm sorry to hear that. And about,' he hesitated, 'about you and John.'

'Yeah.' She put her bag on the floor, unwilling to talk about it.

'Would some cake help?'

'Definitely. If only there was a kind gentleman to bring me some.'

He gave her a mock-salute. 'Consider it done.' He stood up, pulling a fiver out of his jeans.

'I was only joking.' She reached up and took his hand to stop him. It rested in hers for a second too long. She was so unused to being touched. Her cheeks were suddenly blazing and she dropped his hand again, retreating into the safety of taking her coat off and hanging it over the back of her chair.

As she sat down again, she saw a child at the next table

beaming at the sight of a slice of chocolate cake heading her way. If only Seb was that easy to please. She was determined to find a flat with a spare room for him to live in, though she had no idea if he would ever actually use it.

Steve was walking over to the cake counter, coming to a halt behind a group of men wearing suits and the blank expressions of humans in serious need of caffeine. She watched him as he bent his head to choose some cake, noticing the small frown puckering his forehead and the way his hand scratched at his stubble as he surveyed the selection on display. Then he caught her eye and gave her a wicked smile as he grabbed the biggest and most chocolatey piece he could find.

He loped over to the checkout, picking up two forks and a napkin on his way. The old lady on the next table to Abi leant over. 'He's very handsome isn't he? Your young man?'

'Not my young man.' Abi shook her head. 'And not young either, now I come to think of it.'

'Well if he isn't your young man now, then he will be soon.' The woman adjusted the gold cross round her neck. 'And I am never wrong about these things.'

'Never?' Abi looked at her with amusement, surprised to find her sense of humour was still present and correct.

'Well, I was wrong about Harry and Chelsy.' The woman took a delicate sip of tea. 'And about Ashley and Cheryl.'

'I see.' Abi turned away to hide her smile. Outside on Broad Street a group of tourists in matching high-vis jackets saying *Oxford Tours* were taking pictures of the Museum of the History of Science. Its domed turquoise turret gleamed in the sun and two toddlers were jumping on the curving stone steps at its base. Seb had done that once. She could see him now, giggling as she and John had held his chubby little hands.

She was seeing him everywhere.

That little boy had turned eighteen last week. He had barely acknowledged his present and had only eaten a slice of his cake for his gran's sake. It had been the longest day of her life.

Abi turned away from her memories and looked at Steve as he carried the plate triumphantly back towards her, holding a cup and saucer in his other hand.

'Get some of this down you.' He put them on the table and slid back into his chair. 'Earl Grey, the colour of that boring Dulux they always paint school corridors with. Am I right?'

'Yes.' She giggled. 'You are.' She tried it. 'Perfect.' She remembered that morning after getting back from Glastonbury, when he had proudly brought her breakfast in bed. His hair damp from the shower. His black Del Amitri T-shirt over some truly ridiculous orange shorts. The smell of bacon and the splodges of brown sauce spattered all over the plate. His kiss.

It was getting warmer in here.

His eyes glinted with mischief. 'Some things a man never forgets.'

'Oh really? And what else do you remember about me?'

It was so easy being here with him. Forgetting the reality that lay outside the revolving door.

'Toasted marshmallows are your favourite snack.' He sat back, listing on his fingers. 'You hate parsnips, though to be honest that sentence doesn't even compute for me. You hate Kylie but mainly because you always felt she'd stolen the curly hair that should have been yours. Given half a chance, you would eat Frazzles for every single meal. Oh, and your favourite bit of a gig is always the first song, or so you used to tell me anyway. Speaking of which . . .'

'What?'

'How about coming to one later?'

She knew she shouldn't, so she took a mouthful of cake to distract herself. 'God, that's amazing.'

'Thought so.' He reached out a hand towards her, and she quickly hid hers under the table. His fingers dropped back to his lap.

'You've got a very chocolatey chin.' He smiled and brushed at it gently. 'There you go. All gone.'

'Gee, thanks. Now I feel like a malcoordinated six-year-old.'

'I have that effect on all the girls.' He nodded in satisfaction. 'I'm sure that's what first attracted you to me all those years ago.'

'No.' She took another mouthful. 'It was the fact that your mum owned the sweetshop and could get me Chomps for free.'

'I'll take that.' He narrowed his eyes. 'Though I seem to remember that you once decided to take a whole box and hoped she didn't notice.'

'And then I blamed Rob.' Abi giggled. 'God, no wonder he wasn't my biggest fan back when we were young.'

'Ouch.' He winced. 'Watch it. I'm still young at heart, you know.'

'I know.'

'How is Rob?'

She put the fork down. 'Good. We sold two of his paintings last week.' She had caught him several times, standing in the shop staring at the red 'Sold' stickers as if wondering if they were real. She loved seeing the pride on his face.

'That's great.' Steve put his head on one side. 'He must be pleased.'

'Well . . . given that this is Rob, he's obviously busy

predicting it'll all stop soon. But he has bought a new jumper, so that's his dancing-on-tabletops gesture.'

'Yeah, he never was one for shouting things from the hills.' Steve's eyes crinkled as he smiled. 'I remember when he passed his GCSEs and instantly started worrying about his A level resuts.'

'Sounds about right. But he genuinely seems really pleased. He's even managed to talk to Lesley without blushing.'

'Does he *still* have a crush on her?' Steve tapped the table with his hand. 'Wow.'

Abi placed her hand on her heart. 'Love is eternal.'

'Well, good luck to him.' Steve leant towards her again, his voice low. 'Why is that lady staring at us like that?' He jerked his head towards the next table.

'Oh,' Abi replied in a whisper. 'Apparently she thinks you and I are meant for each other.'

'Really?' Part of her was happy when he didn't immediately dismiss the idea. 'Well, that's interesting.'

'Yeah, isn't it?' She didn't know where to look. She noticed that the old lady had DMs on. A woman after her own heart.

'So are you going to come to the gig with me?'

'Tonight?'

'Yes.' He grinned. 'Got anything else planned?'

'Well, you know. I was hoping to spend the evening helping my mum to download security software. It's a real toss-up.'

'It's a great band.' He raised his eyebrows. 'How can you resist?'

'Who is it?'

'Oh, you know. They're newcomers. A mix of Oasis and Green Day.'

'Really?' She wrinkled her nose. 'What the hell does that sound like?'

'It sounds pretty great.' He laughed. 'But then I may be biased.'

'Why?'

'Because I'm the lead singer.'

'You are?'

'Yes.' He grinned. 'And there's space for a maracas player if you're interested.'

'You've been in a band all this time? And you didn't tell me?'

'Well, a man doesn't like to boast.'

She took a deep breath. 'Oh my God, I'd love to hear you.'

'Then come along.' He reached out and took her hand. She glanced nervously out of the window. Knowing her luck, Seb would just happen to be passing.

'Please? I'd love it if you were there. It would give me someone to sing to in the crowd.'

She looked down at their hands, intertwined on the table. At his silver ring. His tanned fingers.

No. This was too much. Too soon.

'I'm sorry, I can't.' Reluctantly she withdrew her hand, only for him to grab it again.

'But it won't be the same without you.'

'I'm sorry.' For once, she felt sure. 'I can't.'

'That dress would have looked great on stage. Just the right shade of purple.'

'Shame.' She mustered a smile. 'But, you know – rock-and-roll superstardom or a night with my mum's computer. It's a no-brainer.'

'Spoilsport.' He forked some cake into his mouth.

For a minute the temptation came back.

Her son's face appeared again in her mind. No. She didn't want to give him any more reasons to hate her. She remembered standing in his room the night she had been diagnosed, breathing in his sleepy scent and hoping with her whole heart that she wouldn't have to leave him. That love was still there and all she could do was keep being around until he returned it again. It didn't matter if he hated her. It didn't matter how long she had to wait.

She felt a swell of determination.

'I need to go.'

'Wait.' Steve reached out a hand. 'Don't go. You've only just got here. I'll miss you.'

She rolled her eyes. 'Don't be a sap. No you won't.' She leant towards him and dropped her voice to a whisper. 'That old lady will have tea with you for sure. Do you want me to ask her?'

He shook his head. 'God, no. I'll never get out of here.'

'OK.' She pushed her chair back and stood up, putting a tenner on the table. 'And thanks for the tea and cake.'

'We're a proper *Swallows and Amazons* story, aren't we?' He got up with her. 'You're so sensible nowadays. Quite a change.'

She looked at him. Weighed things up.

Then she told him.

'I had cancer.' She gave him her widest smile and started to put on her coat. 'It tends to change the way you do things.'

'Wait . . . *What?*' He put a hand to his forehead. 'You can't just spring that on me and then leave.'

'Can't I?' She picked up her bag. 'I thought I just did.'

'Yes, but . . .' His eyes were scanning her face. Her body. They landed on her boobs.

'It was bowel cancer, OK?' Her mouth went dry. She hadn't thought this through. He was the one person who made her feel beautiful. Now she had just thrown all that away.

A beat of silence. She shook her head and started to walk off, only for him to grab her hand.

He pulled her towards him. 'What a woman you are.'

'No.' She was struggling to get free. He was too close. He could see too much.

His voice was barely audible. 'Bloody hell, I'm glad you made it. And I would never have had the slightest idea. You look so bloody beautiful.' And he put his arms aaround her and held her and held her and held her. His hair smelled sweet. His stubble was rough against her face. It was today and twenty years ago and today again, and suddenly she knew how wrong this was. She had waited so long for this feeling of connection. Of being wanted. But it was the wrong arms. The wrong man.

She tried to wriggle away from him, but he held on. 'God, Abi.' He gently kissed her lips. 'God, you blow me away.' And then he was pressing his lips to hers again and she was pulling away but he kept going and her only thought was that she deserved every single word Seb had flung at her.

When she finally managed to escape, someone tapped her on the shoulder. It was the little old lady.

'I told you. I'm never wrong.'

She tripped happily away and Abi's horror grew. Horror at what she was doing. And who she was doing it with.

'Oh God.' She put her hand to her mouth.

'No. Don't start having second thoughts.' His fingers closed hard around hers.

'I've got to go.' She ripped herself away from him.

'Abi.' He caught her arm again.

'I'm sorry. I'm so sorry.' She couldn't even look at him.

'When will I see you again?'

'I can't. I won't.' She finally got away and threw herself into the revolving door. Inevitably it stopped moving and she was trapped, staring at the distress on his face and knowing she was the cause. Then she was running down the steps onto Broad Street, past the bikes and the red postbox and the endlessly enticing window of Blackwell's.

Seb had been right. She was selfish. She was self-centred. She was everything he thought she was.

May

'Get Lucky' by Daft Punk, featuring
Pharrell Williams and Nile Rodgers

This is for Seb. You played it to me first, after all. But it's also for the two of you. My boys.

I may spend too long in the shower and be clinically incapable of walking past a music shop without buying anything, but really I'm all yours. You're it, as far as I'm concerned. All that north, south, east, west shizzle – it's all true. Thank you for looking after me, or at least for letting me have the remote every now and then in between *Match of the Day* fun. Thanks for occasionally watching *The Gilmore Girls* and pretending you don't find it annoying. Above all, thank you for getting on with life while I've been ill and for only telling me the good stuff. I know other things have happened and I know you must have protected me. Thank you. I needed the time to get better and to have a serious chat with this cancer of mine. Hopefully I'll get there, but if not then I can't wait to look down (or up, let's face it) and see you fighting over (or trying to avoid being landed with) my music collection. I love you. And Seb, please don't spend years obsessing about why you don't have a whole song to yourself. It would have been 'Bob the Builder', so think yourself lucky.

Abi

'So, Uncle Rob, are you practising your autograph now that you're a famous artist?' Seb deliberately ignored Abi, saving all his words and smiles for her brother. She was paying him to be here, of course. Paying him to move their stuff into the flat that she hoped he would one day think of as his as well as hers. He hulked another couple of boxes out of the van and started towards the communal front door.

'I'm not famous,' Rob started after him with only one box in his arms. His face was flushed above his rather artisan loose white shirt. 'Or at least only among elderly north Oxford ladies.'

'Don't do yourself down.' Abi patted his shoulder. She had sold two more of his silhouettes this week. Before they had become popular he had strictly been a T-shirt, skinny jeans and Converse man, with the occasional Primark hoodie thrown in for colder days. Now there was some upper chest having an airing and she had spied a large rip in the knee of his jeans. She averted her eyes from the hairy flesh on show, wishing for the first time that there hadn't been an early May heatwave. She had seen quite enough of those legs when they had been growing up. There was no need for more sightings now.

'Really?' Seb grinned at his uncle as he reached the top of the stairs. 'No riders down there in the framing room? Six-packs? Champagne?'

'Nope.' Rob lifted his box onto his shoulder. He was wheezing slightly, even though his new artistic status had seen him break the habit of a lifetime and go jogging in his lunch break. Abi had also seen some ginger tea in the kitchen at the shop, whereas previously he had run on one hundred per cent Tetley. Success was clearly having an effect.

As they reached the landing, the flat's green front door was standing open, and Seb and Rob walked through, putting the boxes down on the ever-decreasing floor space of the living room. It was chaotic and cluttered but the amount of stuff was very welcome indeed, as it covered up the luminous yellow carpet that the landlord had decided would perfectly offset the oppressive orange walls.

Abi loved the place, though. She had known as soon as she walked in that this was the one she wanted. The rent was just about doable on her wage from the shop, and it didn't appear to have mice or the smell of toilets that had plagued so many of her viewings. She loved the huge sash windows that opened onto the hustle of the 'arse end of the Cowley Road', as Lesley had thoughtfully called it. She loved the tree that grew just outside the kitchen window, still covered in the fragile buds of late blossom. She loved her bedroom, with its uneven floor and crooked fireplace and the thought of the life that she would create for herself, piece by piece, over all the years she had left.

It was the flat she was going to build her future in. Hers and Seb's. He had only agreed to move in last night, but it was a new start, and God knows they needed one. She was determined to finally get him to open up once the boxes were unpacked and they had got fish and chips from the shop over the road. For the first time in a long time she felt hopeful. Excited.

She walked into her room, mentally decorating it in yellows and golds. She had bought the bed last week on eBay. It didn't creak when she moved. It didn't look at her and ask her why she wasn't with the man who had shared her life for so long. It was hers and hers alone, and would soon be covered with cheerful IKEA sheets and the bright red 'Duvet Day' blanket Lesley had bought her when Abi had first got ill.

She heard footsteps and walked quickly to the door.

'Are you all right, Seb?'

He paused unwillingly in the doorway, his long hair tied back. A strand had escaped onto his face, and in his tight white T-shirt and baggy jeans he looked overwhelmingly like John. She swallowed, feeling again the ache of his absence.

'What do you want, Mum?' His sullen expression was getting even better with practice. 'I'm here helping, aren't I? Is there something else I'm doing wrong now?'

'I just wanted to talk.' She was so tired of being his enemy. 'That's all. If we're going to be sharing a flat, then we need to—'

'Yeah, well. I won't be around much. So don't worry – I won't be cramping your style. Getting in the way of any plans you might have with *him*.'

'I am not seeing him, Seb.' In fact she had been dodging his calls and ignoring his texts ever since he had kissed her.

'And I'll be in London soon anyway.'

Keep calm, Abi.

'Of course.'

'So? Anything else?' He drummed his fingers against the door frame.

She found the words she needed. 'Yes. I know you're

281

angry with me. And I know you think you have good reason. But the fact is that I just want you to be happy. And you're not. And I wish I could do something about that.'

He shook his head. 'Well you could start by not having an affair with a twat in a leather jacket.'

'I told you, I'm not . . .'

He rolled his eyes. 'You can't even convince yourself, can you?'

She opened her mouth. Closed it.

'I'll get the rest of the stuff, OK?'

'OK.' She sat down on the bed. Her optimism was really struggling here, but she would make this work. Somehow.

Her brother appeared, clearly keen to avoid more box-lifting. 'Are you going to have a housewarming party?'

'Maybe.' She smiled, perfectly well aware of what was going on here. 'Why? Would you like me to?'

'Oh. Well. It's not up to me.' He shrugged. 'I was just wondering.'

She grinned. 'And if I were to have one? Would you like me to invite Lesley?'

He was squirming the way he used to squirm whenever he was made to eat carrots. 'Up to you, of course.' His hand reached up to his hair and dropped again. 'Totally up to you.'

'Right.' Abi grinned. 'OK. I'll see what I can do.'

'Thanks.' He looked visibly relieved. 'But just so you know, I'm busy on Thursdays. I'm teaching an art class.' He couldn't contain the pride on his face.

'Amazing!' Abi whooped. 'You'll knock 'em dead.'

'I don't really know what I'm talking about, but I'll give it a go.' A smile curved across his face.

'You do know what you're talking about. People buy your pictures. That's why they picked you.'

Rob dropped his head. Accepting praise had never been one of his talents. 'Maybe.'

Abi shrugged. 'And I think a housewarming bash is a great idea. Let's totally trash the carpet and then we can rip it out and replace it with something less . . .'

'Psychedelic?'

'Disgusting.' She grinned. 'I mean, I'm all for a bit of colour . . .'

'I think we can see that.' She loved the mischief in her brother's eyes and laughed as she looked down at her neon-green dress.

'Busted.'

'Shall I get some more boxes? I think my arms have recovered now.'

'Mine too.' Abi grinned.

'You carried a tiny one, Abs. Come on. Your arms barely noticed you were carrying anything at all.'

'Hey. Cheeky git. The dishcloths are very important. I was just taking good care of them.'

'Yeah, right.' The two of them walked down the stairs, encountering Seb coming up the opposite way, headphones in. They stood back and waited for him to pass.

Rob leant towards her. 'He'll come round.'

'You reckon?'

'Definitely. Remember when I didn't speak to Mum for two months because she went into my room and cleared out those love letters I got from my French exchange?'

'Yes.' Abi giggled. 'She used to send you flowers and home-made doilies as expressions of her love.'

'Yep.' Rob grimaced. 'I've always been such a hit with the ladies.'

'If you say so.' They reached the van and she picked up

the pots and pans box and staggered under its weight. 'God. I had no idea we had this many.'

'Did John take anything with him?' Rob slung a lamp stand onto his shoulder.

'Yeah. He took the TV, which is just as well as it would have taken up half the living room here. And his many radios. But that was about it really.' She wondered what his place in Cambridge was like. He was already living there part-time, keen to escape the jagged pain of their separation.

She had thought that things would feel better with him gone, but since the kiss with Steve her thoughts about John were only getting stronger. He appeared in her mind every time she heard the sports headlines on the radio, head bent low and hands on the counter as he listened intently for QPR's result. Every time she drove past the Bodleian in the Volvo or walked past the flower stall in the covered market where he had always bought her roses on her birthday. She couldn't even go walking in the Parks any more without thinking of the two of them strolling there, her arm through his, when he brought her out of her chemo cave and into the sunny spring sunlight.

No. She couldn't escape him anywhere except here. Her own flat. Her own front door. She would build a life without him – a life for her and for their son.

'Has he left yet?' Rob held the door open for her with his foot.

'Not completely.' She sighed. 'He's still here a couple of days a week.'

'And you're sure you don't want to stop him?'

'Yes. Totally sure. It's too late.'

'It seems such a shame, given everything you've been through.'

She started to climb the stairs. 'Well, maybe it was all too much. For both of us. Maybe he needs some space.' She reached the top of the stairs, panting. Her fitness regime still needed a bit of work. 'And maybe I do too.'

Even as she spoke, she knew she didn't believe what she was saying. But she gritted her teeth. This was a big day. Her day. Later her parents would come with a bottle of bubbly. Her dad would try to find something to mend, while her mum would start criticising the neighbours. Then her move would truly be complete.

Inside the flat, they could see that Seb was on the phone in his room. Rob put his box down and turned to Abi, face creased with concern.

'Abi.'

'Yes?'

'There's something I've been meaning to ask you.'

'What music you should say you like to impress the ladies?'

'No.' He shook his head. 'I'm happy with my jazz.'

'OK. Just as long as you don't start sporting a pork pie hat.' She pulled a face. 'So what's your question? How to dress so people don't assume you live on the streets?'

'Hilarious.' He shook his head. 'And no again.'

'What is it then?' She started hunting around to see if she could find the kettle.

'Can you talk to Mum and Dad?'

She turned. 'What about?'

'Mum's hands are getting worse – her hips too, so now that you've finally grown up and moved out—'

'Hey!' She shook her head. 'Not fair.'

His eyes gleamed. He seemed taller nowadays. More confident.

'Can you convince them to move? Somewhere sunny?'

'Why me?' She found the kettle and pulled it out.

'Because they're still waiting.'

'For what?'

He had his head on one side, watching her. She straightened up.

'You mean . . .'

'Yes.' He nodded. 'They're waiting to know that you're OK. That you'll be OK without them.'

'But I am. They know that. I . . .'

'I know.' He shook his head. 'But Mum's got this thing in her head about leaving you. She wants to be here just in case.'

Abi stared at him as she realised how tightly cancer still gripped them all. She was only just starting to believe she had days unfurling before her, and her mum and dad were clearly still living life in the brace position.

'Dad mentioned it to me months ago. I forgot to bring it up again.' She felt a stab of guilt. 'Shit. It totally fell out of my head.'

'Don't worry about it. But can you . . .?'

'Yes.' She nodded. 'I'll talk to them. I promise.'

'Thanks.' He walked across and hugged her.

She felt stronger with his arms around her. 'You do know that it might come back, don't you, Rob?'

'It wouldn't dare.' He pulled away. 'I'll beat it up.'

'Oh, well now I feel really safe.'

'Shut up, Batfink.'

'Chill out, Dingbat.'

He was about to go down the stairs but she stopped him.

'While we're on serious topics . . .'

'Yeah?'

'Do you want me to ask Lesley out for you?'

He stiffened. 'How did you know?'

'EVERYBODY knows.'

'Oh. I thought it was just Seb, taking the piss.'

'No.' Abi shook her head. 'I hope you realise what you're taking on, though.'

'Meaning?'

'Ooh, where to start?' Abi drummed her fingers against her chin. 'Lesley does what she wants and says what she thinks and woe betide anyone who doesn't agree with her. Do you know that she never ever let me talk about dying? She said if I did, it would mean I was giving up, and next thing she knew she would be my pall-bearer, coming down the aisle to some terrible Radiohead song or other. And she didn't want that.' She smiled, but there were tears in her eyes as she remembered her friend's fierce determination. 'That's what I mean.'

'I like a woman who knows her own mind.' Rob grinned and took one of the chocolate digestives that were resting on top of the boxes. 'Just as well, growing up with you.'

'You cheeky sod.'

'Shithead.' His smile gave him away.

'Dung breath.'

'Fart brain.' He took a step forward. 'And if I do manage to ask Lesley out . . .'

'*When*.' Abi crunched a digestive.

'*When* I ask her out.' He exhaled. 'It won't be weird? For you and me, I mean. You being her best friend, and all.'

'No it bloody won't.'

'Like when we were little and always played cavemen together, until that mad friend of yours turned up and wanted you to play acrobats all the time and it was really boring.'

'Oh yes.' She smiled. 'You mean Mary Filton?'

'That's the one. The one who would just scream at me until I gave up and went and played with my Lego.'

'Yeah.' Abi giggled. 'Do you know what happened to her?'

'No.' He shook his head. 'Strangely enough, she didn't keep in touch.'

Abi laughed. 'She went off and joined a circus.'

'No?' His eyes were wide.

'Yep.' She thought back to the night Mary had come into the pub in a spangly trapeze outfit, her hair slicked back in diamanté clips. 'She really did it.'

'Well good for her. Her dream came true.'

'Just like you becoming a painter.'

'Eventually.'

'And now you're going to ask Lesley out.'

She hoped her friend fancied him back.

'I hope so.'

'May the force be with you.' She nodded her head and walked over to her phone, which was lying next to the speakers in the corner. She picked a song and pressed 'play', smiling as the room was filled with the opening chords of 'Get Lucky'. This was it. The family favourite. The one song they could all agree on. 'Rolling in the Deep' had enjoyed a moment in the sun, and 'Pala Tute' had been a hit one Greek family holiday, when they had all danced to it like lunatics on the beach as the sun was setting. But this song was the classic. The one everyone really loved. It got John's feet tapping. It got Seb's headphones out of his ears. The ultimate compliment.

John. Damn it, he was everywhere. Even here in her flat on the first day of the rest of her life.

She exhaled. *Enough.*

'Are you OK?' Rob watched her, his head on one side.

'Yeah.' She must think about the future now. 'It's all good.' She stretched her arms above her head. 'How much longer do you think I need to keep that van illegally parked?'

Rob laughed. 'Another half-hour or so, I think.'

'I dunno.' She shook her head. 'You just can't get the help nowadays.' She banged on Seb's door, amused to see it already shut. 'You'd better be revising in there, kiddo.'

He stuck his head out. 'Don't call me kiddo.'

'That's my boy.' She was tempted to really annoy him by ruffling his hair, but decided against it. 'God, I love you.'

'Piss off, Mum.' In conversational terms, it was a real step forward. She smiled to herself. One step at a time. They would get there. Soon he'd be mocking her for her dress sense and things would be back to normal. Well, normal minus John.

Damn. She felt tears pricking her eyes and had to turn away towards the window. Luckily she was right next to the cake box, and she bent down and ripped it open. 'Whoever brings the next box up gets carrot cake.' She turned round. 'Ready, steady, go!'

She had never seen either of them move so fast. Their heavy clomps on the stairs were an absolute guarantee that their new neighbour wouldn't be celebrating their arrival, but Abi didn't care. For now she was in her new home with the May sunshine showing up all the stains on the unwashed windows. This was living. This was heaven.

Nothing was going to change that. Not John. Not the fact that she was going to have to live off baked beans for the rest of the month. Not the fact that she was still only studying psychology via library books and podcasts. It would all come together. Somehow. One day.

She located a knife and bent over to start to cut the cake.

And there it was. The pain. So familiar. And yet so terrifying.

It pierced her for one second. Two.

Then it disappeared.

She took a trembling gasp of air.

Then she unclenched her fists and carried on cutting the cake, forcing herself to breathe as the fear whirled around her, freezing her heart and threatening the very future she was working so hard to build.

Seb

'So when were you going to let me know?'

Seb turned around to see Jess standing behind him, one leg jutting forward and her dark hair flicked defiantly to one side. She looked like a woman going into battle. Only the children fighting over the Nando's ice machine behind her threatened to ruin her style.

Jess stepped forward, blocking his view of the imminent screamfest. 'You could at least have told me.'

Seb shifted his weight to the other foot. 'I haven't seen you.'

'Oh, come on.' She flicked her hair the other way. 'iPhone? Got one?'

'I didn't think you'd want me to get in touch. Not now you're with someone new.' He moved his wooden Nando's rooster from one hand to the other. Jess looked so lovely. Green top. A delicate silver chain around her neck. And those huge dark eyes, still so bright even though he knew she must be revising until 3 a.m. each night.

He could see her digging into her thumb with a nail, and he could sense her distress, buried deep beneath the make-up and the defiance.

Her eyes flicked upwards again. 'What are you having?'

'The peri-peri—'

'Chicken? A whole one?' Now at last she smiled, and he felt his shoulders relax.

'Guzzle, guzzle, that's me.'

He had no idea where on earth that had come from.

He turned, aware that over in the far corner some Year 10 kids were staring at him and pointing. He was now out. Seriously out. Giggles and whispers met him wherever he went. He stared people down until they turned away, telling himself he didn't mind. He wouldn't be around long. He nearly had enough money now. Soon he'd be in London and life would start again.

'Are you OK, Seb? It must have been so difficult . . .' She stopped, and he wanted to reach out and hug her. Still kind, even after all he had done. Behind her the toddlers were now spooling ice cream into their little Nando's pots. The bright pink dessert was in danger of spilling over the sides as one girl with plaits eagerly held hers up, determinedly pulling the lever down for more.

'What is it?' Jess looked behind her. 'Oh.' A smile. 'Do you remember when we used to sit in here for hours while you bankrupted the place with your endless top-ups?'

'Yeah.' He smiled. 'Only as I remember it I was busy wowing you with my romantic one-liners.'

She rolled her eyes in that way he loved. 'Yeah, right.'

'Oh. I'm hurt.' He pressed his hand to his heart.

'Well obviously I was the one impressing you.' She grinned, and he saw that tiny gap between her teeth that he knew she hated.

She folded her arms. 'So how are your exams going?'

'Not bad.' He nodded, aware that she was one of the two people in the world who always knew when he was lying.

'Interesting.' She arched an eyebrow.

'Why?' He knew he sounded defensive.

'Because I heard that you haven't turned up to anything.'

Shit.

'Who told you that?'

'Doesn't matter, does it? What matters is whether it's true.'

'No, it's not.'

'Really?' She shook her head. 'OK, so what was in the biology paper?'

'I can't remember.' Those kids were really starting to annoy him now.

'You can't remember? Or you weren't there?'

'What is this? An interrogation?'

She took a step closer.

'Come on, Seb. We may not have got much out of our time together, but—'

'That's not true.' He shook his head. 'That's not true at all.'

'Isn't it?' She was twisting the strap of her bag between her fingers. 'Because sometimes I wonder why you were with me at all.'

'Are you kidding me?' Suddenly he didn't care about the kids, didn't care about the pointing fingers. He needed to put this right. To help her to believe in herself as much as he did. He couldn't bear the fact that she didn't know how bloody great she was. That she was the reason he had got through his mum's illness without screwing up his grades or his life. That she had helped him through the maze of uncertainty and fear and given him the one thing that he had needed – belief.

He struggled to work out what to say as he remembered her head on his shoulder as they had endured a hundred waiting rooms, full of people just as scared as they were. Without her, he would have cracked. Without her, he would have screwed things up, as would soon be proved by his non-existent A2 results. He was what he had always been destined to be – a pisshead with no friends and no prospects apart from getting on his bike to wobble off and deliver yet another takeaway.

He owed her so much. He had to make this right.

He took her hand. 'Jess, you don't get it, do you? You are amazing. You always will be. But you know now that there were more things going on with me. It wasn't as simple as—'

'So it's true then?' She put her head on one side.

'Yes. I'm gay.'

Naturally the last word coincided with the music system cutting out. On the list of all the things that never happened in Nando's – like running out of chicken or the window seat ever being free – this was right up there. He looked around, feigning a relaxation he definitely didn't feel.

All heads were turned towards them. Great.

He swallowed. Waited for the music to turn back on. Waited for the children to start squealing over the sprinkles again. Waited for a miracle.

It wasn't forthcoming. He didn't know why he was surprised. It wasn't as if he had a strong track record of having Lady Luck in his corner when he needed her.

She was practically tapping her foot now. 'Well?'

'What else do you want me to say?'

No sign of the smile now. Just anger. 'Why didn't you just tell me?'

'I didn't know. Not for ages. I mean, you're going to be a doctor, Jess. You know how it works, don't you? It takes some of us a while to realise.'

'I know that! I just wish I hadn't spent so much time thinking there was something wrong with me. That you didn't fancy me because . . .' She shook her head.

He stepped forward.

'I'm sorry, Jess.'

'So you fucking should be.'

'That's not fair.' Frustration pushed him on. 'I didn't mean to hurt you. Life's not straightforward, you know. You can get the best grades, you can eat the right things, you can know where you're going, and then your mum gets sick.'

'But she's better now. Stop blaming everything on that.'

'Don't you see?' He was gesticulating wildly now. The rooster was having a roller-coaster ride. 'Mum being so ill – it changed everything.' He felt a surge of conviction. 'I know now that you can't take things for granted, just like I know I don't want to waste any more time studying when everything in me is telling me to wait and take some time and bloody process things for a change.'

Yet again his anger was pouring forth and he had no idea how to stop it. He didn't want to be like this. He could see the tears welling in her eyes, but he still couldn't stop.

'Look. I think you're fucking amazing, Jess. I hate myself for hurting you. Don't you get it? But I was never the right guy for you. I'm not your man, or The One, or whatever. I used to believe in all that shit, but not any more. Look at my mum and dad. He's starting again in a sad flat on a ring road. And my mum is busy trying to be nineteen again with her red sheets and her fucking boyfriend.' He shrugged, suddenly exhausted. 'I'm just trying to be me, Jess. That's all I'm aiming at.' He took a heaving breath. 'It's all I can handle.'

Her head was lowered. He leant towards her and whispered in her ear.

'And one final thing. Something I forgot to say before. I'm so proud of you.'

Katie Marsh

'Why?'

'For working so damn hard to be the doctor you want to be.'

She wiped away a tear. 'Thank you.'

He noticed the music had started again. 'Get Lucky'. Song of family car journeys, his dad laughingly protesting about why he wasn't allowed to listen to the cricket. Mum pretending she could sing. Him sitting in the back, pretending he was hating every minute. He'd had no idea how lucky he was.

No point thinking about that now. He wanted to help the girl in front of him. 'You made me stronger and braver and better, Jess. I just want you to believe that. OK?'

She nodded. 'OK.' Her eyes were on the floor but a tiny smile curved across her lips. 'OK.' She tipped her head up and he saw that maybe – one day – they might manage to be friends.

His appetite had gone. Once Jess had gone back over to sit with her friends, he knew he had to get out of here. To be outside, doing the one thing he could do to help himself – earning money. Two hundred more then hello, London, and he could leave all this shit behind.

He checked his App as he got out onto the street and accepted a pick-up from Cornmarket Street. Whoever had ordered was having a very big night. As Seb walked to his bike, he looked around him. The New Theatre one way. Japanese tourists the other.

He took a deep breath. If his mum's illness had taught him anything, it was that you had to make the best of things when you could. Seize the day. He had to get on with it. Right now. Kerching, kerching.

He untangled his bike from the mass of metal on the cycle stand and climbed onto it. Time to go. OneRepublic was blasting through his headphones as he pushed off, weaving his way down George Street, past busy restaurants towards his pick-up. He didn't look left. He didn't look right. Just straight ahead towards the future.

And he didn't see the motorbike. Not until it was much much too late.

His last thought was of his mum. Then his body slammed into the pavement and he lay motionless on his side, the words of 'Good Life' dying on his lips.

Abi

'Any news yet?' John ran in, bright red in the face, his coat hanging from his hand.

'No.' She picked up her bag off the seat next to her so he could sit down. 'Nothing.'

She went back to sitting head down, hands balled into fists in her lap. Her boy. Her wonder boy. She gritted her teeth as a constant reel of family videos kept spooling through her mind. Seb running through the sprinkler in their first ever sliver of garden, eyes wide and mouth open in a joyful shriek. Seb and John racing whooping from the waves on a warm April day in Tenby. Seb declaring that Grandad's shed was now his kingdom and filling it with his toys, and her dad's face when he came home from work and discovered his seedlings and tomato plants out in the freezing cold of a February gale.

She blinked, staring at the cracked waiting-room floor. She had got the call while one of her most difficult customers was busy telling her why she didn't want to pay full price to have her Best Cream Cake certificate framed. Abi had ignored the phone the first time. And the second. But the third time, she had put down the precious certificate, leading to more complaints from Mrs Jeffreys about her lack of professionalism and the standards of customer service nowadays, and answered. She heard sobs. She heard gasps. And then she heard Jess saying the words that no parent ever wants to hear. She had shouted to Rob to come and help and had turned and run, leaving Mrs Jeffreys to mouth angry words at the empty air.

John sat down next to her, and she had to resist the urge to lean on his shoulder, as she had done so many times in the past. He wasn't hers any more.

'What happened?'

'He was knocked off his bike. By a motorbike, apparently.' She closed her eyes as she imagined the shock of the impact. She could see his blond hair flying as he sailed through the air before the crunching thump as he landed on the pavement. She shook her head, trying to force the image away, but it only came back stronger. The breath leaving his body. The shock in his eyes. 'He wasn't wearing his bloody helmet.'

'Shit.' John sighed. 'How many times have we—'

'I know.' Abi stared at the crack in the floor so hard she felt as if it might open up and let her in. It felt like right where she belonged. The window behind her appeared to be some sort of magnifying glass, concentrating all the heat of the day on the back of her neck. She sat up straight, rubbing the spot with her fingers. 'He never listens, does he?' Her voice disintegrated into a sob.

She dug her nails into her palms, but it was too late now. Sitting here brought back too many memories. The plunging nausea as they waited for her results. Lame jokes to kill the time before the next round of bad news came. Tea burning the roof of her mouth. Hands in hers as she realised that her body wasn't her ally any more. She hunched forward once more, unable to hold back the tears. They couldn't be here again. Once they had gone on road trips. On weekends away. On flights to cities with beaches or castles or both. Now this hospital was the magnet drawing them back again and again, taking them into its overheated antiseptic heart.

Her mouth was sandpaper dry and her sobs were building. Her son on the pavement. His crumpled bike. His blood. She could see it all so clearly. And she had been nowhere near him. He had needed her and yet again she had failed him.

She had allowed herself to believe that they had time now. That she could wait for him to open up to her. She of all people should have known that the time was now. That you could never take anything for granted. Her shoulders shook. All she had ever wanted was to make him happy, but she had failed. And now he was helpless underneath bright operating-theatre lights, just as she had been. Needles in his veins. Inert.

She put her hands to her head, suppressing the howl of rage that was rising inside her. Somehow she had coped with all the weeks and months of her own pain, but this was too deep. Too much.

She was struggling to breathe. Then a warm hand curved round her shoulders, and another pressed her fingers. Steady. Strong.

'It's all right, Abi.' John's voice was low and it reassured her the same way it had on countless occasions just as dark as these. 'He's strong, our boy.' She could hear the catch in his voice. 'He always has been. There's no way he's going to let some dodgy motorbike steal his future.'

'He never did like them, did he?' She wiped her nose with the back of her hand.

'No.' John shook his head. 'More of a classic car man, our Seb.'

'Yeah.' She took a breath, thick with guilt and tears. 'What was it he kept asking for every single Christmas?'

John pushed his hair back from his face. 'An Aston Martin Volante.' She glanced at him and saw his eyes were bright with tears. He fought them back as he had a thousand times before and carried on. 'I put a down payment on one once, but I couldn't come up with the rest.'

She managed a shaky laugh. 'And you wonder why your business got into trouble?'

'No.' John dug in his pocket for a tissue and handed it to her. 'I really don't.'

They smiled at each other, and it was such sweet relief, until Abi remembered where they were and put her hand over her mouth to stop herself. Mirth was out of place in this room where fates would be sealed and loved ones might be lost. One woman with auburn hair and glasses was looking searchingly at the man sitting beside her, who was immersed in typing into his mobile phone. Abi had never seen two people looking so lonely. In the far corner a grey-haired woman swore quietly at the water machine, which in keeping with tradition had absolutely no cups. She looked like she was about to kneel down and stick her mouth under the tap when Abi stood up and handed her one from the windowsill.

She smiled. 'I don't know why they keep them up there either.'

'Thank you.' The woman tugged her bag further up her shoulder. 'I was worried I was going to get water all over my face if I just drank straight from the tap. Silly, really.' She sighed. 'Worrying about something like that when my daughter's in there, having all . . .' She stopped. 'You know.'

'I'm so sorry.' Abi tentatively patted her arm. 'I hope she's OK.'

'Yours too.' The woman pressed her lips together in an

attempt at a smile, before bending back down in front of the water machine.

Abi headed back to her green plastic seat.

John was leaning back now, the top button on his shirt undone. He had rolled his tie up and put it in his pocket, so he looked like Saturday John. Weekend John.

She knew him so well. The way he always brushed his bottom teeth before his top. The way he couldn't go away for a weekend without his precious radio packed in his bag. How he never arranged anything on QPR match days so he could remain glued to the TV. How he brought her flowers when she wasn't expecting it and cooked lasagne on dark winter evenings. The way he patiently talked her mum through Skype for the millionth time. His strong arms. His lips on hers.

Everything about him was as familiar as the hiss of the needle when her dad put on a record. The smell of him. The feel of him. It was just such a shame that all those years of loving each other had dissolved into dry kisses and the suffocating silence that descended when intimacy was over.

Still no doctor. She curved her hands over her belly, grateful that the pain of two weeks ago hadn't yet reappeared. Next to her John's leg jiggled up and down. Being with him here as they waited to hear about their son was so familiar. This hospital had taken up too much of their time. There was no escaping the weight of the past settling on her shoulders.

Her heart leapt as a doctor in a white coat strode into the waiting room. A little girl playing in the corner beamed at him and waved her own pink stethoscope, while her mum tried to shush her. Abi could remember Seb bouncing merrily into the kitchen and telling her that she had a broken leg and he was going to fix it with Sellotape and a biscuit. She had never quite worked out how the biscuit was meant to work, but she had enjoyed sharing it with Seb, as he magnanimously gave her a teeny corner while he happily crunched the rest.

Come on, Seb.

The doctor walked across to the grey-haired woman and quietly led her back through the swing door. Everyone else in the room waited for their turn. For the news that could make or break them.

John's fingers were drumming against his thigh, and Abi reached out and took his hand. Their fingers fitted together in the old way, his hand on top of hers.

'How's your new flat?'

'Great, actually.' She had already painted over the living room walls, and was in the process of persuading the landlord to replace the hideous carpet. It was slowly starting to feel like home. She was overspending on pictures from the shop, and Rob had done a huge picture of a girl in silhouette dangling keys in her hand as a thousand flowers exploded behind her. He had called it *Starting Out*, and it hung in pride of place above the fireplace. 'It's on the Cowley Road, near that Indian place we used to go to.'

'Oh, nice. You always liked it down there. All the hubbub. The music booming out of the shops.'

'Yeah.' She squeezed his hand. 'The smell of takeaway in the air. And the swearing from the pub across the street at last orders.'

John inhaled. 'Perfect. Any lock-ins yet?'

She shook her head. 'Not quite. Though obviously it won't be too long till I'm dancing on a bar.'

He stared ahead of him. 'So you're happy? Really happy?'

'Yes.' She glanced towards him, hearing the question he wasn't asking.

'I'm not seeing Steve. Just in case you were wondering.'

'I wasn't.'

Disappointment seeped through her. He had clearly moved on.

God, it was hot in here.

She slid her sandals off and put her feet on the floor, seeking a cool spot. No chance. The floor was boiling. She should have known. She put them back on again and the strap was too fiddly and it took too long and she sat back in her chair in frustration.

'Thanks for telling me.' John turned to her and took her hand again.

'About Steve?'

'Yes.'

'No problem.' She fanned herself with her hand. 'Do you think Seb will be OK?'

'Yes.'

'He'd bloody better be.' She sighed. 'This wasn't how we imagined it would be, is it?'

'Our future? No.' He shook his head. 'We were skipping off into a beautiful sunset, weren't we?'

'Yeah. Though I think there was a rainbow in the mix too.'

'Of course.'

She crossed her legs. 'And perhaps some lush romantic music. Ravel, maybe? Or Debussy.'

'Or maybe just the sound of corn rustling in the fields or the two of us laughing.'

She raised an eyebrow. 'Well, who knew you had a bad movie script in you?'

'I can still surprise you.'

'Like that time when you took me to the Big Apple.'

'Yeah.'

She exhaled. 'Manhattans in Manhattan. The Rockefeller. Me pretending to be a ballerina outside the Met and falling over just as you took the shot.'

'Oh yeah.' There was that smile again. 'Very elegant.'

'If you say so.' She shuddered. 'I live in fear of that bloody photo coming back to haunt me.'

'But I'm the only one with a copy! Don't you trust me?'

Abi tried to ignore her inner monologue, which was being its usual unhelpful self. *I do. I do.*

She had to say something. She had to try.

'John, I . . .' She was just putting the words together in her head when the doors opened again. She was on her feet in seconds, her whole body primed to finally see her son.

'Jess!' She sagged momentarily before drawing the girl into a hug, holding her close as Jess wept onto her shoulder. She stroked the dark cloud of hair and muttered soothing words into her ear. 'It's OK, Jess. Everything will be all right.'

'It's my fault.' Jess took a shuddering breath. 'We were talking, and then he rode off, and now look what's happened.' The last words were lost in a haze of tears.

Abi pulled away and held her at arm's length. 'No. Jess. You stop that. Right now. This isn't anyone's fault – this is just life. Accidents. Illness. It's all so random and there's nothing anyone can do about it. It's just a helmet that wasn't on and a motorbike going too fast. OK? It is nothing to do with you.'

'But—'

'No.' Abi's voice was louder than she had expected. 'No, Jess. Stop.'

'OK.' Jess wiped her eyes, leaving a trail of mascara down her cheek. 'If you say so.'

'I say so.' Abi looked at her. The girl needed something to do. 'Listen, can you call Dan? And the rest of his mates?'

'I don't know . . .' Jess bit her lip.

'It would really help us out.' Jess liked to help. Abi could remember her making endless cups of tea and slices of toast to keep Seb and John going after each round of chemo.

'OK.' Jess's hands were shaking as she got out her phone. 'Of course.' She looked around the room and made the wise decision to head out into the corridor. 'Let me know if anything happens.'

'Of course.' Abi sat down again.

'Why did those two split up again?' John rolled his eyes. 'He must have been mad to lose her.'

'I have no idea.'

Then the swing doors burst open. 'Mrs Cooper?' The blonde doctor had bright red lipstick and a tired smile.

'Yes.' Abi leapt to her feet.

'Can you and . . .' the doctor looked at John, who had also risen, 'and Sebastian's father come with me, please?'

'Yes.' Abi picked up her bag. 'Yes. At last.'

And they walked through the doors and towards their son.

June

'It Won't Be Long Now' from
In the Heights by Lin-Manuel Miranda

One for me. Just for me. I love this show. I love this song. It will get me up for chemo and it will kick me up the arse and give me some hope that one day I'll come back from this and bloody well take the world by storm. Or at least manage to dance on a table again, anyway. I *will* be there to see it in London, and I'll be in the front row and I'll mouth every single sodding word and quite possibly get up and dance too, just for good measure. This song. My heart. My courage.

Abi

A few days later, he was starting to look human again. As they walked into the room, there was always a second when she forgot how to breathe. Today was no different. Seb was lying flat on his back. Still. Helpless.

Then he turned his head and she exhaled.

His voice was a croak. 'The things I have to do to get you two in the same room.'

Tears sprang to her eyes as she moved to the bed. 'Seb.' She tried to put her arms round him, so much easier now the wires and drips had been removed.

'Ow.'

'Sorry.' She leapt back again.

Seb smiled faintly. 'Not quite ready for a group hug yet.'

'I don't care. I'm coming in anyway.' She pressed her face to his, sweet relief flooding through her as she felt the warmth of his skin. She pulled away, tracing his face with her eyes. The long cut running down his left cheek was starting to heal, and his left eye was a puffy riot of colour. His skin was pale but his eyes were alive again.

She kissed him on his cheek. His forehead. His hair. Each time they visited, she had to check that every single bit of him was still there.

'How are you?'

'Not bad.' That slow smile. How she loved it. 'If you discount the broken leg.'

She sat on the edge of the bed and gazed down at him. Her son. Her precious son.

'And the amazing shiner.'

'You can barely see it.'

'Mum, you are a shit liar.'

'Isn't she?' John pulled up a chair. 'My turn.' He sat on the other side of the bed, just in front of the pink curtain separating Seb from his neighbour. He kissed Seb's cheek and sat back again. He had aged over the past week, as Seb steadfastly refused to wake up after his fall and was intensively monitored until he did. So much waiting. So much hoping.

And John had been here so many times before.

Then Seb had woken up and demanded a burger and Abi had known that it would all be OK. And that was when they had talked. Her and Seb, when he was out of danger and they were waiting on the ward for his leg to be reset. John had gone out for a walk and Abi had taken the chance to have things out with her son. No more wasted time. No more misunderstandings.

She had apologised about the night he had seen her with Steve. She had tried to explain what had gone wrong between her and John. And she had made him see how much they both loved him and would support him no matter what choices he made. It took time, but now she knew that he believed her.

Since then something had lifted. He was talking. Smiling. His face was more open than it had been in months.

Her husband, on the other hand, looked exhausted.

'John?' She reached out to him and he turned his face and kissed her hand. She waited for him to put her hand down. He didn't.

A nurse smiled as she pushed the medication trolley past the end of Seb's bed. In the next cubicle somebody laughed. A phone rang behind them.

But Abi couldn't take her eyes from John's.

They both turned their heads as they heard a tapping sound. Seb was feebly banging his empty cup against the water jug. 'Hello. Injured son over here. Can I have some water, please?'

'Of course.' They both leapt into action, reaching for the plastic water jug at the same time and then knocking over the cup.

Seb rolled his eyes. 'God, given the way you two handled that simple task, it's a miracle I'm coordinated enough to ride a bike at all.'

'What do you mean?' John shrugged. 'I was in the third football team at school, you know.' He attempted a smile but didn't quite pull it off.

'Impressive.'

John wagged his finger in mock-indignation. 'And I exercise.'

'Yes. You run. And ride a bike.' Seb rolled his eyes. 'The only sports that require absolutely no coordination apart from travelling in a straight line.'

'For a boy who's just had a major accident you are irritatingly chatty,' John harrumphed loudly.

Abi looked at her boys. At the beating heart of their family. Maybe it wasn't all over. Maybe there was something to save.

She held the straw to Seb's lips and he took a long drink. 'That's better.' He rested back on his pillows. 'Man, you're going to love looking after me, aren't you, Mum?'

She laughed. 'Hmmm. Not sure yet. But you and your crutches are being discharged soon, so we'll soon find out. There'll be grapes and chocolate galore.' She patted him on his good leg, drinking him in.

'I hate grapes.'

'Good point.' She smiled. 'I remember you once shoved one up your nose to try to avoid eating it.'

'Oh God. Did I?'

'Yes. At Anaya Rochdale's sixth birthday party.'

'Trust you to remember that.'

Abi shrugged. 'Well, the rest of my brain is lyrics and cheese toastie cravings, so be grateful I squeezed in some of your precious childhood memories.'

Seb cringed. 'I'd rather it was a more flattering one, though.'

'A more flattering one?' Abi grinned across at John. 'Don't remember any of those.'

Seb shook his head. 'You're meant to be being nice to me. I've just been through major trauma.'

'So? You always used to ask me how I felt just after chemo, when you were doing that bloody science project about the effect of drugs on mood.'

'Oh.' A flush appeared on his cheeks. 'Yeah.' He pleated the sheets with his fingers. 'Listen . . .'

'Yes?'

'I've got something to tell you.'

'As long as it's not yet another request for beer. You know it's not allowed in here.'

'No!' She saw a flicker of frustration cross his face. 'It's bigger than that.'

'OK.' She nodded. 'We're listening. Aren't we John?'

'Yes.' John squeezed her hand.

'OK.' Seb puffed out his cheeks as he exhaled. 'Here goes.'

She settled down next to him, feeling his warmth next to her.

Seb sighed. 'God, this is hard.'

Abi's eyes tangled with John's as they waited. She could hear someone watching *Pointless* in the next bay and it reminded her that she should go and see her parents. Reassure them. They had endured so many shocks recently. Too many.

'Well, there are two things really.'

'Yes?'

The words came out in a rush. 'I didn't turn up to my A2s.'

'What?' John's head turned so fast he must have got whiplash. He was bolt upright in his chair now. 'But I thought we'd talked about this. You were going to . . .'

Abi shook her head and he stopped. She focused on Seb. 'Why?'

'There was a lot happening. And I don't mean seeing you and that guy, or you getting ill.' Seb took a juddering breath. 'This wasn't to do with that.' He looked at the ceiling as if searching for guidance. 'The thing is . . .' He opened his mouth. Closed it. Abi watched him, her imagination catching fire with horrible possibilities. Drug addiction. A criminal record.

She took a breath, forcing herself to wait.

'I'm . . .' He glanced at John, as if genuinely worried his dad might explode. 'I mean, I think I might be . . .' He stopped. 'No.' He looked her straight in the eye. 'I'm gay.'

Abi's first response was relief. He didn't have a police record. He wasn't on crack.

He was gay.

She took his hand.

'What?' The word erupted out of John with all the sensitivity of a rocket launcher.

He didn't appear to be taking it well.

He stood up and walked to the far end of the cubicle. It was so small it didn't take long. He remained there, head bowed, while Abi willed him to turn. To say something. Anything.

'I'm gay,' Seb repeated. His skin matched his pillow as he

looked at his dad's back, his face suddenly so young as he waited for a reaction. 'For ages I tried to pretend I wasn't. But then . . .' His face crumpled and he tailed off. Abi watched as he gathered his strength, wanting to climb into his head and fill it with all the love in her heart. Wanting to make him see how strong he could be. 'But then I realised it's who I am.' His voice trembled. 'It's who I want to be.'

She was so proud of him.

She leant close to him. 'I can't believe I didn't see it. No wonder I never became a psychologist.' She racked her brain for a sign – any sign. Some signal from childhood or kitchen-table conversations or Friday movie nights.

Nothing.

Seb shifted in the bed. 'I didn't see it either, Mum. Not for ages. I didn't want to, I suppose.' His gaze was still fixed on John and his eyes were dark with doubt. 'You know that time I punched a guy at school?'

'Yes.'

'It was because Marc – the guy who lives next door to Gran and Gramps – it was because he kissed me back in September. I punched him because it was easier than telling him I liked it. That's how in denial I was.'

'Wow.' Her heart broke for him. 'And you've been carrying this all year? By yourself? God, you must have been so lonely.'

'Yeah.' He bit his lip. 'But I couldn't say anything. It was too huge. And I knew I was fucking everything up at school, and with Jess. Dragging her through it all, making her feel like crap. Never having the balls to just do the right thing and finish with her.'

She stroked his hair away from his forehead. 'Judging by the number of times she's visited you here, I think she's forgiven you.'

'Maybe.'

John still hadn't turned. Abi didn't understand. Surely he wouldn't have any problem with this.

Then she saw that his shoulders were shaking.

'John?'

'Sorry.' He bent forward and let loose a sob.

'Dad? I'm sorry. I'm really sorry.' Seb looked wildly at Abi, as panicked as the time when he was six and he had lost them both in the supermarket. It had only been a second but those eyes when they found him again. Those tiny arms hanging on to them for dear life. 'I didn't mean to . . .'

John shook his head and turned. 'It's not that, Seb. It's not. It's just . . .' He wiped his face, but more tears came. 'Oh God, I'm really fucking this up, aren't I?'

'Dad?' Seb reached out his hand. 'I'm so sorry.'

John threw himself down at Seb's side. 'What the hell do you have to be sorry about?'

'For screwing up my exams. For giving you so much shit.'

'No.' John rested his head on Seb's for a second. 'We're your parents. You're meant to give us shit. It's what we're here for, isn't it, Abs?'

Abi nodded, swallowing down the lump in her throat. 'Yes, taking shit is definitely number one in the parents' manual.'

'But why are you crying, Dad?'

'Because I'm so damn proud of you.' John wiped his cheeks with the back of his hand.

'Really?'

'Yes.' John kissed him on the forehead, tenderness stamped across his face. 'And because there's been so much . . . life recently. Your accident. Abi. The company. QPR still being shit.'

'Hey.' Seb gently punched his dad on the arm. 'We're having an emotional moment here. Keep QPR out of it.'

'OK.' John reached out for Abi's hand. 'OK.'

Silence fell for a second. Abi looked at her son, promising silently never to let him down again. She would be here. She would help him if she could.

Finally she spoke. 'Of course, don't think this gets you out of giving us grandchildren.' She folded her arms. 'I may not know much about science, but I do know that you can still have kids.'

Seb's grin was back. 'Don't I get a say in that?'

'No.' She shook her head. 'And you'd better have a wedding too. I have dancing to do. And a playlist to make.'

'OK, OK.' He shifted and winced in pain. 'Shit. I forgot. I'm at your mercy. And . . .'

'Yes?' She smiled at him and at John. At the three of them together.

'You're great company and everything, but please can you get me an iPhone charger? I'm a millennial. Not having a phone is like not having blood in my veins.' He pressed his palms together, pleading. 'Pretty please?'

She attempted a frown but knew that her happiness was shining through. 'Only if you promise me a wedding.'

'Mum. I've only just realised I'm gay; give me a second or two before you start pushing me down the aisle.' He was blushing now.

She knew what that meant.

'Is there someone you like?'

'Mum.' He held up one hand.

'There is!' She tracked back through the conversation. 'Is it this Marc guy?'

He shook his head. 'Please. Stop. I'm in plaster and I'm on painkillers. It's not a fair fight.'

'OK.' She sighed regretfully. 'But this isn't over, you know.' She got up and picked up her bag.

'Where are you going?' John stood up too.

'To get a charger for Seb. Then the inquisition can continue.' She grinned.

'You can go too, Dad.' Seb nodded. 'I promise I won't think up any more dramatic announcements while you're gone.'

'You'd better not.' John put his jacket on. 'We don't want to add a cardiac arrest to our hospital collection.'

As they left the ward and walked down the corridor, Abi turned to him. 'Are you OK? About what Seb told us?'

'Yes. Surprised, but . . .' He shrugged. 'I just want him to be happy.'

'Me too.'

'I just hope things aren't harder for him now.'

'I think he'll make the best of things.' Her heart jumped as he held out a hand and took hers. 'Do you want to get a coffee?'

'Here?' She arched an eyebrow as she looked at the tired red tables in the café just along the corridor from the ward.

'Sure.' He ran a hand through his hair. 'Hospitals are our speciality, after all.'

'They are. We should write a guidebook. But first let's get Seb a charger at the shop, or I think he might well and truly go crazy.'

John nodded. 'Good plan.'

'Then coffee, OK?'

'OK.'

She noticed they were still holding hands.

She noticed that she liked it.

'Get a move on.' She pushed him towards the lift, breaking their grip and freeing herself from feelings that she didn't want to think about. Feelings that had probably come far too late.

★　　★　　★

'He seems pretty happy.' John took a sip of his pint.

'Yep.' Abi nodded, pleased by how sure she felt. When they had left him on the ward just now, their son had been glued to his phone while devouring the M&S sandwiches they had brought him. 'I think telling us must have been one of the hardest parts.'

'Shit.' John picked up a Frazzle and popped it in his mouth. 'Doesn't say much for our parenting skills, does it?'

'No.' Abi felt a pang of sadness as she sipped her red wine. 'I think we've been a bit preoccupied.'

'Yeah. Too busy fighting to notice what he was going through.' John shook his head. 'It's not exactly making me feel proud, you know?'

'Me neither.' Abi sighed and leant her elbow on the small wooden table between them. 'Do you think we'll ever feel like we know what we're doing?'

John shook his head. 'No. Given everything that's happened recently, I think it's safe to say that life is one massive blag.'

'I agree.'

'You do?'

'Yes.' She played with the stem of her glass.

'It's been a while since I heard you say that.'

Their eyes met and her body temperature seemed to rise several degrees. She forced herself to look away. Hope was dangerous.

'Can I ask you a question, John?'

'Anything.' He crunched more Frazzles.

She steeled herself. 'When did you know? That we were over?'

He stopped chewing and stared her right in the eyes. 'I still don't know that.'

'You don't?' She could see the honesty on his face. 'Then

why did you never want to touch me? To hold me?' She hated how needy she sounded, but she had to carry on. 'I thought you didn't fancy me any more.'

'I'm so sorry. I never meant to make you feel like that.' He sat back in his chair, pinching the bridge of his nose between his fingers. 'But everything was such a mess and I was so ashamed and I had no one to talk to.'

'You had me.'

'You'd just got your life back! What kind of a guy would I have been if I'd moaned on at you about the company you had helped me to start? Doing that shitty job to keep a regular salary coming in? I wanted you to enjoy your second chance. To do the things you wanted to, and instead I landed you back in your mum's kitchen being told where to put the tea towels.' He fiddled with his coaster. 'I hated myself, Abi. And it was easier to go out and try to rescue things than to look you in the eye. You were so damn forgiving. It was awful.'

'You'd have preferred me to shout at you?'

'Yes.' He pressed his lips into a line. 'That would have been easier. It's what I deserved.'

'But you didn't deliberately screw things up. And it wasn't all your fault. People defaulted. Rachel stole clients. You can't blame it all on yourself, especially when you were trying to help me to stay alive. You were doing it for me.'

He shook his head. 'Yes. And no. Yes, I wanted to help you to get better if I could, but really that was for me. I needed you. I loved you. Noah was gone and the two of you and Seb – you three were my roots. My people. I knew how much it hurt when one of you went and I couldn't let it happen again.'

He glanced at her face and then away. 'I still email him, Abi. Noah. When I'm messed up and confused.'

'You do?'

'Yes.' He shifted in his seat. 'And I know it's pathetic. But I still do it because I can't talk to anyone like I talked to him.' He looked at her and something in her unfurled. 'Apart from you.'

His hand was lying on the table and she dared herself to reach out and take it.

'Apart from me.' She nodded.

'I'm so sorry.'

'Me too.' Her mouth was dry. 'Me too.'

A girl walked over to the old-fashioned jukebox in the corner of the pub, giggling over her shoulder to her friends clustered around a table. She inserted a coin and Abi laughed as she heard the music start.

'"Don't Stop Me Now". Talk about a sign.'

'A sign of what?' The hope on his face made her pulse quicken.

'A sign that it's time for you to see my new flat.' She pulled him to his feet. 'Fancy a walk?'

'Definitely.'

They shared a smile.

'Race you.' She sprinted ahead of him to the door, everything in her glowing when he caught her up and put his hand in hers.

The two of them walked down the Cowley Road.

'This is it.' She stood on the step and waited. Then his arms were round her waist and he was leaning in to kiss her. She closed her eyes. One beat. Two. When he stopped, everything in her wanted to scream 'more'.

His eyes were full of concern. 'Do you think this is a good idea?'

She was aching for his lips on hers. 'Oh for God's sake, of course I do.' She could feel the June breeze on her neck.

She could hear a bus rumbling down the road. She could feel the warmth of him next to her and knew that she wanted nothing more than to get him inside. To wrap herself around him. To remember how he felt and how he tasted.

She reached up and kissed him. Slow. Deep. True.

'See?'

'Yeah.' His voice was husky. 'I see.'

'Thank God for that.' She grinned. 'I was going to whirl my bra around my head, but I thought maybe that would be a step too far.'

'Never.' He dropped light kisses on her neck as she scrabbled to unlock the door. 'Never. Ever. A step too far.'

'Great.' She smiled. 'Then let's go.'

'Yes.' He tripped over the loose carpet on the stairs. Caught himself.

She giggled. 'That's a trap I set for all the hordes of men who come to seduce me.'

'Is it?' He nodded. 'No wonder the hospital is so full.'

She took his hand and practically dragged him up the rest of the stairs. Everything in her wanted this. Everything in her wanted him. She didn't care about the past – she could only think about the here and now. This man. This night.

When she reached her front door, she stopped, confused.

The door was unlocked. Weird.

She pushed it open and stepped inside. She smelt garlic and lemon. The flat was lit by enough candles to cook a hog roast. The oven was on. There was a bottle of wine and two glasses on the small table.

Oh God.

With dread clutching at every nerve, she looked at the figure by the window.

No.

He hadn't.

But he had.

Steve turned. Black shirt, eager eyes.

No.

'Abi. I charmed the landlady to get in here. Played the romantic-boyfriend card.' His eyes crinkled. 'I thought I'd surprise you. After our kiss I . . .'

She turned, hoping somehow to keep John out. To stop him seeing.

Too late.

'Oh my God.' He was deathly pale.

'John. Steve is just leaving.'

'Steve? *The* Steve?' The hurt on his face was unbearable.

'Yes. But it's not how it looks.' She grabbed his arm, but he shook her off. 'I didn't invite him. I didn't know he'd be here.'

'Obviously not.' John was visibly shrinking, walking backwards away from her as if she was a contagious disease. 'Oh my God. I believed you, Abi. I thought that . . .' He clapped his hand to his forehead. 'What a dickhead I am.'

'You're not.' She had no idea how to make him stay. She had no words. No power. 'Look, I'll get rid of him and—'

'Charming.' Steve walked towards them.

'Shut up, Steve!' She didn't move her eyes from John.

'No. Don't get rid of him.' His eyes were bleak. 'I'll go. I think it's better that way, don't you?'

No. She didn't. Her heart was walking out of the room, leaving her with too many candles and a man who didn't know her at all.

'John, I—'

'Goodbye, Abi.'

The last sound she heard was him walking down the stairs. The last until she started to cry.

Seb

'So basically this is just a ruse for making people bring you free drinks, right?'

'Yeah. That's right.' Seb put his hand up to shield his eyes from the glare of the sun. Yes. It really was Marc. Despite the pain in his leg, it was hard not to smile. Keep cool, Seb. Breathe. 'I'm so desperate not to move that I got three metal pins inserted in my thigh, knackered my bike and made myself totally dependent on my mum for two months.' He shook his head. 'Not to mention the whole dicing with death thing.' He sighed. 'Now. Open that can, please. I'm not allowed any more painkillers yet, so it's time for a little something else.'

'Should you be mixing it up like that?' Marc yanked the ring pull off with a satisfying hiss.

'Are you my mum?' Seb stuck his hand out and waited.

'All right.' Marc whistled between his teeth. 'Touchy.'

'Yeah, well.' Seb winced as yet another part of his body reminded him how far he was from being better. 'This is what I'm like when I'm not allowed to play football.'

'Wow. It's going to be a fun summer for you, then.' Marc leant back on his elbows and stared contentedly at the figures on the improvised pitch in front of them.

'Yep.' Part of Seb was hoping that Marc might like to share it.

'You know what I think?' Marc flicked a ladybird off

his jeans. 'I think you did it so you could lie around and talk to me. I think you're glad you can't go over there and kick some goals, or whatever it is you footballers do.'

Seb looked at him in disbelief. 'Oh come on. You must know what the correct bloody term is. I mean, I know you're not into it, but surely somebody forced you to do PE at school or something?' He looked at Marc's toned chest through his tight T-shirt. 'You're in pretty good shape.' Talk about understatement. 'I think you have some secret weights stored underneath your bed and you're up at five every morning giving it some.'

'Nope.' Marc shook his head. 'This is all nature's work.' He grinned and Seb's heart accelerated. 'Nature and nachos.'

Seb smiled. Marc had been one of his first visitors at the hospital and he had been there most days. Something was building between them and Seb couldn't wait to see where it led. 'Wow. You should sell that amazing dietary regime to the Olympic squad.'

'Maybe.' Marc shrugged, a smile tugging at the corner of his mouth. 'Or maybe I'll just stay here getting a tan.'

'Sounds like a good idea to me.' Seb took a long swig of beer as his old mates continued to kick the ball around. Most of them had come to the hospital to see him, but things still weren't quite the same. He pushed away a pang of sadness. They were all starting at uni or apprenticeships soon, while he would be doing his retakes at the shit college down the road from his mum's flat. He hadn't got his results yet, but he knew. Just as he knew that next year he would do himself proud.

A fly had landed on Marc's bleached hair. Seb nearly reached out to flick it away, but didn't quite dare. 'So you're never going to want to talk about who's going to win the Premiere League?'

'Nope.' Marc shook his head. 'No way. Don't even think about it. OK?'

'I think I get the message.' Seb grinned. 'I don't miss much, me.'

'If you say so.' Marc held his gaze and Seb felt a blush rising in his cheeks.

He jerked his eyes away and sipped his beer.

'What are you doing this summer?' He concentrated fiercely on the game.

'I don't know. Got a job, obviously. Catering.' Marc put his can down. 'But apart from that, I think I might see what my ex-next-door-neighbour's doing. Maybe tag along with him?'

'What, Mrs Sully?'

'Yeah, that's right.' Marc's green eyes gleamed. 'I just can't get enough of her and her church lunch-club friends.'

'Sure.' Seb nodded.

'And you?'

'Bugger all.' Seb looked down at his cast. 'Apparently. Though at least I earned enough to renew my Netflix subscription.'

'What's up first? *Better Call Saul?*'

'I think I'll start with that.' Seb glanced at his companion. 'Fancy joining me?'

'Yeah.' Marc nodded. 'I'd like that.'

They shared a smile.

'Are you going to ignore Dan for ever?' Marc pointed across at a figure on the other side of the pitch.

'Well, he seems pretty set on ignoring me.' Seb looked the other way. 'I don't get it. He's treating me like I've got the plague just because I'm gay.' He pulled grass out of the ground with unnecessary venom.

'Well stop being a twat and just talk to him about it.'

'No.'

'Why? Are you chicken?'

'No.' Seb shook his head. 'Definitely not.'

Marc looked at him with amusement. 'You're so old-school.'

'I'm not.' Seb felt a rush of indignation. 'I'm just pissed off.'

'Well I was pissed off aged twelve.' Marc's voice was low. 'When I came out, my dad told me it was just a phase and my mum started ringing every psychologist in the phone book.'

'Oh.' Seb thought of his own parents. The brief struggle on their faces, which had been quickly conquered by love. He realised how lucky he was, despite the broken leg and the fact that his mum had chosen a flat that was up a very narrow flight of stairs.

And of course he was lucky because of the boy sitting next to him, the sunlight highlighting his white-blond hair. Looking at Marc made him happy. Made him brave.

'OK.' He began the very long process of standing up.

Dan was walking away now. Damn.

Seb got hold of a crutch but was unable to lever himself up. 'Shit.' To make matters worse, he knocked his beer over. 'Bollocks!'

'Need a hand?' Marc was up on his feet and put his hands underneath Seb's armpits to support him as he rose. 'Just as well you're so hot.' His breath was warm on Seb's neck. 'Or I wouldn't be so happy to help.'

'Just as well *you're* so hot.' Seb grinned. 'Or I wouldn't be letting you.'

'Why? Don't you like me nursing you? Because I can knock you back down again if you like.' Marc took the crutch in his hand. 'Wouldn't take a second.'

'No thanks.' Seb tucked the crutches under his armpits. 'I'll just be a minute. Don't go anywhere.' He felt a sudden rush of panic. 'You won't, will you?'

'No.' Marc turned back and sat down on the grass. 'I'll just enjoy some more of this.' He tapped the can with his finger. 'And understand a little less of that.' He pointed at the game.

'See you in a bit.' Seb summoned his strength and started to move. Any weights training he had ever done had not helped him to move any more easily with these bloody crutches. Even on dry, flat ground like this his armpits were screeching with pain within seconds, and it would take him about a year to get to where Dan had been five minutes ago. His breath was quickening, but he had to try. After the summer they would go their separate ways, and he didn't want to let all those years of friendship end without some kind of discussion.

Dan looked over his shoulder as he reached the cricket pavilion. Seb saw him registering that his old friend was wobbling across the grass and deciding whether or not to go up the steps and disappear inside. Then he turned and sat on the bench that ran along the front of the building. Seb knew it was his equivalent of a white flag. Dan dug his hands deep in his pockets and laid his head back against the wood until Seb had heaved his way across to him.

'All right?' Seb collapsed beside him, leaning his crutches against the arm and wiping the sweat from his brow.

'Yeah.' Dan kept his eyes closed, the sun lighting the freckles across his cheeks. 'Not bad, considering.'

'Considering what?'

Dan shrugged. 'Considering my dad's moving in with his boyfriend, who insists on calling me "Danny boy".'

'Shit.'

'The only good thing is I'll be at uni soon. It's that or emigration.' Dan checked his phone and Seb could see a series of texts lighting up the screen. 'Or I might head up to Edinburgh for a bit. Work at the festival or something.' He smiled. 'At least it's far enough away that I won't have to listen to Dad's shit.'

'I'm sorry, mate.'

'It's all right.' Dan shrugged. 'No big deal.'

Seb didn't mess around. 'Are you sorry too?'

Dan folded his arms. 'What for?'

'For being such a dick these past couple of months.'

Dan's lower lip jutted forward.

'And for taking out your shit about your dad on me.'

Silence.

Then Dan nodded. 'Sorry, mate.'

Something in Seb lightened. The silence between them lengthened, the silence of summer bike rides or nervous underage pub queues.

Dan glanced at Seb. 'So, are you and that Marc guy an item?'

Seb couldn't help grinning. 'I hope so.'

'He likes his boys injured, then?' Dan reached out and tapped Seb's cast.

'I think I've got a bit more going for me than that.' Seb tipped his head back too, enjoying the warmth on his face.

'What, your incredible sense of humour?'

'Yeah.' Seb nodded. 'And then there's my rugged good looks.'

'You always were an arrogant prick.'

'Yes.' Seb nudged Dan with his elbow. 'But it takes one to know one.'

'Fuck off.' Seb could hear the smile beneath Dan's words. The smile that told him the two of them were OK now.

He knew nothing more would ever be said. That wasn't how it worked. This was about his friend pulling two Coronas out of his backpack and offering one to Seb. Hurts were forgotten. Insults were dust.

'How about you? Got anyone on your radar?' Seb opened his beer and took a huge gulp.

'Yes, as it happens.' His friend looked very pleased with himself, waving his bottle as he talked. 'Do you remember that hot waitress in Cabana's?'

Seb scrolled back through their nights out in that banging pit of a club. The taste of Jägerbombs. The smell of sweat.

'The blonde?'

'No, you fool. The one with black hair.'

Seb shook his head.

'Dressed like Xena the Warrior Princess?'

'Nope.'

'With the massive tits?'

'Wrong again.' Seb shrugged.

'God, you really are gay.' Dan laughed. 'Well, it's her.'

'Right.' Silence fell as they both spent a bit more time with their beers. 'Have you been out with her yet?'

'Still messaging. But soon.' Dan's phone pinged again. 'Very soon. We're talking dates now. We are launch-ready.'

'If you say so.'

'I do.' Dan drummed his fingers on the bottle. 'Is this weird?'

'What? Drinking beer on a bench? No.' Seb shook his head. 'I'd say we're pretty much experts.'

'Shut it.' Dan punched him in the arm and beer threatened to spray all over his plaster. 'You know what I mean. Is it weird us chatting about girls?'

'God, no.' Seb shook his head. 'I've been there, remember? Starting with that mad one in Year 7.'

'Keisha?'

'Yep.' Seb winced. 'She kissed me so hard she bit my lip.'

'Oh God, yeah.' Dan nodded. 'And I went out with her mate Tilly until she ran off with that kid on the gymnastics team.' He thought for a second. 'By the way, I'd probably rather not get into it about guys if that's OK. Who's hot. Who's not. You know.'

'Got it.' Seb put his can down on the arm of the bench and accidentally knocked his crutches over. 'Shit.'

'Want these?' Jess appeared and picked them up. 'Hopalong?'

'Hilarious.' He sat up. 'Hi, Jess.'

'Hi.' She leant down and kissed him on the cheek and he inhaled the sweet smell of CK. She beckoned to a man standing behind her, trying to look like he was doing something important on his phone. 'This is Craig.'

'Hello.' Silence fell as Seb and Dan managed to come out with absolutely no conversation whatsoever. Standard.

'Hi.' Craig slid his phone into the pocket of his jeans. 'How's that Corona going down?'

'Not bad.'

Jess took Craig's hand. 'Fancy a smoke?'

Seb nodded.

'OK.' Dan stood up. 'Let's head over there. Behind the bushes.'

'The usual spot?' Jess couldn't stop smiling as she led the way.

'Yeah. The usual spot.' Seb tucked his crutches under his arms again. He started after Jess and Craig, but then stopped. Did an incredibly slow twelve-point turn. Headed in the opposite direction. 'I'm just going to get someone.'

'OK.' They were halfway across the pitch by now.

Seb worked his way back to Marc, who was lying flat on his back staring at the sky. Around him kids were kicking footballs and drinking from bottles. Someone was playing Sigala on a boom box by the tree, and Seb could feel the bass through his toes. This was it. This was summer.

Even with a cast and crutches, it felt pretty good.

'Fancy heading over there?'

Marc lifted his head. 'Over where?'

Seb didn't exactly want to make an announcement, so he just pointed towards the bushes. 'Do you want to head over and . . . I don't know.' He felt suddenly foolish. 'Meet my friends? Properly, I mean?'

'And why would I want to do that?' Marc's voice held a note of challenge.

'Because I'd like you to.'

'Why?' Marc wasn't going to let this one go.

'Because . . .' *Say it, Seb. Say. It.*

'Because I like you.'

Marc cupped his hand behind his ear. 'I'm sorry. I didn't quite hear that. Could you just say it again?'

Seb thought for a moment. Maybe it was the sun. Maybe it was the beer. But it was time to speak out. 'Because I REALLY LIKE YOU.'

'That's better.' Marc's voice was cool, but his eyes shone. 'That's much better.' He stood up, and now his face was on a level with Seb's. 'Much, much better.'

For a heart-stopping second, Seb thought that Marc would kiss him. Hoped he would kiss him. Hoped with every fibre of his being. But Marc just leant close to his ear and whispered, 'I like you too.'

Then he took Seb's hand, his palm cool and reassuring, and looped Seb's arm around his shoulder. And together they made their way across the cricket pitch, weaving amidst the Frisbees and the footballs and the whoops and the cries. Nobody noticed them. Nobody gave them a second glance.

But with every stumbling step, Seb could feel a jagged piece of his confusing world finally slotting into place. Because to him, this moment was everything he had ever dreamed of.

Abi

'Do you remember the time you fancied that pastry chef?'

'Which pastry chef?' Abi reached for another grape, trying to ignore the rumble of disquiet in her stomach.

'Oh my God, I can't believe you've forgotten about him. The guy with the red hair and the Irish accent?' Lesley's eyes were wide. 'You ruined one whole episode of *Ab Fab* raving about him.' She cut another slice of cheese. 'He had a nose ring and you were seriously contemplating getting one to match.' She took a bite and sat back on the sofa, grinning contentedly. 'Unfortunately you ate so many of his pastries that you weren't exactly giving it your best game on the flirting front.' She laughed. 'I remember you splitting your leather trousers at that shit club in town.'

'Doogies?'

'Ha!' Lesley nodded. 'That's the one. The one where we got locked in the toilet for an hour once and we were too pissed to figure out how to climb out.'

'Well, I was puking, so I wasn't really capable of making escape plans.' Abi swallowed. She pulled her knees up to her chin, hoping that would stop the pain in her stomach. It had only been a couple of hours. It would probably go away.

She took another sip of peppermint tea, not that the first three cups had done any good. She tried to ignore the whispering in her mind as to what it might mean.

'Oh yeah.' Lesley grinned. 'You'd had too many tequilas, as I remember it.'

'Probably.'

'Are you having any of this cheese?' Lesley pushed the board towards her. 'Or not?'

Abi shook her head. 'Definitely not.'

'Are you sure? It's amazing.'

Abi forced a smile onto her face. 'Yeah.' She nodded. 'You have it. I ate quite a lot of it before you arrived.'

'Typical.' Lesley grinned. 'I suppose I'll just have to nobly polish off the rest then.' She picked up a hunk of Brie and bit into it. 'So much for my latest regime.'

'It's all good protein. Very Atkins.' Abi pressed her tummy with her hand. *No. That didn't help.*

'If you ignore the fat content, yes. Still, it's better than that terrible 5:2 diet.' Lesley grimaced. 'I was on it for a month, and those two days a week were dreaded by all who surrounded me. One of my colleagues threatened to leave the firm, it got so bad.'

'I'm surprised your desk wasn't covered in resignations.' Abi shuddered. 'That Duke of Edinburgh trip when we left our Mars bars behind – I honestly thought I might have to kill you to stop your moaning.'

'Starvation doesn't suit me.' Lesley underlined the point by merrily popping the entire portion of quince jelly into her mouth and following it with the remains of the Caerphilly.

'No.' Abi shook her head. 'You're a bit like Seb. Despite being unable to run around at the moment, he still manages to eat me out of house and home. I'm surprised the cheese was still here this evening, to be honest.'

'Well thank God it was.' Lesley patted her stomach. 'I went running this morning, so I've earned it.'

Abi was worrying the cushion between her fingers. Normally a chat with Lesley could make her forget anything. Labour pains. Exam results. Her friend had talked her through them all. But not this.

Today her body felt different. Untrustworthy. Every rumble was a potential sign. Every ache a red flag.

'Abi?'

She blinked. 'What?'

'I just asked you a question.'

'You did?'

'Yes.' Lesley frowned. 'And is it OK with you?'

Abi shook herself back into the conversation. *Indigestion. That was all it was.*

'Is what OK with me?'

'Rob taking me out on a date, of course.' Lesley was staring at her, eyes narrowed. 'Abi, what's going on?'

'Nothing. Nothing.' Abi didn't want to say a word about her worries. She knew where those words might lead. So she smiled and shook her head. 'I was just thinking about the shop.'

'Oh, and there was me thinking you were actually listening to what I was telling you.'

'Sorry.'

Lesley stared at her. 'So. Me and Rob?'

Abi pushed her worries to one side. 'Has he finally managed to ask you out then?'

'What do you mean, finally?'

'Oh my God, Lesley. You can't tell me you had no idea he liked you?'

Lesley's face was so surprised, it was as if Abi was talking a foreign language.

Abi clapped her hand to her forehead. 'Wow. Your radar really is malfunctioning.'

Lesley brushed a crumb of cheese off her lap. 'Well, where were the signs? I saw no signs.'

Abi giggled. 'I suppose they're not that straightforward. I've had a lifetime of watching Rob. When he had a crush on his maths teacher, he demonstrated it by failing to do any of her homework.'

'Interesting approach.'

'And with you he showed his affection by actively avoiding you at parties, and then endlessly staring at you when you were busy talking to other people.'

'Oh.' Lesley pushed the cheeseboard to the other side of the coffee table and sat back again. 'I see.' She crossed her legs and poured more wine. 'It's not a particularly effective approach, is it?'

'Nope.' Abi shifted again as the pain knifed in her stomach. *Come on, peppermint tea.* 'It might explain why Rob has been single for so long.'

'Mmm.' Lesley licked a crumb off her finger. 'Well the other day we were talking in the shop while I was waiting for you, and it turns out that when he gets going he's got quite good chat.'

'Yeah?' Abi smiled. She was happy for her brother. She just hoped that he managed not to panic when confronted with the prospect of an actual night out with the woman he held such a candle for. She prayed he wouldn't start talking about his windowsill herb garden or how long he had owned his trainers – neither of which was exactly winning for the fairer sex.

Another pain. Shit. She could feel panic pushing her pulse into overdrive. She couldn't bear to think about what might happen if she called the clinic – it would be like stepping back into that freezing cancer tunnel with no guiding lights and no exit. A tunnel that led her away from Seb and Rob and Lesley and this flat and into the world in which she had always felt alone, no matter how many people were around her. There were arms to hold her, but it was her body. Her pain.

She swallowed down her fear.

'Did Rob actually ask you out?'

'Well, kind of.' A smile played around Lesley's lips. 'He asked me if I wanted to see *Learning to Drive*. I said yes. Then he kind of ambled his way round to suggesting we might go together.' Her eyes were shining and she was winding a strand of hair around her finger.

Abi smiled. 'Hallelujah. At last.'

Lesley snapped back into her normal sarcastic mode. 'Well, he might be a terrible kisser, so don't get too excited yet.'

'Ewwwwwwww.' Abi shuddered. 'That's my brother you're talking about. Stop that talk of kissing now, my friend.'

'Sorry.' Lesley leant forward and put her hand on Abi's arm. 'Is this too weird? Talking about him?'

'The kissing bit – yes. The rest of it? No.' Abi sighed. 'What does Hope make of it?'

'Well of course he's an artist, so she's over the moon. And she's so busy getting hyped about going to uni in Manchester that frankly I'm not entirely sure she cares.' Lesley squeezed Abi's arm. 'Anyway, let's stop talking about that and talk about you.'

Abi would rather not.

'Are you OK, after . . .' Lesley tailed off.

'After John left?'

'Yes.' Lesley's voice was low. 'I'm so sorry, Abi. You should have called me sooner.'

Abi felt the tears starting again. Damn it. 'Bloody Steve. He had the cheek to get really shitty with me when I kicked him out. Said I'd been leading him on.'

'Once a dick, always a dick.'

'Yeah.' Abi bit her lip. 'I couldn't believe it. I mean, it turns out his girlfriend's still living with him, for God's sake. I was actually stupid enough to go to his place to talk to him the next day, and there she was, all mascara and perfume.' She shuddered. 'I am such a loser.'

'No. He's the loser.'

'Not just him. You were right about the whole thing after all.' Abi stretched her legs out in front of her. The pain was gone. There. She shouldn't have panicked. It had only been wind.

'Lucky guess.' Her friend wrinkled her nose dismissively.

'Don't bullshit me, Lesley. You and I don't do that.'

'Except when you wore that hideous red dress to the school disco. I lied then and told you it suited you.'

'I knew you hated it anyway.'

Lesley glugged some wine. 'I never was good at acting.'

Abi sipped her tea. 'You think I crossed a line with Steve, don't you? Even before we kissed?'

'Yes.' Her friend nodded, her blue eyes serious. 'But I think I was a bit harsh. All that stuff I said.'

'I think you were spot on.'

'Really?'

'Yes.' Abi exhaled. 'Much as I hate to admit it.'

Lesley patted her on the arm. 'Don't be too hard on yourself. But I wish you two had made it. You were always one of *those* couples. The ones people always want to talk to so that a little bit of their magic rubs off on them.' She paused as she took a bite of cheese. 'But after everything you'd just been through – those months and months of you being so sick and not knowing how you'd be from one day to the next – after all that, I honestly thought you two were bulletproof.'

'Apparently not.' Abi shook her head. 'I don't think we knew how to be normal any more. And with all the business stuff too, all that pressure . . .' She felt a lump in her throat. 'It was all too much.'

It sounded so pathetic. She would take a long time to forgive herself for letting things slip through her fingers.

'Yeah. I know.' Lesley had taken her hand and was stroking it with her thumb.

'The Steve stuff was bad, sure, and I got carried away. I let him turn my head.' Abi bit her lip. 'But the fact is that I'm not sure John and I knew how to have a future.'

'What on earth do you mean?'

Abi stared at the swirling purple lampshade she had put up the week before. 'We got so used to there being no tomorrow. We forgot about the everyday shit. The washing in the basket. Changing light bulbs. Filling up the car. Balancing the books. Emptying the bins. If anything killed us, it was that.'

'That and the year of shit you've been through.'

'Yep.' Abi arched an eyebrow. 'Or no shit, in my case.'

'You're making cancer jokes.' Lesley clapped her on the shoulder. 'You are coming on.'

Abi nearly opened her mouth to confide in her friend, but stopped herself. She had just got used to living a normal life. Sara Bareilles was playing on the speakers. She was going to a gig next week. She was booking ahead and widening her horizons. She was running the shop and she had her own place, paying the rent every month with her own money. She had talked to the Open University about psychology courses. There was no way she could bear to risk all that. Not yet. Not when it still felt so sweet.

She sighed. 'Do you know what it was that I liked about Steve?'

'Other than his poetic curls?'

Abi whacked her friend on the leg. 'Yes.'

'Then you've got me. I have no idea.'

'It was that at first he didn't know I'd ever had cancer. He didn't see me the way other people do.'

'Meaning?'

'To him I was just Abi: the girl with the mixtapes and the duffle bag, only with more lines on my face and slightly better clothes. To John – maybe to you – I'm a liability. Someone to worry about. And I hate that.'

'There are worse things than being worried about, you know. It's the flip side of being loved.' Lesley finished her wine. 'And God knows, you are loved.' She held Abi's eyes for a second. 'Though Lord knows why, when you have such a shit sofa.' She rubbed her back. 'Where the hell did you get this from? The dump?'

'IKEA, dickhead. And you can bugger off if you don't like it.'

'No. Wine left. Must stay.' Lesley poured more into her glass, then paused, putting the bottle back down. 'Well done, Abi.'

Abi felt the tears threaten again. 'What for?'

'For keeping going.' Lesley arched an eyebrow. 'Do you think you'll be OK? Without John?'

'I'll get there.' Abi sighed. Considering how little they had spoken for the last few months, it was ridiculous how much she missed him. She missed his toothbrush in its place, his aftershave left open on the bathroom shelf. She missed the sight of him bent over the sports section or swearing at the radio when QPR were playing.

His absence was an aching hole in her life, but she felt a new determination. She wasn't going to waste these days. These months. This second chance.

There was the sound of a door banging and a slow tread on the stairs.

'Is that Seb?' Lesley smiled. 'With his gorgeous new man?'

'Sounds like it.' Abi felt herself relax for the first time. Seb's happiness was her lifeline now.

'Hope says he's lush,' Lesley said. 'Trust Seb. Doesn't go for the losers like we all did when we were eighteen. Heads straight for the potential male model.'

'I know.' Abi stretched her arms over her head. 'And Marc even quotes poetry too.'

'Sickening.' Lesley nestled more deeply into the cushions. 'Well, I'm definitely not going anywhere now.'

'Good.' Abi stood up. 'Back in a minute.'

'Cool.' Lesley was fluffing out her hair. Abi refrained from pointing out that neither of the boys was remotely interested in seeing it all tousled like that. Lesley would figure that one out for herself.

As she closed the bathroom door behind her, the pain skewered her again.

'Shit.' She locked the door and walked to the toilet, praying to every god she could think of as she sat down. Her breath was tight in her chest and her mind resounded to a thousand screams.

She forced her breathing to slow down, whispering to herself. 'Don't be a drama queen. You're just doing a wee.'

She finished and stood back up, glancing down before she flushed.

What she saw made the world slam to a halt.

She looked again, and yes, there they were. Just like

before. Dots of red stark against the white of the toilet bowl.

Grabbing the towel rail, she held on for dear life before sinking to the floor and resting her head on her knees. This couldn't be happening. Not yet. She hadn't even had a year. Not one year.

She couldn't cry. She knelt on the floor, head down, fists clenched, for what seemed like hours.

Outside she heard the laughter of Seb, Marc and Lesley. Her heart clutched with love. So much love. She didn't want to do this to them again. She didn't want to go out and say the words that would turn their evening into a nightmare. She had done that. She had survived it. This was meant to be her time at last.

There was a tap on the door.

'Abi? Are you OK?'

'I'm fine, Lesley. I'll be out in a sec.'

And she knew then. She knew she couldn't do it.

She knew she was going to keep this to herself.

She forced a smile and went out to join them, her heart plunging at the thought of what was coming next.

July

'Sanctus' from *Requiem* by Gabriel Fauré

This one's for life. For the best of it. For the mornings when you wake up and smell coffee and brioche and actually have time to enjoy them before heading off to whatever awaits you. For all the matches where you've scored a goal, Seb. For all the amazing parties you've taken me to, John, but also for the nights where we just sat on a bench in the garden, drinking wine and debating how on earth there is anyone left to kill in *Midsomer Murders*. For Mum's roast lamb and the rare occasions I managed to help her out in her Monday-night University Challenge extravaganza. For the times Dad took me to the record shop for one hour that became five. For Rob and me hiding behind the sofa to try to watch *EastEnders* and forgetting our legs were sticking out. For Lesley and her cocktail jugs and her obsession with Little Mix, though even I have to admit that 'Secret Love Song' is pretty damn brilliant. For musical finales, and Oasis and that Green Day song that I can't listen to without crying. For swimming in the sea and sitting on kitchen tables at parties, and to there always being one more glass in the bottle. Life, I bloody love you. I have no intention of leaving you. I don't care what the devil cancer has to say about it. I'm here to stay.

Abi

'Why are you looking so gloomy, Abi?'

Her mum wiped the sweat from her brow. Despite the fact that the sun had been shining for well over two hours, the heating was still on. Abi knew it would be switched off within seconds of her departure, just as she knew that her mum would never offer her anything to drink except green tea. Right now she was probably bang on point, though Abi wasn't going to tell her that. Not until she knew for sure. She felt a swoop in her tummy at the thought of the call she had made earlier. The calm voice at the other end, becoming slower and kinder as her own tears took hold.

She felt her dad's eyes on her face and rapidly walked to the window.

'Is it because of John?' Her mum put her dad's mug down in front of him. 'You could still go and see him, you know. I'm sure you could work things out.'

Abi had decided not to share the Steve saga. She took a deep breath.

'It's too late, Mum. And when a guy like John chooses to leave, there's not a lot you can do about it.'

Her mum screwed the lid onto a jar of chutney with unnecessary venom. 'I don't understand it.' The jar was unceremoniously dumped in the cupboard and the door slammed shut.

345

'Things had run their course.'

'What a lot of nonsense.' Her mum sliced the tops off a bunch of carrots as viciously as if she was manning a guillotine during the French Revolution. 'You two should have tried harder.'

Abi sighed. There was precisely zero chance of her mum ever really understanding what had happened, and it was probably better that way.

'Anyway, I'm not gloomy, Mum.' She leant her elbows on the kitchen counter. 'I'm just a bit tired.'

'Tired? Why? Have you been overdoing it?' Instantly her mum snapped into nurse mode. Any second now she would be whipping out her thermometer or reaching for the paracetamol pack she kept permanently in her battered black handbag.

'No reason.' Abi spoke in her calmest voice. 'It's just been a busy week, that's all.'

'Hmmm.' Her mum's eyes raked over her face. Abi's acting skills had clearly improved, because her mum appeared to believe her.

'And Dad, I have news.'

His spoon stirred slowly round. 'You do?'

'Yes.' She nodded. 'Rob and I would like to buy the shop from you. We've sold a lot of stock recently, and we think we can make it work, with his painting money too. We'd like to go into partnership, if you're happy to sell, that is.'

His spoon stopped. Tapped against the side of the mug.

'Ahhhh.' He sat back and rested his hands on his knees. 'So that's what the pair of you have been cooking up. I thought there was some kind of conspiracy going on.'

Abi smiled. 'Yes. I remember you told me last year that you two wanted to move away – go somewhere warmer

346

and relax for once. With Mum's arthritis and everything.' Her mum was ominously still. 'I know that the shop was holding you back. And we wanted to help. So Rob's been painting and I've been selling and things are looking good. I can show you the books if you like.'

She ignored the twist of doubt in her gut. The fear that things couldn't be tied up so neatly. That life would have yet more surprises in store when she went in for the tests next week. 'So – we're ready. You can go. We can keep Gryff's Gallery going and everyone's happy.'

'Yes.' He tilted his head as the 'Sanctus' from the Fauré *Requiem* came to an end and the Classic FM announcer introduced the next piece. Then he turned to her mum and smiled. Abi felt a rush of happiness. 'That's wonderful news, isn't it, Carol?'

'No, it isn't.' Her mum's voice was sharp, and she appeared to be trying to chop the garlic into oblivion.

Her dad looked at his wife. 'Why not?'

'You know why not. You can't just sell up. We can't leave. There's . . .' her lip was wobbling, 'paperwork. Taxes. Leases.' The knife was flashing through the air. 'We can't go anywhere.'

'But if the children can buy us out, I don't see what the problem is.'

It was time to step in.

'I think Mum's worried about me, Dad. About the cancer coming back.'

She must not give anything away. Not now. Not yet.

'Oh.' Her dad nodded. 'Of course.'

Abi shrugged. 'And I can understand that.' She was fighting to stay in control. Half of her wanted to confide in them and to cry all the tears she had been storing up these past few days. But not this time. This time she was going to make sure she set them free. No matter what might be going on inside her – what symptoms might be coming or going – she needed to make them see that it was time to leave. Time to live out the retirement of their dreams, rather than waiting for a day that might never come. The day that their daughter was safe. 'But it'll be OK, Mum.'

'No it won't.' The knife was quivering in her mum's hand and her face was wide open, all anguish and doubt. 'I couldn't be living somewhere else, with my feet up in the sun, when it hasn't even been a year yet.' She put the knife down and performed one of her bewildering about-turns. 'And we don't want the taxman coming to get us.'

Abi's voice was firm. 'He won't, Mum.'

Abi could see raw fear on her mum's face. It was the fear she had seen reflected in her own eyes in the hospital toilet mirrors when Seb was hit. The fear of a mum who had realised her child wasn't immortal.

Her mum sank her head onto her chest, leaning on the counter for support. 'It hasn't even been a year,' she repeated. 'It's not the right time.'

Abi felt tears glazing her eyes.

Stay strong. Keep going.

'Mum. I'm not sure it will ever feel like the right time.'

'What do you mean?' Her mum's body jerked into a sob. Abi gently put her hand on her shoulder. She had never known how to reach out to her mum, but now was definitely the right time to try.

She drew her close. 'They never give you the all-clear. We'll never know that it's not going to come back.' She must not think about the pain. The blood. The burden of the knowledge that was threatening to crush her.

Her mum wiped her eyes fiercely. 'Yes, but when you

get to one year, a whole year, that would mean something, wouldn't it?'

Abi knew she wasn't going to get that far. She swallowed back her own sadness and kept breathing. Kept hugging. Kept trying to make her parents believe.

Her mum continued. 'Or two years. Imagine that? Then we could think about changing things a little. We'd feel safer.'

Abi didn't know how to tell her that she couldn't ever imagine feeling safe again. Even if her pains meant nothing. Even if the tests showed that she was still cancer-free. She would be living with cancer for ever. There was no escaping it – all she could do was to keep hoping. Keep walking forward one step at a time.

And now she had to help her parents walk forward too. She tightened her arms around her mum's familiar bony shoulders, drawing her close, trying to encircle her in the love that had kept Abi herself going through all the days of treatment. The love that had held her high.

For once she knew what she wanted. She knew exactly what to say.

'Mum, you can't live like that.'

'I can.' Her mum's voice was tight. 'I can and I will.'

'No, Mum. I won't let you.' Abi squeezed her tight. 'You have to choose not to live like that. You have to choose to be free. *We* have to choose that. Because yes . . .' she was talking to herself now, 'it might come back. It might. And there's nothing I can do about it. And there's nothing you can do about it either.'

She heard her mum inhale and kept speaking. Low and calm. 'I'm doing the best I can, Mum. But we can't control this. And it's a cage, isn't it? Kidding ourselves that we can control what happens next. It's just another cage.'

'A cage?'

'Yes. It traps us.' Things were falling into place now and the words were pouring out of her. 'We think we can eat better, or drink less, or exercise more and we can keep ourselves safe. My cancer won't come back. Seb won't have another accident. None of us will ever get sick again. And we crouch, waiting, desperate to see if we're right. But living is important too. I'm so tired of living life on pause, and I'm not doing it any more, no matter what's around the corner.'

She thought of walking through those clinic doors next week and dug her nails into her palms to stop herself crying. 'And I don't want you to be on pause either. You will always worry about me, I know that. God, you worried about me even when I was at home every night eating Quavers and doing my homework. But this – waiting . . .' She was stroking her mum's hair now. 'If we wait, it means the cancer's won, and it's there every day with us stopping us doing the things we love. Things that would make us happy.'

She gently withdrew herself from her mum's arms and stared into her eyes, touching her pale cheeks as the tears slid down them. 'Stop waiting, Mum. And you too, Dad.' She glanced at him, attempting a smile. 'Though I know perfectly well that you're only doing what she tells you.'

Her dad walked over and put his arms round her. 'Guilty as charged.'

A beat. A hug. Love.

She looked at her mum again. 'Please sell this place. Let us take over the shop. Start again. There are modern inventions like aeroplanes and Skype, you know. There's no getting rid of me. Or Seb.'

'But you need us, Abi.' Her mum's eyes were softer than she had ever seen them.

'It's OK. Seb's old enough to do my DIY now.' Abi grinned and then pulled her mum close again. 'Please. Do something for you. It would make me so happy.'

'I . . .'

'Shh.' Abi hushed her, as her mum had done so many times to her. 'Shh.'

One second passed. Two. Three.

'Just think about it. That's all I ask.'

'I suppose we could get a valuation done.' Her mum's voice quavered with something like hope. 'Just to see.'

'Yes.' Abi nodded. 'Yes, I suppose you could.'

Her mum pulled away. Nodded. Wiped away her tears. 'Gryff, do you have the number for that estate agent that we met at that party last month? The one who didn't have terrible shoes?'

Abi caught her dad's eyes and he gave her a discreet thumbs-up.

Apparently her mum still had eyes in the back of her head. 'What was that for, Gryff?'

'Nothing.' Abi's dad flushed guiltily. 'I'm just pleased, that's all. Can't wait to sunbathe by our pool and annoy everyone here with my holiday tan when we come back for the test match.'

Her mum's voice had found its usual acerbic pitch again. 'Well, you'd better buy yourself some new swimming trunks first. Yours are far too revealing; we don't want to offend the neighbours.'

'Yes, Carol.' Her dad's mouth curved into a smile.

Her mum picked up the knife again, pointing it at him. 'And don't do that humouring-me voice, Gryff.'

'I won't.'

'Or that pretend-meek voice either.'

'OK.'

'Gryff!'

As the two of them settled into their familiar Sunday-lunchtime routine, Abi started to walk away, surprised when her mum reached out and squeezed her hand. Then she kissed her lingeringly on the cheek and let her go, years of love and worry engraved in her smile.

Abi gulped back her tears and walked into the garden. The roses were in full bloom, arching beside the doorway, and she stood for a moment staring at the lush yellow petals with a bee buzzing merrily around them. As she breathed in the smell of summer, a thousand memories crowded through her mind: gin and tonics on a terrace at sunset; the creak of picnic baskets full of cucumber sand-wiches and mini sausage rolls; her and Lesley attempting cartwheels after one too many Pimm's in the Parks on Lesley's thirtieth birthday.

And there were more. Seb dashing out of school for the holidays, arms raised high and a football at his feet. John taking her to Wimbledon, where they sat and drank cham-pagne as Andy Murray took the title. John taking her to Lord's with his biggest clients, only to be horrified at how little she knew – or cared – about cricket. Her summer at Glastonbury, working as a litter picker and sneaking into the backstage area when the Inspiral Carpets were playing. Such happy, happy days.

She went and sat on the bench in the centre of the lawn, drawing her feet up beneath her and staring up into the willow tree. It had been here through all the dramas. All the fighting and the tears. As she looked at the branches cascading down around her, she felt a pulse of strength. She could do this. She could cope with the couches and probing fingers and serious faces. With the discomfort. The pain. She could do it alone this time – at least until she knew what she was dealing with. She couldn't bear to hurt these people, these people who loved her so much.

She put her head in her hands. She would count blades of grass for a while. Block it out a little longer. She was just putting her headphones on when her dad sat down beside her.

'Hello.'

'Hello.' She smiled as his arm curved round her back, as it had a thousand times before. Tears sprang to her eyes and she tried to focus on her counting. One. Two. Two hundred. Two million. Who cared?

'So, are you going to drive yourself to the clinic, or shall I do it?'

'What?' She tipped her face up to look at him.

His eyes stared ahead at the Japanese maple tree that he had tended so lovingly since he had bought it ten years ago. She could see the downturn of his mouth, but he was sparing her his pain. Of course he was. He had had plenty of practice.

'Shall I drive you?' Now he turned towards her and she saw how much fear he was holding in for her sake.

'How did you guess?' Her voice was a whisper.

He shrugged, his fingers fiddling with the frayed ends of his sleeves. 'A dad just knows these things.'

'He does?' Abi was shaking.

'Yes.' He folded her into a hug.

Over his shoulder, Abi saw her mum peering anxiously through the window.

'Does she know too?'

'No.' He shook his head. 'And I can keep it quiet if you want me to.'

'Yes please.' Abi thought of the pain on her mum's face. 'I don't want to upset her if I don't need to. It's bad enough dealing with myself, let alone everyone else, especially now that John's gone.' Her voice broke on the last word.

'You could always let him know.'

'No.' Abi shook her head. 'I'm not having him coming back out of pity.'

'It wouldn't be pity.' Her dad's voice was mild as he sat back against the bench. 'You're too wonderful to be pitied.'

'Not that you're biased.' Abi smiled and wiped the tears from her face.

'Now.' Her dad's knee clicked as he got up. 'Want to help me tie back some overexcited strawberries?'

'Yes please.' Abi stood and stretched. 'That sounds great. And thanks, Dad.'

'My pleasure.' He squeezed her hand. 'And remember. It might not be what you think it is. You're just having some tests. Just in case.'

Abi shook her head. 'I hope you're right.'

'I am. I'm going to be hopeful about this.' He walked over to the strawberry canes. 'Now let's put the radio on and do some gardening.'

And the sun shone and the bees buzzed and Abi got a splinter from a rogue bamboo cane. And the world kept turning. A world in which she had somebody on her side.

Seb

From: CaptainSeb@gmail.com
To: JCooper@TBTglobal.net

Hi Dad,

First up. Skype. FaceTime. Try actually using them sometime. Your butt dialled me last week and I never want to talk to the inside of your back pocket again. Deal?

Now I know you've just started your new job and are probably at that stage where you need to be impressing everyone by pretending you're a good guy, but you have to come home. Now. Don't twat about or let yourself think twice — just do it.

I don't care what happened between you, but Mum needs you. She needs all of us. First it was Gaviscon in her bag. Then that bloody cardigan reappeared. She won't bloody admit it but I hear her hushed phone calls — there are some bonuses to never being able to leave the flat by myself — and I know she's ill again. She's being all chin-up about it but I know the signs. You do too. You'll know what I'm doing now — it's the same old routine. Seeing how much she eats. What she drinks. Whether she winces when she stands up.

You are the one person who knows how shit this feels. Watching her putting on a smile. Watching her waiting for the news that might break her. Watching her being brave.

And no, Dad, I'm not OK. This can't be happening again. Not to her. Not now. Not ever. She doesn't deserve it. Not one bit.

Do you remember that month where she couldn't hug us? When she was having chemo and we both had colds and coughs and she sat there in her room all by herself, listening to that Bob Dylan album on repeat? Well that's how she is now and it scares me. Always staring out of windows or watching me on my phone and then looking away when I catch her eye. She's storing me up. Just in case. And I'm bloody terrified.

She needs you. Fake it if you have to — if you really don't love her any more. But be here. Hold her hand. Be the husband she needs.

And yes, I need you too. Come home, Dad. Now. Nothing could ever be more important than this.

S

Abi

'Mum?' Abi looked at the suitcase at the foot of the stairs. 'I know I didn't eat all my apple pie last time I was here, but packing up my things seems like a bit of an overreaction.'

'Sarcasm is the lowest form of wit, Abigail. One day you will realise that.' Her mum appeared from the kitchen, a tea towel in her hands.

'One day maybe I will.' Abi raised an eyebrow. 'But it's so much fun winding you up.'

'Well, as long as one of us is enjoying herself.' A smile was threatening to ruin her mum's froideur.

'Exactly.' Abi walked over and kissed her on the cheek. She smelt of muffins and Olbas Oil. 'Are you sure your FOR SALE sign is big enough? I think they might not be able to see it from Mars.'

Her mum shook her head. 'You're the one who wanted us to sell, Abi.'

'True.' Abi nodded. 'Is that why you're clearing my stuff out?'

'I just thought you might want some more of your things. For the flat.' Her mum turned and walked back into the kitchen.

'Oh God.' Abi was suddenly full of embarrassment. 'You didn't go rootling around in the underwear I left, did you?'

357

Her mum might well have found things that Abi would rather not think about. The same things she had been hiding since Becky Milligan had taken her into a lurid Soho shop and shown her the way the world worked.

'There was no rootling.' Her mum shook her head. 'I learned long ago not to go hunting around in your things without giving you warning.'

Abi walked into the kitchen, savouring the sweet smell of baking in the air. She moved a chair and sat down at the kitchen table. 'Why? What did you find?' She braced herself for her mum's reply.

'Pink fluffy handcuffs.' Her mum bent down and opened the oven. A rush of warm air steamed up her glasses in its traditional way.

'Oh God. When?'

'Nineteen ninety-three.'

Abi did the maths. 'When I was fifteen?'

'Yes.' Her mum eyed her over her cloudy glasses.

'But you never said anything.'

'No.' She arched her eyebrows. 'I'd learnt by then to pick my battles.'

'I wasn't that bad, was I?'

'Your gran used to call you "fiery".'

'Really?' Abi leant her chin on her hand. 'I remember I liked door-slamming.'

'And dramatic exits.' Her mum put the tray of muffins on the side. 'You were very good at those.'

Abi nodded. 'I used to think it made me look decisive.'

'Well . . .' Her mum gently pressed the top of a muffin with her finger. 'It certainly made you look something.'

'Shall I make some coffee, Mum?'

Her mum glanced at the kitchen clock and shook her head. 'I'm not sure you've got time.'

'But I'm here for Sunday lunch and it's only eleven thirty.' Abi stared at her mum. 'How could I not have time?'

'No reason.' Her mum wiped her hands on her apron. 'Silly me.'

Her mum never called herself silly. Abi watched her, suspicion growing that something was going on. If Dad had told her about the tests she was having, she would kill him. He had promised.

Her mum glanced at the clock again.

'Mum?'

'Yes?' Her mum grappled with the knot behind her and removed her apron. 'I've just got to . . .' she pointed vaguely at the garden, 'go out.' She practically dived through the back door.

Shit. Something was up. Maybe it was time to tell her, but Abi couldn't bear the thought of having to break her heart like that. It was bad enough controlling her own sheer terror at the thought of sitting in front of her surgeon, Miss Seth, on Tuesday and finding out what was to come.

She looked around for clues as to what could be going on. The pile of paper and leaflets on the worktop yielded nothing but the information that her dad had once again proved unable to resist an attempt at the *Times* cryptic crossword. And that her mum had bought yet another *Pointless* book. Obviously the first ten weren't enough.

She moved on to the muddle drawer, which was where her mum told her dad to put all the random objects that he liked bringing into the house. She rifled through it. Nails. Glue. String. A truly bizarre number of packets of Swan matches. Nothing more.

She drummed her fingers against the sideboard as her curiosity grew. She walked to the hall, flicking through the notebook that her mum kept by the phone and glancing at the pinboard that held flyers and photos and the five numbers Dad would need if Mum suddenly dropped dead.

Then the doorbell went. Abi walked towards the door, only to be stopped by her mum moving at a sprint, pushing her out of the way.

'Mum. What the hell . . .?'

Abi watched as her mum opened the door and told a surprised charity collector to go away and never come back.

'What is going on? Who did you think it was?' She planted her hands on her hips as her mum closed the door.

'No one.' Her mum gave an unconvincing shrug that explained why she had never succeeded in her childhood ambition to become an actress. 'I saw them from the garden. I didn't want them wasting your time.'

'I think I could have handled them. He was about ninety, for goodness' sake.'

'Have a muffin.' Her mum practically shoved one in her mouth and disappeared back into the kitchen. Abi stared at the ticking grandfather clock, but it didn't have any answers. The suitcase was waiting by the radiator. It was all she had to go on. She was about to bend down and open it, just to check what was inside, when she heard a key in the door. She looked up. A familiar pair of shoes was just in front of her. As was a familiar pair of jeans.

'John?' She looked up into the relief of his smile.

'No.' He shook his head. 'This isn't heaven. Though I know it might seem like it.'

She caught her breath at those words. They'd been the first things out of his mouth when she'd come round from the general anaesthetic after her first operation, so many months before.

Hope made her tremble. 'What are you doing here?'

He held out his hand and pulled her up, and for a second

their faces were close to one another. Close enough to whisper secrets. Close enough to kiss.

He pulled back. Of course. Disappointment skewered her. 'I thought you were in Cambridge.'

His blue eyes held hers. 'And I thought you didn't love me any more.'

She stared at him. She had to get this right. 'No. God, no. Never. I've done nothing but miss you.'

His smile warmed her.

'Well thank God for that. I was having a shit time in Cambridge anyway.'

She lowered her head. It was too much happiness, but she couldn't do this to him. Not with the pain. The tests. The hospital waiting for her on Tuesday.

It wasn't fair. Not after everything he had been through.

But somehow she was still holding onto his hand.

'Why have you come back, John?'

'To take you away.'

'Away where?' She glanced up, seeing the shaving cut just below his right ear. Seeing the bright eyes. Seeing the lips that she had kissed a thousand times and the lines left by a life of too much heartbreak.

His voice was gentle. 'Away for a couple of nights of adventure.'

The surge of joy was too much. But she couldn't go along with it. She had to protect him, to convince him to turn round and walk away. Whatever had made him come here, he would regret it on Tuesday when she had to walk through those hospital doors again.

One more second. Before she took her hand away. 'A weekend where?'

He smiled. 'Edinburgh. We talked about going there, do you remember? When you were ill?' He put his hand into his pocket and pulled out a picture of Arthur's Seat. 'So let's go and explore it.'

'John . . .' Her heart was too full. The joy of seeing him and the pain of knowing she would have to send him away. 'I can't.'

'You can.'

'But . . .'

'Look, if you're worried I can't afford it, the flights are on air miles and we're staying in a friend's flat. So yes, I can.'

'It's not that.' Regret was tightening her chest. 'It's too late for us.'

'What on earth do you mean?' His hand was stroking her face.

She couldn't tell him. She wouldn't.

'Do you mean the way I left?'

'No.' She could barely breathe. To be so close to him and yet to know that she had to make him walk away.

'I know I should have stayed and listened to you, Abs.' He put his finger underneath her chin and tried to raise it, but she wouldn't let him. She couldn't meet his eyes. If she did, then her resolve would dissolve and she would be clinging to him and begging him to stay.

'Abi, I only went because I thought you didn't want me any more. I was so jealous of that guy – I just couldn't handle the thought of you being with him. And it was easier to leave than to stay and talk.' He shook his head. 'I'm so sorry.'

'Don't be sorry.' Shards of thoughts and feelings were whirling through her mind. 'Please, don't ever be sorry. It was all my fault.'

'Come with me, Abi. Please?'

She had so little strength left. 'I can't.'

He shifted from foot to foot. 'Failed businessman. Jealous prick who runs off at the first sign of trouble. I guess I'm not exactly a stellar contender, am I?'

No. That was too much. 'You are to me.' Finally she looked up. Those blue eyes. That blond hair. That love.

He was so close, she felt herself blush. 'Abi. It's OK. I know what's really going on.' A muscle flickered in his cheek. 'And don't worry. We'll get back in time for your appointment.'

She felt a flash of fear. 'How did you know about that? Was it Dad?'

'No. It was Seb.'

'But I never even told him!'

'Then it's just as well he's an observant kid, isn't it?' John smiled. 'Maybe he'll make a good detective one day.' He put his arms round her. 'Whenever he decides what the hell he's doing. We've got you covered, Abs. Your boys have got you covered.'

She leant against him, feeling the relief as weeks of worry were shared at last. 'Are you sure? It's too much. I don't want to put you through it.'

His fingers moved in a familiar figure-of-eight across the back of her palm.

'It's not too much. It's just what's happening next.' He kissed her lips. Gently. Tenderly. 'And we'll get through it.'

'Will we?'

'Sure.' His mouth trembled but his smile remained. 'We've got form, haven't we?'

She flung her arms around him. 'Thank you.'

'Don't thank me.' He squeezed her tight. 'I love you. And I'm the winner here. I get more time with you and I want to make the most of every single second.'

She nodded. 'OK.'

They stood for a second as the clock ticked and the sun filtered through the window in front of them. They were together. They were strong.

She just needed to check. One more time. 'But are you sure, John?'

'I am if you are.' He pulled her close again.

She thought about it. She needed all of a second.

'Let's go.'

'Done.' He kissed her, and in that kiss she knew that she was loved. She knew that she was wanted. She knew that the world was in its right place again. It didn't matter what came next.

'Wait . . .'

'What now?' He flung his arms wide.

'My clothes. My stuff.' She walked towards the kitchen, before stopping and turning back to him. 'I haven't packed anything.'

'Oh yes you have.' He pointed at the suitcase. 'Or rather, your mum has.'

'Mum?' She felt tears stinging her eyes again. There was too much kindness. Too much love. 'No wonder she was acting weirdly.'

'Weirdly?' Her mum appeared from behind the kitchen door. 'I'll have you know I was being the soul of discretion.'

'Is that what you call it?'

'That's enough out of you, my girl.' Her mum hugged her close. 'Now off you go and have some fun.'

'Will you keep an eye on Seb?'

'He'll keep an eye on us, I expect.' Her mum smiled. 'Though I think it will be our neighbour Marc who's the real draw.'

'True.' Abi smiled. 'Thank you for this.'

'You're welcome. Now bugger off.'

Abi turned to John. 'OK. Mum just swore. It's officially time to leave.'

'Great.' John opened the front door. 'Now I'm guessing you might have a few tunes ready for the drive to the airport. Am I right?'

'Damn right.' Abi put on her sunglasses and stepped out into the sunshine. Edinburgh. The hospital. John. Seb.

This wasn't life coming full circle. This was another bend in the road. It might be cancer. It might not. But whatever came, she knew that she was strong enough to meet it. With them. For them. For all the people who loved her.

August

'Into Your Arms' by The Lemonheads

For my family. All of you. Yes, that includes you, Lesley. This song sums it up for me. I've lost count of the number of times you've taken me in your arms and made me understand how much love surrounds me. Thank you. Already since my diagnosis I have so much to be grateful for. Thank you for the soup (Mum), the records (Dad), the movies (Seb), the boxed sets (Rob), the books (Lesley) and the everything else (John). Not to be too 'Wind Beneath my Wings' about it, but you are the reason I wake up in the morning and the reason I get out of my pyjamas and stagger to the sofa. The reason I will drink those disgusting smoothies and why I will take every single tablet they give me like the mild-mannered lamb I most certainly am not. For you lot I'll go through anything.

So this is your thank you. Thank you for loving me enough to rally around me, and apologies in advance for my mood swings, my rage and my endless bloody swearing. You must love me a lot, but, as Seb said when he was small, I love you all to the Clangers and back. And praise doesn't come much higher than that.

Abi

'So. Here we are again.' She stared at the cream door that stood between her present and her future.

Nearly two years ago she had been sitting on this blue plastic chair, waiting to see Miss Seth, just as she was doing now. Back then she had been calm, sure for some reason that her ongoing stomach pains were nothing to worry about. She had been looking forward to a big Saturday night out and listening to Keane's *Hopes and Fears* and drinking Coke out of the can. She had been thinking about their trip to Ireland the next weekend, and whether Seb would run rings around his gran.

Now her brain was on one track. One terrifying track.

An arm curved round her shoulders. 'How are you doing?'

She smiled at her husband. 'OK.' She looked down at her toes with their chipped nail varnish. 'I was just thinking I need to buy some new nail polish.'

He raised an eyebrow. 'Of course you were.'

She leant into him, just as Seb hobbled through the door, a canvas bag hanging over his shoulder. He leant his crutches against the wall and lowered himself into the chair on the other side of Abi, lifting his cast up and propping it on the opposite seat.

She looked sideways. 'What's in the bag?'

'Your favourite.' Seb smiled.

'What? Merlot?' Her smile felt stiff.

'She's funny.' Seb looked over her head at John. 'You've got to hand it to her. She's still trying to crack the funnies, even now.'

John leant back in his seat. 'Even if they aren't particularly funny.'

'Hey!' She punched him in the side. 'You're meant to be nurturing me. Supporting me through this traumatic experience. You know?'

'Oh yes.' John nodded. 'Nurturing.' He shook his head in pretend disbelief. 'Nope. No idea what that means.'

She rolled her eyes at him, but this time her smile was real. 'You know what I mean. You two are here to quietly support me. To sit there holding my hand with a scenic tear falling down your cheek – that kind of thing.'

He closed his fingers round hers. 'What? Like this?' He squinted. 'Working on the tear, babe. Working on the tear.'

'You're rubbish.' She looked at the clock on the wall. The hands had barely moved. 'You'd better step it up on the nurturing, you two, OK?' She looked at their faces and felt a wave of love overwhelm her. They knew she didn't want sympathy. Didn't want pity. Emotion here – in this room – would suffocate her, whereas their banter kept her at a distance from the scans and the results that were sitting on the surgeon's desk right now. The results that might put an end to her blossoming happiness.

'Well . . .' Seb reached into his bag. 'I think this is pretty damn nurturing.' He pulled out a raisin scone. Then a plate. Then a knife. Finally a little pot of clotted cream and a ramekin of jam.

Despite the heat, the yellow walls and the uncomfortable chair, Abi felt saliva leap to her mouth.

'I suppose I could squeeze in a quick bite.' She nodded. 'I mean, only because you've gone to so much trouble.'

'How kind of you.' Seb carefully laid the scone on a plate and layered it with cream and jam.

'You know, the jam should go on first.' John shook his head in disapproval. 'I don't know why you do it that way round.' He leant towards Abi. 'He must have been badly brought up – I blame his mum.'

'My dad always cuts the scone into three so he can squeeze more cream on.' Abi smiled as Seb handed her half. She bit into it, sighing in delight. 'This was Mum's doing, wasn't it?'

John cupped his hand to his ear. 'Pardon? I'm sorry, I can't hear you through all that chomping.'

Abi swallowed the first delicious mouthful. 'Shut up, I'm eating.' She was surprised by how hungry she was. Normally she was unable to eat on the day of an appointment, and this morning had been no exception. Even swallowing her vitamin tablet had been a struggle. Anticipation seethed in her veins. Her mouth was dry. Her heart was racing.

'Charming.' Seb shook his head. 'I bring you vital nourishment and you just tell me to shut up.'

'Actually . . .' Abi took another bite. God, it was good. 'Actually I think you'll find that I'm telling your dad to shut up.'

'Details, details.' Seb shook his head and looked at the water cooler in the corner. 'No cups again, I see.' He nodded. 'Good to see traditions are alive and well in here.'

'Yeah. They're trying to make us feel at home.' John laughed. 'Very kind of them.'

Abi dedicated herself to her scone as the two of them chatted football over her head. QPR might pull it off next season, it seemed. At last. And as they talked and laughed in lowered hospital voices, she knew that she had never felt more loved. Never felt more precious.

A song started to weave its way into her mind, and before too long she was humming it in between bites of scone. The final song on her survival playlist. The song of family. The arms that were always there. The hearts that were always open. The invisible ties that held her up and kept her strong.

'Oh God, she's singing. And eating. This is only going to go one way.' John leant forward and turned his head towards her. 'There will be crumbs.'

'There will.' Seb looked towards the door. 'I hope no one else tries to join us until she's got this out of her system.'

Abi kept singing, her voice getting louder with every word.

'Oh . . .' Seb feigned panic. 'The scone is on the lap. The scone is down.'

John joined in. 'This is bad, people, this is BAD.'

Abi sang on, smiling more widely with every note. She wasn't in tune, but she didn't care. She didn't need a drink in her hand or the glow of a karaoke screen. She didn't need chips, or high heels, or bright red lipstick. She just needed these two men at her side and this song in her heart. Her voice was quiet, but it was sure.

'Yeah, Abi. Get on down.' John was tapping his foot.

Seb looked at him despairingly. 'No one says "get on down" now, Dad. No one.'

'I don't care.' John shrugged. 'It's what I say when my wife is murdering The Lemonheads in a hospital waiting room. So you can just . . .' He cast around for a suitable insult and clearly failed. 'You can just lump it.'

Seb made one of his finest dismissive faces, but Abi didn't care. She was nearly at the end now. The bit where the band were whirling around in the woods in their fuzzy nineties video. Her arms were in the air, and then she handed the rest of the scone to Seb and stood up. Her pretend microphone was in her hand and nothing on earth was going to stop her. She needed them to hear these words. She needed them to hear how much she meant them.

'Mum!' Seb looked like a child who was rather hoping he had been adopted.

'Oh God.' John's hand was over his eyes.

Abi came to the end and beamed at them both. She blinked. Saw the peeling paint. The crack in the ceiling. She realised she was not a pop star on tour in New York's Madison Square Gardens. Instead she was a cancer survivor. And she was pretty damn proud of it.

The door opened and adrenaline jolted her back into the present.

'Mrs Cooper?'

'Yes?' Her voice appeared to have gone up an octave.

Miss Seth smiled, and Abi saw the humanity beneath the white coat and the perfect bun. Her black hair was flecked with grey, but her eyes were bright behind her glasses.

'Would you like to come with me?'

The fears were overwhelming now, and Abi stood there for a second, immobilised, helpless before a future that terrified her. She knew now what her body could do. What she might hear once she was sitting in front of the surgeon's desk, with all the pieces of her bound up in a yellow file with her name written on the front. A book of fear and pain and stolen days.

She didn't want those notes to get any bigger. Not yet. Not when she had so much to live for. These two. Her brother, who texted and called this morning, and who was waiting with Lesley at the shop for news of how she had got on. Her mum and dad, quietly pottering around their house pretending they weren't on standby for whatever result came through. Marc, who had spent last night at their flat and made them breakfast this morning, and who had looked after Seb with a quiet attention that melted Abi's heart.

John and Seb were watching her. Waiting. She looked at Miss Seth's face, trying to gauge what news she might have. The surgeon gave nothing away. Not a flicker to tell Abi what her fate might be.

Abi stuck her chin out. 'Just coming.' She looked at her two boys, remembering the letter she had written to them so many months before. A letter that told them how much she loved them. That they were the reason she was trying to live.

They still were. And she could be brave for them now, just as she had been before. 'Are you two coming with me?'

'Me too?' Seb flushed and sat up in his chair.

'Definitely.' She kissed him on the top of his head. 'You're big enough now. And certainly ugly enough.'

'Hey.' He shook his head as he started to lever himself up. 'A wise woman once told me never to be rude about people's looks.'

'Did she?' Abi smiled. 'She must have been amazing.'

'She's all right.' He was up now, and hopped to his crutches, tucking them under his arms. 'I like having her around.'

For a second tears threatened again. No. She would not cry. Not at maybes. Not at what-ifs.

A warm hand slipped into hers. 'All right, Abs?' John's smile gave her strength. 'Shall we go through?'

'Yes.' She nodded. 'Yes. Let's go.'

'Your wish is my command.' John led her towards the open door as Miss Seth turned and crossed the corridor towards the consulting room.

Abi took one step. Two. Three.

She was back. It was all the same. The yellow blinds that didn't close far enough to stop the sun shining in. The delightful car park view. The smell of TCP. She glanced at her husband and saw a spasm of fear cross his face.

She squeezed his hand as they sat down, and then she reached for Seb's too. She frowned as Miss Seth looked at the folder in front of her and took a breath.

Her pulse spiralled.

The surgeon looked at her, steepling her fingers into a V.

'OK, Mrs Cooper, let's talk about your test results.'

Abi was so tense she couldn't even manage a nod.

'Are you ready?'

Abi swallowed. 'Yes. Yes, I'm ready.'

And there, with the sun in her eyes and the two hands that meant more than anything resting in hers, she learnt what her future would hold.

Acknowledgements

I am so grateful to everyone who has helped me while I've been writing this book.

Thank you to the wonderful team at Hodder, who work so creatively and tirelessly to get my books out there on the shelves. I am endlessly indebted to Emily Kitchin, my wise and incisive editor, and to the dream team of Naomi Berwin and Emma Knight. Thank you to Jane Selley and also to Joanne Myler and Malena Valcárcel for the truly beautiful cover, which is everything I could have dreamt of and more. I would never be here publishing my third book without the amazing Hannah Ferguson, who is my agent, my champion and my friend – many many thanks and hugs to her.

I am so grateful to everyone who has helped me to research this book. Thank you to the clinicians who have advised me throughout and who have corrected my wilder imaginings with clarity and tact: thanks to Miss Bubby Thava, Anna Ingram and Dr Fiona Kyle for their insight and their time. All mistakes are entirely my own work. Thank you to Kate Bolton, Mel Hedges, Phillippa Burt and Chris Burt for their honesty and patience in answering my endless questions – I am very much in awe of them all.

Thank you to Melissa Vanger, Carlie Line and Nerrie McSween for telling me how to run an art shop and to

Alex Lawrence, Alex Simpson, Noah Chulu Chinn and Francesca Viragh for helping me in my attempt to get in touch with all things teenage – I know it was a tough job. Thanks are also due to Ali and Jonathan Crowther, Sandra Iskander, Hugo Mortimer-Harvey, Diana de Grunwald, Clare Hill, Tamara Bathgate, Jo Farrell, Rob Beaugie, Tanya de Grunwald, Damian Higgins, Suzanne Lawrence, Ed Purnell and Karen Tierney.

I have been boosted by so much support from the book community. Thanks in no particular order to: Nina Pottell, Anne Cater and the Book Connectors, John Fish, Michelle Ryles, Anne Williams, Laura Lovelock, Kelly Spillane, Kaisha Holloway, everyone at TBC, Jo Barton, Sophie Hedley, Sharon Wilden, Victoria Goldman, Linda Hill and Agi Klar.

I have a trusty gang of inspirational writers who keep me on track – huge thanks to Isabelle Broom, Cesca Major, Kirsty Greenwood, Lisa Dickenson, Cressida McLaughlin, Miranda Dickinson, Sarah Turner, Amanda Jennings, Louise Beech and Kim Curran.

I am enormously thankful to my friends and family for their patience and encouragement. Thanks to mum and dad, to Richard and Tammy, and – of course – to my girls: Kate Holder, Rhian Fox, Claire Pollard, Helen Winterton, Nijma Khan, Alice Jarvis, Myoung Rhee and Jo Rose.

Finally, all my love and thanks to Max, football editor and husband extraordinaire. One day I will meet a deadline without drama. Promise. And – of course – to Evie, for laughs, cuddles and for being the point of it all.